HARD RAIN
By Andy Waddell

Riverside Press

Santa Cruz, California

HARD RAIN

First edition. May 4, 2024.

Copyright © 2024 Andy Waddell.

Written by Andy Waddell.

To Maria, for everything.

"Oh, what did you see, my blue-eyed son?
Oh, what did you see, my darling young one?"
-Bob Dylan, from "A Hard Rain's Gonna Fall"

BOOK ONE

THE EXPERIMENT

"The doubts of day-time
and the doubts of night-time,
the curious whether and how, /
Whether that which appears so is so,
or is it all flashes and specks?"
Walt Whitman,
from "There Was a Child Went Forth"

Franc could see the red light blinking in the upper left corner of his vision, but he had more important things to attend to. Kerdilaoch's hammer had shattered his shield and broken all the bones in his left arm, and ever since then the dwarf had been pursuing him, driving him into a narrow ravine with no means of escape.

"Pox puppy!" he taunted from the entrance to the gorge, "Come out like a man, Zelphar, if man ye be!"

"Eat shit, Nigel" Franc muttered under his breath and heard Zelphar's sonorous baritone intone, "I defy thee, Kerdilaoch, thou villain!"

Sharp rocks pained his feet, his legs were getting shredded in the briars, and he regretted his choice of avatar. Zelphar wore only a tunic and some sort of slippers. On this type of terrain, he had no speed advantage at all. Without a shield, he had no hope in hand-to-hand combat, and his most powerful weapon, his bow, required two strong arms.

The smart move, probably, would be to surrender. He was in trouble already, why make it worse? He kept climbing, but turned his attention to the red light, which was now flashing urgently.

He knew who it was before he opened it. Only one person could break through the gamelock filter. A simple flickwink left eye and the words "Where are you?" hung before him, stretching across his field of vision. Beyond and through the letters, the rocks and brambles of the canyon paled and pixelated, and he could see just past them the shadowy outlines of walls and a dim figure of a teenage boy walking in place.

The effect was dizzying. A faint tinge of nausea rose below his breastbone, and Franc closed his eyes. Everything disappeared but the words. He stood still and tried to push the image of Kerdiloach's hammer out of his mind long enough to answer the text. He squeezed his already shut right eye and a menu of replies dropped down. Without bothering to read it, he chose the first one and flicked his index finger to send, and when he did, the words before him disappeared, the red light blinked out, and he opened his eyes to resume his retreat.

But entering GR was as disorienting as leaving it. The colors dazzled him; everything was brighter than IRL, lit by two suns; every object sharply defined, undiluted by the dust and fog of inattention. It always took a couple of minutes to adjust, to stop staring dumbly, but he didn't have a couple of minutes. He began walking without looking ahead and immediately stumbled.

"Damn it!" he cried as his shin scraped across a tree root, tumbling him face first into the trunk, but the sound he heard of course was Zelphar's voice shouting, "Zounds!"

Nigel was laughing at him, he knew. He heard Kerdiloach's mocking bark quite close at hand, "O ho!" he cried in a bass voice so different from Nigel's usual tenor, "Art thou drunk as well as slow–witted?"

The dwarf was close enough now that he could see the drops of sweat dripping down the ends of his greasy hair. His grin was wide, and his eyes had murder in them.

Franc turned and tried to scale the rocky cliff, but didn't make much progress with only one good arm. He had barely ascended two meters when the pounding began. Scorning to climb, the dwarf was forcing his prey to come to him, slamming the sandstone with his enormous hammer, carving massive divots and shaking the entire cliff. Franc felt his footing go and grabbed a root protruding from the rock. He dangled by one arm, sure that the next moment would bring the death blow.

But nothing happened. He hung there a minute, feeling the tendons in his shoulder stretch, and then looked down to see Kerdilaoch trapped by an avalanche of his own making.

The dwarf was cursing loudly, calling him a "pribbling, crook–pated haggard," whatever that was, and struggling to extricate himself from a mound of stones.

No bragging this time, no monologuing speech. Franc let go, slid down the cliff, and removed Shinokagami from its sheath. As soon as he reached him, before the little man could lift his hammer, Franc brought his sword down with a slashing downward blow that caught Kerdilaoch's neck just below the helmet and left his head dangling by a thread.

Franc bent to his work, he didn't have much time. Blood was cascading from the dwarf's neck. Soon all his life force would be drained, and Nigel would snap awake. He knew what that would be like: he'd find himself lying on the floor with a throbbing neck. The pang in his neck would disappear almost immediately, but for a terrible second he'd still feel that rage, the adrenalin–filled need for revenge; he'd turn instinctively toward the actual Franc and start to lunge for him, but before any harm could be done, his receptors would flood with dopamine and serotonin and he'd laugh aloud, you couldn't help it. But then he'd shut the whole thing down, so Franc knew he had to grab whatever he could before that happened.

He patted down the still–warm corpse until he found it: a small pouch hanging between his shoulder blades. He yanked off the bag and peered in, but could barely see the diamonds and rubies glittering inside

Again, he raised his sword. He wanted the hammer. Anything in his possession when the game ended would remain with him when it rebooted. If he could remove Kerdiloach's main weapon, he would remove him as a threat forever; he'd essentially kill an immortal avatar. Technically, the character would still be alive, he'd rise again when the game restarted, but no one would play him. He'd wander the landscape randomly, hiding himself when any player came near, or possibly forced into slave labor, like the armless centaur Franc had once found hitched to a supply wagon.

He could see right away that the hammer wasn't *in* his hand, it *was* his hand. There was obviously only one way to get it, but as he raised his sword, a cascade of scarlet droplets splashed on his face and he instinctively turned his head away. Before he could turn back, the corpse at his feet was gone. Reality cracked, and he found himself kneeling on a black turntable in Nigel's game room with the sound of his giggling cackle in his ears. Everything had vanished but a residual sense of warm wetness, and he reached up and wiped a sleeve across his clean, dry face.

Already the game was fading like a dream, but he remembered enough to know that Nigel had no reason to be laughing; he should be furious, although of course the chip would never allow you to feel fury IRL.

Franc's heart was still pounding with rage and the exertion of wielding the nonexistent sword, and a wave of dizziness passed through him as his pulse dropped rapidly to normal. But his brain was bathed with dopamine and his whole being suffused with a warmth of calm contentment. He smiled despite himself, and when he turned to face the friend who so recently had been a foe, a laugh escaped his lips.

"You suck, Dude," he said, and they both laughed.

. . . .

Nigel was rich, and even his game room was beautiful. One entire wall was nothing but a giant window, and the light filtered through a grove of redwoods that made up the back yard. Franc watched two squirrels chasing each other up the closest trunk and tried to turn his mind off.

The problem was, he knew too much. He knew that the warmth he was feeling, the giddy glee, was not real—not the way the tree was anyway. It existed inside himself only, nothing more than a skillful manipulation of the body's chemistry. And he knew for a fact that it wouldn't last, so he could never simply enjoy it the way he once had; he had to think, and thinking killed everything. Even now, before the elation in his body even had a chance to fade, the old sadness entered his brain, and rather than just living in this moment of joy, his brain was busy thinking about the fact that it in less than a minute, he would return to the flat calm he had experienced since he was first chipped when he was ten years old.

Franc could remember being scared in the waiting room, and his mother reassuring him that the procedure would not hurt at all. But it wasn't the pain that he feared. He had overheard the arguments, and he knew that his grandfather, who was not a worrier and who never told his daughter what to do, was dead set against implantation before the age of 18. His mother just kept repeating that he was stuck in the past, that it had been proven safe, and that Frankie, as she called him, would not be allowed to advance to Middle Academy without a chip. And that was that.

Franc never understood what his grandfather's objections had been, but he knew they were important enough to make him raise his voice, something he had never heard before. And he knew that Grandpa was smart—he'd been to work with him and seen the respect he was given by the other programmers. He definitely knew more about such things than his mother did, so it seemed most likely that he was right.

But he wasn't. The chip was great. Sure there was an adjustment period, and he had to learn to master all the commands, but having his emotions under control felt like a superpower. Suddenly it was easy to be "good," to be the mature young man everyone wanted him to be. No longer would he slam the door and scream "no fair!" about things that did not matter. He never cried again. The grownups were right; there was nothing to cry about.

Life with a chip was so calm, so effortless that he wondered how he'd ever lived without it. Or rather, he didn't wonder at all, he simply forgot, shuffled off his old self like a lobster shedding his exoskeleton, and forgot he'd ever been a prisoner to emotions beyond his control. He had younger cousins, so occasionally he'd see them squealing in delight or melting down in tears, and he knew enough to be patient with them. Excess emotion was a defect, and politeness required you to pretend you hadn't noticed. He would nod sympathetically like the adults, all the time thinking, "I was never like that." Life without a chip wouldn't make any sense at all.

In school, Health and Hygiene lesses reinforced this. Less after less had preached the vital importance of chip maintainprotocs: weekly checks, semi-annual upgrades, recalibrates whenever necessary. "The chip is not just an eye to the world," the T-voi℠ said repeatedly, "It's not just a toy, a gaming device, a way to learn and be. The chip is vital to maintaining bodily function. Without the chip, our bodies would wither and die. This is why our ancestors seldom lived past their 100th birthdays."

But as he moved into the upper grades and the lesses became more technical and started explaining the actual brain chemistry, the way the chip heightened or suppressed the body's natural endogenous opioids, he began having questions. He had long noticed, for instance, that he felt particularly calm and relaxed during the daily bulletins from the V.T.B., the Venture Trade Bureau, and he could see by the expressions on their faces that his classmates felt the same. He'd always figured it was because this part of the curriculum wasn't subject to tests or grades, but maybe something else was going on.

And why could he never experience in real life the highs and lows he felt in the game? He knew it sounded crazy, but one afternoon he asked his grandfather something he definitely couldn't ask anyone else: how could he know whether this world was real at all?

"Maybe I'm really Zelphar, and this is a game," he told him.

He expected him to be annoyed, or maybe concerned about his sanity, but Grandpa just said, "'Last night I dreamt I was a butterfly. Today, am I a butterfly, dreaming I'm a man?'"

"Huh?"

"Chuang-Tzu, Chinese philosopher, 2500 years ago. It's not a new question," as if that answered it.

"Oh."

"I have my own answer," Grandpa went on, "If you want it."

"What?"

"If this were a dream, or a game, would it be so boring?" and he laughed.

So he forgot about it, sort of, went on with his life, and then one day, Health and Hygiene was covering the historical context of the modern system. Like all lesses, it wasn't boring, exactly, but soothing. But when the Classi™ showed what life was like before the endorphin distribution centers were controlled by the chip, Franc felt roused, like a shakeawake when your mom gets tired of calling you in the morning and presses her override. The Classi™ was showing pix, pix they claimed were not shopped, of screaming people in a white room with women dressed in white. Their bodies were strange—parts were missing, legs mostly. But you could tell they were not much older than Franc. The T-voi™ said they were soldiers in a war. But what was really interesting, what made Franc sit up, was that the T-voi™ said they were in a state of constantly feeling pang. Their faces were contorted, the cords in their necks strained. "Imagine," the T-voi™ said, "Bumping your shin, or pulling your hair, but instead of a quick pang, followed by a message on your Mindsi™, imagine the pang continuing and continuing for hours or days or even years! They called this, 'pain.' That's what it would be like without the endorphin distribution capabilities programmed into your chip."

The concept seemed so impossible—constant pang. Of course, like most kids he had played around with the receptors now and then, poking a scab, for instance, over and over, trying to get a "dorpho–high" or maybe just to feel that pricking, poking sensation as the scab raises up, to see that drop of red, to savor the salty iron taste. But the chips were too smart. Blood: the sight of blood, the taste even and the Mindsi™ would start that flashing, small and dim, then brighter, blinding finally, impossible to ignore. He'd heard, of course, of kids pushing through it—that was the term—"pushing", pushing till the faint. They said the faint was a sleep like flying. But that would activate the override, naturally, and signal your parents' sensors, and nobody wants that.

"Any pang lasting longer than a minute," the T-voi™ went on, "Indicates the need for recalibration and should be reported immediately to your parent, or directly to a physician. The same applies also to emotional states. No heightened emotion, whether sadness, anger, or even joy, should last more than one minute. If leveling does not occur by then, lingering emotions should be reported immediately." The historical images of people exhibiting ridiculous expressions of different moods faded away and were replaced by two extremely earnest teens in discussion with an older man in a lab coat.

"But why joy?" asked the girl.

"Yeah," added the boy, "If the chip can make us feel happy, why not feel happy all the time?"

"Well," the man said in a winking voice, "If we were all blissed out all the time, I doubt if we'd get any work done." The laughter that followed this "joke" was so fake that Franc felt almost sick to his stomach. "But seriously, research has shown that emotions only exist in relativity to each other. A brain flooded with the proper dose of endorphins does feel joy, but kept at that level, it will soon feel nothing at all. Only by leveling to the norm can we ensure that you are able to feel the full range of emotions. After all, it's a great big, beautiful world out there, and you want to be able to enjoy it all!" A montage followed showing the boy and girl experiencing various emotions: high–fiving after winning a race, mourning the loss of a pet dog, kissing under the glow of an enormous moon.

Franc felt sure the first explanation—the joke—was the real truth. No society would function long without work, and it seemed logical that the V.T.B. would want people who were contented, but not so high on life that they forget to show for their shifts. But his question, which of course he never could ask, was not about long–lasting joy but sorrow. "Why not feel sad?" he wanted to say, "What if the world is sad?" Like the people they just showed with the dead dog. After a minute, the dog's still dead, isn't he?

Because he'd been having lingering emotions for months now, a dark lens between himself and the world, and he hadn't told anybody. He knew he should; he'd been recalibrated many times before when he'd been overly blue, and one time when a weird glee had seized him for no reason and he couldn't stop giggling in class. But this was different; he didn't want to cure it.

For one thing, it wasn't hurting anyone. He was still going to school, still working for his grandfather, still socializing with his friends. As far as he could tell, not a single soul had noticed any difference in him at all. So why should he have to tell anyone that it felt sometimes like there were two of him, one living his life and another observing it at the same time? One smiling when his mother came home from work, the other wondering if he is really glad to see her or whether some official algorithm has decided it is good for society to have strong familial bonds so all teenage brains should release dopamine in the presence of their mothers.

He might be "happier" if he could shut off his brain, just stop noticing things, stop feeling separate from the rest of the world, stop wondering about what is really real. But he wanted to know, and he had a plan to find out. Tonight, he thought. Tonight, before I chicken out again.

He looked over at Nigel. He could see he was scrolling through his feed while he talked to him.

"Dude, I am going to smash you so hard next time! No mercy!" as if he'd ever given any.

"Maybe pick an avatar taller than a hobbit," Franc began, but a bell in his head pushed out the rest of the sentence. "Oh shit," he said, "It's my mom."

Nigel's eyes widened. "She's *calling* you?"

In answer, Franc held up his palm toward his friend. He directed his attention to the toolbar at the bottom of his field of vision and flickwinked on the symbol that looked like a red bridge. "Hi Mom," he said.

"Young man, where are you?" said a voice that filled his head. "Your grandfather has been expecting you."

"Yeah, sorry. I'm at Nigel's. We were playing a game."

"You promised your grandfather you'd be home by four at the latest. You *promised* him."

"Yeah, I know. I'm on my way."

"He's got deadlines, you know. People depend on him."

"Yeah I—"

"And he depends on you."

"I know. I'm leaving now."

"We'll talk about this later."

"Okay, Mom. love y—" but she was gone.

He dropped his hand and Nigel began to speak. "Yikes dude! Scale of one to ten, how bad?"

"Oh, only a six, maybe. Still, I probably won't be able to play for a week or so." At least he hoped so; that was his plan.

"Bummer. Oh well, see you tomorrow." His attention was already back on his feed.

Franc's grandfather sat at his antique desk in front of two enormous monitors, pounding away on a stained keyboard, the letters of which had worn off long ago. He didn't bother asking where Franc had been; he just continued to type with one hand while he pulled out a gold pocket watch with his other hand and held it up to show him.

"Yeah, sorry. Don't worry, I'll do the hours."

His grandfather didn't bother to respond. If it had been his mother, he would have worried. When she pulled the silent treatment, you knew she was really angry. Grandpa was different; if he didn't have something to say, he just kept his mouth shut.

The office was the grimmest room Franc could imagine, a lead–lined cave with a metal mesh across the window, but it was the one place on earth where he felt most comfortable. Nothing ever changed there. His grandfather forbade anyone to clean it, and he wasn't exactly a neat freak so there was a distinct, but not unpleasant odor of old man. He still used a pencil to plan his programs and his desk was littered with scraps of paper covered with an indecipherable scrawl. Franc's desk, a piece of plywood on top of two sawhorses, was meant to be temporary six years earlier, but he'd gotten used to it and didn't want to change.

When he shut the door behind him, half the display on his Mindsi™ snapped off. No more notifications, no texts, emails, appointment reminders. Everything was calm and quiet. He switched on his monitors and sat down in the same chair he'd used for as long as he remembered. The only sound was the clatter of the keyboard and the hum of the frames. They were the only family he knew who still had their own frame room. The cloud had made them obsolete, but Grandpa still used it for his work. There were programming apps for the Mindsi™, but, according to Grandpa, they were inferior. He liked control. According to him, using Phorum™, with its multiple shortcuts, was OK for lazy people, but even they needed to be able to at least read the underlying code. And he had taught Franc some of the ancient languages: Java, C++, Python, even some SQL and PHP.

The lessons had begun early, before he even had his chip. In those days, Franc had idolized his grandfather, had followed him room to room, had wanted to copy his every move so in order to get some work done, Grandpa had fitted little Franc up with his own "big boy computer," an ancient Dell with the best technology available half a century earlier. And he had even stripped out most of that capability, running it on Linux, severing it not only from the cloud, but from their own frame so the boy could not damage anything, no matter what keys he banged. Grandpa set up a simple animation program. Little dancing bears and ponies and elves would randomly appear and disappear at random. Franc, dutifully tapping the keys, was led to believe that it was typing that brought forth the miracle.

Later, from kids on the playground, Franc had learned about real games and had begged his grandfather for 20 credits to purchase one. Grandpa said, "You want a game? I'll make you a game. When you can beat it, I'll give you those credits." He sat down at Franc's ancient computer and began typing away. All Franc could see was a blur of lines of code. In a few minutes, his new game appeared: Tic Tac Toe.

And it was actually fun, for a while. It wasn't too long until he could "almost beat it" almost every time. Grandpa was unimpressed. "Cat's game don't count," he said.

Hours a day, Franc tried every combination of x's and o's, but nothing worked, until one day he had an idea. He was staring over his grandfather's shoulder, watching the blurred lines of code fly up the screen.

"How do you see that?" he asked, pointing at the screen.

"What do you mean?

"On there." He pointed at his own screen, the Tic Tac Toe game half finished.

"You want to see that," he pointed at his screen, "on there?"

Franc nodded.

"How do you know it's there?"

"I saw you put it," he said.

"I'll show you," he said, "but I don't have time to explain it." And he showed him the combination of keys which, when pressed, made the normal display disappear, replaced by the long list of characters the child had no idea how to read.

But he tried. He stared at the list. He knew how to use the arrow keys, and he could scroll up and down the lines. He couldn't read them, but he could see which were longer or shorter. He noticed that many started with the same letters. The old man went back to his work, but he kept turning back from time to time to view this curious sight, a child so young staring for so long at lines of code. Finally, as he had expected, the boy said, "How do you change it back?"

"Okay," he said, "I'll get your game back."

"No, *how* do you get it back?" the boy insisted, so he showed him that combination of keystrokes, and the game reappeared. When he looked back from his work again, he could see Little Frankie toggling back and forth between game and code. He'd make a move in the game, then look back to see if anything was different. Back and forth with a curious, unchildlike curiosity.

Grandpa had always been kind to Franc, but for the first time, he was *interested* in him. The longer it lasted, the harder it was for him to concentrate on his work. After a while, he stopped trying and just stared at his little grandson with his furrowed brow.

"Do you want to ask me anything?" he suggested kindly, but the child just said "Not yet" and continued toggling and staring.

The next morning, when Grandpa had entered his office, he was startled to see Franc already there. An orange bear pirouetted on the screen. Franc spun around.

"This isn't a game," he said. "It doesn't matter what I push." And he walked out to spend time with his mother; she wasn't a cheat.

But he was back that afternoon, staring somberly over Grandpa's shoulder. Two programs were open at once. The lines on the right one were changing, flying upwards as Grandpa typed on the keyboard. But Franc could see that from time to time, large sections of the left side changed color just before the right side grew rapidly. He watched carefully, trying to concentrate on a single line as it changed color, and sure enough, just as he had expected, that same line appeared on the right.

"How do you do that?" he asked.

"What?"

"Move it, move stuff from there to there."

So he showed him, showed him how to highlight, how to copy, how to paste, and the rest of the day, the little boy copied lines of code from the dancing bear program to the Tic Tac Toe program to see what would happen. Sometimes, nothing occurred; more often, the program shut down. In either case, Franc would delete the new code and start over. His grandpa watched, impressed by his patience. "I'll teach this one to program," he thought.

But in the afternoon the child went to the park with his mother and played happily on the slide and swings. When he came back, he went to his room and made growling sounds with his dinosaurs.

"He's forgotten all about it," thought Grandpa. But the next morning, when he entered his office he found a grinning Franc waiting for him.

"You gotta buy me the game. I can beat it!"

"But that's imposs... let me see."

Franc began a new game. He placed an X in the top left corner. The computer responded with an O middle left. Franc took the center, but rather than blocking, the computer took the middle right. Triumphantly, Franc put down his X and a big red line suddenly appeared, joining the X's.

He had hacked the game, broken it actually. And now his grandpa was really interested in him. He got his credits and his first game, but more importantly, his grandfather began teaching him, teaching a child to code before he could even really read.

By the time Franc was 10, he was working for his grandpa on weekends and holidays, doing QA, searching for bugs in the code, most of which the old man had inserted on purpose to keep him on his toes. But one day, when he was 13, Franc had flagged an entire section that was perfect as far as his grandfather was concerned.

"It's not a bug exactly," he told him. "It works, but it's so awkward."

Grandpa looked up.

"Look, if you make these functions recursive, you don't need all these steps." He typed in a few dozen new lines of code, then deleted a few hundred lines his grandfather had written.

Grandpa was quiet for some time, reading and rereading.

"Your version is superior," he said finally.

From that point on, they were partners—four hours a day in the summer and every other day during the school year. He didn't think a young person should work any more hours than that. Even if Franc was right in the middle of something, Grandpa would force him to stop at noon. "Enjoy your youth" he'd say. He had spent his teen years washing cement trucks and scrubbing floors at his father's business ten hours a day all summer long, and he had always resented it.

The work wasn't unpleasant at all. QA was still boring, but he was pretty good at it and he didn't mind too much because it was real and it needed to be done, unlike schoolwork, which was just work for the sake of working. And Grandpa always gave him a few tasks that were a bit more challenging. Most of these involved repairing security breaches and figuring out how the hackers had entered the system. Franc liked dismantling a problem and finding a solution, and when his Grandpa had described it to him as a war, that they were constantly under siege, it had made it seem very important, and just a little fun. It wasn't up there with slicing off a dragon's head, but he did have a feeling of accomplishment when he wrote a successful patch, a sense of scoring one for the team.

One day he had asked who the other side was, who was attacking the system, and his grandfather had hesitated, which was unusual for him. He respected Franc and was unusually honest with him for an adult, but this time he seemed to be holding back.

"Who? Well, actually. . ." he began, but after a pause just said, "Lot of bad actors, who knows?"

Franc thought it was most likely kids like him, just causing trouble, like these two guys who had got kicked out of his school for the malware they had written when they were supposed to be doing schoolwork. But that was boring; it was more fun to imagine his enemy as a criminal mastermind, impossibly rich, with an elite team of hackers laboring in a gleaming palace of technology on a remote island guarded by a private army.

Today's hack was pretty simple, actually just a variation on the same problem he'd seen many times before so he imagined instead a power-mad terrorist intent on world destruction operating out of a filthy cave in some country he'd never heard of, not terribly sophisticated technically, but determined and evil. It was dumb, he knew, but it made his job just a little more fun.

He was still working on the patch when his grandfather stood up. "Almost dinner time. You'd better ask what you can do," he said as he walked out the door. Franc typed a few more lines, then hustled after him and started setting the table without waiting to be asked.

Dinner was fried rice with veggies and a lecture, but it wasn't too bad, just the usual: blah blah blah, disappointed, blah blah blah, promised, blah blah blah blah blah... It didn't take too much brainpower to nod and uh huh at all the right times, and compliment the food and show interest in his mother's day while scrolling through his feed and answering his friend's texts. There was a close moment when a vid Nigel sent to him made him laugh, but he managed to play it off like he had breathed in a grain of rice and he coughed until the urge to chuckle faded. In the end, it was exactly what he thought: straight home every day for a week, no battling his friends in the game. It worked out just as he'd planned.

After dinner they all withdrew to their corners. Franc had seen old movies where whole families would stay in one room all evening, chattering away, but that had never been their way, at least not since he was a little boy. His mother sat on the sofa with the cat curled up on her lap and read a book, an actual paper book, and his grandfather went up to his room and played a song that was ancient before he was born on a guitar with a shiny metal plate in the center. He played it with a tube of glass over one finger and slid up and down the neck with a mournful wail while his thin voice croaked out "I'm home at morning, face full of frown, I know that Baby, you been running around."

Franc normally would be sitting on his bed, his head propped up on giant pillows, watching vids or chatboxing with his friends. But tonight, of course, he had to finish his work. Most of it was pretty straightforward, but he was distracted and made several mistakes that he had to go back and fix, so he ended up working longer than he had planned.

And he wasn't done yet. He logged out of his operating system, then double-clicked on a seemingly random spot on the screen, and a hitherto invisible icon appeared. He had created a back door, a login that left no record and that allowed him access to portions of the operating system that his grandfather thought were beyond his control. There was a file hidden there, a large file. For an entire week—the last time he'd been grounded—Franc had recced every waking moment. He had an entire week of the most tedious footage imaginable: eating breakfast, sitting in class, etc. And he had hacked the outgoing feed loop from his chip. For seven days, if his mother, or anyone else, were to snoop on him, they would see only the activities of a normal, boring week.

Everyone knew your parents could do this, jump in whenever they wanted to see your feed, essentially to see and hear whatever you were seeing and hearing at that moment. You could go incog of course for the bathroom or other activities you didn't want to share, but too much would be suspicious—he definitely couldn't incog a week. Franc's mom swore she would never use it, never invade his privacy, and he believed her, mostly. But better safe than sorry.

One more thing to do. He opened another file, a program he had written. This was an autoreply for any texts or emails he would receive in the next week.

He had pored over his replies from the previous weeks and come up with this system: Anything from his mom without punctuation would get "k", "sure" or "np" randomly applied. Texts or emails from Mom that ended with a question mark would receive "not sure" "hmm" or "sure I guess" back. Three questions in a row or an exclamation mark would yield "Sorry Mom, I'll talk to you about this in person" followed by no response.

For his friends, all his replies were memes: the toddler staring at his shit-covered finger with the caption "what the hell is this?", the vid of the hippo stuck in the bog with "I'll get back to you", the cartoon rat with the bug-out eyes, the one with the bored little girl with a T-Rex behind her, the police car rolling off the wharf, the hungry rabbit with the dick-shaped carrot, etc. The program just pulled out one randomly. A question mark response got another one. Two questions in a row would get the message: "Dude, I'll talk to you in person. Hold on."

He loaded the program and checked it over one time. Of course it had never been tested, but he was pretty sure it would work. He pressed "run", exited the program, and logged out.

"Tonight," he thought. "Tonight, I'll really do it, no chickening out."

He waited until he was sure they were asleep. He'd lived in the same house his whole life so he knew every squeaky floorboard by heart and he maneuvered cautiously down the hallway and across the living room to what had once been a fireplace. A framed portrait of his ancestor, his grandfather's great-grandfather or something, glowered down at him from the mantle. Next to the picture were two artifacts. The first was a strange wire device with two pieces of glass that its former owner was wearing strapped over his eyes in the picture. The other was something called a "straight razor." Grandpa had laughed when Franc had asked if some were gay. He had demonstrated the sharpness of the blade on a piece of paper, and then returned it to its case. Ironically, the face in the frame was covered with bushy hair, like an animal so he didn't seem to have gotten much use out of the razor.

He tiptoed back to his bathroom, closed the door behind him, waved at the light to brighten it, laid the razor down carefully on the sink, and took off his shirt. While he wrapped a towel around his waist, he stared at himself in the mirror. His nose was bigger than ever. He leaned in toward the glass where could see it in the two side mirrors; it seemed to be growing. When he opened the case and folded out the blade, he could see that his hand was trembling. His Adam's apple danced when he swallowed unconsciously. He knew what he was about to do wasn't wise, but he couldn't back out now. He tried not to think about his mother's reaction when she inevitably found out. He could hear her voice in his head, telling him how disappointed she was, but he could hear another voice as well saying "Now, now, now!"

He had planned the operation meticulously and of course researched the depth and quadrants of the placement. But still, as his grandfather always said, "Shit happens" and you can never be completely sure of anything. He'd seen it done in a doctor's office, a special instrument made a tiny incision and aspirated a few drops of blood and it was over. This wouldn't be exactly the same, but the principle should apply. He shut his eyes and rolled his eyeballs to the lower left to open the toolbar and flicked his finger at the Mezr™ icon. When he opened his eyes again, a grid appeared in his vision. He looked at the blade and could see that it was 15.2 centimeters long and 1.9 centimeters wide. He zoomed onto the point, the outward corner, and set a distance of five millimeters. Instantly, a bright red arc appeared, a little quarter circle. "Okay," he thought, "No deeper than that."

He picked up the blade and leaned as far as he could into the place where the two mirrors met. With his left hand, he folded back his ear, revealing the black dot he had made that morning with his Sharpie. His stomach spasmed and his hand trembled, but the voice said, "Now, now, now!" and he did it. He plunged the blade in, careful to stop when the red line on the blade met his skin. But at that moment red was everywhere, It surged out, dripping down the blade, and he feared that he'd gone too deep.

Still, he went through with it, levering the blade deftly against what felt like a tiny obstruction, and suddenly everything changed. His Mindsi™ snapped off like a light when you leave a room. The grid disappeared, and it was hard for him to even tell where exactly in that red mess the incision was, let alone where the chip was. He rubbed his bloody fingers together, but could not feel even a tiny bump. Unable anymore to zoom, he could only assume it must be there.

Franc had never seen so much blood at one time and his heart started to pound. He listened for footsteps, but he heard only the air, the whirr and whine of the frames in the next room, nothing. If the chip were in, his mom would have knocked down the door by now. Franc told himself to relax, to ignore the pang, to stop the blood before it dripped down to his pants, but all he could think of was finding the chip; if he lost it, everything was ruined. Besides, he wanted to see it.

Still holding his bloody hand up so as not to drop it accidentally, he grabbed a wad of toilet paper with his left hand and held it to his neck. He reached his right hand towards the ceiling and hunched his shoulder up to hold it long enough for him to grab the hand mirror and lay it down flat. Then he switched back to holding the paper with his left and let his right arm down. He held his hand carefully over the mirror and let the blood drip onto the silver surface. He examined each drop as it fell but saw nothing. Unable to zoom anymore, he tried his sense of touch. He lay his palm flat on the mirror and slid it along the glass, spreading the blood out into a long smear—still nothing.

Franc held the blade downward over the mirror and with thumb and forefinger ran down the length, squeegeeing off the blood that remained. Again, he examined carefully every drop but saw nothing.

He began to feel faint, and it did not feel like flying. He dropped the razor in the sink, sat down on the toilet seat, and put his head between his knees, as he had learned in Scouts. For the first time, the reality of what he had done hit him. What made him think he'd get away with this, and why did he want to? The pang that had started in his neck had moved to his head and seemed to pang harder with each heartbeat.

Franc tried to control his breathing. He thought of his grandfather and his chanting. Grandpa sat each morning in basically a closet moaning softly over and over the same syllable. When he was just a kid, Franc had found him once and panicked that he had suffered a stroke. He had run to his mom with the news, but she said not to worry. He was meditating, she said, and her only explanation was that Grandpa was old–fashioned. She said it was how people had leveled in the old days before the Mindsi™ made all that obsolete. She told him it was nothing to be concerned about, but he must never tell anyone; they wouldn't understand.

Now, staring at his reflection in the bloody mirror, he saw his face was pale, drops of sweat beading at the forehead. His stomach churned and he felt his dinner moving back up towards his throat. He knew that nothing could rouse his mother faster than the sound of retching. She would burst in, ready to plaster her warm palm onto his clammy forehead, to coo those soothing words, "It's all right, let it out. It's all right." But then she'd see—the blood, the mirror, the wound on the neck—and it would all be over. She wouldn't turn him in, of course. She'd make up some story about a slipped razor—a foolish youth playing with a dangerous object. No doctor would believe it, but just plausible enough, combined with her iron, maternal glare, to let him know it wasn't worth his while, to let it pass, leave it unrecorded, reinstall the chip and chalk it up as an "accident."

Part of him wanted nothing else, to let himself be taken up and mothered and just return to "normal." Everything would be as it was before—back at school—no difference, except now watched closer than ever before, his mother monitoring her Materfeed™ daily, hourly even, for aberration, for signs he was becoming like his father.

Franc's mind whirled. Now done, the thing could not be undone. It would only be a matter of time before he was caught. He wasn't worried about the law—his family was too well-connected for that—but just the embarrassment of stupidity. He'd pulled his chip, his lifeline, his store of knowledge, his communication with the rest of humanity—and for what? The hand against his neck jerked spasmodically, the fingers digging into the wound. And the pang was somehow manageable now. He found he could feel pang, pain, and still think at the same time.

He opened his eyes. A drop of blood stood out red against the white tile. Franc was struck with the perfect roundness of the droplet. It was as if he'd never seen one before. Everything else faded as he examined the light glimmering in this little piece of himself there on the floor. They say inside you blood is blue. It turns red in reaction to the air. Imagine seeing blue dripping from a wound! Grandpa had once told him they weren't bluebloods. "We've got where we are by work and smarts," he had said. How strange it seemed now that Franc hadn't bothered to click the Instadict™ or even ask him what he meant. He got the gist and dropped it. Now, the phrase troubled him. Was his blood different from others? He could see his grandfather in himself, and his mother, obviously, but he must be half his father's blood as well. Reaching out he smeared the red across the tile. The smear, like a tiny I, stretched out thinly. What part of this red was from the one they never spoke of?

Franc had always thought, even told people, that he'd never met his father. He knew lots of kids without fathers—only donors—and while he wasn't exactly sure if that was how it had happened, he had a strong feeling he had never met the man.

But once, his mom had surprised him. He had asked her about a memory. He was young—three, four? They were at the beach, Baker Beach probably, and he had spent the days running in and out of the white water, being knocked about. A man, his grandpa in his memory, had picked him up. Holding him tight against his chest, he had marched right into the massive breakers, letting the waves crash across his back to shield Franc from the spray. Then they were in another world, floating in the dark water. The sea, no longer crashing, rolled quietly up and down. That slow rolling in the cold, cold water, and the feeling of being totally secure—warm even—in this man's arms was crisp in his mind, but one day he realized he'd never seen his grandfather swim. He hated the beach—"Waste of time," he said. Franc told his mom the memory. Was it a dream? he wanted to know.

"No," she whispered. "That wasn't a dream. That was your father."

And that was all she said. When he asked what happened, where he was, she'd only said, "He's gone. It was a long time ago. Let it go." And it must have been a long time ago; he searched his own drive for the very first vids he ever recced; Mom was there, and Grandpa, even his friend Nigel—he'd forgotten how fat Nigel was back then—but no one else.

He remembered his mother had had a MyFace™ page back when that was still a thing. Hacking in was easy, but there was nothing there. She must have really hated him when he left; her page was scrubbed clean. He found some baby pics of himself and shaky vids of crawling, stuff like that, but way fewer than he would have thought, and nothing with a father.

One pic caught his eye. His mother was holding a baby—obviously him—and smiling. She looked so young, impossibly young, and beautiful, not just Mom beautiful but actually beautiful. Something about the lighting, the background, told him that this was taken by a professional. But the framing was odd. He zoomed in on the right side of the pic; it was just slightly blurred.

He opened it again with PicDissect™ and searched for earlier versions, and then he saw him. He was smiling so broadly, he looked like he'd never be unhappy again. He had straight, light brown hair like Franc, and his blue eyes, nothing like his mother and grandfather with their dark, Portuguese faces. Franc's hand went unconsciously to his nose. The man in front of him had the same prominent bridge, almost a hook.

He looked back at the eyes. The smile was real, no question about it. He was happy. They were happy, once.

Franc looked around the bathroom. He shook his head to try and clear his thoughts. He pulled the tissue away from the wound and the blood seemed to pour. And that's when he blacked out.

The first thing he saw when he came to was the blue porcelain of the toilet rising above him. The pool of blood under his neck had flowed toward the tank, coating his right cheek with a crimson film. He was cold and he felt queasy still, but he was calm, calmer than he had ever remembered being. All fear and anxiety had dissolved and at least for this one moment it was enough to stay still, to feel the cold, hard tiles, to smell the bathroom aroma of cleanser and piss. To not think.

It was quiet. He could hear his own slow breathing. The silence was strange, but it took Franc a moment to realize why: no music. How long had it been? How old was he when he turned his setting to "constant"? Every waking moment since he was, what twelve?, had been accompanied by a steady feed of the latest songs, a second pulse of bass notes thrumming through his bones. Without it, the world seemed too harsh, like a lamp with no shade.

His "plan" was over, of course. It seemed stupid now. Could he really expect to last a week without his Mindsi™ functioning? But now, without the chip, even unconnected, it was completely hopeless. He wouldn't be able to open the door to his own house, wouldn't get through the school gate. The whole thing was ridiculous. All he could do now was to confess to his mother, let others handle it.

But still, she couldn't see this. He would clean up the blood, clean up himself. Wait until morning.

The hand mirror was in front of him on the floor. Broken of course. Franc sat up and felt the dizziness return. He thought he might throw up, or just pass out again. He put his head between his knees again and waited for the feeling to pass. From that angle, he could see himself in the cracked glass.

He wasn't bleeding any more, but he was quite a sight with dried blood caked on his neck.

Suddenly, he laughed. He couldn't help it. He covered his mouth so he wouldn't wake his mother, and he laughed. His shoulders shook and tears stood in his eyes, and all the while he watched himself in the cracked glass. It was the face of a mad man, and he laughed so hard that drool collected at the corners of his mouth.

His grandfather had told him a story once. They were walking across the Golden Gate Bridge and Franc had asked about the rusty netting between them and the water. He couldn't figure out what animal they were trying to catch. Plus, it was full of holes. Ragged shreds of metal trailed below them, although he could see that in other places the net was intact. Grandpa explained that in the old days it had been a popular place for suicide. The net would catch people before they fell to their deaths.

"I guess they wanted to go out in a beautiful place," he said.

"But why did they want to die?"

"God knows, it wasn't a rational decision. People weren't rational back then. We didn't have any way in those days to make people think. Might be what they called temporary insanity.

"Actually," he went on, "there's a story I read—true supposedly. Before they built this barrier, one guy jumped off the bridge—you know he wanted to die, but for some reason he didn't. They say hitting the water from this high is like hitting cement, but from some fluke he didn't die. Must have broken some bones—I don't remember. But anyway, he found himself alive, in the water, and a boat just happened to be passing by so he called out and they pulled him onboard. But the thing I remember most is that afterwards when they asked him why he had done it, he said, 'As soon as I jumped, I realized there was absolutely nothing wrong with my life, except the fact that I had just jumped off the Golden Gate Bridge.'"

That's how Franc felt. He wasn't stupid. He knew he was lucky. He lived in a house with a view of the bay. He had security and love. His family had provided him with the best chip available, one that could unlock almost any door, could take him to the highest levels of society. And he had just gouged it out and thrown it away.

His head hung down now. The face in the cracked glass sank. He let himself cry. If you're going to be crazy, might as well go all out. He hadn't cried like this, with tears, since he couldn't remember when. His head hurt and he wanted to stop, but he couldn't. He knew he no longer had the receptors to tamp down extreme emotion, but he didn't know it would be like this, tears streaming down his face like a pre–chip child.

One tear fell onto the mirror. It stood out like a dewdrop, and through it Franc could see something. His first thought was a mote of dust, a grain of sand. But it was too dark, too blocky. Looking closer, he saw a tiny cube with almost microscopic wires.

Wide awake now, he picked up the mirror and stood slowly, never taking his eyes off the tiny drop. He placed it delicately on the counter and then reached for the alcohol and cotton ball. He cleaned the area directly around the wound and dried it. He stared again at the tiny god on the broken mirror. He put one finger into the wet spot, and he could feel the chip, like a piece of fine grit. He pushed until he felt it poking into his skin, and when he pulled away, he could feel it come with him. He took his other hand and rubbed across the glass, but there was nothing there. He knew he had to act quickly.

An Invisibandage™ was laid out on the sink. His hand was shaking, he was shivering, but he managed to transfer his tiny treasure onto the pad and, with utter care, fearing it might drop, apply it to his neck. You could still see a small red spot, but he would cover that with Zitcrayon™ tomorrow morning. The rest of him was a mess. Smears of blood along his cheek and down his bony shoulders and chest. Suddenly he was freezing. Lying on the tile had sucked the warmth out of him. He longed for his warm bed, but he had things to do first. He pulled on his hoodie and got to work.

He was pretty sure that as long as the chip was physically present, even unattached, it should work for automatic functions, like passing through security. But he needed to check. He went into his room and slid open the window as quietly as he could. He grabbed the screen by its little plastic tab and pulled it upwards out of its slot, then dropped it down, only just barely catching it before it fell outside. He turned it sideways, then pulled it into the room and leaned it against the bed. He sat on the windowsill for a minute before he jumped. How would he get back in if it didn't work?

Oh well, he thought and kicked his legs out, landing on the ground with a thud he hoped no one could hear. He looked up to see a shape disappear around the side of the house. Franc held his breath, expecting the Patrol to descend on him, but there was nothing. Just to be on the safe side, he sat a minute behind the camellia bush and listened. The whole block was silent. Fog was rushing up the headlands, and the muddy ground was freezing on his bare feet. No one was out. Probably just the raccoons.

Franc crept around to the front of the house and up to the door. This is it, he thought. If the chip's not there, the alarm will go off, Mom will wake up, the whole thing will be over. His heart beat as if he'd been in the middle of a game, even though he was only walking. He stopped a moment and tried to will his heart to slow down, but he couldn't. That is very strange, he thought.

Three steps up, still quiet. Two strides across the porch, and he heard the whirr and scratch of the bolt sliding, the gasp of seals deflating. The door opened. He had done it.

He closed the door as softly as he could, but still his mother called out from her room. "Franc?"

"Yeah, Mom"

"Did you go outside?"

"I thought I heard the cat out there"

"Mai-cat? She's with me."

"Okay, sorry. Night Mom" and he crossed the room and into the hall.

His heart was still pounding when he entered the bathroom and he almost cried out when he turned the corner and saw his reflection. His face was still covered in dried blood and there were splatters of blood all over the room. Frank took a cloth and began to wash furiously. If his mom came in to check on what he had been up to, he was screwed.

But she stayed in her room. She believed him, or maybe she was just too tired for a fight. Franc was tired too. By the time he'd cleaned up, put back his screen and closed his window, he was exhausted. He climbed into bed and enjoyed the warmth of the covers. But there were no sensors anymore to detect by time and place that sleep should occur, no mental override to block out extraneous thoughts, no prescribed release of melatonin. He was in bed, but awake. It was very strange, but not unpleasant. He lay there thinking. The whole thing was crazy. He'd fucked up for sure. But at least he had the chip. Could he live a week without his Mindsi™? He didn't know, and it wasn't smart to find out.

But he'd already jumped off the Golden Gate Bridge. He might as well enjoy the trip down.

He dreamt of her again. The same dream, just a face hanging over him, a voice, "Are you okay?" Long, shiny black hair, glowing dark skin. And the eyes! Too big to be real, too dark, too perfect. They filled the screen of his mind. "Are you okay?" so soothing—a real question, not just polite. And those eyes looking at him like he'd never been looked at before, like he was the only person in the universe.

And that was just how it had been, he knew it. He felt it. But the doctor told him it was a hallucination brought on by trauma. Which made sense, he had to admit. He had experienced trauma, and plus, if it was real, who was she? No one in his class looked like her. In the weeks since the incident, he'd been staring at every girl in the school. Many had black hair, and a few had skin like milk chocolate. But no one had those eyes.

Even the voice "Are you okay?" the voice that haunted his dreams like a song stuck in your head. "Are you okay?" It was a melody he heard in his sleep, never in daylight.

So it made sense, what the doctor said, even though it felt so wrong. It was a hallucination. The blow to the head, hard enough to knock loose his chip and shut off his Mindsi™, had created the "memory." It had never happened.

What had happened was stupid. You can see it if you tube, "Doofus Gets Kicked in Head." It was all Nigel's fault, as usual. He had been bragging that the kick he always did in the game, a flying roundhouse we'd all seen him use to deliver the death blow, that he could do it in real life. Not Gargantua high, like in the game, but as high as a person, higher even. Vladi called bull and wanted to bet. He bet him fifteen credits he couldn't kick an apple off someone's head like the story guy with the arrow.

You'll never guess who someone was. It was stupid, very stupid, as he'd been told many times since by the doctor, by his mom, by school officials, by countless commenters who used much more colorful language than the others had. It was stupid, but Nigel was Franc's best mate. And actually, he really was good at acrobatic kicks and flips, so he volunteered to hold the apple on his head. A side bet developed that Franc would flinch.

"I believe in you, man" is only one of the many stupid things that Franc had said in his lifetime, but it's the one he'll be remembered for. As millions have seen, he does not flinch. The vid shows just his head, the apple teetering. The crowd is jeering. Franc is yelling, "You can do this, man! You can do this!" And then the famous words, "I believe in you, man." And then a size 12 foot enters the frame and the vid goes slo–mo. It looks like the eyes and cheeks ripple towards the shoe while the rest of the head goes the other way.

A shoe company got the rights and made those ads. You've definitely seen those. Same set up, same slo–mo, but each week a different shoe is shopped in, and just at the moment of impact the logo: "KICKS: we believe in you, man!"

It was by far the most famous Franc had ever been, or ever would be, he thought. A depressing realization.

He even wondered if the hallucination—the voice, the eyes—had been a trick by the Mindsi™, a defense mechanism against the embarrassment because it was true he hadn't been bothered near as much as you would think. He heard the laughter, but all he cared about was finding her, which he never did, of course. No one else had seen her (His "friends" had all run) and Franc never set eyes on her again.

He had no record either, not even the 30 second auto–rec. The force of the kick had dislodged the chip from its neural network. Franc had woken from his blackout with no Mindsi™ at all. There was blackness, then the voice, the eyes, then blackness again. When he came to he was in the hospital. The Mindsi™ was working again, of course, and after a series of tests, he was on his way. The doctor told him such hallucinations were very common with an injury like his. There was no voice, no girl.

He awoke feeling hungover. The front door was closing. Soon he heard the soft whine of the car pulling out. He was late, no time for breakfast. Nigel would be here any minute. That was one thing he hadn't thought of. He now had no alarm, no way to tell what time it was.

In the bathroom, the insanity of the night before came back. There was the razor and the case. He looked at himself in the mirror. There, just below the ear, he could see the brown–red spot. He grabbed his Zitcrayon™ just as a car pulled up outside. Nigel was waiting. He'd start honking soon, that was Nigel.

Franc threw on his clothes and rushed out, pausing just a moment to return the razor, making sure he replaced it exactly in its spot. The bushy face of his ancestor scowled at him.

• • • •

"**D**ude, you see it?" Nigel said by way of greeting. He was dressed, of course, like Franc in the same blue–gray uniform, the same black shoes, same stupid tie. His blond hair was cut close to the skull—too close for regulations. Minimum half-inch hair at all times, but Nigel and his crew were always pushing it, cutting off a little more, trying to get away with something. They had temp–tatted messages on the backs of their heads with phosphorescent ink and had sewn miniature black lights into their collars. The teachers couldn't figure out why everyone laughed if the classroom lights ever dimmed.

"What?" asked Franc, strapping himself in the seat across from him.

"Simon's vid," he said.

"Oh yeah," lied Franc. "It was great."

"Hilarious!"

"Stupid!"

"Yeah."

The car pulled down the driveway and turned without pausing into the street, slipping neatly into the slot. Franc looked at the cars next to him, metal boxes moving along efficiently, the people in them staring vacantly. Franc looked back at his friend. He was smiling, but the look in his eyes was the same as all the others.

"How 'bout this one?" said Nigel, looking up for the first time. Franc realized suddenly that he was waiting. "Oh" he grunted, then forced himself to look up and left, "Got it," he said. When he looked back again his friend had the same blank, watching face.

It occurred to him that this might be easier than he had thought. Why had he been so worried about covering that little spot? Nigel would never have noticed. No one really looked at anyone anyway.

He had never noticed before about how much of his time with his friends was spent like this: watching vids together, just sitting in the same room with the same blank stares on their faces. It wasn't even necessary to see the vid. All Franc had to do was watch his friend and wait to react. Knowing Nigel, there were really only two possible reactions. The vid was either "hilarious" or "gross." One called for a laugh, the other for a groan. If it was both disgusting and funny, you groaned first then laughed really hard. He'd just watch Nigel and react the same. And if, for some reason, he was unsure, he'd say "That was sick!" which would cover it.

At school it would be harder. Some vids call for an "Aaah!" reaction, either "Aaah!" cute or "Aaah!" sad, but Nigel wouldn't have shared one of those. Boys watched those vids—he knew he did—but they did not share them, or only with girls to show their sensitive side.

With a different friend, maybe the vid would call for "Wow, that's something to think about," but with Nigel—well sure enough, he burst out with a laugh so sudden it was like a sneeze, followed by "Oh man, watch this!" and soon an even bigger laugh.

Franc went for the snort laugh, easier to fake, followed by "Oh man!" when it appeared the vid had ended.

"That was fucking hilarious," he said. The two sat a moment, grinning at each other. This was friendship.

They were stuck in traffic now at the gate that divided The Pres, where they lived, and the city proper. Sensors picked up the identity of the car itself and the first gate opened. Only when that gate had fully closed did the bot arm sensors reach into the vehicle itself to sense the identity of the passengers. It was a pain, mostly; no one really cared who *left* The Pres, but they had to do the same procedure coming and going anyway. Nigel didn't even look up, so he didn't see the bead of sweat forming on Franc's upper lip. It shouldn't take this long, he thought, it never takes this long. But the arm withdrew as quickly as it had entered, the window rolled itself up, and they were on their way.

"I need to calm down," he told himself.

When they passed the end of Golden Gate Park, Franc saw what looked like bundles of old clothes all over the slope and in the bushes. One of the bundles sat up, and he could see that these were people sleeping on bits of cardboard and covered over with old coats and tattered blankets.

"Dude! Have you ever seen that before?"

Nigel looked up. "Dude, we went there on a field trip in like fourth grade."

"No, I mean the people."

"What people?" but by that time they were a block away.

They passed a long line of people standing in what he could have sworn had been a vacant lot only yesterday. At one end there was a red tent with a long table in front where three women were ladling something into bowls out of a giant pot.

"What the hell is going on?" he thought, but Nigel only sat calmly, eyes up and to the left. Franc could see his right eye winking from time to time. "He's liking things," he thought.

The car turned down 17th toward Market. Traffic slowed to a crawl as they neared the Mission Gate. Franc could see hundreds of people now in makeshift tents. Others walked near the car in actual rags, like he'd seen in old–time pictures in his history lesses. A family appeared to be living in an old car. A Patrol van was pulled up; something was going on.

As they drew up beside, Franc saw the officer in the van give a signal. Suddenly a group of guards in brown uniforms like Franc had never seen before surrounded the car. A man jumped out, knife in hand and three of the guards began beating him with their clubs, while two more reached into the car and pulled a baby from the arms of a screaming mother. One was prying her fingers off the child while the other smashed the woman in the head.

"Look at that!" Franc blurted.

"Oh wow," said Nigel. "It still has a steering wheel! My grandma had one of those."

The car rolled inexorably on, no more interested in police matters than Nigel. Out in the sunlight there were fewer, but all the way to school, on benches, in doorways, down alleys, he could see pockets of people shuffling along like tired ghosts. Stooped, dirty, their faces covered with hair, they looked like another species.

At Castro they came to a stop at the Mission Gate, again a two–stage process. The car's sensor opened the first gate, and then the robot arms checked the passengers, but there must have been a glitch because now there were actual humans operating the security.

The outer gate began to open but stopped suddenly after only a few inches. From both sides of the street a mob had swarmed right in front of their car. They threw their bodies against the gate, pushing with all their strength to widen the gap, while the outside guards in brown uniforms shouted and swung their clubs. Within a minute, the rioters had succumbed. Their heads banged on the asphalt as they were dragged off by their feet.

One man had made it through the gap. Franc could see him sprinting, trying to reach the inner gate before it slammed shut. But the inner guards were waiting. One slammed him in the stomach, while the other took a home run swing at the back of his head. Franc could see them high–five each other before they dragged the body out of the road.

The gate opened all the way, and they drove to the checkpoint.

Their windows rolled down. A middle–aged man in a black uniform leaned in and looked at both of them as he waved his sensor.

"Heading to school, boys?"

Franc couldn't help staring past him. One of the men in brown was wiping blood off his baton. "Yessir"

"Well good for you. We need more educated people these days, that's for sure."

"Um hm.'

"Ok, proceed. Have a good day!"

Two blocks later, they pulled up through the school gate and up to the moving sidewalk. They got out and the car whisked away.

"Mm," said Nigel, looking up. "New banner."

L ast week the banner read "Spacetime™ Academy for the Gifted (A Subsidiary of V.T.B. International): Learn from Each Other." The week before it was "Spacetime™ Academy for the Gifted (A Subsidiary of V.T.B. International): Socialization **Is** Education." The week before that it was "Spacetime™ Academy for the Gifted (A Subsidiary of V.T.B. International): Open Your Eyes, The Answers Are in Front of You."

Franc looked up, expecting huge red letters across the white façade, But what he saw was dirty stucco, and letters, no color at all, etched on the wall: "Mission High School."

He didn't have time to ponder this as Kelli and Jasleen were calling them over. Jasleen was Nigel's girl so Kelli and Franc had to stand there awkwardly while they engaged in some school–forbidden PDA. It was even more awkward because just a month ago the two of them would have been going at it as well. They were friends now, had been friends before and were again. No big deal. Drama minimum, but still it was awkward.

They turned away and pretended to be fascinated by two freshies who were obviously in the middle of a game battle, also against the rules. Standing five feet apart, they were swinging arms, kicking. He'd seen these two battle before, and they were pretty decent. If he had his Mindsi™, Franc might have tapped into the game, seen it as the two fighters did, an epic battle between two gigantic superfoes. As it was, it just looked silly. He recognized the game by the fighting style. The smaller, chubbier kid had taken the dragon avatar, Megasaur. He kept turning circles, leading with his ass. Franc knew the movement was effective; it was how you activated the dragon's tail with its fang–like spike, but seeing a pudgy 14-year-old swing his butt around was hilarious, especially combined with the little kid dragon face he couldn't help making.

Kelli laughed and Franc turned towards her. It was good to hear her laugh, a real laugh like when they were kids, not a performance like so much these days. She looked different somehow. Her eyes were smaller, with little circles under them. Her skin was no longer perfectly smooth; he could see tiny bumps and blotches.

"She's filtering," he thought. He knew this was a thing, sending out a signal to change your appearance to those nearby, but he didn't realize normal girls like Kelli were doing it. For one thing, it cost a lot of credits, and for another thing, why? Kelli looked great; she had always looked great.

He looked back at Nigel and Jasleen who had come up for air and were engaged in some heated, secret conversation. Franc could see that Jasleen was filtering too. Her lips were smaller, paler. Maybe they all do it.

When he turned back to look at Kelli, he felt a twinge of sadness. Honestly, he liked her better this way, with the bumps and blotches. She was the Kelli he had known before, the one he had played hide and seek with.

"Dude," he said, taking her hand. "Let's grab a cookie, I'm starving." For a minute, holding her hand as they crossed the quad felt so nice and natural, but he forced himself to let go. He didn't want to give her the wrong idea.

"You want one?" he asked as they approached the snack shack. This would be the second test of the separated chip. The snack shack was automated. The chip let you in, and if you had enough credits on your account, would let you out with food.

"No thanks," Kelli said just as Franc slammed into the glass door. He pushed with his shoulder, but it would not budge. He began to panic. If he couldn't even get food, his little experiment was doomed to fail, and quick.

"Sign says 'pull,' Genius" Kelli laughed. "I'll wait for you out here."

And it worked like a charm. Chip unlocked the door. Chip opened the cookie case. Chip charged two cookies to his account. Chip sent a message to his mother informing her about his junk food habit, but oh well, he could deal with that later.

He held the cookies out to her. "I know you said you didn't want one, but we both know you'd eat half of mine, and I'm hungry!"

Kelli laughed and chose the peanut butter cookie as he knew she would. They leaned against the trophy case and chewed. It was so nice, so comfortable, that Franc wondered if he had made a mistake breaking up with her.

What did he want? She was pretty, but more than that, she was nice. They had fun together. He definitely had not wanted to hurt her, but he knew he had, although she seemed to be doing OK. Rumor had her going out with a college guy, although he wasn't sure if that was true, and he didn't ask.

All he had known at the time was that he felt trapped. Trapped with a nice person, yeah, but even a golden prison is still a prison. It was all just too inevitable. Everyone, all his friends, even his mother, kept saying, "Why not ask Kelli to the dance, she's such a nice girl?" Everyone just assumed they'd be together, him too he guessed. Probably her as well. "You're 16," they all seemed to say, "You can't just be friends." But he had the feeling he was on a treadmill and he wanted off, so one day he asked her, "Could we go back to the way we were?" which hadn't been an easy transition, but they'd done it.

As they ate, they watched the people going by. Franc could see now that almost all the girls, and quite a few of the boys, looked different without his Mindsi™. Acne was the most noticeable, but he also saw scars, moles, crooked teeth. The class president strutted by and Franc was shocked by the size of his nose. Unconsciously, his hand went up to his own face.

"Do you think I should filter?" he blurted.

"What?"

"Do you think I should filter? I mean my nose is pretty big, and I have this tooth," he lifted his upper lip, "that sticks out."

"No! You look..." she broke off. She breathed out through her nose and shook her head sharply. She looked angry, or annoyed. Without thinking, Franc leaned back, his eyes widened.

"You idiot," she laughed. "You're not supposed to ask your ex-girlfriend about your looks! Why don't you know stuff like that?"

"I don't know," he said. And that was the truth.

Kelli's head jerked up. All down the hallway Franc could see the same move of the head, hear a slight sigh. It was time for class. Some students were already hustling, others holding back. Time for a last laugh, a last kiss. Frank shoved the rest of the cookie in his mouth.

"See ya" Kelli said as she hurried off.

First class. Health and Hygiene, good old health and hyge, very relaxing. Ms. Mcgreechy was in front welcoming everyone as they came in, but Franc recognized the vacant look in her eyes. She was probably watching her cats on a nanny cam or something.

"Five minutes!" she yelled, "Back in the gym in five."

Five minutes meant ten, and everyone knew it. Movement was leisurely to say the least. As soon as he had turned the corner, out of sight of the teacher, Franc felt a scrape on the back of his heel. Someone had given him a "flat tire," and when he turned back to see who it was, he got a hand on his back, pushing him over.

"Watch out, dude! You're blocking traffic."

The person who had said this was stepping over him, would have stepped on him actually if he hadn't rolled out of the way quickly. He knew the voice; it was Bruno who had done this move or something like it on him since middle school. Not painful, but humiliating. Nigel came up behind him and helped him up.

"Don't stress," he whispered, "he's an asshole."

But Franc wasn't listening. He was staring at Bruno who had paused at the end of the hall to look back and laugh with his friends. It was him all right, but where was the scar across his cheek he supposedly got in a knife fight with two dudes last summer? Where was the skull tattoo on his neck? And where was the beef? His arms looked like, well, like Franc's arms.

"Don't stare, dude," whispered Nigel, "He's gonna get pissed."

And indeed, there was Bruno, striding up to him. "Who you looking at, you little trick?" But Franc was so amazed he forgot to flinch, just stared into those milky blue eyes, thinking "He looks like a choir boy."

So when Bruno came at him, chest out, Franc smiled. He couldn't help it. Relief, maybe, or just surprise, but all of a sudden it all seemed hilarious. Bruno, school, this whole world he hadn't seen before. "Whoa, dude, slow down!" he said.

And it worked. The calmness, the smile, all of it threw Bruno off and for a moment he didn't know what to do. It was beautiful, like out of a kid vid—stand up to the bully and he'll back down. The thought made Franc laugh out loud.

And that's when Bruno hit him. Apparently you don't need muscles or scars or a neck tattoo to be a violent son of a bitch. The roundhouse caught him in the side of the head and knocked him back into Nigel.

"Still think it's funny?" he said, rearing back for another punch.

"No, not at all," said Franc, stepping back.

"Thought so" he said, and walked away.

The laughter was even louder now, and when they had turned the corner into the locker room, Nigel said, "What the hell is wrong with you?"

Of course he had no answer. Franc said nothing as they walked into the locker room. Fortunately, their lockers were on the other side from Bruno and his friends. They changed in silence, then Nigel said, "Are you fucking nuts?"

Again Franc said nothing. Because the answer was yes. Yes, he was nuts. He was seeing things no one else saw; isn't that the definition of insanity? He just looked back at his friend and raised one eyebrow.

"You're an idiot. I should have punched you myself." And they both smiled.

"Hurry, everyone! Take your spots," called out McGreechy, and they spread out in pairs. At 8:37 an involuntary groan was heard all around the gym. Franc could not help being amused. All around him people looked startled—punch drunk. The Classi™ had snapped off all their vids and games and chats, and even though they knew it was coming, they acted surprised.

Then they began moving in unison. Hands out, bending to the toes, then hands flat on the floor, feet kicked out behind, a series of stretches and calisthenics. Franc watched the girl in front of him and did whatever she did.

A few times, he messed up, went up instead of down, lost concentration. This was another test for him. Without a screen, without the soothing voice giving the instructions, he didn't really know what to do and if it were noticed, it would be hard to explain.

But he needn't have worried. One time McGreech did walk up and down the rows, but he could see by the grin on her face that one of her cats must've done something cute. She passed by without noticing him watching her.

He knew the other students were all looking at two screens: in one, a woman in a leotard was leading them through the motions; in the other, words, images, a voice instructing them about something. Probably something about chip maintenance, or telling them "Don't Rec It!" That was the new campaign this year. "The cloud is full!" with a pic of a thunderhead, dark and menacing. They were trying to get kids to stop posting so much, stop reccing everything. Good luck with that. Half of Franc's friends were reccers. They kept the camera going all day, 'cause you never know what you'll miss, what might go viral. Getting punched just now, that was up already he was sure. Nigel wouldn't have posted it, but at least one of those kids in the hall did, he was sure.

Actually, Nigel probably had uploaded the "fight." He uploaded everything. He probably posted their drive to school. For a second, Franc worried. Nigel hadn't noticed anything, but someone watching might find it weird to see him staring out the window, getting freaked out. Once again it hit him how doomed his little experiment was. It's true people don't notice much, but they do notice some things.

On the other hand, 90% of what was recced was never even looked at. They'd scroll, they'd even like it, but they wouldn't actually watch something as boring as "Heading to School." A kick in the head, yeah, but a ride in the car—no way.

Suddenly, the class began to run. Ms. McGreechy had opened the side double doors and the students were streaming out. Franc ran with them, crossing the black top and heading to the track. Four circuits they ran, pausing only to glance back from time to time with frightened eyes. What was it this time, he wondered. Bears? Zombies? Everyone was being chased by something, and he knew from experience that even though you knew it was fake, it was impossible to not be at least a little frightened. If your heart rate dropped, whatever was chasing you got closer, no matter how fast you ran. It was fun. Franc had always liked this part of class, so he was surprised to see what looked like real terror in the eyes of his classmates. He caught up with Nigel and touched his hand, but when Nigel looked back, he didn't like what he saw and took off like a rocket, which should have been funny but somehow wasn't.

The end of the run was always the same. Windchimes tinkled and whatever had been chasing you, tigers or wolves, dissolved into bunnies and butterflies, and everybody laughed. You couldn't help it. You knew it was corny, but the relief was too great.

They all walked back to the gym, chatting and laughing. This was really Franc's favorite part of his entire school day. The fright, the run, the relief, the silly recognition that at least on some level you'd been fooled again: it always brought down everyone's defenses. For a few minutes it was elementary school again, when everyone in class was your friend.

By the time they'd crossed the blacktop all that was wearing off. People were wandering off the straight path back, trying to stay close enough not to be noticed, but far enough to catch the edge of the network, check their messages, find out what they'd missed in the last half hour.

Back inside, back to their spots. Not really a workout now, just slow stretches. Even without the Mindsi™ he could hear the soothing music, the T-voi™ droning on. And just when you thought you might nod off, the real T-Voi, McGreechy herself yelling out, "OK, up on your feet. Face your partner! Come on, 'Socialization **is** Education.'"

Franc's partner was a boy named Edgar. They were friends, kinda. They had been in Scouts together a long time ago. Unbelievably earnest, Edgar absorbed the lesses like they were his mother's dying words. He was always eager to discuss so Franc breathed easy; he wouldn't have to say much.

Almost every class Franc had ended each day this way. This part of class was always spoken of as the most important. Paired off, they were to look directly into each other's eyes. Looking away, especially a glance to the left where the now–disabled message center would be, meant losing a point. As the ten-minute discussion countdown clock wound down, the message light would glow brighter and brighter, more insistent. Even though he knew it was disabled and there would be no actual messages there, Franc had never made it the whole ten minutes without looking. And the only partner he'd ever had who had made it was this one.

"Partner nearest the door begins," shouted the teacher.

That was Franc who, of course, had nothing to say, but he was prepared for this. "So," he asked politely, "What part of the less did you find most important?"

"Oh my, good question," and he was off. "Well of course we've heard it before, but I'm always struck with the idea of the cloud getting full. We all know how important it is to purge our files, unnecessary stuff, but sometimes I forget. One time, my messages were over 1,000."

"Uh huh," grunted Franc. He still had stuff from Middle Academy. He was probably in the 100,000 range.

"I mean, I don't know what will happen when the cloud is full, but . . ."

"It'll rain," interrupted Franc.

"What?"

"That's what my grandpa says. He's the one, well he's one of the ones, who built the cloud. I mean there was a cloud, but they figured how to put the droplets between the droplets."

"What does that mean?"

"It has to do with Kubernetes superclusters. Multidimensional matrices, things like that."

"I've never even heard of that."

"Well, we're not supposed to learn storage until senior year. I just know about it because I work for him sometimes. But anyway, nothing's infinite. He says it won't happen soon, but if they don't come up with something, the cloud will fill and it will rain."

"Rain?"

"Not literally, but picture a cloud. It's just billions of little droplets hanging in the air. So picture each droplet is a file, like a vid, or a message, or even the security code on your door. Well, rain would mean the cloud would drop some, so you know, you'd look for a pic or something, and it wouldn't be there; it'd be dropped. Like rain."

"But what would..."

"Grandpa says most of it is crap anyway. It's supposed to hold the important stuff and drop the crap, but..."

He realized that Edgar was really listening to him, not just trying to score a point.

"But what?"

"Well, it's never been tested, I mean, how could they?"

History class was most people's least favorite. "Pointless" was the most common comment. But Franc liked it.

Mostly, he liked seeing all those pics from a gone world. All those lives, all that struggle, for what? He liked to picture himself back then, maybe a soldier in the Civil War. Those guys charged across huge fields with guns that only fired one bullet while people shot cannons at them. It was hard to imagine ever doing something like that.

Anyway, he didn't hate it the way the others did, and he didn't hate old Mr. Lewis either, even though he actually talked to the class himself instead of using the T-Voi™, which was weird. What the others really hated were the questions he'd shout out midlecture. The T-voi™ just went on no matter what, but Lewis would interrupt himself to call on individual students about material he had just covered.

One time Franc had been daydreaming in class, lost in contemplation of the pictures flashing before him, when Mr. Lewis had suddenly shouted, "Franc, which world leaders were in attendance at the Yalta conference?"

Without hesitation, Franc had answered, "Wheelchair, Bulldog, and Mustache." The class laughed, although few got the joke. They leaned forward, eager to see him get in trouble, but Lewis had only smiled and said, "Very good, but let's see if we can nail down the information a little better. Ula, same question."

And of course Ula got it right, but even though he was polite and praised her, it wasn't hard to detect just a little disgust in Mr. Lewis's face as he watched her eyes moving down and to the right, and the slow, measured speed of her response as she repeated the Wikinotes. Also, how else would she know Stalin's middle name?

Today there was a sub so Franc was in luck. Mr. Lewis was old, and he moved slowly, but Franc had a strange feeling that if anyone would notice him acting weirdly, it would be him. When class started, the sub read some message about paying special attention blah blah blah, then it started. Franc slunk down in his chair and spent the next half hour staring at the back of Cheryl Jay's head. Cheryl had black hair, but she was nothing like the girl of his dream. For one thing, her voice was screechy, especially her laugh. He looked around, as subtly as he could, at the girls in the class. The filtering was obvious, now that he really looked. Almost every girl in his range of vision looked different than they had the day before. Eyes were smaller, skin less smooth. One girl next to him seemed to sense him looking and turned to look back at him. The day before her eyes had been almost Manga big. Today, they looked normal, like his own. And her breasts were smaller too, Franc thought.

He forced himself to look back at Cheryl's head. The desire to stare at everything, everyone, and see the really real was overpowering. It was like seeing them all for the first time, and to him they looked perfect. Why would anyone want cartoon eyes and a pointy nose? Without the filters, the girls looked more like themselves, like they did in elementary. Freer.

From time to time the class groaned. Another grim one. That was the other thing that people did not like about history that Franc did like. Everything in the past was so horrible, well almost everything. People were ignorant, dirty, dressed in weird clothes, and they were always doing something terrible. Blowing people up, starving the masses, ruling with an iron fist. He would never forget one image: a huge stack of human hands. What the hell was wrong with people?

That seemed to be the real lesson of history class: thank God we live now.

Ten minutes left in class and the sub was standing before the class holding a piece of paper, of all things, and a pencil. The less had apparently stopped early. Around him people were stirring, whispering.

"Alex Anderson?" she said, "Which countries were involved in the Opium War?" Alex answered correctly, obviously, and the sub made a mark with a pencil next to his name. They were all correct, which is why only a really old–fashioned teacher like Lewis was still asking questions. It was just an exercise in repetition.

"Suzanne Brown? What was the . . ." She was going in order, he realized. Probably won't get to him anyway. He relaxed. It would be over soon. He went back to dreaming.

But suddenly, Franc was aware that people were looking at him. He heard his name repeated.

"Franc Sousa?"

"Uh yeah?"

"Which Chinese city was divided into European zones?"

He hesitated. He didn't know, obviously, but that wasn't an answer he could give. He was just about to throw a fake coughing fit when he realized: she didn't know either.

"Ding How," he said smoothly, using the name of the restaurant where his family got take–out.

"OK," she said, and made the mark.

• • • •

The rest of the morning was even easier. He actually fell asleep in econ and no one noticed. And in bio there was a terrarium next to him with a snake. Ms. Ewald had dropped a mouse in that morning and Franc spent the whole period watching the poor creature waiting for the strike, which strangely never came. The snake wasn't hungry.

He was starting to feel like going a week without his Mindsi™ wouldn't be so bad after all. Sure, he was missing out on some info about photosynthesis or bubble markets or whatever, but it was amazing how little he cared about that.

His afternoon classes would be a breeze: art and programming, both classes where you weren't supposed to use your Mindsi™ at all. Art was an "experience" class where you just drew pictures or sculpted with clay, and the programming teacher had the same philosophy as his grandfather: back to basics. Plus, a few years ago there had been problems with student programs being released directly onto the cloud. Two kids wrote code to make vids "shudder," essentially repeating frames. When it was released, the "Shudder Bomb" became one of the worst viruses in history. It attached to random vid files and made them hundreds of times longer. It was weeks before it was completely patched and removed. That was the first time people started to worry about the cloud collapsing. Anyway, they were expelled (arrested, according to rumor) and ever since, programming was held in a windowless, lead–lined room with absolutely no connection to the outside. No one had email, chat, vids, or even access to Wikiknowledge. Franc would be fine there. It was his easiest class. The other kids struggled, and their parents were always on their case because it was the "most important." But, thanks to Grandpa, Franc had no problem; he was the star pupil.

It was only the social part that was hard. He finally understood the motto, "Socialization *is* Education." It was hard talking to people, being with people, who didn't see the world the way he did. The desire to tell someone—Nigel at least—about what he was seeing, what was really going on, was overpowering. But how could he? Even if he asked him to stop reccing for a minute, that would be enough, maybe, to trigger an override. Perhaps he was paranoid, but he had a feeling that saying, "Dude, turn off the rec, I've got something to tell you" would trigger a backup camera, or at least audio. And if they heard the words "removed my chip," he was pretty sure the Patrol would be alerted. No, he couldn't tell anyone, just nod and laugh and hope he wasn't noticed.

If he could make it through lunch, he could make it through anything.

• • • •

The cafeteria was packed by the time Franc got there. Nigel, Jasleen, and Kelli were already at their usual spot, and Franc waved as he came in.

The line was long and slow. Spacetime™ was supposed to be a fancy school so they had food actually cooked on campus, supposedly the last school in the state not to use MREs. So the food was better, but slower, and served up by people who didn't exactly improve your appetite. It's mean to say, but the cafeteria workers, with their light blue hairnets and gloves, were downright ugly. It was a big joke at the school. The worst insult you could make was to call someone, or call their mom, a "lunchlady." Kids would even make these comments right in line, even while they were being served, but the lunchladies never seemed to notice, just chatted away to each other in their harsh–sounding language.

As he edged his way up the line, Franc stared around him, his eyes darting from face to face around the room. He was looking for *her*, even though he knew it was hopeless. He'd looked at every girl in the school already, and the sensible part of his brain knew that the girl of his dreams was just that: a dream.

When it was his turn, Franc pointed at the Feak™, the vegan steak substitute, and was shuffling along, following his tray to the mashed potatoes, when something made him look up. The server at the end, the one who passed out dessert, had shouted back to the kitchen for another tray of pudding bowls.

"They're speaking English," thought Franc, looking up. The lunchladies were all different. Must be a new crew. Same ugly uniforms, same ugly hairnets, but their faces were just average, regular faces, like looking at your mom's friends. Not exactly gorgeous, but not ugly like the day before. And as they worked, they chatted to each other—in English. "What happened to the foreigners?" he wondered.

By the time he had his mashed potatoes and his green beans, and he reached the pudding, he had to stand and wait a minute because the boy in front of him had gotten the last one. The kitchen door opened and a young woman, a teenager actually, backed through the door carrying an enormous tray loaded down with pudding bowls. The server lifted the empty tray, and the young woman clanked down the full one in its place.

As she grabbed the empty tray, just before turning back for the kitchen, she looked up at Franc for just a second.

It was her.

Her flowing hair was trapped in the hairnet, but it was her, he knew it. Those eyes, the eyes of his dream, there was no mistaking them. For the briefest moment, she looked back, straight into his own eyes, before wheeling around and heading for the door.

But Franc called out, "Excuse me, Miss?"

And that's when everyone stared. The servers looked up in unison. No one had ever spoken to them. The students were not just shocked but annoyed.

"Dude, move it!" said the boy behind him.

But Franc did not move. She had turned back. Even in that ridiculous uniform, that stupid hairnet, she was beautiful. He wanted to reach out to her, to tell her about his dream, how he'd been looking for her every day, how he felt in his heart that she was a part of his destiny.

Instead, he said, "You work here?"

"What do you think?

"I'm . . . I'm the guy. . ."

"I know who you are," she answered, and, with just a hint of a smile on her lips, she turned away.

"Wait!" he called, "What's your name?"

And this time it was a real smile. "Maya."

"Maya," he said, "That's a beautiful name."

"Dude!" the boy behind him said, "Calm down!" and everybody laughed. For the students in line, annoyance had changed to amazement as this crazy kid was acting like Romeo of the year to a lunch lady who obviously answered in gibberish. But as it went on, the intensity of his gaze was so perfect with the absurdity of the situation that everyone cracked up. They couldn't help it.

"Wait!" he yelled, and the laughter got louder, "Don't go!" But she was gone already back into the kitchen.

By the time he got to his seat, his friends had already seen the vid. All around the cafeteria, you'd hear roars of laughter going up as different kids saw it for the first time. For the second time, Franc was viral, except this time they were laughing with him. He was a comic genius, a guy who'd do anything for a laugh.

Even in his agitation over seeing her, Franc realized he'd have to play along. Of course he had been going for a laugh, nothing else made sense. He "watched" the vid, of course, and laughed with them. And when he barely touched his food and spent his meal craning his neck to see her, they laughed even louder. But when he did catch a glimpse of her, and thought he saw tears in her eyes, he leaped to his feet. Nigel pulled him back down.

"Dude, you're going to get in trouble. Don't overdo it."

Plus, it was time for class and Franc was swept out of the cafeteria by a wave of students. People he didn't even know were slapping him on the back as he crossed the quad.

"Fucking hilarious!"

• • • •

Civic Duty, his next class, was a misery. It took all his effort to maintain a blank, bored face like all the other students as he "listened" to the less. He had found her, but now what? How could he talk to her, how would she talk to him? They lived in two different worlds.

Crazy plans went through his head. They'd run away together, live in the woods, some place without cameras, without chips, without people. As if. Franc didn't know anything about the woods or even really how to get there. And why would she want to go with him?

Why would she even talk to him after seeing a whole cafeteria of people laughing. Of course, she must think it was a joke aimed at her. She spoke English—they all spoke English. They'd heard them all along, all the stupid comments kids have said about them. She must have thought this was just one more jerk, worse than the others, singling her out for a laugh.

He had hurt her, he was sure of it now. He felt it in the pit of his stomach. She had seen him afterwards, laughing with his table of friends. He could see it now from her perspective. Stuck up rich kids. Stuck up chippers, laughing at her, looking down at her.

She hated him, he knew it.

By the time the rest of the class emerged from their less cocoons, wiser than Franc about some law or something, it was hard for him to even keep his head up. He walked to his next class in a sort of a daze. He couldn't see the point of finishing the day, couldn't see the point of school, but he was on autopilot, moving down the hall without question. Like everyone else.

All along the hall people he didn't even know recognized him from the vid, called out, slapped his shoulder. He didn't care about them. He saw now that he had never cared. But he smiled anyway, he gave them the nod of recognition, he high-fived the ones who high-fived him. He couldn't help it.

He didn't even have to try to fake it; it was automatic. He felt the rush of fame despite himself. When some kid he barely knew clasped his hand and said, "Dude!" he couldn't help feeling good at that moment. But when the moment passed, he felt worse than before.

None of it mattered. None of these people mattered. Meming didn't matter. Nothing that had seemed so important the day before mattered to him anymore.

To get to art you had to pass the cafeteria. It was closed now, obviously, but when he looked in, he could see movement inside. They were cleaning, picking up the mess the students had made. She must be in there, he thought. He put his face up to the glass. Was that her?

Franc banged on the glass. "I'm sorry!" he yelled. The crowd behind him laughed. People were stopping, expecting another show. He banged again and was about to shout when the door popped open and a head of short-cropped gray hair leaned out and told him to go away and stop bothering the poor girl.

"I just want to say I'm sorry. I didn't mean to embarrass her."

"Embarrass her? Young man, you've put her in danger. You've put yourself in danger. Now go away, and don't come back!"

The door slammed shut and the crowd behind him roared with laughter. He heard a voice yell, "Don't give up! The custodian's available!" He looked back, saw their expectant faces, turned away. There was a murmur of disappointment. He put his head down and trudged on.

. . . .

Art was not a less like the other classes, it was active. Research had shown that developing brains still needed interaction with physical objects. Otherwise the right hemisphere atrophied. Early chippers had begun to lose spatial awareness and became disoriented when having to deal with non–virtual reality, so all students were required to take at least one class of doing instead of learning.

Ms. Mirabella, the teacher, greeted them as they walked in. She was almost as old as Mr. Lewis, with gray hair tied up in a bun on top of her head.

"Grab your canvases," she said, "If you haven't finished your still life, gather round the bowl. Those already finished, work on your perspective lesson."

Franc went into the storeroom for his canvas. It wasn't any good, but he enjoyed working on it. He liked the splotches of color on the palette. He liked the atmosphere of the class, usually. Students chatted while they worked; Ms. Mirabella did not mind. She was, as always, working on her own painting and seemed able to completely tune them out.

But today, Franc did not want to talk to anyone. He took the easel near the teacher. He looked at the bowl of fruit and flowers they were supposed to be painting. He looked at his own painting. They weren't as similar as he would have liked. Not that it mattered. He could have painted the banana blue and his teacher would have been thrilled. He looked at her canvas. She was the only teacher he'd ever heard of who did the work right alongside the students, class after class adding more details until she'd produced what appeared to be a photograph, but better, realer somehow. She always included at least one thing that wasn't actually there but which blended in so well that it looked like it *should have* been there. Today it was a frog, one of those maybe poison ones from the rainforest, peeping out of the top of the vase just below the hydrangea.

If you were too obviously not getting anything done, too obviously watching vids or playing games, or just talking too much, she'd come up beside you, stand there so calmly and just gaze intently at your picture. Then she'd pull out her own brush. Sometimes, if someone was really struggling, she would give a tip, gently point out how better to shade the edges or correct dimensions that were obviously off. But if the problem was laziness, (and this had happened to Franc many times) out would come the brush and before you even noticed sometimes, something would appear on your canvas – an angel on the windowsill, a flying saucer buzzing over your dog's head, something bizarre and unexpected. This meant a demerit – a lower score. You could paint it out, of course, but Franc always left her little additions right where she left them, because they were so beautiful.

"Hey, Ms. Mirabella," he said suddenly, "How many times do you think you've done this?"

"Done what?"

"Painted a bowl of fruit or something."

"Just once."

"What?"

"All the others were just studies—practice. Today I'll paint my masterpiece."

He looked up to see if she was joking; it was impossible to tell. He looked back at his sad canvas. The flowers were oversized, the wrong shade, the apple looked dull. He could no longer zoom, that was part of it. You weren't supposed to rely on zoom and Mezr™ and all the other tools, according to Ms. Mirabella. "Just look," she'd always say, "This is a class in seeing. See what you see, paint what you see." But to Franc, and everyone else, he supposed, that had never made sense anyway. Why would you not zoom if you could zoom? How could you get proportion with just your eye?

So he knew today would be a challenge, and it was, but not the way he had anticipated. When he picked up his palette and faced the arrangement of fruit and flowers he was meant to be painting, he understood Ms. Mirabella for the first time. Everything looked so real, so vivid, so alive! He realized he had never really seen them before, never really looked at anything, not since childhood anyway when he used to lie in the grass and watch the clouds spin by above him. He picked up his brush, eager to try and recreate the beauty he saw, but when he tried to paint, he saw that his hand was trembling.

"Pull yourself together!" he thought, but he had no idea how. He looked at his classmates. Fortunately, no one seemed to notice.

He tried again, but again his hand shook so he could barely hold his brush. Suddenly, he felt the teacher's hand on his arm. He looked up and found himself staring into two large, gray eyes. Calmly, she said, "Franc, why don't you take a little walk. Get yourself a drink of water."

She knew! He didn't know how she knew, but she knew.

"Um, okay," he said, heading for the door. For a moment he had an impulse to run as if the Patrol were already there, but he forced himself to walk, to stroll really, to act like he didn't have a care in the world.

He made his way to the restroom, which Thank God was empty, for once. He locked himself in a stall and sat down, staring at, but not seeing, the stupid messages carved there. He could still see old Ms. M's eyes before him. Her look wasn't an accusation. If anything, she was saying, "Your secret's safe with me." He felt certain, the more he thought about it, that he didn't need to worry about her at all.

So why was he still shaking? More than ever, he was aware of everything he was missing, in this case, mood stabilizers. He knew the chip regulated dopamine and adrenaline to keep you on an even keel, but he had no idea how much he needed them. What if he were to start crying in class? The whole thing was just too much. He felt dizzy. A week was crazy. One day and he was losing it already. What was he going to prove? He felt the world crashing in on him, and he was no match for it. He'd go home, he'd talk to his mom. He'd go back to normal.

Even better, he'd talk to his grandfather. Grandpa would know what to do. He had contacts; there would be no report. They wouldn't let that happen to the family. They'd get the chip reinstalled and things would be normal again—he'd be normal, he'd feel the same things everyone else felt, he'd see what they saw.

He'd forget her, somehow.

But even as he said it, he knew he had to see her once more. He left the bathroom and walked back to the cafeteria. Looking through the windows, he saw an empty room; they were gone. He walked the length of the building looking in the whole time, but nothing.

Around the back, he found a fenced–in area he had never before noticed. He pressed his face up to the crack, but saw only two dumpsters, one brown and one green. He was about to walk away when the door opened and two women came out pushing a cart loaded with plastic trash bags. They were talking as they came.

"How can you say that? He's worse than all of them, laughing at you like that!"

"I didn't say he was good, I said he was cute."

"Cute? He's an idiot."

"They're all idiots," she said. "School for the Blind!"

"Chippers!" said the older woman over her shoulder, as she headed back for another load, leaving the younger one to sort the bags into the two dumpsters.

It was her. The day was hot, and sweat dripped down her forehead. She still had on those stupid rubber gloves and that ridiculous hairnet, but nothing could hide her beauty. When she turned toward the recycling bin, he could see tears on her cheeks.

Franc stood frozen for a minute. He knew that he should go, that he'd done enough damage already, but he also knew that after he was rechipped, he'd never see her again. He began to climb the fence. At the top, he looked around, but no one was watching. He dropped down and walked up behind her. As he came close he could hear her humming softly to herself.

"Maya," he said as softly as he could. She jumped and spun around, slapping him across the face with her gloved hand. He reached up to block the left hand, which was coming in fast. He grabbed her wrist and held it.

The fright in her eyes changed to anger and she came back with another right, clomping him smack across the side of his head before he managed to grab that hand too. She opened her mouth as if to scream, but she could see him now, a face so mournful, a caged puppy, and she whispered instead.

"What are you doing here?"

"I had to say I'm sorry. I . . . I never meant, I wasn't being funny."

He was looking now straight into those eyes, the eyes of his dream. He felt her arms relax and he let go, but as he dropped his hand, she grabbed it.

"You're an idiot."

"I know."

And then she smiled, and the corners of her eyes crinkled.

"You're so stupid."

"I know."

And she laughed, a real, open–throated laugh. He could see her perfect white teeth.

"It's so ridiculous!" she said, and he answered "I know" again. He felt like a tremendous stone had just been rolled off his chest, and the happiness he felt at that moment showed him that he had never really been happy before.

But suddenly, he saw fear in her eyes. "She's coming! Hide!"

Franc looked around. There was only one place. He jumped into the dumpster.

It wasn't until that moment that Franc pondered the wastefulness of his society. His landing, on a pile of sealed trash bags, had been easy enough, but immediately he was overwhelmed by the smell of other people's uneaten food. Through the plastic, he could see, and smell, half–empty milk cartons, torn bits of bread, stale green beans. So much waste. Whatever happened to the clean plate club? It was like staring into an open, chewing mouth.

When the first bag broke, Franc had only two thoughts in his head: Who doesn't finish their pudding? and Why did today have to be rice pudding day? Franc had always liked rice pudding, but he knew that little pleasure was gone forever as soon as he saw it splash and dribble down the side of the dumpster, saw it puddle at the bottom, and felt himself sinking towards it.

Another bag broke, and it was abundantly clear that the beef stew was not a big hit. A substance too dark to be vomit, but otherwise indistinguishable from it, poured out.

But it was the unmistakable stench of broccoli that really concerned him.

"Broccoli was yesterday!" he thought, looking around in a panic. He saw then a ladder welded to the side, probably to enable people to climb inside to clean out the dumpster when empty. He lunged for it, ripping open two more bags in the process. Having grabbed the top rung, he dragged his feet across, through the rice pudding, though mercifully avoiding the rancid broccoli. Careful to stay out of sight, he walked his feet up out of the muck as high as he could, where he remained crouched, back to the trash like a swimmer about to race the backstroke.

"What was that?" he heard someone say.

"Rats," Maya answered, "I think they're back."

Having already hit panic mode, Franc had no bandwidth left to obsess about this latest fact. He was too busy listening.

"Maya, I spoke to The Committee. They're going to relocate you."

"But..."

"You've been recced. They know your name. It's too dangerous."

"But they didn't understand what I said. They can't."

"He did. And they heard him say it. You're going back to Oakland. To the docks."

"What about him?"

"He'll be fine. He'll come back tomorrow with a chip like a good boy and his memory will be synced up. He'll never know you existed."

"I guess."

"But you'll be OK, don't worry. Oh, and set a new trap before you leave, okay?"

He could hear footsteps fading off, a door slam. "You can come out now" and then he was out and standing before her again. Her eyebrows were trying to eat her nose, and her head was down.

He had no idea what to say, so he reached out and kissed her instead. She reached up her gloved hands and pulled his face toward her even more tightly.

Suddenly, she turned her head. He could feel the tears on her cheeks as she burrowed her face into his shoulder. Her hands slid down his back and they held each other tightly.

"We'll never see each other again," he said.

"I may see you, but you won't see me."

"None of this makes sense!" He pulled back. "There has to be a way."

Her pause gave him his answer, the one he already knew. There was no way. They were from two worlds, two universes.

Maya laughed. "You're disgusting," she said. She took a rag from her back pocket and began cleaning him off. She rubbed a pudding stain on his shirt and repeated, "You're disgusting."

When she was done, when he was as clean as a dirty rag could make him, Maya pulled herself up to her full height.

"You've got to go," she said simply.

Franc leaned in for another kiss.

"No!" she said, "You have to go now!" and she turned and walked back into the building. He watched her go, then climbed back over the fence.

He couldn't see any point in going back to class, so he just sat, staring, his back against the dumpster fence, until school ended.

Nigel was in his usual spot, snogging with Jasleen. Kelli sat on the same bench, her back to them, chatting with a girl Franc didn't know. He sat between them, trying to look anywhere else.

Suddenly, the squelchy sound of locked lips stopped.

"Hold on a sec," he heard Jasleen say. He looked over. She was holding her palm towards Nigel while her eyes dashed back and forth furiously.

"Text," he thought, "Probably her mom." He wondered if Jasleen's mother had dropped in on her cam feed. They all do it, it's no secret, though most, like his own mom swore they never would. Of course minors had no legal privacy, but still, just thinking about it was kind of gross. He remembered back to when he and Kelli were hot and heavy. More than once his mother had chatted him or emailed at inopportune times. Might have been a coincidence, but he always wondered.

"Dude," Nigel whispered, "Come on over and we'll battle." He glanced in his girlfriend's direction. "Sounds like she's going to have to head home."

Even though he knew it was expected, and that he'd do the same in Nigel's shoes, Franc felt a vague resentment about being second choice. In some ways, it only made him even more aware that he and Nigel weren't as tight as they used to be.

"Can't," he replied, "Grounded."

"Oh well, join us from home."

"I'll try."

Nigel's car was inching up alongside the moving sidewalk. When they approached, the door opened, and after a wave and a blown kiss, they got inside.

As they drove home, Nigel chattered about some dude in his Mandarin class who said *wáng bā* instead of *wǎng bā*. Which meant bastard instead of internet bar. It was "hilarious," he said and he made Franc "watch" the vid so he could see the teacher's face turn red.

It took all of Franc's effort to play along, to laugh at the right spot. And when Nigel brought up again how hilarious he had been at lunch, he felt like he was beginning to hate his best friend. The constant laughter, the easy way he pried himself off his girl and changed the subject like she was nothing. He was beginning to hate friendship itself. It was all in the past. Nigel wasn't friends with *him*; he didn't even notice him. He was friends with the kid on the playground in fifth grade, the kid having a sleepover in the tree fort, the kid who didn't laugh at him when he wet his pants at school, who threw water on both of them so he could blame it on a water fight. That kid didn't exist anymore.

He took a really good look at Nigel, trying to imagine seeing him for the first time, without the ghost of the child he had been. Nigel was looking up and right, watching a vid he'd just been sent. He had the same happy look of expectation he'd had when he was six and his mother brought out a plate of cookies.

And outside the window, just past his head, Franc could see them again. Hordes of shuffling misery, dragging their blankets, peering out of doorways, hollow-eyed. They passed a factory, and he could see the workers lined up waiting for their shift. Several of them looked to be about 12 years old.

This time, when Nigel laughed and looked up expectantly, Franc couldn't even manage a smile. It felt like they were having a party in a cemetery, ignoring the sobbing of the bereaved all around them.

"What's wrong?"

"I think I'm going to puke."

Nigel used his override and the car pulled to the side of the road. The door opened, and Franc found himself kneeling by the back of the car, puking for real. Great spasms shook him, and even after his whole lunch was in the gutter, he still retched. His forehead was covered with beads of sweat.

When the heaves subsided, he looked up and saw Nigel beside him. He was his friend after all.

"You okay, dude?"

"Yeah. Must be something I ate. Just give me a minute."

He got up and leaned against the car. The metal was warm in the sun. He looked around. It wasn't too bad here, not scary. They were in front of a large apartment building. A woman stood on the porch shaking dust from a rug.

She looked at them suspiciously. Clearly, this wasn't an everyday occurrence. A bunch of little kids had paused their hopscotch game to stare at them.

"Let's go," whispered Nigel. "This place is weird."

· · · ·

His front door shut behind him with a sucking sound. He could hear the gears of the lock turning, the bolt sliding back into its slot, a whirr as the seal reinflated, then silence. The distant hum of traffic, even the hoo–hooing of the mourning doves—all of the sounds he wasn't even aware of hearing—shut off as with a switch. It was so quiet he could hear the cat's claws click on the kitchen floor two rooms away, and from his office the tap–tapping of Grandpa's ancient keyboard.

He'd never noticed before how calm his house was, how serene, how sealed–off from the world. He sat for a moment and looked out the window. The Bay Bridge poked its head above the fog, and he could see the Oakland Hills beyond. He felt so comfortable, so protected, like he never wanted to open his front door ever again.

Here, in the quiet of his home, the solution seemed so easy. Confess. Confess and be cured. Rejoin and learn to forget. Maya was right; she might see him again, but he'd never see her. That's just the way life is, all he had to do, all he could do, was accept it.

When he pictured her face, those eyes, he felt a pain that was actually physical. But if he truly forgot, if they could erase it all from his mind forever, would it matter?

He looked at the door of his grandfather's office. He'd be working now. He didn't like to be disturbed, and anyhow Franc was suddenly aware of the taint of vomit on his teeth.

As he brushed, he stared at himself in the mirror. His nose looked huge to him now, his crooked tooth an immense deformity. But he liked his eyes. People would think it was weird if he ever said it out loud, but Franc had always admired his own eyes. He'd heard his blue eyes complimented for as long as he could remember. Older ladies never failed to comment on his long, black eyelashes. "So unfair!' they'd say.

He leaned up to the glass and stared at his own eyes. They looked different to him. Before, he liked the word "mischievous" when he thought about his eyes. Now they seemed weary, older. Wise?

On the counter lay the broken hand mirror. He should have gotten rid of that, but it didn't matter anymore. He'd tell his grandpa everything. Not his mom. She'd find out, of course, but he wouldn't tell her first. She'd be understanding, comforting, but he didn't want comfort—he wanted information. Grandpa would tell him he was stupid, but he'd also answer a few questions.

He walked back to his room. There was nothing to do without his chip, and he started to wish this was a work day. Normally, he'd be in the back yard where there was more room, battling with his friends. Or he'd lie in bed and watch vids. All the usual fails and pranks, but he also liked really old movies—comedies. *Dumb and Dumber*, *Pee Wee's Big Adventure*, even really ancient stuff like Laurel and Hardy or *The Little Rascals*. He liked 2-D, something his friends couldn't understand at all. They were funny, all right, but they also gave a glimpse into a world that was gone forever.

Lying on his bed, even without his chip, images flickered across his mind. He saw two men in overalls moving a piano upstairs. Saw a boy with an enormous cowlick burping up soap bubbles, heard "the most annoying sound in the world."

The next thing he knew, the front door closed, and his mom called out, "Anybody home?" It was dark in his room. He sat up, and the light went on.

"Hi, Mom," he called out, "I'm in here."

His mother appeared in the doorway. She looked weary. He could see lines around her eyes, deep ridges between her brows. Her hair was turning gray.

"She filters too," he thought.

"Were you napping?" she said, "I heard you up last night. "Maybe we should get your chip checked. That's not normal for a boy your age. Do you feel all right?"

"I'm fine," he said, getting up. "Just tired."

"Well, dinner will be ready soon. Can you go out and pick some lettuce?"

That was another weird thing about his family. Everyone else he knew ate packets. They were delicious, and it took like two minutes to prepare a whole meal. But his mom was following the latest trend; she was a "realist," insisting on eating only (or at least mostly) food that was "real," things that had never been sealed in plastic, did not come from the factory. She believed it kept her "grounded." It all seemed like a waste of time to Franc, and some of the stuff was gross. One day, there was a bug crawling in the salad. Grandpa just pinched it between his thumb and forefinger, tossed the smush on the table next to his plate, and kept eating. "At least we know it's real," his mom had said.

So it was out to the greenhouse for him, while his mom started cooking something with tofu or goat cheese or godknowswhat. He walked past the patio, into the garden, but rather than stopping at the greenhouse, he went further, past the plum and apple trees, to the pines that edged the property. Looking up, he could barely make out in the dim light the tree fort where he and Nigel used to play and dream. It had been his world in those days, this yard. Through the dark branches, he could see a single star.

The old wooden pallets nailed to the trunk for a ladder were still there, and Franc began to climb. He wriggled through the trap door and pulled himself up onto the platform. He was startled to find the whole structure was barely seven feet above the ground. It had seemed so immense!

He stood and looked east. The lights of the city glowed beyond the wall. Behind him he could hear the low, familiar tones of the fog horn. "How long has that been going on?" he thought. The fog hadn't reached them yet, but below them, he knew, it was rolling in, obscuring the bottom of the Golden Gate, enclosing the headlands. Soon the whole bridge would disappear. When he was a child, he had loved to watch the fog roll in. It felt like you could disappear, turn into cloud.

He thought about his grandpa's story, about the jumpers from the bridge. It must have been the fog, he thought. He felt sure no one had made that leap on a sunny day, but in the fog it didn't seem so crazy to just drop into nothing, to disappear.

He listened for a moment to the mournful home–home of the fog horn. It was the sound of his childhood, his nightly lullaby, but it seemed to him that it had been years since he had heard it. When had it stopped? How old had he been when the outdoors had stopped being a place of wonder and had become the everyday, something you had to get through to reach your destination?

"She must be wondering where I am," he thought.

He climbed back down and completed his errand, picking a head of lettuce and a few radishes as well. His mother didn't look up from her chopping when he entered. She just gave a little half nod toward the big pot of water on the counter. Frank dunked the lettuce in and swirled it around a few times before placing it on the drainer board.

"Can you hear the fog horn?" he asked, and his mother answered "Hm." She grabbed the lettuce, tore off the bottom, and dropped the rest back into the pot, washing it vigorously before taking it out and shaking the leaves over the sink and laying them on a dishtowel.

Franc stood still and watched her. She looked small. The line between her brows was deep. He'd never noticed before that her resting face was worried. Had she always been like that? It seemed to him to be something about motherhood itself, although he couldn't picture Nigel's mom ever worried. She was always flying to Vegas with some new boyfriend, leaving Nigel alone. But Franc's mom, never. Every night she stood behind that kitchen island, washing, chopping. The thought that she might prefer something else had never once entered Franc's mind.

"Hey Mom, how was work?" She was an administrator of some sort for the V.T.B.

"What?" she looked up. "Oh fine." Her eyes were flitting up and down, upper right quadrant. She was doing emails. Work.

"Go tell Grandpa dinner will be ready in ten minutes."

Grandpa sat as usual, leaning towards the two giant monitors, typing rapidly. Before Franc could speak, he held up one hand as he continued to type with the other. Lines of red and yellow code slid up the screen. His back was bent, more than Franc had ever noticed, but the gesture, the posture, was the same as Franc had seen every day of his life.

But when he finally stopped typing and swiveled round Franc gasped.

"Didn't anyone ever tell you it's impolite to stare?"

The voice was his grandfather, but the creature before him was something else—shrunken, twisted, with only thin wisps of hair on a milk–white scalp. The smile was the same, the corners of his mouth curved slightly—more sarcastic than amused—but the teeth were yellow and crooked.

But what really had Franc transfixed was the eye, or rather the gaping hole where his right eye had been the night before.

"Like what you see?" Grandpa asked calmly. "Go ahead, 'Feast your eyes, glut your soul on my accursed ugliness!'"

"Um... Mom says dinner's almost ready."

"Wonderful" he answered, "We'll have so much to talk about!"

"**S**o," said his mother, as she put a plate in front of Franc, "How was school?"

"Umm, fine"

"Did you learn anything today?"

"Um, not really."

"How's that Kelli? She's so nice."

"Fine, I guess."

"Oh! I ran into Oscar Gonzales' mom at work."

"Who?"

"Remember? He was on your soccer team. Pee Wee league? His dad was from Redding, where Grandpa was born?"

"I have no idea who you're talking about."

"Well he goes to Mitty—I guess they're Catholic. He still plays soccer. He's on the school team."

"Oh"

"You ever think about taking that up again?"

"Mom, I was terrible."

"You just need to practice. I think more fresh air would be good for you."

Franc couldn't even imagine a good response to this. He took a spoonful of potatoes while his mom went on. She was full of news. It seemed Aunt Becky had a new boyfriend or maybe she had just broken up, he wasn't sure. He found it hard to follow because every time he looked up he could see his grandfather staring at him. He had a look in his eye of cruel amusement, like a cat watching a mouse struggle to escape. He chewed his salad with an open mouth and Franc could not look away from the green leaves and yellow teeth. He was enjoying himself.

They were both wondering the same thing: when would she notice?

But she kept on. Franc watched her talk. The lines in her face were still there, of course, but relaxed. This was calming for her, this was what she enjoyed. When was the last time he had really listened to his mother talk? Usually, he would be messaging his friends or watching a vid with half an eye.

She had gone onto another of his long–forgotten teammates and what had become of his parents, when Franc broke in.

"Hey Mom, didn't you play sports when you were my age?"

"Oh yes! Not soccer, though. I played a sport called softball. No one plays it now. In those days boys played baseball and girls played softball—the same really except the ball was bigger and you pitched underhand. Course now they play baseball same as the boys. Seems crazy looking back—a whole separate sport. And girls' hands are smaller, so why a bigger ball?"

And on she went. She moved on to explain about cheerleaders (all girls apparently) and football (all boys) and how the whole thing really made no sense, "but we had fun, and honestly I can't remember even thinking about it."

Suddenly, she looked up and saw her audience sitting curiously quiet, not listening, but waiting.

"What?" She studied Franc's face. It looked different—pale. "Are you feeling okay, Honey?"

"Me? I'm fine."

Grandpa cut in. "We have something to tell you."

Here it comes, thought Franc, the tears, the worry.

"Franc's going to miss school tomorrow. I'm taking him to Campus with me."

"Really? Why?"

"Oh, career exploration. Want to show him off to my colleagues. We'll spend the day, have lunch. Sounds fun, right Franc?"

"Um, yeah," he said. He had no idea what was going on, but apparently there would be no maternal tears, and that was all he cared about at the time. "I can make up my schoolwork easy."

"Well, I don't know."

"I'll take good care of the boy."

"I know."

"Then it's settled. We'll take The Beast."

"Oh no, that's not safe. Take my car."

"It's perfectly safe. Are you saying I can't drive?

"No, but . . ."

"Franc, clear these dishes and bring in whatever whole–grain tofu–based nonsense is passing for dessert these days."

And so it went. They ate their dessert—which was in fact tofu–based and tasted like it—and talked of other things.

"You know, you shouldn't be eating this at all, young man. You had two of those big school cookies today."

"Ah, Mom, I was hungry, and besides, one of them was for Kelli."

"Oh! Are you two . . .?"

"No! She's my friend, that's all."

"Such a nice girl—and so pretty!"

"I know she's nice."

"Well then, what's the problem?"

"No problem, it's just ..."

Franc's mom's eyes narrowed. Her voice softened. "You know, if there's anything you want to tell me. . . "

"I'm not gay! Not that there's anything wrong with it."

"Of course not."

"We're just friends now—leave it at that."

"Mmhmm," she said, not convinced, then changed the subject. "They say 'heavy fog tomorrow,'" they being the weather update she could see in the lower right quadrant. "Are you sure you want to drive that thing?"

Franc relaxed. His relationship status—even the question of whether and why he should miss school—was forgotten, lost in their age–old argument, the foolish stubbornness of certain people to continue driving manually after it has been proven unsafe compared to the latest systems.

They were still arguing when Franc excused himself and went to his room. Once again, there was nothing to do. No games, no vids, no chatting, nothing. Franc found himself staring out the window. The trees were waving in the wind, but he wasn't really watching them. He was thinking—couldn't help but think—about everything. The razor plunging into his neck, the strange crowds on the streets, his grandfather's gaping eye socket, his moth-er's blind love. And her. His mind kept circling back to her—those eyes, that voice, her lips. He'd never see her again, and there was nothing he could do about it. All these images swirled in his mind and he had no control, no way to distract himself.

Why had he done it? What could it prove? He wanted to know what was real, but he found himself more confused than ever.

Suddenly, he saw something move under the pine tree in the front of the house. An umbrella opened, and a man walked out of the shadow of the trunk. He walked the length of the house, and then turned and walked back. When he neared Franc's window, he tilted the umbrella back and peered straight at him.

Without thinking, Franc jumped back away from the window. His heart was pounding. Who could this be? He started for the door to tell his mom, but hesitated. As the words formed in his mind, he could hear how ridiculous they sounded. He could hear her response. "He's on the sidewalk? Probably a neighbor taking a walk."

Franc returned to the window. No one was there, and the fact that his pulse was still pounding made him feel like an idiot.

A scratching sound at his door, followed by a yowl, distracted him. Mai-cat was there when he opened it, looking very impatient. She came in and rubbed against his legs, meowing pitifully.

"What's the matter?" he asked, picking her up, "Did they forget to feed you?"

The cat squirmed out of his grip and jumped to the floor. Franc followed her into the kitchen where there was indeed an empty bowl. He pulled a glass container from the fridge and emptied it into the bowl, thinking for the thousandth time "Who makes their own cat food?"

Mai-cat bit happily into the stinky pile, and Franc began to wonder where his mother was. He padded up the stairs and looked down the hall. The door to her bedroom was open. "Mom?" he called as he walked down the hall, but all he saw was a still-made bed. A photo of him holding Mai-cat's predecessor was on the nightstand. Was he four? Five?

But no Mom. Franc went back downstairs. When he passed Grandpa's room and saw it was also empty, he knew there was only one place they could be.

Outside Grandpa's office, Franc stood and tried to listen.

"It has to be done soon, of course, but while I'm out. . ."

"Why would he take such a risk?"

"Oh come on, Amanda, you know. We've both seen this coming—discontented, moody—I knew something was up when he broke it off with that Kelli girl. Algorithm selects the perfect mate, and he slaps it away. Any normal kid wouldn't be worrying about true love, or whatever's in his head. He'd be too busy trying to fuck her."

"Dad!"

"Sorry. But him? He questions, he ponders. We both know where that comes from. Don't act surprised."

His mother did not answer. He could hear the unmistakable sound of sobbing.

Grandpa's voice was softer now. "He'll be fine. I'll take care of it. Believe me, they need him."

The doorknob moved—someone was leaning on the other end—and Franc took off back to his room. He lay on his bed, listening to his own heart beat.

He wondered if he could ever get used to this sensation, that his own heart was a creature inside him over which he had no control. No way to command a calm, no automatic flood of relaxing chemicals. No way even to call on a distraction. Right now he'd happily watch that vid of being kicked in the face. Nothing to do but lie in bed and *feel* the pain, the regret, the worry,

His breath was ragged, almost painful, but he found that this was one thing he could control. He forced himself to breathe slowly and beat by beat his heart began to slow. He closed his eyes and began to count each exhalation, and by the time he reached twenty, he felt calmer. All his problems were still there, waiting for him, but at this moment all he needed to do was breathe.

And when he opened his eyes, it was like seeing his own room for the first time. It was a dork's room, a nobody's room. Besides some vaguely "boy" stuff his mom had picked out years ago, it looked like every other room in the house. Why had he never bothered to even put up one poster?

There was a quiet knock at the door, and the knob turned.

"Franc?"

"Yeah?"

"Can I come in?"

There was no need to answer this as she was already in. Franc stood, ready for the tears, for the "Why would you?"s, the "What were you thinking?"s, but before he could speak, his mother held up a hand and said brightly, "Can I use your bathroom? I'm in a hurry." And without waiting for an answer, went in.

But the door was barely closed when it opened again.

"OK," she said, "I'm on incog. Let's talk."

"Incog? Adults have that? Why? Who could tap in?"

"You can't be too sure. But we don't have much time. We need to talk."

She sat down on his bed, so he sat beside her. "I'm sorry," he began, but she cut him off.

"We don't have time. Tell me, what did you see?"

"What?"

"Without the chip. What's it like? Is it relaxing?"

"No, it's scary, kind of. Weird. Well, sort of relaxing. Quiet."

She was leaning forward, her body twisted around so as to look him straight in the face. In this light, and so up close, those wrinkles at the corners of her eyes stood out clearly. There were two deep lines between her brows, like a mask of worry.

"But what did you see?"

And he told her about how so many kids were filtering, and he could see her cheeks redden as her own vanity was revealed. Then the bigger story, the throngs of people on the street, the hollow–eyed misery he had seen strewn across the city. About seeing the baby ripped from the mother's arms.

"Why would they want to take a baby?" he asked.

"Well, could be many reasons. Unfit mother, not caring for it, something. But there are rumors."

"What?"

"Well you know fertility is way low, which is maybe good 'cause we live so long. So a lot of people adopt."

"Okay."

"The rumor is that V.T.B. has ways of sensing positive genetic configurations and that they're using this to supply babies for adoption from people who can't provide for them."

"By force?"

"It's just a rumor."

"But all the others?"

"You're too young, but I remember seeing what you're talking about—the chipless. You'd see them whenever you had to cross town. And they'd even bang on the car, begging food. Children even. Women with babies. You could hear them crying through the glass. Without a chip, in the city there's no work. Can't get through any doors. You need the basic chip just to sweep floors.

"Rumor was they'd cull them, take out the ones that bothered people, keep the population down. Some said they were transported out to work the fields—you don't need a chip to pick lettuce. But others said there was a permanent solution.

"I knew it!" she interrupted herself, "I knew they hadn't solved anything."

"What do you mean? Who?"

"And then one day the streets were empty. They newsfed us that they'd solved the problem, manufactured enough chips for every man, woman and child. Everyone from now on would be happy and productive. We'd all live forever, well hundreds of years anyway. No one knows yet."

"What do you mean, enough chips? Everyone has a chip. I know they're not all PlusTens™ like we have, but the basics, the health functions, everyone has."

"You think so? Do you know how many people there are? Even if they could produce that many chips, I don't think they would. Where would we all go? Life span used to be 70 years. Even if we only live to 140, that's double the population.

"I knew it! The problem was too big, I knew they couldn't solve it. They just programmed us not to see. You know," her voice dropped. "Your father predicted this."

"My father?"

"Do you know what cancer was? Your dad was the one who managed to program cell level diagnosis into the chip. It takes massive bandwidth. Constant diagnosis of the entire body to detect any mutations. Before a tumor can even begin to form, the chip sends antibodies to destroy it. No more cancer. You don't know what that means, but my mom died from it—your grandma. It was horrible. Wasting away, crying in pain. When he told me what he'd accomplished, I was so happy. He was too, for a while.

"But then he started to get really depressed. He'd say, 'We've created a new species. 10% will live hundreds of years—forever maybe—and the other 90% will just die. How long before they figure it out? How long before they rise up?'

"It bothered him tremendously, the failure to manufacture more, to spread the benefit. But it was too expensive. 'Be practical,' they told him."

"10%? That's all?"

Her voice dropped again. "Actually, he was over–optimistic. It's closer to 1%. "

"What?"

"Less, actually. He accused the chief of genocide. Said not preventing death while you can is the same thing. And then he disappeared."

"Disappeared? What do you mean?

"You know what disappeared means!" she snapped. Tears were running down the lines of her face, those lines he'd not seen yesterday.

"I don't know . . . He's gone . . . It's not safe to talk about." And for a few horrible minutes Franc just sat and listened to her sob. He felt he should do something, hug her maybe, but he didn't know what, so he stared down at his own hands.

'Honey, I'm sorry." She ran a sleeve across her eyes and lifted her head. "It just seemed better to forget. You were so young, and after a while, you just stopped asking. One day he was here, and the next he wasn't. He went to work, and the car came back alone."

"Where did he work?"

"Same place as your grandpa," she said. "Look, I have to go." She pulled him into a hug and her cheeks smeared his face with tears.

The warmth of his mother's body, the softness of her flesh, seemed to break something inside him. He started to tremble.

"It'll be OK, I promise," she whispered. "We'll talk again soon." And then she left.

Morning came as an unpleasant surprise. He'd been having the falling dream again. Over and over throughout the night—hundreds of times it seemed—he'd feel himself falling and will himself to wake up. If you hit bottom in your dreams, you die. Every kid knows that. And each time, he'd wake in the dark, heart pounding and nothing he could do about it.

In his dream he was himself, but not. He felt full–sized, but somehow he was a baby being ripped from his mother's arms and dropped from the Golden Gate Bridge. He saw it from all angles: he was the officer pulling on the tiny arms, while at the same time he could feel the child slipping from his grip, and always he was the innocent infant looking up at his mother's face as he fell, fell, fell.

It seemed he had only finally dropped into really deep sleep when he felt something tugging at his arm. He opened his eyes and found his mother staring at him.

"Honey?"

"Huh?"

"I have to go. Grandpa's in his room."

"Okay."

"You know the person we were talking about last night?"

"Huh? Oh yeah."

"He left something for you."

"What?"

She handed him a small rectangle of cardboard in a plastic sleeve. There was a picture on it of a man in an old–fashioned baseball uniform with a big padded vest with a helmet and mask on throwing a baseball. At the bottom were the words "RAILRIDERS" in a funny font and then "SCRANTON/

WILKES–BARRE" in boldface. Down the left side was "#45 EDDY RO-
DRIGUEZ" and the word "CATCHER."

"What is it? Why?"

His mother shrugged. "Boys used to collect those. You're a boy. He had a
bunch of them, hundreds, but he sold them all, I thought. But later I found
this one in a drawer with a note that said 'Franc." It must have been a special
one I guess."

"Um, Okay, thanks."

"I should have given it to you earlier. Well, I've gotta run. Have fun with
your grandpa," and she was gone.

Franc sat on the edge of the bed and stared at the card in his hands. What
did it mean? He didn't know much about baseball. He had played one season
of little league, and sometimes his grandpa had taken him to see the Giants,
but that's about it. He'd never heard of this team, let alone the player. Was it
rare, and therefore valuable?

He stared at the card, expecting something to happen, some message
from beyond the grave, or from wherever his dad was if he wasn't dead. The
year on the card was 2017. Did that mean something? What happened that
year? Or the team, the Railriders, could that be the clue? But what?

· · · ·

Grandpa stood at the stove frying sausages when Franc emerged from his
room.

"Grab a plate." he said without turning his head, "And put four slices in
the toaster. Coffee's on the stove. Pour me one, will you?"

Franc dropped the brown bread into the slots. He then pulled out two
mugs. He didn't actually like the taste of coffee, but he loved the smell and
the feel of it in his hands. For his grandfather's cup he reached into the fridge
and pulled out a small glass bottle—actual cow's milk. He had some connection and had it flown in once a week, his only extravagance.

The white and black swirled together in the mug, and Franc watched the
merging clouds. He poured normal oat milk into his own.

"Eat up," Grandpa said, placing the hot skillet directly on the table, something that drove his mother crazy. "It smells like meat at least. Close your eyes and picture a pig."

That was his sense of humor.

Franc forked two sausages and transferred them onto a plate. He pulled his two slices out of the toaster and spread "I Can't Believe" on them.

"Big day today," Grandpa said with his mouth full. "You're going to see some things."

They chewed in silence for some time. They had always communicated mostly without words, and he knew it was better to wait than to ask questions. Whatever he was going to see, besides the doctor who would reinsert the chip, he'd just have to find out when it happened. His mind went back to the baseball card.

"Hey Grandpa," he began. "You're a baseball fan. Who's Eddy Rodriguez."

"Who?"

"Eddy Rodriguez."

"Are you sure you got the name right? Was it Alex Rodriguez? How'd you hear the name?"

"Oh, you know, my history teacher, Mr. Lewis, he's always making little references to sports. He said I was like Eddy Rodriguez. 'You're a real Eddy Rodriguez,' he said."

"Wow, that's a deep cut." Grandpa's eyes were scanning right and down, he was Wikying and playing off like he knew, just like a kid. "Mostly minor league. Why did he say it? Did you succeed at something right away? This guy Rodriguez homered his first time at bat in the majors."

"Um," Franc said noncommittally.

"Did you flame out?"

"What?"

"You know, quick success followed by failure. He only played four days for the Padres, then it was back to the minors."

"Maybe?"

"You probably got the name wrong. He's not enough of a player to remember. But his life was interesting. It says his family . . ." He gave up the pretense of knowing. "It says his family escaped in a little boat. Almost died at sea."

"Escaped what?"

"Cuba. They were so desperate for freedom they tried to make it to Florida in a little rowboat or something. Had to eat coffee beans to survive. I think you must have the wrong guy. Maybe it was Alex Rodriguez. That's a compliment. He went out with Madonna."

"Um, Okay."

"You clean up," he said, getting up. I'm going to meditate for 14 minutes."

Franc loaded the dishes on the belt and pressed the button. He dropped the frying pan in the super heater and grabbed the table–bot off the top shelf and placed it on the table, where it began its meandering munching.

He walked to the edge of the living room where he could see down the hall to his grandpa's closet. The old man was sitting straight upright, like an idol in a niche. There was nothing to do, and Franc's mind began to wander like the table–bot, moving through the recent events randomly, stopping to chew, then moving on.

He could see the tents, the lines waiting for food, the steam rising from the giant pots. Nigel's smiling face, the guards, swinging their batons, could hear the skulls cracking. But that must be his imagination. He had been inside the car; he couldn't hear anything. Was the whole thing in his mind only?

He thought of her again, Maya. He knew he'd never see her again, and his heart ached for the loss of something it never had in the first place.

Before long he could hear his grandfather's shuffle in the hall. "Franc!" he yelled, "I'd like to see you in the office."

He was at his massive desk when Franc entered, typing furiously as usual. Franc sat in his usual chair and glanced at the screen. It looked different from the usual code. Leaning forward, he recognized the distinctive key strokes of "SirChee™," a commercial add–on shortcut of the type usually scorned by his grandfather. He was running a query of some kind.

He was just about to ask what the search was when his grandfather turned towards him and he could see now up–close that wound, that red–black hole in his face. Grandpa noticed his expression and said, "Oh, for god's sake, just ignore it, can't you?"

But Franc continued to stare so the old man, sighing loudly, began rummaging through the drawers of the ancient desk. There, among the papers and junk, he found what he was looking for: a black disc of cloth attached to an elastic string. He slipped the elastic around his head and pulled the black over his wound.

"Better?" he asked, and Franc knew not to answer. "We've got to talk before we go. You've seen some things. You're going to see more today. You did a stupid thing, you know that, but done is done, so we might as well go whole hog and unveil everything. It'll make you better at your job."

"My job?"

"In the future. You have to have at least an idea of the shit we're in if you're going to fix it."

"What? Where are we going? I thought you were taking me for reattachment."

"Well yes, but later. But while we're out there, you can't react to what you see, and for god's sake don't ask me questions."

"Okay, but where?"

"Never mind that now. First things first. What have you seen already?"

"You mean?"

"Yesterday, just tell me about it." And then he did something strange, something Franc had never seen him do before. He turned off the monitors.

Franc had never seen this room, hardly ever seen his grandfather, without that blue glow, and the room suddenly felt very cold and quiet, like a tomb. And as he told his story: the chipless hordes wandering, the battle at the gate, even the baby ripped from its mother's arms, Grandpa leaned in and fixed Franc in a one–eyed stare, but he showed no surprise, no emotion whatsoever.

He found himself dramatizing—acting out the screams of the mother— to get some rise out of the old man, but nothing.

"Why would they do that?" he asked for the second time. "Why would they take someone's baby?"

"Not supposed to be there."

"What?"

"Technically, the whole city is a chip zone. All that camping, begging you saw—strictly against the law. But no one wants to enforce, costs more to put them in jail. It's been a problem for a long time. Some wanted to eliminate the problem finally but . . ."

"Eliminate how?"

"You know how." Grandpa's one eye stared straight into his own, and he knew it was true. There was only one way to eradicate such a problem completely. His mind went back to something Mr. Lewis had said once, 'For every problem, there is a solution that is easy, final and wrong,' or something like that. He was quoting someone.

"But calmer heads prevailed, or more timid anyhow, and they decided on sterilization."

"What?"

"One simple, intradermal injection for every female. It didn't solve the problem short–term of course, but by the time your children, certainly your grandchildren, are riding to school there won't be any ugliness to see. And if we come up with a transport system big enough to bring in all the chip–minus workers every day—already most commute from the East Bay anyway—then we can take down the walls within the city limits. All of San Francisco will be chip–plus only."

"Mom said the kid might be adopted by . . . by people like us."

"Possible. Infertility's still a problem. Women live longer, but their reproductive window hasn't changed. Could be a black market for babies."

"You mean they're selling..."

"Could be, I don't know. I hope so for the kid's sake. You saw enough in one day to tell you that. Anyway, kid shouldn't be there. They must have breached the city walls somehow. And supply and demand will always meet, they say. Go on with your story."

When they got to the battle at the Mission Gate, Franc found himself exaggerating the horrors that he had seen; the blood spurted in his retelling. But still his grandfather was unmoved. Suddenly a thought occurred to him.

"Hey, how do they see them?"

"What?"

"How do the officers, the guys with the clubs, how do they see them. We can't see the chipless, how do they?"

"Well, first place chip–minuses aren't shielded from unpleasant sights the same way you and I are. It's considered good policy to remind them that their lives could be worse. In the second place, the guys you saw with the brown uniforms, they're chipless themselves."

"What? Then why do they...?"

"Oh please, nothing could be simpler. Law of supply and demand. When something is scarce, it becomes more valuable. What's the one thing the chipless lack, even more than food, medicine, and shelter?"

"What?"

"Power. Power is a mighty scarce commodity. Give a little of it away, and these guys will beat their own grandmothers to keep it. And they'll never charge that gate themselves either. Why should they? They're kings in their little world."

"That's all they get?"

"Oh no, they get whatever they can steal from those who have almost nothing. They get first in the chow line. Apparently, they get stray babies, as you saw. And they have a place to live—no tents. It's a building in the Tenderloin, right on the edge of the chip–minus neighborhood. You can see it from the Nob Hill wall. I'll show it to you. It's guarded like Fort Knox. They're living on scraps, but God help anyone who tries to take those scraps! What you saw at the gate is nothing compared to what those boys'd do if some chipless fool, or even a chip–minus, were to try to get through that door. They have guns, real ones, and the V.T.B. looks the other way.

"And best of all, is that all of the anger, all of the envy of the rest of the chipless, all the gnashing of teeth over unfairness, is directed at the guards. They see us drive by across their territory, passing from gate to gate, but we're just as unreal to them as they are to us—a different species. But the fucker with the club, that guy was just like them two minutes ago, and nothing would make the chipless happier than dragging those guys back to their level.

"But go on. What happened at school. Did you do anything different? Anything that made people notice? Did anyone rec you?"

"Well they didn't know what was up, they thought it was a joke, but..." And he told him, even though he did not want to, the whole story of lunch, the lunch ladies, Maya.

"Why would they do that? Why make us think they're ugly and don't even speak English?"

"Why? Isn't it obvious? You're living why. You fell in love—good for you! How's that working out for you? And suppose it all had gone smoothly, then what? You guys get married and live happily ever after? What'll you tell your little wifey? 'Oh by the way, I'm going to outlive you by a couple hundred years, maybe forever.'? She'll love that. The pressure to issue upgrades is already too much—never going to happen."

"Why not? Why can't they make more chips?"

"They can make them, I suppose, or at least more. But where does it end? How many can we sustain? Are we going to allow the population to climb until we're committing cannibalism? Or stop reproduction altogether and live forever in endless old age? And don't forget, those chip–minuses, like your little girlfriend. . ."

He broke off, seeing the anger in Franc's face. "But seriously," he began again, "chip–minuses perform tasks that need doing. There's nothing wrong with work, but are they going to want to keep working for hundreds of years? No, there's no choice. No upgrade. The supply must be limited for the sake of society."

"But"

"We can't solve this now. Let's just do one thing at a time. So, it was lunchtime, huh? Ok to be safe, I'll just go 11:30 to 1:30."

He switched back on his monitors and began typing.

"What are you doing?"

"Erasing all the vid and audio files from all of your classmates during that time frame. I'll replace them with whatever they posted during that time one week before. I'm using a program I found on my hard drive," he winked his single eye," a very elegant program I might add. Can't have any evidence of your foolishness hanging around."

"People will still have their memories."

"You think so?"

And he pressed RUN. Query code flew up the screen. Find Replace Find Replace thousands of times and, as Franc watched, bit by bit part of himself disappeared forever.

M om called it The Beast for a reason. The jet black 1966 Ford Galaxie was a relic, but a very powerful one. It had belonged to Franc's great–great–grandfather. Not only did it require a driver, it ran on gasoline, which Grandpa had trucked in once a year (another connection of his) and stored in a huge tank beneath the garage, despite his daughter's plea that he'd "blow them all to hell." It required a key to start it, and Grandpa kept it on a chain with a chrome skull that matched The Beast's custom stick shift.

He pumped the right pedal twice before jamming down the left one and turning the key. The Beast roared and coughed out a cloud of smoke.

"You know, Grandpa, I don't often agree with Mom."

"Don't start," he said, pulling the stick towards him as far as it would go, then shoving it up toward the dash.

"But there are reasons no one drives these anymore."

They reversed down the driveway through the cloud of smoke. In the wide area, he spun the wheel until they were facing the street.

"Yeah, there are reasons." He threw it into first and popped the clutch, leaving a patch of expensive rubber on the driveway.

"The main reason is that everyone's a pussy."

He turned up the street without hesitating, forcing a normal car to squeal on its brakes. Embarrassed, Franc tried a friendly wave at the people behind him. "He can't help it," he tried to convey with the wave, "He's senile."

Actually, another argument against driving The Beast was that no matter how much horsepower it had under the hood, it couldn't drive any faster than anyone else. The line of traffic proceeded at a stately 25 mph until it slowed at the North Gate.

As they passed through, Franc looked around, expecting to see hordes of hungry people trying to push their way in, but everything was calm.

Outside The Pres, they sped up along Lombard Highway, before taking a right up Van Ness. They passed a vacant lot full of disheveled tents. Leaning against a fire hydrant was a bearded man with a needle hanging from his arm.

"They're not here yet," said Grandpa, pulling over near City Hall.

"Who?" but his question was answered as three armored cars seemed to materialize out of nowhere. One pulled in front of them, one behind, and one stayed to their left. They started up, moving into the middle lane and the fourth pulled up on their right. They were close enough that Franc could see the eyes behind the gunsight.

"What's going on?"

"I told you your grandpa's a big shot. The V.T.B. doesn't like to take chances."

"Where are we going?"

"Across the bridge."

"The Bay Bridge!?" No one crossed that bridge. Oh sure workers, chip–minuses, crossed every day in armored buses, but he had never heard anyone just driving across. Why would you? He'd been to HQ—"Campus" they called it—when he was a child, but they'd taken a helicopter.

He looked at the green dome of City Hall rising above the stainless steel wall that encircled it. Along the bottom of the wall every inch was covered with human misery. Apparently, these people lacked even tents. They were stacked like cordwood, covered with plastic sheets.

Near the freeway, they stopped at a red light. He could see an armored bus unloading people at some sort of factory. To get in they had to pass through yet another encampment. At the head of the workers line, four burly guys marched straight ahead, swinging their lunch pails, smashing anyone their way in. The crowd divided like the sea for Israel and in they went to work.

A convoy of worker buses was crossing the intersection, making a left from downtown, heading for East Bay. "Night shift?" he wondered.

Across the street, a giant ad for some hair care product stretched the length of an old brick building. Something was moving in front of it. Franc could see two people in black dangling from ropes. As he watched, they began unfurling some sort of giant tarp.

"Look at that!" said Franc as the tarp dropped, revealing a banner in huge block letters that said only "#UPGRADE."

"Oh not again!" said Grandpa. "When are they going to give up?"

The light changed, and they moved on. Franc swiveled in his seat and stared at the two figures who were now climbing back up the ropes. Suddenly a swarm of what looked at that distance like huge bees surrounded the climbers. One man kept climbing and disappeared over the top of the facade, but the man closest to Franc began to jerk madly, as if in pain. The last Franc saw, he was dangling limply.

The convoy turned up the onramp. "Was that an advertisement?" asked Franc.

"A protest. You can't advertise what you don't have."

The bridge rose up before them. The city gate was bigger, more high–tech. It could scan cars going by at 20 miles per hour. As they passed, Franc looked down at the array of dikes along the waterfront. He could see the roller coaster at Dike 39 where they'd gone when he was a kid.

"Oh oh," said Grandpa.

"What?"

"We're pulling off at Treasure Island. There's some delay. E.B.I.'s blocking the bridge or something."

"E.B.I.?"

"East Bay Independence Movement."

"What do they want?"

"Attention."

They took the offramp for Yerba Buena. Only the really old called it Treasure Island anymore. The real island, the one made by nature, was Yerba Buena. Treasure Island was a man–made island that housed a Navy Base at one time. Grandpa's father or grandfather or someone had been stationed there. But the barracks and everything else had been underwater for ages, at least as long as Franc could remember. At low tide you could paddle around the barnacle–covered walls. They had gone on a scout trip, and Franc and Nigel had kayaked through one window and out the other, something they had been strictly forbidden to do. One sudden surge and you could be trapped. They were in what must have been a chapel or dining room when a wave dropped them on the rock–strewn floor. The next slapped them against the side wall and all the way up to the ceiling where Franc had smacked his head. Paddling out the window into the sunlight with blood streaming down his eyes was one of the greatest moments of his childhood. They had laughed so hard, and when they got back to the troop, it was the first time he had ever felt like kids were looking at him with admiration. Sure, it cost him 30 credits when his mom found out, but it was worth it.

The convoy had pulled into a parking lot for a massive housing complex. The building was new and shiny, with a fantastic view of the city across the bay. Technically, they were still in San Francisco, but outside the city gates so he knew it couldn't be chip–plusses, but it seemed too nice for chip–minus.

"Who lives here?" he asked.

"Management."

"Like Mom?"

"No, middle management, worker managers." But immediately his gaze shot left and then up. "No," he barked, "I don't want to go back. I told you what I want. Is your memory that short? Well, figure it out!"

He reached across to the glove box and pulled out a white cloth and a small, unmarked bottle. He poured some foul–smelling black stuff onto the rag and began polishing the stick shift.

"They've reversed traffic. Westbound is using this level now. When they clear one lane, we'll drive across the upper deck, which should be fun. Nice day for it. We're just waiting for the dozer."

"What?"

He didn't answer, just kept serenely polishing. When the shifter was as shiny as it could be, he started on his key fob. Franc stared at some kind of bush outside his window. Something was moving in it, some animal. With the engine off, the crashing in the undergrowth was loud. Visions of mountain lions flashed through his head, but the culprit, when it flitted into the light, was only a small brown bird.

"Here" and Grandpa was passing him the bottle and rag again. He put the key back in the ignition and The Beast roared once more. The little bird didn't even look up. The convoy started. They had to make a U-turn at the end of the lot, so they went one at a time. As the lead car turned and filed past, Franc could see that the turret gunner looked asleep.

As they approached the bridge, buses began to move. One after another, they lumbered down the offramp to take their places waiting in the parking lot. Franc could see the line stretched back, probably all the way to the city.

They drove up the offramp, past the big NO ENTRY sign onto the upper deck where they again pulled over and waited. The residential towers of Oakland were clearly visible from here. The "Seven Sisters," they were called when they were built, according to the Civics less Franc remembered. A triumph of urban planning, they said, these seven structures each housing 100,000 people single–handedly solved the East Bay housing shortage. Each building had its own shopping mall with a grocery store, gym, restaurant: everything anyone could need. Each complex was built around a huge bus terminal for easy transport to work, and since none of the workers had private cars, it was very easy to patrol. Anyone found off the property was probably up to no good and could be picked up.

Franc looked at the massive concrete structures and noticed the narrow windows. It occurred to him that in a building that large, most apartments must be on the inside with no windows at all. People must work pretty hard to make management, move up to Yerba Buena.

The beast began to tremble. Franc's first thought was "earthquake," but his grandfather showed no reaction at all, except impatience."Finally," he said.

The rumbling grew louder as they were passed by a massive truck, two lanes wide, with three axles, huge knobbed tires and steel sides 20 feet high. The front was shaped like a wedge. When it passed, they started up again. They crossed the crown of the bridge and could see the obstacle.

Three buses were parked perpendicular, end to end, across the lanes. In front of them was a human chain—people in black masks, literally chained together. Each held up a red letter. Together, they spelled out D E C O L O N I Z E O A K L A N D. The chain was bolted and locked to each person and on each end to the guard rails. In the center, between the two words, a Patrol officer in a welding mask was cutting one of the links. Sparks flew over the adjacent protestors who were wincing in pain or fear.

But in a minute, it was over. The link snapped and officers at each end pulled sharply at the ends of the chain. Some of the protestors were obviously not ready for this and tumbled down, only to be dragged along the pavement by the others. Those in the center started to run for the edge as the dozer closed in on them.

It aimed for the front of one bus, rear of the other. The buses shuddered, and for a second, it looked like they would flip over, but with a screech of metal on metal and squealing tires, the dozer pushed right through. The convoy followed through the gap. Franc could see the terrified looks on the passengers' faces, although one young man was clearly laughing.

Free from the obstruction, and with no traffic at all, the Convoy roared to life. They flew down the bridge at 90.

"You see why I want to drive myself?" he grinned.

"To go fast?"

"Well that too," Franc grinned back. He had to admit it was fun. Looking over, he could see the needle inching up to 100.

"No. For safety. You think those buses were factory–programmed to stop halfway across the bridge? Somebody built an override. Three buses simultaneously going off track. That's a feat."

"How would they do it?"

"I can think of three ways, all pretty scary. First, some mechanic swapped the chips during maintenance. I doubt it. Whoever did it would certainly get caught, and how could they know all three buses would even be on the bridge at the same time?

"The second possibility, maybe most likely, is malware, inserted remotely by a passenger. Three buses, three transmitters, very small and very powerful. That's bad, that's very bad. It would mean the encryption is toast. Bad news for the security boys."

"Who could do that?"

"The hack? Lots of people. I could. You could. But the really scary possibility..."

"What?"

"Well I'm assuming the hack takes time. I'm assuming the perpetrators need to be on the bus or at least driving next to it to maintain signal long enough to hack in. That's why I'm saying three transmitters. That's why I'm thinking the terrorists are on the bus. But what if they're really powerful? What if momentary contact is enough to load it onto the system? Then it

could be done remotely. Someone in a passing ship could make all those buses just turn and plunge off the bridge. Or imagine in the city overriding a
whole intersection."

They were on 80 now heading north by Emeryville and back in traffic.
Franc looked back at San Francisco. You had to admit, it was beautiful at a
distance. The rounded glass obelisk of V.T.B. headquarters towered above.
His mom would be inside, probably running a meeting or something. He was
never sure exactly what it was she did for a living.

"Hell," said Grandpa. "I might get one myself just so I can get these idiots
in front of me to speed up."

The turrets of Telegraph Wall look down from an impressive height onto the approaching roadway. The square stones look like they've been there since the Middle Ages, and although Franc knew that was impossible, he was still surprised when they passed through and his grandfather pointed to the moat and said "I used to get pizza right there."

"What?"

"This used to be a neighborhood. Old houses, shops, lot of chipless roaming around begging. It was a shithole, but the pizza was very cheap, very good. Real cheese."

They were alone now; the escorts left them at the Berkeley gate. Grandpa was driving slowly for once.

"So you remember the wall being built? What is it even here for?"

"He wanted it. Old Man Altshuler. He's the one who took the place private. He just liked castles, I guess, so he built one. Those were the days when they were getting things done."

They were coming into the campus proper now. Grandpa gestured at the green lawns, the old oaks, the ivy-covered buildings. "All this," he said "was mostly just wasted. People studying philosophy, history, art. Altshuler made it productive."

It didn't look productive. Franc knew the stugrammers worked hard, 12 to 20 hours a day, but you would never know it to see them lounging about, shoving junk food in their faces, walking arm in arm, laughing. Smiles were everywhere, except for one couple who must have had a fight. The guy looked down sadly, while the girl sat bolt upright, still as a statue, staring blankly. She held her hand up palm facing him. "Wow, that's cold!" thought Franc.

A group of five or six were standing in a circle facing each other. They were kicking a small object back and forth. Grandpa saw them too. He grinned. "Oh god," he said, "some things never change!"

They were pulling into the parking lot. Grandpa backed The Beast into the only space big enough and soon they were walking up to New Evans Hall, the biggest, newest building on campus. The door opened automatically, a voice said "Welcome, Dr. Sousa," and soon they were greeted by a very serious–looking young woman who said, "Dr. Lippman is expecting you."

"Come on up," said Grandpa to Franc. "I'll introduce you, then make yourself scarce. I'll meet you later at the Campanile."

The elevator raced up the outside of the building, and Franc was fascinated to watch the ground drop beneath them. They zoomed above the trees, and he gripped the rail as they shot up. Fog covered the bay, but he could make out the towers of the Golden Gate Bridge, stubbornly orange against the white billows.

The door opened to quiet and light. He expected the bustle of the old office, but saw only a few sofas around a fountain with a column of water. Ceilings 15 meters high hung above the glass walls, letting in a soft blue light. Through the far wall, Franc could see the Berkeley hills.

A tall, well–dressed man and two equally tall, and equally well–dressed women were approaching.

"Dr. Sousa," the man said, warmly extending his hand, "So good to see you again." Franc could see that, like most adults, his eyes did not match his smile. "Please allow me to introduce Dr. Yoshii and Dr. Milhaupt."

"My pleasure," said Grandpa, shaking their hands, but showing no pleasure at all. "Where is Dr. King?"

"She won't be joining us."

"Oh, I see."

"And this is?"

"This is Franc, my grandson. He was just leaving."

The tall man took Franc's hand, and having shaken it, pulled him into the room. "Not at all. Let him look around. See what the future may hold, if he plays his cards right." A hand on Franc's back ushered him in and pushed him toward the window. "Nice view, hmm."

It was that. He couldn't help but be drawn toward the window. The drop below was dizzying. Franc loved the feeling: a war between your brain, which told you that of course everything was okay, and your senses, which screamed for a return to safety. He wished his mom had been there. She would have gasped and pleaded for him to go back. That would have been much more fun.

"Pretty nice, eh? Look around, enjoy yourself."

The fog was lifting out there, he could tell. More of the bridge was now visible, and he could just make out movement on the road deck on the Marin side. Downtown was easy to see, and Sutro Tower of course, but he was surprised to see two bumps too far out to be a part of the city.

"That must be the Farallons," he said to no one. Dr. Lippman had walked away. He was talking to Grandpa who looked more scowly than ever. He broke away from the others and headed for the coffee. Dr. Lippmann stayed where he was. He had a curious smile on his face, and Franc had the strange feeling it was directed at him. Meanwhile, everyone was heading to the sofas and chairs, so he did so too, taking the seat beside his grandfather. He took a cup of coffee to be polite and stirred in some cream and sugar. There was a plate of pastries, and he grabbed a sticky bun covered in nuts. The others did the same and soon the room was filled with munching and slurping and mmm's and polite "please pass me"s, all except for Grandpa who just sat still, sipping his coffee like a man waiting for a late train.

"Your grandson has really grown up," said Dr. Lippmann, "My compliments. Last time I saw him was in the old building." Turning to Franc he said, "Quite an upgrade, eh?

"Do you know what makes this possible?" he went on,

"Well I guess ., ,. "

"Productivity," he said before Franc could finish. "Productivity. The programs we produce here—many designed by your grandfather—are the bedrock of the entire economy. So why shouldn't we indulge a bit?"

Franc smiled and took another bite.

"When our next chip is mass-produced, productivity will be through the roof. We've already got the chip–minuses working at 99% capacity, now for the chip–plusses. Of course it's harder to do. You take some worker in a widget factory. It's not too difficult to screen out non–widget thoughts (during work hours, of course—beyond that everyone's thoughts are their own business). The results are incontrovertible. Industrial accidents are down 97% We've literally saved thousands of lives. Now that's something to be proud of!

"With chip–plusses, it's more complicated. The areas of cognition necessary for intellectual work have always seemed too variable for autofocussing to work. Better to let a few stray thoughts through than to screen out necessary ideas. After all, how could anyone invent something new without daydreaming?

"You, for instance, does your mind ever wander?" He was talking to Franc.

"Me?" he answered with such obvious confusion that everyone laughed, even Grandpa.

"Exactly! No need for embarrassment. We all do. But the new chip—and the test data is extremely encouraging—will gently refocus your thoughts, not eliminate them, of course not, but refocus. Like a kindergarten teacher with an unruly student."

Dr. Yoshii and Dr. Milhaupt laughed politely. Franc smiled.

"You know, Franc, we've seen your stuff, and honestly, we're very impressed. Frankly, I think you're wasting your time in that school."

"What?"

"You could start here tomorrow, but I suppose you're happy there?"

Was he? For some reason, the only thing he could think of was Bruno stepping on the back of his heel.

"Franc will stay home, with us, until the proper time." Grandpa stated flatly.

"Oh of course, of course. But just think about it. It's nice here, and all the stugrammers are getting the newest chip. It's a massive upgrade."

"That chip is not ready and you know it," Grandpa broke in. "Dr. King said it needed further testing."

"Dr. King was overly cautious, and at any rate, she's not here," said Dr. Lippmann.

Grandpa turned to Franc. "Okay, you've had your pastry, now scat. You know where to meet up. We've got business to attend to."

* * * *

The campanile is an old bell tower that probably was the tallest thing on campus in the old days. At the bottom is a kind of courtyard, very cool and green, and Franc sat down on an old stone bench and watched the people. Everyone looked happy. Groups strolled past, talking excitedly about some sort of "Big Game" and there were multiple couples so intent on each other that they seemed to be unaware of anything else. Two guys walked by arguing loudly, but even they seemed happy, as if the argument itself were only a type of competition. And further out, in the open area, he recognized the kicks and turns of actual gamers.

Why shouldn't he start now, tomorrow? Obviously, he'd have to be rechipped first, but face it, that's going to happen no matter what. Maybe they'd have to wait for the wound to heal so no one would know, but after that, why not? He'd miss Nigel and Kelli and his mother. And her, of course, but he'd miss her no matter where he was. If this was to be his future anyway, why not get to it?

A couple opposite him were at it hot and heavy. He tried not to watch, but he had nothing else to do and they didn't seem to mind. He was about to walk away, give them some privacy, when he witnessed something strange. Right in the middle of it, with the hands and the tongues and the heavy breathing, with no warning at all, the guy pulled back and sat completely upright as still as a statue. He held his left palm toward the girl who seemed to sag with disappointment. But all she did was pick up her bag and walk away.

The man's eyes were flashing in the upper right quadrant, and Franc thought, "That must be one hell of an important text!" But even stranger, the hand stayed where it was, still warning off the passions of someone who wasn't even there. His eyes were still flicking furiously, while the fingers of his right hand undulated like a pianist dreaming of a performance.

It was unnerving somehow; watching it felt like even more of an invasion of privacy than watching the couple. Franc stood up and walked away. He found a spot on the other side of the tower. He sat under an ancient oak and tried to puzzle out everything, but his mind wandered. It was like Dr. Lipmann said: he couldn't control it, like a vid he couldn't shut off, but one with a virus that mashed up the order. Maybe it would be better with the new chip, with the teacher to keep you on track.

He leaned against the trunk but felt something sticky on the back of his head. He turned around and saw red sap dripping down from the black branch above. It stuck to his fingers when he reached back. He felt in his pockets for a tissue and his fingers closed on the baseball card. He used the plastic sleeve to scrape the gunk off the back of his head, then wiped it off on the grass. In the process, the card bent, and when he tried to bend it back, he saw the edges of the card were coming apart. Between the layers of white, he could clearly see a layer of gray now splitting in two, opening like a pouch. The glue, as he supposed the gray stuff was, looked familiar somehow. He put a finger into the slot and scratched it.

There was no mistaking it—it was lead, the same stuff painted on the walls of his computer class and Grandpa's office. He flattened the card again and removed it from its sleeve. It looked completely flat. Franc put finger and thumb on the top corners and pressed gently. The pouch opened like a mouth. He held the opening toward the light and peered in, but he could see nothing. He held it upside down over his palm, but nothing came out except a tiny lump of some waxy substance.

This was his inheritance! A meaningless card with a secret container for a booger! It was funny, you had to admit that, but the feeling was somewhat different. He sat completely still, trying to think, but the only thing that ran through his mind was a longing to return to how things were, to go back to before yesterday when life was normal, when he was normal.

He dropped the booger back in its pouch and returned it to the plastic sleeve. When he got home, he'd show his mom. "See!" he'd tell her, "See what a lunatic you married? Thanks for the present!"

• • • •

Grandpa was standing over him. "Are you asleep? C'mon, we've got to get going."

They didn't talk as they walked to the car, his grandfather moving faster than normal. They passed a bench where two people sat staring like statues, their left hands raised, palms out. None of the passersby seemed to notice anything out of the ordinary, but Grandpa stopped and stared for a minute. His brows knit, and one side of his upper lip began to rise. He looked as if he were about to say something but seemed to change his mind.

They passed a grassy glade, and Franc could see the gamers twisting and kicking. He saw groups of friends lounging as before, but now he noticed others, a dozen or so dotted here and there sitting stock still staring into space. One young man in a tie–dyed t-shirt wasn't even sitting. He just stood there in the sun with one hand raised as if he were directing traffic. At his feet was a small knit bean bag.

"Jesus!" said Grandpa. And with a change of tone as if he'd just made a decision, "Let's hit the head before we go—long drive."

They turned and went up a marble staircase into a very old building. The heavy oak door creaked and opened into an empty hallway, quiet and echoey, that smelled like dust. Franc was heading for the urinal when he noticed his grandfather doing something strange. He was peering under the stall doors. He straightened himself up and said, "Listen up! Things have changed. We're not going home, not straight home."

"Why not?"

"We're going to Livermore to see the boss. Things have changed, there's been a shake–up. They want your grandpa to play ball, but I don't want to. They're off the rails. Young punks think they know everything. Bypassing psych, bypassing med. There is a process," Grandpa was ranting, "There is a process for a reason! The boss himself laid down those priorities. Health and wellbeing first and foremost. It's rule number one! And they show me a holomessage where he contradicts all that and expect me to believe it? I want to talk to the man face to face, then we'll see!

"Meanwhile, we'd better pee. It'll be a long drive."

Franc had seen his grandfather go off before about slow drivers or fake meat products, stuff like that, but he'd never seen anything like this. When they were washing their hands, he watched him in the mirror and saw that he was actually shaking. If he didn't know any better, Franc would have thought that Grandpa was scared.

The old man looked up and saw him staring. "Frankie," he said very slowly, "Listen carefully. Whatever happens, don't let them install that new chip! Not now. In a year, there'll be changes. There will be testing. People will listen to reason, I'm sure. I can't be the only one who objects to this. There will be changes for sure." He was speaking in a reassuring tone that Franc had not heard since he was child and had woken up from a nightmare.

And that is when he began to be afraid.

They left campus the wrong way, heading due east, away from the bay. Grandpa took a series of small streets winding east and south along the edge of the hills. There was no escort now. At an intersection, he did a strange thing. He turned off the engine. One moment The Beast was roaring and choking, the next was stillness. It was a quiet, residential area and all Franc could hear was his own breathing and someone's sprinklers pattering. Grandpa gave him a quizzical look as if to say, "Do you hear that?" and he did: a far–off buzz like a swarm of bees outside a window.

Grandpa started the engine again and drove off, more slowly now, and then he did the second strange thing. As he drove, he reached out the window with his left hand and began violently tugging the side mirror back and forth until it snapped off in his hand. When he drew his hand, with the mirror, back into the window, Franc could see that he had cut or scratched his wrist. Blood trickled down his arm as he held the mirror up.

He took both hands off the wheel for a second to shift the mirror so that he was holding it from the back. Then he held it out the window, angled up, and nodded grimly. Without a word, Grandpa handed the mirror to him and pointed up. Franc copied him, angling the mirror so he could see the sky. At first he saw only gray clouds and a swirl of light, but suddenly, there it was: a surveillance drone hovering directly above.

Grandpa made a turn, and gave Franc that same quizzical glance. He checked the mirror and nodded. The drone had turned right along with them.

The third strange thing would not have been strange for anyone else. Grandpa simply said, "Buckle up." Franc looked back at him to see if he was serious. Calmer now, Grandpa was quietly wiping his bloody wrist on his pants. He wasn't joking.

"What about you?" he asked.

"Mine's broken. Buckle up."

Grandpa didn't believe in seatbelts. It was one of his standard rants about constriction and freedom and people being pussies nowadays. There weren't any in the back seat where Franc usually sat, and the only person he'd ever seen use one was his mother. He reached back and tried to remember how she'd hooked it up. They were on a highway now, heading toward the Caldecott Tunnel. By the time he'd managed to pull the belt across his chest and waist and latch it, they were inside, and Grandpa was driving very strangely. He slowed way down and straddled the line, forcing two lanes behind him to slow down as well.

He looked at Franc and jerked his head up questioningly. This time he saw only dirty concrete passing ever more slowly as they came almost to a halt. He looked back and shook his head. Grandpa smiled and jerked the wheel to the left. He gunned the engine and the tires spun and smoked as The Beast slid directly into the slot between two oncoming cars. There was a squeal of brakes, and they ended up in the right lane coming out of the tunnel. In a flash, they were in brightness. Franc checked the mirror again and gave the thumbs up.

They were speeding now, weaving in and out of cars. Franc could see the puzzled looks on the passengers' faces to see this antique monstrosity leaving them in the dust. By the time they were back to the freeway, Grandpa was grinning like a schoolboy, Franc too.

But rather than heading south to the Bay Bridge, Grandpa careened onto 80 North. Franc's concept of geography was a bit shaky, but when they started to cross the Richmond Bridge, he knew they had given up on Livermore. Apparently, it was too dangerous, or maybe Grandpa just decided the old man wouldn't help anyway. They raced over the bridge at 90. San Quentin loomed on their left, the old brick castle looking particularly gloomy in the gathering fog.

When they merged onto 101 South, Franc knew they weren't going anywhere but home. The long way, sure, but they'd avoid the danger of the Bay Bridge, instead coming in across the good old Golden Gate. Marin was familiar ground to Franc and he began to relax. Grandpa seemed to feel it too. He wasn't grinning anymore, but neither did he have that haunted look.

He stopped weaving through traffic and just took his place in line, trying to blend in as well as an ancient muscle car could.

Franc was playing with the little mirror, staring at his own reflection. The concave glass stretched his features. His nose looked longer than ever.

"Hey beauty queen," Grandpa said and jerked his head up again. Franc put the mirror out the window again, but the wind at this speed made it hard to hold steady. It was a couple minutes before he saw it this time. He turned back and nodded, but Grandpa just shrugged. "They're just surveillance. We're going home. No one could object to that. They just want to be sure, probably."

And they just continued to drive, sticking solidly in the flow of traffic. From time to time, Franc would stick the mirror out and check on their traveling companion. It seemed to be higher now. Perhaps whoever had decided they weren't such a threat after all. Soon Sausalito rolled by on the left. The fog was thick, but he could make out the shapes of the houseboats and remembered his mother taking him there to visit his friend who lived on the water. They'd be home soon and everything would return to the way it used to be. In one week it would be his birthday. He'd have his friends over, they'd eat cake. Everything would be normal again.

The right lane had started to slow and as they headed toward the Elon Musk Tunnel, they passed a line of cars full of annoyed–looking people who all seemed to be wondering what the delay was all about. The left lane, where they were, was empty. Grandpa slowed way down and tried to merge right. But there was no space at all. The cars crept along nose to tail and would not yield.

"There must be some problem up ahead," Grandpa said. Franc stuck the mirror out again, but the surveillance drone was gone. In its place, a much larger drone, one with wings, hovered. This one was black and enormous and had what looked like two giant bullets on its underside.

"Grandpa!" shouted Franc, handing him the mirror. He took one look and stomped on the pedal.

In the tunnel, he slowed again, almost to a stop, but this time no traffic backed up behind them.

"Well, we've pissed someone off, that's for sure. That's military grade."

The Beast came to a complete halt. The right lane was now creeping past them. Franc could see the passengers staring at them.

"They won't fall for the same trick twice," said Grandpa. "Besides where would we go?" He seemed to be reaching a decision. "They're probably just trying to scare us. They wouldn't do anything so close to the city." And turning to Franc, "Hold on," and he stepped on it, leaving a plume of black smoke behind them.

They came out of the tunnel into blinding light. The wind around the headlands had carved out the fog from just this spot. It must have just happened because the roadway was still wet. The sun flashed up like a million diamonds, and Franc had just enough time to register the strangeness that he could still appreciate beauty at a time like this.

The other cars were exiting the road, still nose to tail. The Beast flew on alone down the empty, shimmering highway, and Franc could see that there were no longer any cars approaching from the city. They must have all been shunted off as well.

"If we can make it to the bridge..." said Grandpa to himself, staring up with the mirror, as the car drifted into the right lane and onto the shoulder. The dial said 110 when Grandpa, still looking up, slammed on the brakes and jerked the wheel to the left. There was a blinding flash just in front of them as The Beast fishtailed and flipped. It rolled over three times, landing on its roof. Despite the harness, Franc's head slammed against the door of the car while his shoulder felt like it had been wrenched from the socket. Still, as he hung upside down, his overwhelming feeling was elation. They had done it! They had cheated Death!

Then he noticed his grandfather. Head and shoulders were sticking through what had been the windshield, while his back twisted towards Franc in an impossible angle. Franc pressed the button on his seat belt and fell to the roof. He scrambled through the broken glass and over to what was left of his grandfather. But he was breathing! And when Franc came close, Grandpa tried to speak,

"Angel eye...Ange ...eye."

And that was it. He could feel no heartbeat. The eye was open still, but it looked different—blind. He brought his face very close, but there was no breath.

For the briefest moment the thought flashed through Franc's mind that he should be feeling emotion. He had loved his grandfather after all. But all his feelings were physical: the pain in his head and shoulder, and on his knees and hands where the gritty bits of broken glass were pressing on him. The smell of gasoline was everywhere, even on his clothes. And his ears were filled with a high–pitched tone, that quickly gave way to a buzzing, a whirring. Where had he heard that before?

It was back! The drone was coming back for another try, lower this time. Franc scrambled out from under the car and jumped over the median. He lay flat, tight against it, just as the bomb dropped.

The explosion was so powerful it pushed the concrete median three feet and Franc with it. Looking up, he saw an enormous fireball engulf the drone, which crashed, burning, to the pavement.

Franc looked around. There were no cars, no people anywhere. He knew he had to get out of there. Sausalito was closer, but all he could think of was that he wanted to get home, so he ran to the walkway and headed toward the bridge. He ran faster than he ever had in health and hyge. The roadway climbed and soon he was far above the land below. When he got to the first tower, he looked back. At first, all he could see was fog, but when the wind blew, the plume of black smoke was clearly visible.

And then something crossed his line of sight, a bird, he thought, flying west to east, ocean to bay, a few hundred yards away. And then again a few minutes later, closer this time, the same bird or one just like it, flying in from the Pacific. And then a third time, closer still, and he knew it wasn't any bird. The surveillance drone was back, and it was searching, flying in narrowing circles, each pass taking it closer to its goal.

Franc ran around the tower and huddled against it, looking for a place to hide. There wasn't any, but maybe if he lay flat in the shadow of the walkway fence, the fog was thick enough that he wouldn't be seen.

But what if it wasn't seeing at all, or not just seeing anyway? What if it had the capacity ro pick up a signal, the tiny ping, the little "I am here" that his chip was sending out every few seconds. Normally this only traveled a few feet, enough to open doors and get through gates. But who knew what they could do?

His hand went unconsciously to his neck. Could he do it? Rip it off and throw it over the edge? And then what? Beg in the streets? Better to join Grandpa.

A buzzing noise flitted past. He wasn't sure how far, but it wouldn't be long now. He pinched the pad of the invisibandage between his thumb and forefinger and pulled. All that was left was to reach between the bars of the railing and open his hand. The bandage would float in the breeze, land in the cold, cold water and disappear.

But what if it didn't drop? What about updrafts? What if landed on a cross piece a few feet below, close enough for the signal to still be picked up? Again the buzzing sounded, closer, and still he hesitated.

Suddenly an idea came to him. With his left hand, he reached in his pocket and pulled out the plastic sleeve. He pinched the edges and the pouch popped open. He shoved the bandage in and put it back in his pocket just as the drone passed by within 50 yards of him.

Franc lay still waiting for the next pass, but this time the buzzing came from the south. It had passed him by! He waited a while and resumed his journey. He began to envision success. He pictured a tree whose branches extended over the wall into the Pres. He'd shinny up the trunk, drop down the other side and sneak into his back door. He could see his mom's face when he told her what had happened. That would be tough, but she'd know what to do. There must be something.

And that was when he heard it, the buzzing again. It was coming back, and much faster this time. No more widening spirals, it was coming straight toward him. He'd been spotted. He looked around. He was midspan now, No towers, nothing to get under or behind. He looked over the railing, Through the thick fog, he could barely make out the dark water below.

Franc looked up and down the bridge for something, anything to save him, but was entirely alone. He knew there was only one solution. He climbed up on the railing and took one look back at the approaching drone. And then he jumped.

BOOK TWO

THE BOAT

*"[T]hen all collapsed, and the great shroud
of the sea rolled on as it rolled
five thousand years before."*
-Herman Melville, from Moby Dick

I can row, but Momma won't let me. Never on the real ocean. Only on the back waters when maybe we have caught some crab so she's in a good mood and it's still a long way till dawn, and the tide is right so each sloop of the oar sends you sailing along so easy. Those are the good times when Momma is nice, and it's calm—no giant ships blowing their horns, just the sloop–sloop of the oars, the skittle–skat of crab claws on wood, and Momma's voice, singing clear but quiet: "I am a poor wayfaring stranger," and I join in on "traveling through this world of woe." That's her song.

But not tonight. Tonight we've gone through the gate. Had to, no fish in the bay. Rowed all the way to the Farallons for one tiny rockfish and now she's fighting tide, dodging along the rocks, trying to catch some eddy and still not smash, so she doesn't want to hear me when I say it's still there, the leg I saw in the rusty net that hangs from the bridge. I saw it when we passed the first time, and I told Momma but she said "Hush" and told me I had to keep a sharp eye out. "That's your job," she said, and I said, "I'm doing my job. Why keep a sharp eye when you don't want to see what I see?" but she said hush again and that I knew what she meant so I closed my mouth. But here it is again, and I forget to hush.

Course Momma can't see nothing, her back is facing, but after we pass she looks up and starts to stare. I turn around. You can see the whole person now. The rest of him stretches back toward the bridge. He isn't moving. Momma lets go her oar for a second and crosses herself. "Poor thing," she says, shaking her head.

We don't trade or even smoke the fish that night. Too small. After we tie up to the rock, we pull the old kelp–covered rope. It always seems to take forever, but Momma says "Deep is safe" and has stones attached to drop it to the bottom. But finally it bobs up, a long, white ladder, twice as tall as Momma, that we have to use when the tide is low. She leans it up against our castle and I climb up with the fish and the water and my pelican feather I have to carry always. Four high points of piled–up rocks and bricks make up our castle with a tarp stretched across. The top of the tarp is full of dried kelp and old plastic bits so no one will ever know we're here, even if they look. It's our castle only and Momma is the queen, Queen Yvette, and I am Princess Umi. I climb under the tarp and drop the fish in the pot and start to blow on the coal. It's a good day and the coal still glows. I drop dried kelp on it and blow and blow and Momma will be so happy when she sees we don't have to eat cold fish again.

I'm putting splinters of driftwood on when Momma climbs under the tarp. She's breathing hard. The boat is heavy and it's hard to pull it up against the rocks and cover it with kelp. And then lower the ladder again. But I can see she is happy to see the flame and smell the burning kelp of home.

Momma's scraping scales when I ask her. The scales flake off silver and pretty, into the box where we keep them until they're dry enough to burn. She turns the knife and slices into the belly and pulls out the guts. She hands me my share, and we both chew quietly while she cuts up the rest of the fish. This one's tiny, probably the smallest rock I remember, but it will make two days anyway. She filets out the meat and hangs the head, bones and tail on the rock behind her. She lays the meat carefully on a piece of an old screen door we found. I'm the one who saw it. I look out sharp. We burned the broken wood long ago, but Momma saved a big long piece—don't know why. The screen is good for all kinds of things, and right now a piece of it sizzles over the flames.

"How'd he get up there? Honey, I don't know. Once upon a time lots of folks jumped from that bridge. It's why they have the net. But a lot of chipless folk, like you and me, kept jumping anyway. The net'd stop them, but some of them would just climb over the net and keep going. Others would just lie there with broken bones and such, and wait to be picked up. Or they'd try to go up the tower, but there's no way to climb up from there, or down. Inside the towers it crosses like this," and she held up her hands like an X, "You've seen it. Looks like you could climb that. But you can't get to it from the out-side. They'd either fall or quit, just lay there hollering for help. Help from the

Patrollers! I'd rather jump. And anyway, the V.T.B. just stopped picking them up. Made a law against it."

She turned the fish with her fingers. "When I was a girl, there were bones in that net. But now the whole bridge is chip–only, so I don't know how that man got up there."

"But why did the people want to jump? Where were they going?"

Momma takes the screen off the fire and starts to blow on it. She is quiet for a long time, then she looks up, right at me.

"Honey," she says, "They wanted to die. They just gave up. But you re-member the verse I taught you?"

"The Lord detesteth a quitter."

"And don't forget it."

• • • •

I wake up in the middle of the day and Momma is peering through a crack in the rock. She's not looking at the island like we sometimes do, at the ruins of the prison. Momma says before the big one our castle was part of that island. She's looking out the other crack, at the bridge. She looks sad and I ask her why, but she just says, "Hush." I try to snuggle up and lean against her chest, but she cries out sharp like a gull. She says she's sore from rowing. She shifts me over and strokes my hair until I fall back asleep.

• • • •

We leave early that night when the sky is still red. Momma don't like to show in light, but the nights are getting shorter and sometimes you have to row a long way to get the fish. But anyway, it's still easy to see the bridge when we pass. I look sharp, but the leg is gone. I look back and forth but can't see anything.

"Momma, he's not there!"

She takes her hand off the right oar and lets the current swing the boat sideways. She raises her arm and points to the spot we saw him the night be-fore, then swings it slowly to the left till it's pointing at a dark shape lying face down on the crossbeam, over the part where there is no net, a good half a cast length from where it had been.

"He ain't no quitter," Momma says.

. . . .

We blank tonight. Nothing by pole, nothing by net. Crab pots empty. And Momma don't like to blank so we stay out longer than maybe we ought. The tide is strong against us and the sky is getting light so she's pulling hard, sweating even though it's so cold. But still, when we pass, she holds off a minute and we both look up.

I spot him first. He's almost over to the tower. With the light behind us I can see him clear. He's on his stomach on the cross piece, but he's moving. His arms are held out past his head and he's pulling, inching his way forward. I look at the tower. Momma was right. I can't see a way up or down from there.

When I look back at Momma there are tears in her eyes. I ask her what's the matter, but she just tells me hush and takes up rowing once again.

. . . .

The coals are out, and I know we have no more matches. When Momma climbs in under the tarp and sees my face black with ash from blowing, she starts to cry again.

"I don't mind, Momma," I tell her, "Now we don't have to wait to eat!" and I pull down the rockfish carcass. I break the spine and start sucking on the juices inside. I hand the head half to Momma and start nibbling the bits of meat clinging to the tail. I get some scales in my mouth, but I don't let Momma know. I'm a big girl.

"Mmm," I say, "this is good!"

. . . .

I wake up with my stomach grumbling and there she is again, staring. I climb in her lap and look through the crack. He hasn't moved much. He's at the north tower, but he's just laying there, not climbing up or down.

"He's stuck," Momma says, "or . . ." And she strokes my hair, but I don't go to sleep. Just lean against her and listen to her heart beat.

. . . .

That evening Momma does something she's never done before. After we load up the boat, and I get in, she doesn't sink the ladder. Instead, she takes out her knife and cuts the cords that bind it to the big stones. She takes three empty water jugs and ties them to three of the rungs, then she throws the ladder off the rock. She ties the end of the ladder rope to the gunwale, then unties the hawser and casts off.

We row off to the gate, and the ladder bobs along behind.

"Here," she says when we've gone a ways. She hands me the fishing line and a piece of driftwood. "Now make this fast, and no granny knots!"

She doesn't have to hurt my feelings. I know my knots. But I don't say nothing, just set to tying. The piece is a funny shape, kind of a crooked cross, so just to be on the safe side, I first tie two bowlines at cross angles, then double timber hitches around each of the four branches. I draw the line crossway to the center and join them in a reef knot. I hold the result up to Momma. She nods and says, "I couldn'ta done better myself."

My face feels hot. She's never said anything like that before.

"Now you remember the fisherman's knot? I need you to tie the end of that fishing line to that." She points to the lank end hanging from the gunwale cleat. "Do it twice. It's got to hold."

So I do. It takes a couple tries because it's weird with a big rope and a little thin line, but I do it, and I hold it up Momma nods. "Ok, look sharp! Is our friend still up there?"

"Yeah," I say. The moon is out, and I can see him clear. "But he's not moving."

Momma pulls back on the oars and looks up herself. Then she does something she's never done before: she yells.

"Hey!" she shouts, then "Hey!" again, even louder.

That's when he moves. His head swivels round. I can see his face. "He's moving Momma!" I shout, and she answers "Hush!" out of habit, I think. She looks as excited as I am. Suddenly an arm sticks out and waves around.

The tide is sweeping us past the tower island, and Momma stops back-oaring and turns around. She rows us back toward home a good ways before turning back.

"Honey?" she says, "I need you to take the oars. Row towards home."

"But what about?" I begin, but she just says, "Row!" so I do. I slide into her place, facing the bridge and row toward home. But we keep going out to sea!

"Little harder, Honey," says Momma and I pull as hard as I can. We keep slipping towards the bridge, but Momma doesn't seem too concerned. She just loops the fishing line through the eyelet at the top. She coils up the rest of the line and holds it flat against the bottom of the pole. Then she stands up and starts to swing. The drift swings back and forth, then shoots up and out toward the bridge. Momma can cast far. She's strong. But I don't know if she ever tried casting up before. The wood falls short by a long ways.

I try the best I can, but by the time she pulls it out again and winds up the line, we're passing the tower, heading to sea.

"No worries, little one," she says, handing me the pole. "Hold this. Coil up the line. Let me row now," and she takes over the bench, pulling hard until we're far back, too far for a cast. But by the time we switch spots, she's in range.

But this one is short too. And the next one, and the next, and the next, and the next. Momma is sweating. She takes off her jacket. In the moonlight, I can see a red spot on her shirt. We row back again. "One more try," she tells me.

"Lord," she prays aloud, "You created me and the earth and the seven seas. I'm asking you Lord to still this boat, to make my arm strong and my aim straight. Amen" And then to me, "Honey, I know you're tired but I need you to pull. Pull hard."

We're drifting, but I pull. I lean back and pull harder than I ever have, and the boat stops still. The bridge doesn't get closer, it doesn't get farther. Momma stands and swings. I see the wood lifting high, higher. It strikes the bridge a couple of feet above the man, and falls. A hand grabs out, but the wood keeps falling.

TWO

Momma sees it too. I hear that same seagull cry, and then she folds, drops her head down. The pole clatters to the deck.

Momma is holding her chest.

We're drifting now. The oars are slippery in my hands. The right one slaps the water. We're turning.

Momma looks at the concrete walls of the tower island we're floating to. But she doesn't do anything, just stares at it as if she's going to just let us crash. She breathes out slow and hard through her nose, then looks up once again.

I try back–oaring to straighten out, avoid the smash, when all of sudden Momma is praising the Lord and pushing me from the bench. She grabs the oars and pulls hard and soon we're back far enough for me to see. The moon is strong now, and I can see that piece of drift hanging. I look up at the man. His arms are moving. The wood is rising.

"Alleluia!" cries Momma again. There are tears in her eyes.

We switch again, and again I'm told to row for home, but this time she says, "It's okay if we drift a bit. I just need a little time."

So I row while Momma goes about uncleating the ladder rope. She tugs on the ladder end till the rope is slack, then stretches out like a cross and measures out two lengths. Then she pulls out her knife and cuts the rope.

"Momma, what are you doing?"

She throws the cut end into the water and cleats off the ladder end again.

"I thought you were giving him the ladder!" I say.

"Move over," she says and takes the oars. "Fishing line won't hold it. Not 100% sure it'll hold the rope. Besides, we need that ladder. "

We're drawing near the tower island once again. This time Momma slides past it and pulls back. She draws up alongside the lower level, and uncleats the hawser line. There is a tie–up there, a staple in the concrete, and Momma passes the mooring line through it. She pulls it back until the boat is tight with the side of the tower and hands it to me. "Hold tight," she says.

Then she uncleats the ladder line. The tide is pulling the ladder past us. It tugs on the lines, trying to get out to sea. Momma reels it in until the line is slack, then ties it with a bowline to the staple. She then reels it in the rest of the way and hoists it out of the water, leaning it with the bottom on the lower level, the top almost up to the higher level.

"Okay," she says, "Let go Honey." And she sits down and starts rowing, but after only a few strokes, she stops. She looks to the north, she looks to the south. Then she puts oars up and gets down from the bench. She lays down with her back against the prow.

"We're going to just let it drift," she says. "Get out the squid. Tie it on the line. But first, hand me that sail, will you?"

I do what I'm told. We hardly ever actually sail, unless conditions are just right, which they definitely aren't. But I get it out anyway from its place in the stern and hand it to her. She bunches it up and puts it behind her back and pulls one flap across her front like a blanket.

We keep the squid, and the other lures, in a box under the bench. Momma made them all. This one has arms of white plastic from a bag we found. There's red spots on it that Momma says is the name of a big trading store way up in Sacramento. Many days rowing, she says. Maybe it's just a story.

I get the line and tie on a casting stone about a foot up, then tie the squid on the end. The other end is already tied to our just–in–case rock we keep at the bottom of the boat. It's so heavy Momma always complains when she's putting it in and out of the boat. It keeps us from rocking too much and with the line tied even if she dropped the pole, we'd get it back, but Momma's never dropped it yet.

She still hasn't got up so I thread the line through the eyelets and under the pieces of sail cloth tacked on halfway down and at the bottom. I pull the cap off the bar that holds the can and slide it off. This is a new can, you can still see a little bit of the tomato picture. I wind the line around and around it till there's no slack, slide it back on its rod and put the cap back on. I hold the pole out to her, but it's like she can't be bothered. "You cast it, Honey," and this is something she never says, not unless we've already got at least one already.

I get one foot up on the bench, just like Momma does, and hold the pole as high up with my left hand as I can. My right hand is over the sail cloth clamping the line tight and I concentrate on letting go of that hand when the squid is flying but not before.

And I do, first try. It's not far like Momma's, but like she says, "It's a big ocean, how much difference could it make?"

"Good one, Honey. Hand me the pole and lay back with me. You can see some stars now."

We're barely moving, just rocking up and down. The boat is pointing now back to home and we're looking away, out over the black water, the glow of the city behind us. Momma wedges the end of the pole under her side and pulls me down under the sail.

"Okay, Honey, which one's Arcturus?" and I have to look for it. Part of the Dipper is behind a cloud so it takes me a while, but I find it and follow the front of the cup. "There," I say and Momma tells me I'm a smart girl. She's combing through my hair with her fingers, and it makes me sleepy. She starts to sing so quiet and sweet I don't join in for my part. I just want to hear her sing and look at the stars twinkle.

> "I am a poor, wayfaring stranger
> Traveling through this world of woe,
> But there's no sickness, toil or danger
> In that bright world to which I go...."

And next thing I know I'm dreaming again about the bright world. This time I'm on a beach and the sun is so bright I'm covering my eyes, but I can still see. It's beautiful with red flowers and green grass, but I'm looking at the dark ocean. Our boat is there, and Momma's in it and I am too, waving.

I wake up wondering how a person could wave to herself. There is a noise, a skitter–skat, and I know the line's going out.

"Momma!" I cry and she grabs the pole, but she must be tired because she misses the sail cloth and the line cuts her hand. I can see the blood, but Momma doesn't say anything, just shifts her grip and squeezes hard. The can is spinning and Momma gets herself up and turned around so she can step on it. When she does, the boat lurches and the pole almost snaps, so she has to ease off and let it run a bit.

"She's a big one," Momma says, "We're going to have to tire her out. She sits on the bench, keeping her feet pushed hard on the can. The wind is up, and that means fog's coming. Already, you can't see the stars. Momma smiles at me. "Sing your song, Honey" and starts the beat, knocking the pole on the bottom of the boat, Knock Knock-knock, Knock Knock-knock, and I sing the song she taught me, her lullaby song.

"Lord, whom wind and waves obey
Guide us through the watery way
In the hollow of Thy hand
Guide us safely back to land."

And while I sing she reels the fish in a little bit at a time. When the line slackens, she jerks the pole back, then back–pedals fast on the can, reeling in as much as she can before it's pulling again. By the time she's pulling solid, walking back hard and slow on the can, bringing the tired fish in, the horn is sounding on the bridge, "Home. Home. Home." And it's pea soup as Momma says by the time the poor creature is flopping and flipping at the bottom of the boat.

It's a salmon, for real, and Momma praises the Lord in her secret language before she takes her knife out from its sheath on her leg and stabs it in the back of the head. "Get the basin," she says, and when I do, she flops the fish head in and makes two cuts behind the gills and one puncture in the tail. I know the blood is red, but it looks black oozing into the basin.

"We've got to move," she says and then I hear it too, the breakers on Baker Beach. Momma leans back and pulls hard, straight away from the roar, but she doesn't go far before she turns. You can't see a thing now, but I know we're heading towards the fog horn and sure enough I soon see the flashing red at the top of the bridge.

"What do you say, we head back early?" she says and I grin. One salmon is a good catch, enough to trade and eat.

• • • •

"The ladder's gone!" I yell to Momma, who cranes her neck around to get a look then goes back to her rowing. And pretty soon I see it bobbing around, smashing up against the concrete. I tell Momma and she tells me to look sharp.

"Is there anything else in the water?

"Anything else?"

"Just look sharp," she says, but nothing's there.

Momma pulls alongside the tower and I hold the mooring line while she fishes out the ladder and stands it again. "Maybe the wind knocked it down," she says. We're both looking up to where the tower disappears into the fog.

"Hey!" she yells, and we listen to the wind for a while before she casts off again and continues rowing.

We're heading cityside so I know she's nervous. She doesn't want to hear how pretty the lights are or questions about the shiny buildings. I'm to hush; we're here on business. She hands me the sailcloth and I climb under it and stay flat. No one is to know I'm here. I don't know why.

Once, she stops rowing. I peek under the cloth and I see her take a long look at shore. Then she starts again but slower, the oars barely slapping the water. The roll is so small here we're barely moving up and down at all and the air feels different, closed in, and I know we're under the wharf.

There's no fishermen at Fisherman's Wharf, just some things called restaurants, which Momma says are for chippers too lazy to cook. The side of the boat creaks, and I know she's tied up to the pilings. And then she's gone. I feel the boat rise, and even though I know I shouldn't, I take a peek and see her legs disappearing through the trap door at the top of the ladder.

I hear voices, angry then laughing. She's up there a long time, and when she comes back down, she smells funny and she's carrying a flashlight, like we used to have.

"Here," she says, handing it to me. "Hold this. Shine it on the fish." I do, and she starts to clean it. She slices open the belly, but stops suddenly. "Look at this!"

It's roe. A sack of perfect pink eggs as long as her forearm. "Get the jar," she says, "And the bag." She tips the end of the roe sack into the jar and cuts it off. The rest goes into the plastic bag for the restaurant. "Rich folks love this stuff," she says.

Before I put the lid on the jar, I reach in and pull a little handful out. Momma sees me, but she smiles. She reaches over and pulls a glop out of my hand and for a few minutes we just sit there happily, rolling the pretty pink balls onto our tongues and popping them against the roofs of our mouths, each one a little salty explosion.

"I'm trading for something special today," she says, pulling the rest of the guts out and dropping them in the basin. She cuts off the head lower than usual, three fingers below the gills. We'll be eating good tonight. Then she cuts off the tail, again leaving three fingers of meat. "She's a big one." she says. "They won't miss it."

She flops the body of the fish into the cloth sack, grabs the plastic bag with the roe and tells me to stow the basin. But before she climbs the ladder again she says, "Hold on," and takes the flashlight from me. She dips it in the basin and pulls it out dripping with blood. She turns it on and off a few times, then winks at me.

"Oops," she says, and climbs out of the boat.

I stow the basin and climb back under the tarp. In a few minutes, there's a clunk on the deck. Six big water jars lowered by a rope followed by Momma with a huge sack over her shoulder climbing down one handed. She unclips the jugs and gives a whistle and the rope pulls up and the trap door clanks shut and for a second it's completely dark again. But suddenly there's a light shining in Momma's hand. She hands it to me and says, "Wipe this off. What do you know, they said they didn't want it anymore," and she chuckles. She's smart, Momma.

"We did good, Baby Girl," she says, dumping out the sack. There's flour and oil and carrots and onions and potatoes and even oranges. She puts the flour in the dry box, dumps the rest back in the sack and hands it to me. "Stow that in the back and get back under" as she starts rowing.

When we're out in the channel again, Momma says to come out. "Look at this." She pulls something orange and plastic out of her pants pocket. She holds it out towards me and rubs her thumb across the top. A flame pops up!

"We won't need matches for quite a while," she says. "Oh, I almost forgot! I've got something for you." She reaches into her pocket and pulls out a brown disc about as big as the palm of my hand and gives it to me.

"What is it?"

"Called a cookie. Try it." And then I know that all I want to do forever is to eat cookies, my new favoritest thing in the entire world. I take the smallest baby bites to make it last, and when it's almost gone, I look up and see Momma's hardly rowing at all. She's just staring at me eating the cookie. I see then that she didn't have any for herself.

"Momma, I'm sorry. You want some?"

"No, that's for you. It was your lucky cast that got us that salmon. Besides, I've had them before. Good, huh?"

I nod and grin and shove the last of the cookie in my mouth. I want to stay like this, happy, forever. But Momma starts to frown. She leans back into her oars and says, "One last thing to do. Let's hope we haven't used up all our luck."

• • • •

I'm looking sharp so I see the ladder before we get to it. It's on our side of the bridge, bobbing at the end of its rope, trying to get back home. She rows right past it, into the channel and past the tower. There's nothing on the lower level, but at the top of the concrete wall I see a shape, and there's an arm dangling.

"Momma!" I say too loud, and she hushes me, but I know she's just as excited as I am. She brings the boat about and I hand her the mooring line, which she threads through the staple once again. I hold tight to the line she hands me, and she starts to drag on the other line, heaving back to pull the ladder in.

The arm disappears, and a head pops out. He has a black hood on and his skin looks so white it almost glows in the darkness. He tries to yell, but it's more of a croak and not very loud, but Momma still says, "Hush!" holding up her hand palm out. She goes back to pulling on the rope, and in a minute, she's hoisting out the ladder, standing it once more against the concrete wall. It doesn't quite reach him, but he sees it and starts to move. Two legs stick out, feet up, and I can see already that one of the legs sticks out the wrong way. I see his hands reach up and grab the remains of an old fence. The legs slowly turn feet down and start to move down the wall. He's on his stomach, holding the bottom of the fence now, but it's not enough. He grabs the top of the wall and eases backward, until one foot touches the top rung then slides his body further till his face is against the edge, and his one foot is holding him up.

The other leg is twisted and useless. There's no way he can stand on it. He lets go of the wall with his right hand and tries to reach for the top of the ladder, but he can't make it. I think he's going to tumble off, but the hand goes back up and he stands still for a long time, no movement but the flapping of his hoodie in the wind. Momma climbs out of the boat. She grabs the bottom of the ladder, I guess she's going to climb up, carry him down? But just at that moment, he goes for it, takes his foot off the rung and starts to lower himself down. I see his foot waving just above the next rung, and then he's falling. His foot catches between the rungs, but the rest of him falls backwards. Momma tries to hold the ladder, but it twists out of her hands and we just watch as man and ladder fly backwards over us and land in the water.

Momma jumps back in the boat and unties the ladder rope. "Let go!" she yells at me, meaning the hawser line and I do. She hands me the ladder rope and says "Cleat it" and starts rowing after the desperate, splashing creature caught up in our ladder.

He's untangled himself by the time we get there and turned to face us. He waves one arm and waits. He's not splashing anymore. Momma pulls up alongside and grabs him by the collar, but he's too big to land so she yells for me to reel in the ladder. She lets go of his collar and pulls the end of the ladder on board. He gets the idea and climbs up right away. He moves better up than down.

Even so he flops face first onto the deck. I know I'm not supposed to show a light, but I grab the flashlight and shine it on him. He's just a boy! Or maybe a very young man. His eyes are light–colored and they have big dark circles under them. He's shivering and breathing hard and opening his mouth like a fish.

"Water," he says and I reach for a jug.

"Turn that off. Haven't you got any sense?" So I do, and then it's black again, just the sloop–sloop of the oars, the glub–glub of drinking and then the clickety of chattering teeth.

Ηis name is Frankie, and he's funny. His eyes are blue, and his nose is big and pointy, and his teeth are pure white and straight when he smiles. And he smiles a lot.

He tells stories about a big monster named Gargantua and a dragon called Megasaur. He made me a doll called Princess Loomy out of driftwood and dry kelp. Gargantua and Megasaur are always attacking Princess Loomy's castle. Sometimes her brave knights protect her, but sometimes she gets tired of waiting and fights herself. She can spin and flip and kick Gargantua right in the face. He talks in different voices for all the people. Gargantua's voice is rough and gravelly like breakers on a rocky beach, and Princess Loomy's voice is high and singy and she says made–up words like prithee and my liege.

Momma rolls her eyes and tells us to hush up when we're giggling too loud, but I know she likes him. He's strong, and he helps a lot. Momma don't have to raise or lower the ladder anymore, or drag the boat up and cover it with kelp every morning. He pulls in the nets and the crab pots by himself, and now he's the one climbing the ladder to make the trades. She doesn't even row anymore. He pulls harder and faster than she does.

But he can't row straight. We zig–zag across the bay now, with Momma and me all the time yelling "Port!" or "Starboard" at him and laughing and teasing him when he goes the wrong way. And he still ties granny knots half the time. How could anyone get so old and know so little? He can't pick out Arcturus, or even the Dipper, and he doesn't have a song of his own, so I let him share mine.

I ask him what he learned in school, and what he used to do, but he just says, "Nothing useful." He does know about the shiny buildings and little boxes that fly a person right to the top and how the cars go across the bridge so fast and why the lights of the city shine so bright. But Momma always frowns and mutters, and he changes the subject.

I asked him why he was up on the bridge, and he said, "Enjoying the view" and laughed. But I see his face when we row under the bridge at night.

He always looks up, and his eyebrows wrinkle together. And when we're asleep, him and Momma back to back, me in Momma's arms, he'll cry out all of a sudden and shake, and I heard him tell Momma, when they thought I was asleep, that he dreams about falling.

So I don't ask him anymore. I asked Momma once, when Frankie was outside stowing the boat, and she said "The Lord delivered him unto us in our hour of need," but I remember him shaking and gasping at the bottom of the boat and said it seemed more like we was delivered in his hour of need, and Momma said, "That too."

• • • •

That first night he just lay in the boat while I scrambled out to tie up and Momma hauled out the ladder and tied it again to its sinking stones before leaning it up against the castle. Then I climbed up and down while Momma handed up the goods to store, and then carried up the fish basin herself. She knelt down and started the fire with the lighter, then told me to stay there and feed it and climbed back down again. I built up a little pile of dried kelp and made a tent of the smallest, driest drift I could find in the stack. Black smoke rose and the orange glow disappeared, but I blew on it and soon the flames were licking up the driftwood. When I was sure it wouldn't die, I climbed back to the top of the ladder and looked down. He was still in the bottom of the boat, not moving. Momma's voice was low and hard, and she took one of the oars and started poking him with it.

"Get up now! Get out of this boat!" But he just lay there looking up. "Now!" and she smacked him with the oar.

So he moved. Pulled himself up to the gunwale, then over the side, onto the rocks. "Now climb that ladder! Go!" and I thought she was going to smack him again, but he started moving, crawling with one leg and two arms across the rocks to the bottom of the ladder. When he got there, he looked up at me and back at Momma. She raised up the oar again, and he started climbing.

I could see Momma staring at me, and I went back to the fire. I made a tent of bigger sticks around the yellow flame and blew again. The inner pile fell in on itself and sparks flew up the chimney hole. Already the castle was getting warmer. When I could see the new wood glowing I went back to the ladder again.

He was moving. His hands were shaking so bad it looked like he might fall, but he kept on, reaching up to pull himself up just enough to get the knee of his good leg on the next rung, then reaching up more to pull that knee high enough that the foot could stand. Hand hand foot, hand hand knee, hand hand foot, he inched his way up towards me until he was looking me right in the face and I scrambled back down to get out of the way. He didn't swing around like a normal person, just dropped over face–first and slid down the wall, and then he just lay there, all crumpled, staring into space. He looked just like the salmon after Momma stabbed it in the back of the head, and when Momma appeared at the top of the ladder holding the sail I told her I thought he was dead, but she just said "Hush up Darling" and continued casting off the ladder and sinking it again.

When she was done, she looked at him for a minute, then went to the fire and spread the screen across the uprights. She piled even more wood on and then got the fish basin. She took out the head and tail and hung them from the wall, then poured the blood and guts into the big can and set it on the screen. She took a drink from one of the water jugs and poured some in the can, then pulled an onion from the bag and cut both ends off. The papery peel she threw in the fire, then cut two slices off and handed one to me. The rest she dropped into the can, then for a minute we both just sat there, chewing our onion and staring at the strange creature shivering on the floor of our castle.

"Stay right here and stir," she told me, handing me the stirring stick. I did what I was told, while she went over and kicked him right in the side. "Momma!" I said, but she paid no attention. "Don't you go to sleep!," she hissed at him. "Sit up and take off those wet things!"

And he did. Pretty soon wet clothes were dripping into the fire, sending smelly steam everywhere. Momma had pulled off his shoes and socks and was tugging off his pants despite his cries of pain. And now he was on our sleeping tarp wrapped in both blankets, and Momma was piling the sail cloth on top of that. She bunched up the spare tarp and pushed it up behind him, making him sit up. Her voice was softer now. "No sleep, not yet."

She pulled her sleeves down past her hands and picked up the cooking can. She poured some in the bowl and put it back on the screen.

"You and I will have to wait just a bit," she told me. She brought the bowl over to him and blew on it before holding it to his mouth. "Drink this. It'll give you strength." And he did. He choked on the first swallow, but Momma just pulled back the bowl a bit, then started again.

By the time the bowl was empty, he wasn't shivering so bad. "Thank you," he said.

"Okay, child, there's just one more thing, then you can sleep, okay?"

"Okay"

She took a length of rope and looped it around his back twice. She wrapped one end around his wrist and tied a knot

"What are you doing?" he asked.

"I'm going to fix your leg, and it's going to hurt. A lot. I need a place to brace, and I need to make sure you won't hurt me or my daughter, so I'm going to tie your arms across your stomach. Do you trust me?"

"No!" he said, then laughed. "Okay, lady, go for it."

So she did, cinched both arms tight, folded at the elbows across his stomach. Then she called me over. When I got there, she was taking away the tarp from behind his back.

"Okay, you can lie back now. You'll be asleep soon. Umi, come here by his head." Then she said "Now open your mouth. C'mon, open it. Now bite down."

She had put a piece of driftwood in his mouth and he was trying to spit it out, but she held it firmly. She took my hand and put it on the drift. "Hold his head down, Honey. Use your weight. We don't want him breaking a tooth."

He started shaking his head, trying to get away. Seemed like he was going to bite me, but Momma yelled at him. "Don't you hurt my child! She's trying to help you! Now lie still!" And he quieted down instantly. I didn't even need to push. He looked at me and closed one eye.

Momma folded back the blankets to show the twisted leg. It was all black and purple. She ran her hand along it and Frankie bit down hard, but he held still. Then she lay down beside him, her head down by the fire. She put her bare foot on his crossed arms and grabbed his lower leg with both hands.

"Okay, One, Two..." and then Frankie's whole body shook. He bit hard and screamed in the back of his throat and water came out of his eyes.

And then he was still. His eyes closed and every muscle relaxed.

"Okay, Honey, you can let go."

"Is he dead?"

"No, just asleep. He'll probably sleep for a long time." She ran her hand along his leg, smiling. "We did good, Honey. We did good." She got up and took the can off the fire and filled the bowl. "C'mon, Sweetie, you have first bowl. I have more work to do."

I took the wood out of his mouth and looked at the teeth marks on both sides. He wasn't dead. I could see him breathing. I wiped the tears off his cheeks and got up.

While I ate, she went into the corner and came back with a straight piece of wood, part of the screen door I found so long ago. She broke it over one of the sitting rocks and brought the two pieces over and held them up along the purple leg. She untied his arms, then took the rope and tied one piece of wood on each side of his leg. Then she pulled the blankets back down and the sail. She even piled on the spare tarp.

"Poor boy's frozen half to death," she said as she put more wood on the fire. She took the bowl from me and filled it again. Then we sat and watched the flames while she slurped. When she finished, she put the bowl down and pulled me over into her lap. We both stared at the new member of our family.

"Good thing you look sharp," Momma said.

FOUR

"Are you okay?"* whisper quiet, but I hear it clear over the rumble of the passing cars, the roar of the wind. "Are you okay?" and I raise my head from the steel. She's there, her face as big as a billboard, and I can see the city through her pupils. A truck passes above, and I'm wobbling, and I grip the rivet so tight it cuts into my palms. Now I see her all at once, head to toe, glowing white robes and behind her a flutter of feathers. The steel is shaking harder and I look down, a passing ship like a bathtub toy. I'm slipping and I press my back against the girder but I don't feel it anymore. "Are you okay?" again and I try to scream, "NO!" but no sound will come but my chattering teeth. She's reaching out her hand and I let go of my grip first the left hand, then both. Then I'm falling. The hand, the robe, the wings are gone. I grab for the bridge but it's only air and the ocean is rushing up to me, but now it's an eye, grandpa's gory socket, and I'm disappearing into the red darkness. I cry out for help, but all I hear is him laughing, and I slip right through into fog, just falling, falling.*

But I don't hit bottom. I'm awakened by pain; I kicked in my sleep and now my leg is throbbing with each beat of my heart. I reach down to touch my leg. Something is strapped onto it, some piece of wood. The cord is cutting into my bare flesh, and I rub it gently, but it hurts even more when I touch it. The pain is so intense that it takes me a moment to realize something else: I'm lying next to a stranger, wearing only my underwear!

I'm under a blanket with some kind of stiff cloth on top of that, and I roll and see the back of a head of dusty black hair. Her arm is out, over the covers, and she's wearing a filthy sweater that might have been white a long time ago. I roll back and scooch away, but I'm against a rock and there's no place for me to go.

It's day, but the light is dim and green. I'm in some sort of cave, it smells of sweat and smoke and rotten fish. The walls are jumbled stones and broken cinder blocks and the wind whistles through the cracks. A gust flutters the ceiling; it must be a cloth of some kind.

I'm breathing hard, and my heart is beating so loudly I'm afraid she'll wake. I feel each beat as a hammer on my thigh, but I can't control it, can't slow down the panic rising in me, can't think.

I need to get out, to get back. Mom must be worried half to death; her father dead, and her son missing, disappeared like his father before him. But no, not worried—sad, because they would have told her we both died in that explosion, no that mechanical failure, that's what they'll say. Operating an unsafe vehicle, endangering the lives of others, brilliant but arrogant, you know how he was. They may not say it, but she'll fill it in, *I told him a thousand times that thing was unsafe and why was he coming that way anyway?* So sorry for your loss, they'll say. And she'll be alone.

Or maybe? No, they wouldn't think that, would they? They'd know that she had nothing to do with all this, with whatever Grandpa was mixed up in. She works for them! They'd know, they wouldn't suspect her, interrogate her. No, she is alone; she's sad; that's bad enough.

Why didn't I just jump? No pain, no worry, no thinking, just join the sea, melt away. I remember the cold steel against my cheek, the slow climb down, the fall, the freezing water. Cold down to the bones, shaking, shivering, numbing cold.

But not cold anymore. Heat radiates from the body next to me. Only the stone is cold, pressing in my side. I scooch back. It's warm. It's soothing. Even the smell is soothing, the rich, animal smell of human beings. My breathing slows. There's nothing I can do. Nothing I must do. Nothing.

• • • •

"Are you okay?" It's the girl from last night, but she looks smaller, younger in the daylight. Two pigtails poke out of her pink hoodie, black against her thin, white cheeks.

"Honey, I told you, let him sleep."

"But he's awake, Momma, his eyes are open."

"Well back off a little. Let him sit up." But she doesn't move.

"What's your name?"

"Franc, Frankie," I say. My voice is hoarse and croaky. "What's yours?"

"Umi. My momma's Yvette," she says.

"Give him some room!" and a hand pushes the girl back. The woman—Yvette—comes forward. "Don't be scared," she says. "You hungry? I'm cooking. Fog came in thick this afternoon. No one'll see the smoke."

Suddenly, she looks like she's just remembered something. "Umi," she says, "Put another piece of drift on the fire, a small one." Then she pulls the top cloth off me and stretches it out arm's length.

"There's a jar behind you. Do whatever you need to do." And she turns her back, still holding the cloth out, making a little partition.

I turn around and see what she means. A five liter jar wrapped in a rope net sits against the wall. It's partly full, and when I open the lid, the smell knocks me back. But I do what I need to do. What other choice do I have? And after I replace the lid and return the jar to its spot, I turn around and look at this woman's, Yvette's, back. Her shirt and pants are dirty, stained like everything else in here, but there's a delicacy, something so civilized, in this simple gesture, patiently holding up a cloth, doing her best to give me dignity, to make me comfortable. I am her guest.

I pull the blanket back up and clear my throat. She turns around briskly, businesslike, folding up the cloth and says, "Your sweatshirt is still wet, but we have something that will fit you."

She dips an old rag into a can of water on the fire. "Here," she says, "clean yourself up." The rag looks as dirty as everything else, but it's steaming and feels wonderful held against my face. I drop the blanket around my waist and wash my whole upper body. The girl is watching me, shyly peering from behind her mother's legs, but I find I don't care. The water, the warmth, and I'm starting to feel like myself again.

She comes back with my t-shirt and an old, gray sweater, stretched out at the sleeves. There is a brown stain on the chest, but I put them both on anyway. The shirt is still a little damp, it's cold against my skin, but the sweater is wool and feels warm immediately. It's scratchy but comforting. The smell takes me back to elementary school, I don't know why, coatroom on a rainy day?

"Better check that leg. Do I need to tie you up again?"

"What? No, that's okay."

She laughs. "Just kidding." She folds the blanket back and begins to examine the leg.

"I'm going to loosen the splint, but don't move your leg until I tie it back on." And then she's reaching up to my thigh and tugging on the cords. I grit my teeth not to yell, but I can't help making a weird animal noise through my nose when the first knot loosens and the blood rushes in.

Umi looks scared by the sound so I force myself to smile at her. I raise one eyebrow and waggle it up and down and she giggles.

The second knot is coming undone and the urge to bend my leg is overwhelming, but I grip the blanket in my fist and stay still. The marks of the rope are clear on my purple leg. She undoes the last two and pulls away the boards. She runs her hand gingerly up and down.

"Looks good, nice and straight, but you won't be walking for a while. I'm going to try and make this splint a little more comfortable, but you've got at least a couple weeks of pain ahead of you."

"Well, if you could drop me on shore, I could..." but she only smiles.

"We both know that's not a good idea. No, you'll be staying with us for a while." and to Umi, "Get me that old flour sack in the corner."

She rips the sack into four strips and arranges them, two on the thigh, two on the calf, each one just above or below the rope marks. Lifting my leg gently, she slips the cloths under and pulls them up and overlays them on top. Then she gets the boards and lines them up on each side of my leg. Her touch is gentle, but the slight knock of wood against my thigh makes me gasp, and when I think of those ropes cinching up again, I feel my heart race despite myself.

"Take slow breaths," she says. And turning to Umi, "Sing your song, okay Honey?"

She picks up one of the splint boards and raps it gently on the stone floor: knock, knock-knock; knock, knock-knock, and then the cave is filled with the voice of an angel. Pure and clear, the tones float in the air like no music I've ever heard before, and it is so strange to see this skinny little ragamuffin singing this ancient–sounding tune, her little cupid mouth forming archaic words I can't quite understand.

> "Lord whom wind and waves obey
> Guide us through the watery way"

My breath does slow; I give in to the rocking rhythm, I can't help it. Yvette cinches up the ropes one by one, and I gasp each time, but without panic. My mind is on the music, floating back in time, it seems. The worst is over, and the pain just a reminder that I'm going to live after all.

> "Save, till all these tempests end,
> All who on thy love depend;
> Waft our happy spirits o'er;
> Land us on the heavenly shore"

The song ends. She's been singing with her eyes closed, more like a prayer or a dream than a performance, but with the last words she opens them and sees me staring at her. Her eyes widen and she frowns, and I realize suddenly that tears are sliding down my cheeks. She comes around her mom and kneels next to me. She puts her arm around me.

"It's okay," she says.

Yvette is tying the last knot, but her eyes are fixed on her daughter. She smiles. Her teeth are yellow and crooked, but her eyes crinkle in the corner. It's a smile of pride, of contentment. I smile back. I can't help it.

"Okay, all done. Breakfast time," and she goes back to the fire. "Umi, honey, come here. Peel this."

Umi takes her arm off my neck. I turn and see her staring at me, like a doctor checking if I'm well enough to be left alone. She tucks her hand in her sleeve and wipes my cheeks before she goes to her mother and takes the orange she is holding out. She bites the end of it and begins to peel. When she is done, she places the fruit on a flat piece of driftwood, then divides the peel into three piles and hands one to me and one to her mom who pops a piece in her mouth and starts chewing. Umi does the same, and they both stare at me, their faces neutral, waiting.

"C'mon, you don't want to get scurvy," Yvette says, "Plus, it makes the fruit taste sweeter."

So I do it, thinking "This is my life now—orange peels for breakfast, hot blood for dinner," but it's not too bad. Bitter, but it cleans the teeth. And when she breaks the rest of it into sections, and gives me the largest, it does taste sweeter, juicier than any orange I've eaten in my life.

And now she's cutting up pink chunks of meat of some sort and placing them on a metal screen over the fire.

"Hope you like salmon," she says.

I do. My family had salmon once a year, my grandfather's birthday, and even for someone as well connected as he is—was—it was an extravagance, flown in from Alaska or Greenland or something. I had no idea there were still salmon here in the bay.

She turns the pieces with her fingers, Umi comes back and sits next to me.

"You have a big nose," she says, and I laugh. I'm expecting Yvette to scold her, to say "No Honey, that's not nice" or something like that, but they both just smile. Umi's grin reveals a missing canine.

"Yeah, I guess I do, and you have a hole in your smile" which makes her grin even more.

She reaches out and touches my nose, her other hand going to her own for comparison. I stick out my tongue and she laughs.

"What were you doing up on the bridge?"

I hesitate. What can I say? I look over at Yvette. She shakes her head slightly, the corners of her mouth turned down.

"Just looking at the view," I answer. She rolls her eyes, but lets it drop.

Yvette is putting the salmon chunks on little flat pieces of wood. There are three little piles. She takes the smallest one and gestures to Umi, who brings me the largest. We eat without ceremony. No one talks.

The first piece burns my fingers, so I put it back down and blow on it. I see tiny flecks of ash clinging to the skin, and when it's cool enough to bite I sense a slight dusting of sand and salt from the driftwood plate, but it's delicious. As I chew, I'm overwhelmed with longing for my mother. I finally understand her "realist" beliefs about food, her insistence on feeding us greens just ripped from the soil, her disdain for the packets all the other kids' families ate. She would have loved this. No sauce, no spice, not even any lemon, but a flavor and a texture so vivid you can't help but picture the fish itself and the cold, dark water from which it came.

We're done in only a couple minutes, and I know enough not to ask for more. Mother and daughter are both so thin it's obvious there's no food to spare.

"That was delicious," I say as Umi gathers back the plates. "Can I do anything to help?"

"Not today," she says. She is cleaning the wooden dishes in a curious way, holding them face down in the flames, pulling them away just before they light. "Today you need to rest. That's your job. Umi and I will be heading out soon. If you're cold, you can keep the fire going; otherwise, let it go out. We're running low on wood, but if the fog holds, we'll stop on Angel and gather some more."

"Angel?"

"Angel Island," says the girl. "It's so fun! We get out of the boat and walk on the beach and everything,"

"Maybe," says her mother. "Don't count your chickens."

Umi leans towards me. Her voice gets quiet. "Sometimes we see lights, then we don't go. One time we heard voices, so we got out quick."

Mother and daughter begin getting ready for their night of fishing. Yvette leans out of the "window" and looks around before reeling in a rope. Yard by yard she pulls and the hemp snake grows and coils at her feet. The last section is clearly harder. She grunts as she heaves the line, and I can hear a clattering on the rocks outside. Meanwhile Umi gathers another coil of rope, a metal basin, a knife, extra fishing line, the oars. No one tells her what to do or even to do anything at all. She stands behind her mother, watching her final efforts. There is a bang and a scrape and the top of the ladder appears.

Yvette climbs out and Umi begins passing things to her, then climbs out herself. A bang, a scrape and a splash and I know the boat is in the water. A moment later, the ladder creaks and Yvette's head appears,

"We'll be back before daybreak. Try to get some sleep."

Once again, I thank her and ask to be dropped ashore. "I don't mean to be a burden." Take me to Fort Point, and I'll be fine."

"No, you won't," she says. "You can't even walk yet, and where would you go?"

I start to answer, but she just laughs. "We both know you weren't up there for the view."

FIVE

I tell her everything, of course. Long days, lying next to her while Umi sleeps, my story seeps out, a couple drops at first, then a splash, and soon everything I've known and done is pouring out of me. I've never talked like this—at length—in my life. And I've never been listened to like this, not just patiently, but eagerly, as if her life might depend on some little detail I've left out.

The part that interests her the most is Grandpa's dying words. She has me tell it again and again. She wants me to describe the look in his eye, the tone of his voice. To her, it's clear that Grandpa was transitioning to the next world. The idea of looking an angel in the eye appeals to her. She wants me to say that at the end he looked blissful. Or at least peaceful.

But I don't know. Grandpa wasn't a believer. If he saw something on the other side, I guess his expression would have been surprise. I don't say it, but I feel if he did see an angel's eye, it was nothing but a hallucination.

Even that is hard to picture. Grandpa's mind was so clear, so sharp, I can't see him being out of touch with reality, even in his last moments. I can't see him wasting his last breath describing a vision. No, he was trying to tell me something.

I go over and over that last day, replaying the conversations that I overheard, trying to figure out exactly why the V.T.B. would want to kill my grandfather.

Yvette listens patiently, but her response shocks me. "What makes you so sure he was the target?" she asks.

"What?"

"Well, what did the professor say? They've 'seen your work'? They've been watching you."

"Okay, but..."

"Your grandfather isn't the one who took out his chip, who rejected their way of life.. He's not the one who met with an enemy agent."

"What? Who?"

"Isn't it obvious? 'The Committee has decided to move you. You've been seen.' Isn't that what you heard? What did you think that was? The food service union? The woman told you that you'd endangered her—Maya. What else could she have meant?"

"But…"

"You might be right. You'd know better than I would, of course. But I'm surprised it never crossed your mind."

"But they offered me a place on campus."

"Of course. You're an asset. You do the thing—the coding—and you're good at it. They want to use you. But only if they can control you. They don't want anybody else to use you. What did your grandpa say about the buses, about changing their instructions, reprogramming them for chaos? You asked who could do such a thing. What was his answer?"

The fog horn is blowing "home, home, home" and in between the blasts I can hear the little whistles of Umi's sleep. *She can't be right. Is it my fault, the whole thing?*

"Grandpa was an important person," I say. "I'm a nobody.

· · · ·

It's not easy to accept being dead, but I finally do. The first weeks, as my leg healed, I'd lie alone at night and imagine going home. I'd go ashore, swim if I had to, and make my way to the Presidio wall. There are trees there, pines, that grow along the north wall. Their limbs stretch across to join the branches of the elms across the street. I pictured myself climbing across the branches like a squirrel. I'd drop in unnoticed into the woods we played in, Nigel and me, when we were kids. I know the back ways, I'd only have to go a block or two on the street. Late at night that should be pretty safe. And then I'd be home.

And here my plan ended. I still had my chip in its baseball card case. If salt water hadn't destroyed it, it might still open the door, but wouldn't that trip some sort of alert? Unless the V.T.B. was absolutely certain of my death, wouldn't they be on the lookout for any use of the chip? I thought about climbing the fence, tapping on a window. Or maybe just waiting in the greenhouse until evening when she'd come to get her lettuce. It was hard to picture either meeting without hearing my mother scream. If they're monitoring her feed, they'd be sure to program an algorithm looking for unusual heart palpitations, triggering an auto-rec. Incog wouldn't help, they'd know.

And then there is the other possibility. I go in the door, I tap on the glass, I wait in the greenhouse, and no one's home. Weeds strangle the vegetables, thick dust coats everything. Mai-cat wanders in and out of the cat door, mewing piteously.

When my leg is well enough that I can climb the ladder and join them in the boat, I beg Yvette to row in close, let me look. She doesn't want to, but she does. Our neighbors, the Zelevanskys, have an unusual house topped with a glass pyramid. I look for it as she rows, but trees and buildings block my view. Suddenly, as we pass the marina, I see it. I look to the right: there's the tall, thin modern block of our other neighbors' house—the Changs—but in between, where I should be, only darkness. Three nights in a row we check, three nights of disappointment. But on the third night, later, lying in the boat looking up at the stars, waiting for something to bite, the fog clears and Umi shows me the dipper, points out Arcturus, and I'm not listening exactly, but just hearing, like music, the tones of her voice, and I think, "It's not so bad, being dead."

A dead man is free. No need to accomplish anything, worry about anything. No need to fight injustice or enforce order. No need to know what side you're on.

Is my mother dead, or locked in some dark cell? Nothing I can do about it. And if she's not, if she's safe at home, if she just is not turning on her lights, well then her only hope to stay safe is to stay away from dangerous dead men like me.

Franc is dead, long live Frankie. That night I ask to row home.

SIX

It's a hard life, and once the novelty wears off, a bit boring. I don't mind the work, and even with my bum leg I can pull harder, lift more than Yvette, who gets weaker every day. She "superintends" now, and I call her "Boss." Her biggest threat is, "Do you want me to get up and do it for you?" and at first, that threat was real. I'd struggle pulling the boat ashore or reeling in the sunken ladder, and she'd lose patience and take over—zoop, the boat was up on the rocks, the ladder too, and I'd stand there like a weakling idiot. She still talks a good game, but now I don't know. When I'm rowing, she leans against the prow sometimes as if just lifting her head to see is just too much work. And when we return to the island, she creeps up the ladder and then just lies still while Umi and I prepare the food.

Umi's fun. Her thoughts, her emotions, are so pure. She loves me in a way I've never been loved before, and sometimes it's awkward. My mother loved me, of course, and so did my grandfather, and I know they both respected me. But Umi looks up to me. In her eyes, I'm the bravest and strongest ever, which I'm definitely not. And the smartest, which I am about some things, but only because I've seen a few things that she can only imagine. I made the mistake of describing the glass elevator of Evans Hall, and for weeks it was all she could talk about. She's only seen machinery at a distance, and a "view" from above is something she can only imagine in reverse. Yvette frowns when I mention anything about city life that is in any way appealing, so I stick to funny stories, like getting kicked in the head and falling into the trash bin. But it's hard to never mention sunshine, or trees, or driving in a car: things she'll never know.

It's a beautiful world, the bay at night, surrounded by the lights of the city, and even more beautiful beyond the gate, engulfed in fog, rolling with the waves, like dissolving into the water itself. One night we saw a huge flock of gulls, wheeling and diving in a frenzy for a giant school of sardines. Yvette ordered me to row fast, and she and Umi pulled out the net, but just when we arrived, and they began lowering for the fish, an immense being from another world emerged, a humpback whale lunging straight up, maybe 20 feet out of the water, gulping thousands of the tiny fish at once. Even Yvette had never seen one so close, and we all screamed when we were hit by the splash as it returned to its world. The fish were gone, of course, and we were all three soaked and freezing, but we whooped and hollered and laughed, and I felt more alive at that moment than I had ever felt in my life.

But other times it's dull, monotonous. We sit in silence for hours and I get tired of my own thoughts; they swirl around my brain beyond my control, the same stupid stories, the same futile longing for a do–over. Sometimes I really wish I had a vid to distract me, or even a wiki entry, some dumb fact that doesn't matter but is still fun to learn. I can't help feeling this is not my life, that I'm meant to be doing something, part of something bigger.

I still ask to be set ashore, especially when the food runs low. I thought I'd be sick of fish, but the bigger problem is the many, many nights when we blank—catch nothing at all. Then it's potato soup again, and not much of it. I can't help feeling guilty about taking a third of not enough food for two. When we got down to boiled kelp for three days in a row, I insisted. I waited until Umi was asleep to bring it up again.

"Look, we need to go ashore, if not all of us, then just me. Maybe you can get enough food for two, I don't know. But if I stay, we'll starve to death."

"We won't starve. We've gone hungry before. We'll catch something tonight, you'll see."

"You're better off without me," I said.

"No, we're not, and you know it. How long till I can't climb the ladder?"

"Well, all of us then. I know you don't want her in the city," I said, dropping my voice. "It's bad there, I know. I saw. But I saw food at least."

Yvette was quiet for a long time.

"We can't let her starve," I began again.

"No!" she hissed. "Umi is never going to live on the street. I'll flip the boat first."

"Okay, but."

"You've got to promise me! You'll never take her there, even after I'm gone. Promise!"

My cheeks were wet again. I couldn't help it. "Okay, I promise, but we have to do something."

"We'll catch something tonight. You'll see."

And she turned back on her side and put her arm around Umi. I lay there for a long time, staring at the tarp above me slowly getting lighter. Then I turned on my side as well. I put my arm over her shoulder, buried my face in her hair. Breathed in her scent.

• • • •

She was right, we did catch something that night. A new spot I'd never seen before, around the city, under the bridge and past the ballpark. All the way to Hunter's Point, she made me row, and then dropped line in a part of the bay that looked exactly like all the rest as far as I was concerned.

"There's a shoal here," she said when I asked. "A shallow spot, sandy by the outflow. This used to be a river mouth long ago."

We were quiet that night. No songs, no stories. Too close to shore, and anyway we were all tired and weak. We were trolling, so my job was to row slowly back and forth. From time to time, a plane would pass, taking off for God knows where, and Umi would gasp every time. I tried in a whisper to explain how something so heavy could fly, but as soon as I began, I realized I didn't know what I was talking about. I was just about to resort to the old "magic" story, when the fish struck.

Yvette and I switched spots. She began to row out towards deep water, while I grabbed the pole and started to reel it in. I followed orders about when to pull hard, and when to let it swim. Bit by bit, I walked the tin can back, rolling in the line until finally something big and white rose out of the water. I was just wondering how to pull the whole fish out without breaking the line, when Umi, smacked it with the gaff and together we flopped it into the boat, a big, flat, white ghost of a fish.

"Halibut!" she said, pulling out the gaff and smacking the club end on the fish's back. It lay still, and Yvette leaned over to look at it.

"Praise the Lord!" she whispered. "This one's worth a lot. Let's go trade it right now. We can get maybe five pounds of potatoes, plus two or three of carrots. Maybe some onions. Some flour."

"Let me do it," I said. I was on the bench, rowing again.

"What?"

"I'm going to do the trading."

"Well, I'm not sure..."

"I'm sure," I said, and the tone of my voice surprised me. I was giving a command.

Because I had been thinking. What did I have to offer? Some strength, sure, but do I really know how to fish? I can't even row straight. And I've never bartered before either, but I did have one big advantage over Yvette. I've been to restaurants, and I know how much they charge for a piece of fish.

All the way there, she gave me her list. "Don't forget, five pounds of potatoes, some oil, some carrots, some onions. A little fruit if you can. Maybe some greens. Oh, and sometimes they have old bread! Get some of that!"

When we were moored under the wharf, I stuffed the halibut in a sack and climbed the ladder. I pushed up the trapdoor and found myself in a kitchen storeroom. Through an open doorway, I could see the kitchen. Two large, greasy men in hairnets sat beside an overturned crate, playing cards.

The aroma of the evening's meal was in the air, so many smells: garlic, and roasting meat, fried onions, and hot bread. Saliva gathered on my tongue, but I made an effort to look uninterested.

"I'm Yvette's friend," I said. "I've got something for you." I put my sack on the counter and opened it to show the contents. I could see their eyes widen when I laid out my demands.

"You're crazy," one of them said, laughing.

"That's twice the normal," said the other.

"That's right," I said, "And that's not all," and I told them my other demand.

"There's no way in hell." the first one said.

"Okay, have it your way," I said, and picked up the sack.

By the time I was at the ladder, the laughter had stopped.

"Be reasonable" was the last thing I heard as I began to descend. I could see Yvette smile up at me, but her smile faded when she saw the bag.

"What's happening?" she asked.

"Cast off," I said, sitting at the bench, tossing the sack on the floor of the boat.

"But"

"Cast off."

A head hung upside down from the hatch. "Yvette? Who is this guy? He's crazy."

"Cast off." But she didn't move. Her head swiveled back and she looked at me. It was the only time I ever saw her look uncertain.

"Cast off!"

"Okay, okay," said the voice from above. "Seven pounds of potatoes, three of carrots, two of greens, two bags of onions, one bag of oranges."

Yvette's eyes widened.

"You heard what I want, and don't forget the other thing."

"Be reasonable!"

"Cast off."

"But what are we going to eat?"

"We're going to eat halibut. It's delicious. Cast off!" And she did. She shook her head, but she uncleated the line and I began to row.

The yelling started as soon as we started to move, but I took three long strokes, before I back–paddled and looked up as if I'd just heard them.

"Okay, you win! We'll get it!"

Soon I was climbing up and down the ladder, burdened down. 15 gallons of water, 10 pounds of potatoes. 5 pounds of carrots, 3 pounds of chard, 4 bags of onions, 2 sacks of oranges, 3 loaves of bread, a small bottle of oil, and a pound of flour. Yvette said nothing, but I could see Umi's face peering out of her hiding place, grinning.

When the last bit was stowed, I said, "I've got to go back up. It might be a little while."

I climbed down for the last time holding a paper sack, cinched tight at the top, a grease stain on the side. I handed it to Yvette, and we cast off. As I rowed, I could see her sniffing the bag and smiling. She shook her head at me as at a naughty child.

When we were far enough off for Umi to come out, I let the boat drift.

"I'm not waiting anymore," I said. "Open the bag."

She reached in and pulled out what her nose had already told her she would: three bags of french fries and three hamburgers.

"Well," she said, "I guess we won't starve."

SEVEN

"**One, one zero, one one,** one zero zero, one zero one, one one zero, one one one, one zero zero zero, one zero zero one, one zero one zero, one zero one one, one one zero zero, one one zero one, one one one one, one zero zero zero zero, one zero zero zero one, one zero zero one zero, one zero zero one one, one zero one zero zero."

Umi is counting her fingers and her toes. In binary. Yvette is biting her tongue. She can't stand all this "nonsense" as she calls it. The regular counting was bad enough. Lots of kids like to count everything, or just count up to a hundred, or maybe a thousand, to show off. I can remember trying to count to infinity. Grandpa just closed his office door and put on headphones. He was supposed to be watching me.

But this is worse, even I admit it, all those zeroes and ones droning on. I get a kick out of hearing her, but I know it really is annoying. And it's my fault.

We were talking about dreams, like we do every afternoon. Umi's are the best. Always adventures in the "bright world" as she calls it, they're a mix of real stuff she's heard about—cats, elevators, flowers—and her imagination. They always start vague; often they're "really scary" but when they start to peter out, she looks left and says, "and" and then some new fantastic detail flies out and soon she's in a wonderland of purple flowers and green cats with hair that sweeps the forest floor when they walk. And Momma, she's usually there. Me too.

Yvette tells her dreams like a list—no story at all. "Night. Rowing. Strong current. Light, blinding. Gentle voice. 'Stay calm.' I'm awake." Then follows immediately with her interpretations, which are usually practical—"Crab pots tonight"—and sometimes quite surprising. A salmon she hooked in her dream was her mother, she was sure, and its gasping and flailing in the boat, just her way to communicate. "Stay home tonight," the fish 'said' to her. And she did. Sent us out alone.

As for me, most often I remember nothing. If I do remember, it's the falling dream again, and I don't want to share. Sometimes I make up a silly story to amuse Umi, but usually, I just say, "No dreams," which they can't understand at all.

But then I had one so vivid I had to tell it. In my dream I was tiny, small enough to crawl inside my own ear. I was trying to get to my brain; I had to tell it something, and it was so important to get there and deliver the message, but by the time I woke up I couldn't remember what the message was. I'm not sure I ever knew. But I still felt that urgency.

Inside my head was a corridor with thousands, millions of doors. My heart jerked and I lurched left through a door and I hurried down a new hallway past several doors and then left again into another hallway, another set of doors. Every doorway led to another corridor, with another million doors.

But I had no control over which door I opened, which path I took. I lost all sense of east and west and north and south, even up and down because some of the doors were in the ceiling and some on the floor. I was exhausted and I felt I'd never get there, never deliver my message, but I kept going, going, turn after turn, with no control over where I was heading—no way to stay on the correct path, or maybe there wasn't one.

And then my self separated. I could see myself from outside, from afar, going and going—random turn right, left, up, down. I could see I was in something like a cube made up of millions of little cubes, a mesh, like a stack of screens.

But my other self, the watcher one, could travel freely. I could see myself and my herky–jerky turns, but my other self could slide in and out through the gaps in the screen like a sparrow flying through the monkey bars.

It's so hard to describe, but while I was flying I could still feel, in my body, every turn my other self made, could still feel the urging and weariness of those random rights and lefts and ups and downs. But I, the watcher I, the flying I, wasn't there anymore. I was flying into a building, a giant, dirty block with bright lights.

It was a factory, and a long line of men wearing identical gray aprons, a line so long that I couldn't see the end, were standing at table, swinging hammers. Each strike would drive a spike into the table, but another would pop up at the same time right next to it. Then they'd hit that one and the first would pop back up. The men near me were quite lazy, they only swung the hammers now and then, but as I went down the table I saw the hammers coming down faster. And with every hammer strike I could feel in my body a pull or a jerk, and I knew that my other self was turning left right up down and the further I went along the workbench the faster the hammers flew. At the end of the little table the strikes were so fast it was just a roar and I could see that the men swinging the hammers were tired and sweaty, like I was. And the table they were striking was covered with blood.

I woke up covered in sweat, my heart was racing.

The interpretation was obvious to Yvette. A door is an opportunity, a turn is a decision. She didn't need to say more. But what opportunity and what decision? Where to drop the line? Which lure is the best? No. I have no opportunities and my decisions were made for me.

"Of course," she said, "It seems that way now."

We sat in silence for a few minutes. I didn't feel like arguing. How could I explain it to someone who never had a chip? I was literally programmed. I was running smoothly, then I glitched.

"The real question is what was the message? What were you trying to tell yourself?"

"I don't . . ."

"Well think about it. And what were the hammers? I'd say the heart because of the blood, the beating. But why so many"

"Well. . ."

"Divided affection? You don't know where your heart lies. That's true isn't it? You're still thinking about leaving us."

Umi looked up sharply. This was news to her. I tried to smile at her, to wink and make it a joke, but she's too smart. It's true, I had been thinking lately, 'What next?' I just let the comment lie.

We sat in silence for a while. A freighter was passing our island, close enough to cast a shadow. Could we stow away? I wondered. Sneak on in the dark, take on new lives in a foreign land?

"But I can't understand," she went on. "Why so many? And why were the ones close to you lazy and the ones far down the line working so hard?"

"Binary."

"What?"

"Base two. Ones and zeroes. It's how computers work."

"How?" This time it was Umi.

"Well, a computer is a machine. It's just switches. A switch is either off or on. You know, like your flashlight? We say ones and zeroes, but really it's off and on, so they use the binary number system."

Yvette gave me about a minute to wax poetic about the glories of base two numbering before she interrupted me.

"And we need to know this because…?" She never pretends to be interested when she's not. "Somehow, I've been able to use a flashlight without this knowledge."

So I hushed up, as she would say. We sat and listened to the fog horn in the distance. Then Umi said, "Did you learn it in school?"

"Well, yeah, we learned it."

"Teach me."

I glanced at Yvette, but she just rolled her eyes and returned her attention to the net she was repairing so I went ahead.

"Well, like I said, binary is a number system that uses only ones and zeroes. You know how we count onetwothreefourfivesixseveneightnineten? And you know how you write ten as one zero? And you know how after ten, it just starts over? Eleven is ten one. We write 'one one' right? And twelve is one two, and so on?"

On our excursions to the beach on Angel Island to gather firewood, I had collected twenty-four flat, round stones. I had blackened half of them with ash on one side and had taught Umi how to play checkers on a grid I scratched into the dirt. I laid them out in three rows, two sets of ten, one set of four.

"How many checkers?"

"Twenty-four." She didn't bother counting. We've played a lot of checkers.

"Okay, and how many in this row?"

A moment's hesitation, then, "Ten"

"And this one?"

"Ten."

"And this one?"

"Four."

"Right, so twenty-four is two tens, and four ones. And we write two four, right?'

"Mmhm"

"And I could show you it like this, right?" I flashed open my hands twice, then held up four fingers.

Umi grinned, She'd never seen anyone do this, but she got it immediately.

"How many is this?" I asked, then opened my hands seven times, followed by just the pinky and the ring fingers of my right hand."

"Seventy-two?"

"You know it!" She's really quick. "Okay, that's base ten. That seems normal to us, right? Because we've got ten fingers. But did you know there's an animal called a sloth that only has three fingers on each hand?" I held up both hands with the pinkies and rings tucked in.

"Really?"

"Yeah, they're very slow—I'll tell you about them later—but if Mrs. Sloth asks how many, and Mr. Sloth does this," I flashed open my hands two times, but with only three fingers on each hand. The third time, the left hand was a fist while the right had just the thumb and the pointer out. "What number would she write down?"

Umi was quiet. "I couldn't count them that fast."

"Look we go" and I flashed my full hands twice, followed by four fingers, "And we call it twenty-four. One." I flashed my open hands and flashed them again. "Two" One hand this time with the thumb tucked in. "And four. Two four. Twenty-four. Right?"

She nodded. "So when the sloth goes" and repeated my sloth sign language "What's the number Mrs. Sloth writes down?"

"Twenty-two?"

"Exactly!"

"It's fourteen!" cried a voice from the other side of the cave. "Don't lie to the child!"

So she was listening! "Well to a human, you're right." I said, "In base ten, it would be fourteen. But Umi here can count like a human, but also like a sloth!"

Umi said nothing. She glowed with this new–found ability.

"It's nonsense!" Yvette muttered, but I went on.

"Okay, Umi, suppose there was an animal with only one finger on each hand."

"Okay.

"And one creature goes" And this time I flashed both hands once only, and with only one finger on each hand. The second flash was just a single finger. "Okay, how many was that?"

"Eleven?"

And I grabbed her in a hug, I couldn't help it. Never been to school, and I know I wasn't that smart at her age.

Yvette was livid. "That was three!" And she was right, of course, in her way, but we didn't let that get in the way of our hug. This is our thing. Me and Umi. Our little game. I let go of her, but stayed close. I leaned in and whispered, "In binary, you count like this: one, ten, eleven, one hundred, one-o-one, one eleven, one thousand."

She was amazed. She's counted to a thousand before, I've heard her. "But actually," I go on, "you don't say it that way because it's confusing. You say 'one, one zero, one one, one zero zero like that. But here, let me show you something."

I went back to our checkers. I separated out the black ones and laid eight of them in one line.

"Now one thing I never told you is that if a zero is before a number, it doesn't mean anything. Zero is nothing, right? After a number, it means something. One zero is?"

"Ten."

"Right. And one zero zero?"

"A hundred"

"Right. So after a number, or in the middle of a big number, the zero is important. But before a number, it doesn't mean anything. Zero one is one. And zero zero one is one. And zero zero zero zero zero zero zero one is?"

"One!"

"Exactly. So look. All these black checkers are zeroes, right? And when I turn it over on the light side, that's a one, okay?"

She nodded. I flipped the stone back over. "Okay, I want you to count one to ten on your fingers slowly, just the regular counting okay? And I'll count it off in binary. Okay? Go."

"One," she said, holding up her thumb the way Grandpa would count. And I flipped over the rock on the far right and said, "one."

"Two," she said, and I flipped the rock over again, along with the one to its left.

"One zero," pointing to the rocks as I said it.

And so it went.

When she said "ten" I said "one zero one zero" and pointed. And then for the hell of it, I did six more because at 16, I knew I'd flip five rocks at once. One black to light, four lights to black.

"In a computer, each flip is a switch. In my dream, each time a hammer struck, I made a turn. I switched. The lazy guys, they were down here." I pointed to the stones that hadn't yet been touched. "They hardly have to work at all. But the ones at this end, they were hitting so fast," and I flipped a couple of stones back and forth, "that you could barely see what they were doing. Do you see what I mean?"

Umi nodded her head, but Yvette shook hers.

"I think you're both nuts."

· · · ·

Next morning, I couldn't sleep. Yvette was snoring quietly, Umi in her arms, but I was staring at the tarp above me growing lighter and greener. I've never completely adjusted to being nocturnal.

What was the message? What was I trying to tell myself? She's not wrong, Yvette. Hammers beating, blood. A heart makes sense. And divided affection? Is there any other kind?

But I'm right too. It's binary. I'm in those corridors again. Left, right, up, down. No control, a maze of mesh. I crawled inside my own brain and what was there? A chip.

I never meant to live forever without it. Just a week. I don't want to die young, but now I will. Is that the dream? Just my neurons mourning the loss?

I closed my eyes and pictured an ant crawling up my own neck. It summited the jawline and made its way through the forest of my sideburns. It came to the mouth of a cave and hesitated, then entered.

Now I'm the ant and again I've got that urgency. I must get to my brain, but I don't want to. The thought of those doors, those endless corridors, fills me with dread. I'm weary already, and afraid. I hear the hammers in the distance. A pair of doors appears before me. A boom rips my ribcage and I feel myself pivot to the right, but as I start to go, I see that the left door looks familiar. My hand is still on the right doorknob, but I turn anyway. I feel my flesh rip as I turn. I step through my body, which is not an ant's and feels like it never was. I come out larger, but tender, prickly, more vulnerable. I glance back and see that what I thought was me was only a shell. I've molted, like a lobster.

I open the door on the left and find it familiar, a small, dark room where an old man with an eyepatch sits in front of two enormous monitors.

"You want a game? I'll make you a game. When you can beat it, I'll give you those credits."

He's talking to a boy, a boy unbelievably small and young. He looks at his grandfather with total trust.

On the screen, lines of red type fly upwards, but I can slow them down, see them all.

"My God," I think, "It's Fortran. He's using Fortran!" It's like writing a novel in hieroglyphics. But I can follow it. Those long–ago lessons return and I see every step. When he hits "run," I wake up.

I can still see the lines of code in my mind. I scroll through them. It would work. I know it would work, although, of course, I can't test it.

I turn to Yvette. She's on her back now, staring at the tarp overhead. Her head is swept back, and I can see the scar on her neck just below her ear.

"Yvette," I whisper. "I can program—you know, code—in my sleep!"

"That's nice," she says through gritted teeth. A vein throbs in her temples. There are tears in her eyes.

EIGHT

"We were here before the Bay was here."

We're in calm waters, up past the big boats where rich people live, and we're telling stories again. The moon is out, and we've got four lines in, trolling for bottom feeders. and Frankie's rowing slowly. He looks up. "What?" he says.

"We're Native San Franciscans, Umi and I," Momma says. I know what story she's going to tell.

"Me too," he says, "third generation."

She snorts a little laugh. The moonlight is dim but I can see her roll her eyes. She shakes her head and her long, black hair ripples. She has a streak of gray, but you can't see it in this light.

"No, we're Petlenuc."

"What?"

"Ramaytush? Yelamu?"

He shrugs.

"Ohlone?"

"Oh, Native San Franciscans. Capital N Natives."

"Of course. We lived in the marshes, where Crissy Field was. Do you remember that?"

"Where?"

"Next to the Marina Dike. You can still make out the area at low tide, if you know what to look for. The old sea wall is still there. But the marshes, the village of Petlenuc, you can't see without imagination. But that's where we lived. We were fishermen, even back then, but also hunters. Herds of elk and deer roamed the hills.

"You forgot the bears," I tell her.

"And bears," she says.

"The day they came we were expecting them," she says and he asks "Who?" but she just keeps going. She knows how to tell it.

"Well we were expecting something anyway. It was the third day of mourning. Our brother was passing over. Three days before, the men had found Mother Grizzly and her cub sharing his flesh, and now, after his bones had been three days in the earth, we waited by the side of the marsh to see what our brother would become.

"So we were expecting something, like I said" The boat turns and the moon is shining on Frankie's face. His hair is longer now, past his eyes, and there's fuzzy fur growing on his cheeks. "Some animal to come drink at the stream, and then we'd know our brother had made it across the dark water to the land of light. If we saw a deer, we'd know Brother would be swift and graceful in his new home; if an elk, he would be strong. Some hoped the raccoon would arrive, because that would mean Brother would be clever in the bright world. I was praying for a bear so I would know that he would never feel fear again.

"So we were waiting and watching when we saw them—De Anza and his men. It was sunny that day, and their swords and lances shone. We admired the strange drapings that covered their bodies, but our eyes were on the animals. Thick elk with no antlers and longer necks and faces and the men sat atop.

"People say the Indians, that's what they call us, the Indians, when they first saw men on horseback, that we thought they were one creature with four legs and two heads—and arms I guess. Nonsense! Can't they see we have eyes like them?

"Even at a distance, we knew, we could see these were men, like us, and we could see their friendship with the new elk gave them power. But we weren't afraid. They came slowly, openly. No war party ever did that.

"They stopped at the top of the hills when they saw our smoke. They leaned heads together and didn't seem to know what to do. Our runners were just about to go greet them when a man in a shining hat raised his arm, then swung it down fast, as if he were throwing something at us. Down the dunes they came, slowly at first, but when the horses smelled water, they began to run. The men tried to hold them back, but they came on anyway, plunging into the marsh, throwing up great splashes of mud, until they were deep enough to thrust their heads in and drink. Deer and elk wade into water slowly, looking around before they lower their heads, but these creatures seemed to have no fear. We knew our brother would be strong and swift and fearless. He wouldn't be clever like the raccoon, but brains give you headaches, as we used to say. So we cheered to see these new animals. We cheered when the Spanish arrived. Can you believe it? So much for the gift of prophecy!"

"Is this some kind of . . . you know, like myth?"

Momma looks up at him and opens her mouth like she's going to say something, but she clamps it shut. I can hear her breathe out through her nose like she does when she loses her temper, but she doesn't say anything. After a minute, she goes on.

"The Spanish were happy to hear our cheers. They climbed down off their horses and opened one of the packs. They gave us beads, one handful for each man. My father gave his to my mother, and she gave one each to me and my sister. They were blue and green balls, hard like shells, but clear like moon jellies. I remember holding mine up to my eye and the strangeness of seeing the world in this new, distorted way."

"What do you mean, you remember?" he says, and Momma shakes her head.

"Don't interrupt. When it's your turn, you can speak." I've heard that before, and I know he'd better hush. Momma's getting angry.

Frankie's face is in shadow now, so I can't tell what he's thinking. I look over at Momma, expecting to see her eyebrows clumped together, but she doesn't look angry at all, just tired, like she used to be after a night of rowing. She leans her head back against the prow and closes her eyes, but goes on with her story.

"Father knew right away he needed to give these strangers a gift in return better than the one they had given. He went into the lodge and came back carrying big hunks of salmon that were hanging there. He brought them to the man in the shining helmet. Of course, he took the first bite and politely opened his mouth to show the chewed fish so our guests would know they weren't being poisoned. He gestured at the ground, inviting them to sit and share the food. He placed the salmon in my mother's basket and put it in front of them. The man in the shiny helmet smiled. He bowed politely, then turned and shouted something to the men behind him. He sat down in front of the basket, and as he did, he took off his shiny hat. We were astounded to see a head with no hair on it. I giggled, and Momma grabbed my hand and squeezed it hard.

"We were so busy being amused by De Anza's bald head that we didn't notice the approach of another man, this one also bald on top, but with a single band of hair around his head. He was wearing a plain brown robe with a rope tied around his middle and he was carrying a long stick with a carving at the top of it. When he came close and we could see the figure carved in the dark wood, I heard people gasp. Father bowed his head, and I saw others do the same. One woman began to wail and beat her chest in sympathy.

"We were looking at a crucifix, of course. Even as young as I was, I could see the four sacred directions and a Shaman in the center enduring the agony of a vision. Father Font was amazed at this outpouring of religion from a bunch of savages. He chanted words we didn't understand, then sat down next to De Anza and began to eat.

"And that's our 'Thanksgiving' story."

"But what happened?"

"What do you mean what happened? You know what happened. They built a fort, a presidio. You know, you grew up there. They built a mission, well we built it really. They killed the game. No more elk, no more bear. They chopped down trees, they drove away the deer. They drained the marsh. Starvation drove most of us to the mission.

"That's the way it happened. I can see it as clearly as I can see you. Clearer really. You think memory is just, what would you say, data. It's just yours, you save it or erase it. But there are memories deep inside you. Memories from before you were born. They say the victor writes the history, but for the defeated you have only stories."

We sit quiet for a long time. Frankie turns the boat and starts edging towards home. He's still just trolling, but nothing's biting. Momma's staring right at me, I can feel it. I look back at her. I don't know what she wants. She's biting one side of her bottom lip. She looks back at Frankie, begins again.

"You know, I went to school like you. Well maybe not like you, but I went to school. And we learned history too. But I never heard one word there about my people."

"You went to school. Momma?" She never told me that.

"What kind of school?" Frankie asks.

"An orphanage. Holy Angels Orphan Asylum, out near Stockton."

"Where?" I ask.

"Far away, Honey," she says, "Farther than the very end of the bay. Before that, we lived in the city, in the Tenderloin. We weren't supposed to be there. Chip–minus only, but Momma'd found a hidden place in the basement behind the furnace and no one really bothered us. One day she left, told me to wait. She was going to get medicine. She'd done that lots of times, gone out and come back a few hours later with her medicine. But this time she never came back.

"I know now what happened, why she never returned, but at the time I thought she just didn't want me anymore. And that hurt more than anything, more than the hunger pains in my stomach."

"But why didn't she come back?" I ask.

"She died, Honey. I know that now. Now I know a mother would never, never leave her child."

I look up and she's shaking. There are tears in her eyes. I go to put my arm around her, but she grabs me first. She wraps her arms about me and squeezes.

"A mother would never leave her child," she says again. "Never."

We're quiet then. She leans her head down and smells the top of my head.

"Only death. Only death could make a mother do that. I know that now, but I was a child, younger than you, Sweetie, and I was very, very scared. There were bad men in our alley, men who hurt children. Momma had shown them to me and that's why I should never play outside without her. But there was nothing to eat, not even any water left so I had to do something. I climbed out the basement window, ran down the alley, past the doors where the bad men lived, and down into the street.

"No one paid any attention to me. I wandered down to Powell Street. I ate some pizza crust from a garbage can. It was foggy, and I leaned back my head and caught drops of water dripping from an awning. I was cold, and I had no shoes, but no one asked me, 'Hey Little Girl, do you need some help?' No one noticed me at all.

"Then I heard something. Someone was singing, 'I am a poor, wayfaring stranger,' and I came closer. When the song stopped, a lady started preaching. I didn't understand what she was saying, but I came up through the crowd to hear. When she saw me, she stopped, right in the middle of her sentence. She looked at me, and then at the crowd around me to see who I belonged with. Then she walked over to me and bent down. 'Little one,' she said, 'are you here alone?' and I started to cry, I couldn't help it.

"She got down on her knees and gave me a hug. 'Don't worry,' she said 'Don't worry, we'll take care of you.' And they did. It wasn't so bad, although the other girls hated it. We worked the fields in the morning, weeding, picking fruit—stuff like that—and in the afternoon when it was too hot to work, we had our lessons. We learned to read and do numbers, and even a little history like I said.

Lots of kids never tried at all. They figured they'd be spending their days picking tomatoes anyway—not much else a chipless kid can do. But I knew that a few, the best students, would get chipped, and that meant a good job, cleaning offices in the city, or maybe even a mechanic.

"To be honest, I didn't even know what a chip was, but I wanted one. I didn't like the country. I always wanted to return to San Francisco. My home. Ha! But that's what I wanted, God knows why, so I worked and I listened, and that's how I got my chip."

"You had a chip?"

"I had many chips. But the chip–minuses don't do much, just make you a zombie during the work day and feed you a lot of government announcements and ads for stuff you'll never be able to afford. But when I finally got my chip–plus, I didn't care about the games or the vids, I only wanted Wiki. I looked up Petlenuc, and guess what it said?"

"What do you mean, you had many chips?"

"It said the last of our people died in 1842! What a joke! We're right here!"

"Okay, but?"

"I had many chips, like I said. Many. I had a port in my neck. I was a tester, a test subject."

"A port?"

"So they could switch the chips in and out quicker. They were working out the kinks, that's what they called it. One chip would give you blinding headaches, another would make you nauseous, dizzy. But mostly they worked fine. It was better than cleaning offices anyway. It was boring, and it was annoying being hooked up to wires and monitors all day. But there was a lot of nothing time, and I liked watching the vids—kind of like dreaming.

"And even though the wiki was wrong about us being dead, at least we were there. Petlenuc was a word I'd only heard my mother say, and I had started to wonder if she'd made it up. All she ever told me was that we belonged in the city, that we were Petlenuc and that our people lived in the marshes by Crissy Field, and when I searched it, there we were, just a word on a map, but we were there."

"What do you mean, that's all she told you?" he says, "She didn't tell you that story about Brother and the arrival of the Spanish?"

Momma doesn't answer. She's leaning back again.

"So, you just made it up?"

"Oh Frankie," she says, "All stories are made up. You know that."

NINE

"Have you told her?"
"She knows."
"But have you told her?"
"She knows. She just doesn't know she knows."
"You need to talk to her."
"She knows," she says again. "She just doesn't know she knows."

I bite my tongue. She's her daughter after all, not mine. And maybe she's right. She must know. She knows her mother hasn't been out with us in weeks. Months? And we don't come home to hot food, like we did for a while. She's lying down when we leave, and she's lying down when we return. She doesn't remind us anymore to hide the boat properly or make sure the ladder is completely sunk. She no longer even gives her predictions about the best place to cast our lines. Even her dreams are too weak now to yield up the secrets of the deep.

Umi's seen all this. She sees the sunken cheeks, the wall–eyed stare. And it's hard to say about someone you love, but she has to have noticed the smell, as if she's rotting away. She's not stupid, she knows her mother is sick; it's mostly what she talks about. Every other sentence begins with "When Momma gets better . . ." And she makes me row to every bit of flotsam, every piece of drift or floating feather. Some she rejects. With a waft of her hand (I told her how queens wave and talk) she says "Row on, Sir! No need to stop!" in a bad imitation of my bad imitation British accent. But anything remotely beautiful or interesting must be brought aboard and presented later to her mother with an explanation of its magical healing properties.

Back home she chatters to Yvette about the adventures we've had, not all strictly speaking true, while she ladles broth down her throat or makes her suck the marrow from the spine of a mackerel.

"It's going to be so fun when you come with us tonight," she'll say. "We'll catch another salmon for sure." And Yvette says nothing, doesn't smile or frown, just stares in that way she has that seems to say, "We'll see."

She takes good care of her mother, but otherwise seems to be the same carefree girl she always was. She still begs for stories about Princess Loomy, and if I'm too tired or not in the mood, she sits by the far wall and plays by herself with the ugly, ridiculous doll I made her. I used to be so amused to hear her quietly tell herself a little story and act it out, but now it makes me ache to see it.

"She knows, but she just doesn't know she knows" isn't good enough for me, and one night, even though I said I wouldn't, I tried to bring up the subject. She just began to sing, and when I thought she was done and I tried again, she smiled and pointed to the sky. "That's Arcturus," she said, "We're going east!"

And now it's too late, it seems to me. I've never seen someone die, but I'm pretty sure it would look like this. She hasn't eaten, and only drunk a sip or two of water, in days. We didn't go fishing last night, or the night before despite the objections of both of them, one a thin whisper, a single word: "Go," the other a giggle about how silly I am, but I refused. I sat right where I was, holding her hand and just said, "No." So we've just sat here, day and night listening to the rasp and gurgle of each breath. We've piled up the sailcloths behind her to sit her up, which seems to help, but she still sounds sometimes like someone breathing under water.

Not even Umi could cajole her into a spoonful of soup this morning, but this didn't seem to trouble her. "Momma's not hungry now," she announced as if I didn't know and turned her attention to her latest project: her mother's hair. She's braiding it into thin plaits, weaving into it all the magic feathers she's collected for her. Shiny black cormorant feathers ring her face, followed by a row of seagull, then back to cormorant, alternating black and gray all around her head. Her special feathers, the pelicans, she's saved for the top. She works their tips into the hair at the back and pulls them forward across the top, making a little hat.

Yvette opens her eyes and looks at her daughter. "I'm making you beautiful, Momma," she says. Her mother then does something she hasn't done in weeks. She smiles.

I keep the fire going all night long. It's not cold, really, but I can't stand that much dark. Besides, it gives me something to do. Umi begins the evening snuggled against her mother, chattering on about all the fun they'll have next time they walk the beach at Angel Island and the big fish they'll catch and trade for cookies and remember the salmon, Momma, that I caught and how you got me that cookie? And on and on. But Yvette says nothing. Her eyes are closed now, most of the time, though from time to time she startle–wakes and stares at us as if she's about to say something, but she never does.

After hours of this, Umi moves to the other side of the fire. She turns her back to us and plays with her doll. I can't blame her, but she's telling herself a story and her voice begins to rise. Soon she's loud, too loud, and too happy, and I want to smack her. I'm holding Yvette's hand, as I have been for hours, and I feel her squeeze.

Her eyes are open, and her lips are moving. I lean over, but I can't hear what she's saying, Umi's giggling over her own private joke.

"Umi!" I shout, "Shut up! Your momma's trying to talk!" And I regret it as soon as I do it. She doesn't cry, just looks back at me so confused and hurt and doesn't say a word.

Yvette is looking at me with what seems like reproach. Her lips are moving, and I lean in again.

"Sing," she whispers, "My. Song."

"Umi, honey?" I say. "Your momma wants you to sing her song." She's angry with me, I can see that, but she begins anyway.

"I am a pooooor" she holds the note four whole measures before she goes on "wayfaring stranger."

Same song, but so different now at this tempo, from this single voice. Out on the water, with both of them belting it out, the song rolls along. I've heard the words enough to know what it's about, but the sound is rousing, happy almost. Now, penned in by stone, each note, stretched out, rings like an organ pipe. Umi closes her eyes. It's like a prayer, like a voice from a dream. As she sings I can see her body relax, and I think the song's not for Yvette at all, but for us. It's her last gift, helping us through.

When she gets to the end of the second verse, to the line that goes, "I'm going there to see my mother" her voice cracks. She tries to go on with, "She said she'd meet me when I come," but she stops. Her eyes open, and she looks straight across the fire at her mother's face. There's a question in the air, and Yvette nods, ever so slightly. And that is the worst moment of my life. When I witness a heart break.

Her shoulders slump, and a wail comes from her throat like nothing I've ever heard. She drops her doll and runs around the fire to us. She plunges into me with her whole body, hissing "Get out of the way!" and pushes me aside, takes my place.

Now it's my turn on the other side of the cave. I turn my back, I can't get far enough away, but it doesn't matter. I'm not there anymore, I've ceased to exist. There's only mother and daughter and a sadness so deep it's drowning us all.

I try to control my breathing, to calm myself down, but it's no use because I'm angry. I'm sad too of course, but angry above all—at her for not preparing her daughter for this moment, for leaving it to me to pick up the pieces. I'm scared because I have no idea how I can take responsibility for this child, but mostly I'm angry at a world where there is no justice.

Hours go by. I keep my back turned as much as I can, but when I'm tending the fire, I can't help but look. Umi's sitting up now, holding her mother's hand, staring into space. I kneel down by her other side and try to take her hand, but she slaps it away without even looking up. So I go back to my end of the cave.

Yvette's breathing is louder, raspier than ever. I try to count between breaths to see if they're slowing down, but my mind wanders. I keep going back to the story she told me, about being a test subject, a guinea pig.

"You know why they picked me?" she asked one day out of the blue. We were lying under the blankets, listening to the rain on the tarp.

"Who?" She didn't answer right away. She was listening. In the quiet, we both could hear the even breathing of a sleeping child. She went on, whispering.

"The lab, the doctors."

"OK, why?"

"My genes; they scanned my genes. They scanned all of our genes, but mine, and a few of the others, they were specially interested in. We had just what they were looking for. Lucky us."

"What was it?"

"Cancer. I had the genes. Ticking time bomb. I had the gene for breast cancer and one day it would switch itself on. Only question was when. But there was a new chip coming they were all excited about. Gonna end cancer forever, defuse the bomb inside me. That's how they explained it to me.

"One doctor was really nice. Dr. Soo. He'd talk with us, not just about symptoms, but about life, you know. We'd had many chats, he and I. To tell you the truth, he was sweet on me.

"So when he told me I was getting the chip, I was thrilled. Him too. It didn't feel any different from the other chips, but there was a lot more physical monitoring, a lot more blood drawn. That was okay, but I started to notice that Dr. Soo wasn't smiling anymore. He wasn't chatting with anyone, and when I'd try to catch his eye, he'd always look down.

"Then one night, very late, I was asleep, and I heard someone whispering, 'Get up'. It was him. He waved for me to follow him, so I did. He opened the door to a little lead–lined closet they had for special equipment, and I followed him in. To tell you the truth I thought... Well anyway, when we got inside, I could see it wasn't romance in his mind. He was white as a sheet. 'I have to tell you,' he said, 'I'm not supposed to, but I have to tell you, you're in the control group.'

"Well that was disappointing, but I always knew it was possible. That's how testing goes. Half get it and half don't so they can tell if it's working. 'Oh well,' I said, 'I'm back to square one, I guess.' But he was so upset he was like trembling. 'You don't understand,' he said, 'They're not waiting. They can't wait 40 years to see who gets it and who doesn't. They're flipping the switch.'"

"What?"

"Turning on the gene," she said, "Giving all of us cancer. If the chip worked, half of us wouldn't get it. But the control group. . .

"So I got out. I gouged out the port with the chip in it and hid in a hamper of dirty laundry. I joined those huddled masses you saw standing in the soup line, fighting every night for a good patch of sidewalk to sleep on.

"But I never gave up. I never give up. And one day when I was down by Hunter's Point, and I saw something in the mud flats. It was a boat with no one on it, no one around. Somebody must have got stranded by the tide and just abandoned it. I sludged through the mud to it and climbed aboard. All I was looking for was a hiding spot to sleep without being kicked by some patroller. But a few hours later I woke up to the most wonderful feeling. I was floating. I'd never been in a boat before, but I wasn't afraid. I just let the currents take me wherever they wanted to go. I figured anywhere was better than where I was right then.

"So here I am. Here we are. For a long time, I thought maybe I'd dodged a bullet. Maybe I pulled it out before the switch happened because I felt good for so long. But. . . Frankie, you've got to take care of her. Swear you will."

I swore I would, and I will, but how? She's taught us, it's true, what we need to know, how to eke a living from the water, things she learned herself by trial and error: where to drop the long lines with the heavy sinkers, where to drop the nets for the herring, where the crabs congregate on the bottom. She's taught us how to hide, how you can live right next to a city and not be seen at all. We can do it, I guess, bring in enough fish to stay alive.

But I keep feeling I'm not meant for this. I've been coding in my head now for months each morning before I sleep, going back through programs I wrote for school, the work I did for Grandpa, seeing them complete like maps. I now understand my grandfather's pencil outlines, all his work with the Kubernetes matrices, squeezing giant files into tiny spaces—the drops between the drops. Without being lost in the details, I see now more efficient ways of combining and condensing the elements. And ways to disrupt them, to corrupt the system, turn it on its head. What a waste of time! I'm probably fooling myself anyway, thinking these programs I'm "writing" could ever run. I'm probably missing steps I'm not even aware of. And even if they're perfect, so what? I might as well try counting to infinity. I can't see a future where it'll ever be of any use.

My only choice is to carry on. Row the boat, drop the line, row the boat, try again. The thought of it makes me feel weary. Because how long? How long could we go on? My mind keeps going back to something else Yvette said. She was running through a list of things I needed to take care of after she was gone. Suddenly, she said, "Wait ten years."

"What?" I asked.

"Just wait ten years—twelve would even be better."

"For what?"

"In ten years, if you want, you and Umi can, you know, get married."

"What?"

"You know what I mean."

I said nothing. I felt sick to my stomach.

"Frankie," she said. "Life has to go on."

Now, just remembering it, I feel sick again. Life has to go on. Ten years from now, twelve years, fifty years. Can this really be my future?

Because I've been thinking lately. About Grandpa's last words. I think I know what he meant; I know where I have to go. I've known for a long time. But it's a risk. If I'm wrong, it could be the end of everything. Is that a choice I can make for two people?

It's too much for my mind to deal with. I go back to counting the intervals between her breaths. Ten seconds, ten seconds, forty-five seconds, then a gasp, then ten seconds, ten seconds, ten seconds. Then I'm asleep on my side, back to the fire, my head on a flat stone.

It's daylight when I wake up. Umi's standing over me. She doesn't look angry anymore, just disappointed, like I've let her down.

"She's gone," she says.

"What?"

Her voice is flat. A simple statement of fact. "Her spirit. Her spirit's gone. Her body's still here of course."

I look back. She's lying flat now. I go to her. I kneel down next to her and take her hand. It's cold. Umi's right, she isn't there anymore. I expect to feel, I don't know, overwhelmed, but I don't. I don't feel anything, not right now anyway. Her hair has been carefully arranged, each feather aligned in perfect rows surrounding her face.

"She looks beautiful," I say.

TEN

It rains all afternoon. An open boat is miserable in the rain. We've been caught suddenly by showers before, and it's no fun rowing home drenched and freezing while Umi bails with a cut–open water jug. When we know it's going to rain, we stay home. Better to starve a day than die by hypothermia. But this is one errand we can't avoid or postpone.

She's going to be buried at sea, of course. I tell Umi what I plan to do, what Yvette had said she wanted. I see her clamp her jaws. She wants to say, "Why didn't she tell me what she wanted?" but she doesn't. She only says, "I get to pick the spot."

"Okay."

"I know right where she wants to go."

I tell her that in the old days, sailors would be sewn into bags of sail cloth and weighted with stones. She shakes her head.

"Momma don't like waste," she says flatly. "She wouldn't like us cutting up a sail."

• • • •

Late afternoon as the sun is dropping, the wind kicks up and blows the storm past us. It's hard going that night, rowing through the gate. The swell is up, and the gusts are so strong sometimes I feel like we're not moving at all. I want to say, "We can drop her anywhere," but I bite my tongue and put my back into it. After two days stuck inside, it feels good to use my body.

I've been hearing the trumpet blasts of an incoming ship grow louder and louder, but I'm shocked to see, when I look back over my shoulder, that Umi's sent us up the same channel.

"Umi!" I yell, but she only looks up at the massive machine bearing down on us, then returns to what she's been doing. She's taken her mother's shoes off and she's tying a bowline around her ankle. We're alongside the tower I climbed down so long ago, it seems, and I turn and head straight for it.

The wake of the freighter picks us up and smacks us against the brick-work. My left oar is useless, and I don't have time to fend us off. We lurch right, then left, and for a moment it seems we'll overturn, but the same wave pulls us right back toward the ship, sucking us toward the gigantic rotors, and for a moment I feel like we'll be caught in a whirlpool, but I backpaddle hard and the ship just passes us by, sounding its horn one final time.

I pull hard, five long strokes straight for open ocean, before I stop and try to catch my breath. I look at Umi. The knot is tied, but she's taking the lank end and she's coiling it around and around, turning it into an anklet or some-thing. She's perfectly calm, and I think, "She did it on purpose." I remember Yvette threatening to flip the boat if I ever tried to take them ashore in the city.

"Maybe they're right," I think. "Maybe it would be the best thing."

The bridge rises before me, the red light flashing at the top of the tower. To my right the backside of the Pres, the lights of evening, and further on, the glow and twinkle of the Sunset. Each light a person, and all of them trapped in their own heads. Everyone thinks they're the center of the universe, but out here, on the edge of the immense Pacific, you know you're a speck, that you could just disappear and life would go on just fine without you.

The wind is pushing us back towards the bridge. I swivel in my seat. No ships on the horizon. Just darkness and the deep. I turn and see Umi looking at me. It feels like she knows what I've been thinking.

"Fifty strokes out," she says, "And then hard to port."

I do what she says, then stop to rub my hands.

"Keep going," she orders, so I do. She's tying loose loops on the other end of the rope, and when she finishes, she starts to look around. I row on. I have no idea what she's looking for.

Suddenly she jumps up on the bench.

"Stop. This is the spot."

For the life of me, I can't see how it's any different from any other spot we rowed past, but I don't say anything, just put up the oars and wait.

"Here," she points, "Pick up the just–in–case." She means the large stone we keep in the bottom of the boat for ballast. I do what I'm told, and she pulls two loops around it and cinches them tight. She tugs back and forth until she's satisfied.

"Okay, put that down. Help me lift her body."

"Do you want to say a few words first?"

"About what?"

"You know, say goodbye?"

She looks at me with pity. This is clearly the stupidest thing she's ever heard. She reaches under her mother's arms, tries to lift. I go to help, and together, we get her torso onto the gunwale. With all three of us on one side, the boat begins to tip so I take a step back, I kneel in the bottom of the keel and push, and she flips into the water with a splash.

She floats, of course, and her feathered hair spreads out around her like a crown. We're drifting and the rope slowly uncoils, slipping over the gunwale after her. I hoist the heavy stone. I take a half–step forward, the boat rocking. I extend my arms. All I have to do now is let go.

"Goodbye Yvette," I say. "Thank you."

I look over at Umi, she must want to say something. But she's not even looking up. She's crouched, doing something with the rope. When she comes up I see she's made a loop, a slip–knot. She puts her wrist through it, steps on the rope and stands, cinching it tight.

Before I can think, before I can bring the weight back down into the boat, she's standing on the gunwale. She leans forward, and with a lurch of the boat, she jumps.

The rocking topples me to my knees, and the rock slips out of my hands and plunks in the water with a tremendous splash. I lean over the gunwale just in time to see Umi trying to swim to her mother when the weight drags her under.

I dive in, trying to catch her before she disappears, but I come up empty. No Umi, no rope. Everything is blackness and cold—so cold that for a moment I don't know why I'm there until something smacks me in the back of the head. It's Yvette, hurrying after her daughter. I grab her sweatshirt, but it starts to come off as I pull, and she keeps heading down. I reach for another hold and my hands close on flesh. It's slick and slimy, but I dig in my claws and pull myself downwards, down her body, down her leg to the ankle. When I have the rope in my hand I turn and kick up as hard as I can, but I can feel we're still going down. I am pulling on the rope, hand over hand, trying to get to her, when she kicks me in the face. She's flailing, trying to get away from me, or maybe trying to get away from the rope, her body fighting to live despite herself.

One final pull and I'm at her arm. I tug at the knot and the skinny wrist slips out. I hold it tight and swim upwards as hard as I can. I break the surface, spouting like a whale; I've forgotten to exhale under the water. Umi's head is out as well, but she's not breathing. I flip her on her back, put my arm across her chest and begin side–stroking for the boat. My clothes feel like cement, and light as she is, it's hard swimming with only one free arm. But those long–ago lessons kick in and we move. The boat is only maybe 20 yards away, pointing towards us, but the wind is taking it to shore.

When we finally get there I realize none of my scout lessons have pre-pared me for this. We practiced rescues, but there was always someone in the boat to grab the victim by the life vest and pull him in. I swim to the side of the boat and reach up. I kick as hard as I can while I pull. The gunwale low-ers, but when I try pushing Umi over the lip we start to ship water, the whole boat starts to flip on its side. and I can feel it sinking.

So I swim to the stern and try climbing up the square back. Again I try to lift her out of the water, but the side is too high. I try climbing in myself while carrying her, but I'm just not strong enough.

"Umi!" I yell. I know I could do it if she'd just wake up, but I get no re-sponse. My only chance is to climb in first, then lift her in. But she'll drift away while I'm doing it, and then what? I only know one thing for sure: If I do not get into this boat I will certainly die, and I know that I do not want to die, not now.

But I will not let her go. I grab one of her pigtails and put it in my mouth. I bite down hard, then let go of the rest of her and slip under so that she's flopping on my back. I reach up with both hands and grab the stern. I kick and pull until my chest is up against the edge. I put one arm, then the other over so I'm hanging from my armpits. I need to keep pushing, to pull myself straight up and over, but the pigtail is slipping, her weight out of the water is too much. Instead, I drop my left side and swing my right leg up as hard as I can. I feel her slip off my back, and I bite down harder. I cannot lose her. Without the weight, I manage to get my foot on board, then my whole leg. One final push and both legs are in, and the rest of me follows. Just my head and neck are still hanging overboard.

I can see her now. She's face down, not moving. I grab her by the hoodie and pull. She's so light, so small. I reach under her arms and just lift her all the way into the boat. We've shipped a lot of water, and she lands in a puddle. I pull her out and lay her on the bench.

This part we did learn in Scouts. I may not remember everything, but I can try. I tilt her head back, pinch her nose, put my mouth over hers and blow. Her chest rises, then falls. I try again, then go to chest compressions. One, two, three, four, five, six, seven on up to thirty counting in my head, while out loud I yell her name. "Umi! Umi! Umi!" over and over. Two more breaths, and while I'm puffing into her, a wave lifts us up. I hear a roaring noise; we're drifting into the surf zone. One, two, three, four, five, six, seven, I keep going, but another wave catches us broadside and we're heading stern first for the rocks.

I jump into the rowing bench and unlock the oars. Three hard strokes and another wave smacks the bow. We're too heavy with water to ride over it, so we plow straight through, and suddenly we're filled almost to the gunwales. But she stays afloat and I pull hard ten more long strokes and we're out of the surf zone.

Umi's off the bench, floating against the stern. I drop the oars and pull her roughly back. She's so tiny, almost weightless. The water's higher than the bench, but I lay her down anyway. I need a surface to push against. Once again, I place my mouth on her blue lips and blow, but this time I feel pressure coming back at me. She's puking, but I can't turn her head; she'll be underwater, so I pick her up and hold her face down. She coughs and more water spills into the boat. She's shaking her head now. I turn her over. Her eyes are open.

I stand up and hug her to me. Behind me the open ocean and a biting wind; before me the swell rising over rocks. It's Baker Beach where I played as a child on those rare sunny San Francisco days. And I'm here again, in the middle of the night, freezing cold, my hands cramping, standing in an old rowboat that's almost filled with water. Almost.

She's not talking yet, but I can see her eyes, and she's taking everything in. I hoist her up on my hip and hold her with my left hand while I grab the bailer and start shoveling out water as fast as I can, and I'm singing while I work, singing the only song I can remember from my childhood. "Row, row, row your boat/ Gently down the stream."

When the water's down to a manageable few inches, I put her back down on the bench. I hunt up the old sailcloth. It's also soaking wet, of course, but I know that it's better than nothing. I wrap her up like a mummy and lay her back down on the bench. Her teeth are chattering, but she's trying to tell me something. I lean in.

"Momma's a bear," she says.

Hours later, after the fastest rowing I've ever done, when we're finally home and out of our wet clothes and wrapped in blankets, when the fire's roaring and we're drinking hot water with an onion in it, which was all the dinner I could muster, when her teeth have finally stopped chattering and both of us have almost stopped shaking, I ask her what she meant.

"I saw Momma," she says as flatly as any fact, "in the bright world."

"Really?"

"She was in a big, sunny field, all kinds of flowers. She was beautiful. Her hurtie," she touches her own chest, "was gone, and she smiled at me. But when I ran to her, she got angry. She yelled, 'You're not supposed to be here!' I kept running to her, but she was changing. Hair was growing all over her, and she was on four legs all of a sudden. She was a bear. A great big, beautiful bear. But she was still Momma, so I still wanted to be with her, but the bear said 'No!' and growled and charged at me with its teeth, and then I was in the boat puking."

We sit still, quietly sipping our hot water, then she says, "I'm glad Momma's a bear. She'll be a good bear."

"Yes, she will."

"Momma could be really scary sometimes."

"Yes, she could."

THE STORM

"Remember that on any world
the wind eventually wears away the stone,
because the stone can only crumble;
the wind can change."
-A.C. Crispin, from Time for Yesterday

"One two three four, I declare a thumb war. Five six seven eight, try to keep your thumb straight."

Akilah swung her thumb back and forth across her forefinger. Her wrist was completely motionless, her fist like a rock although she could tell by the loose grip of his fingers that Chibi was cheating as usual. His wrist was raised, his whole arm swinging back and forth in a desperate attempt to get a better angle, a higher perch for his stubby thumb to stab downwards and capture hers.

They both knew he wouldn't be able to do it. Akilah's thumb was long and thin, like the rest of her, and it moved swiftly and silently like she did. The lights of Marin across the bay gave little light to the island and even less in the bushes where they were sitting, but Chibi stared intently at the moon of her thumbnail as it moved. Again and again it paused in the center, teasing him, daring him to strike, but he knew that one. The moment he pounced, he knew she'd parry, roll over him and pin him in an instant.

His only chance, the way he beat her that one time, was to time it perfectly, attack just as she changed direction and squeeze with all his might. But she was too fast. He only grazed the edge of her thumb, which whipped around and trapped his so hard it hurt.

"No fair!"

She said nothing, just kept her eyes on the beach below them. She was watching—they were both supposed to be watching—two people who had beached a little rowboat and were walking around. One was tall and thin and the other very small, a child. She'd seen them many times before, usually with a third person, at Perles, but last week Ace had spotted them all around the other side at China Cove and the week before that, they'd actually landed at the dock at Ayala. Carla said all they did was walk around peering in windows.

Now they were here, at Sand Springs, closer to base than anyone had come in quite a while, and Akilah felt uneasy. She knew there was no way anyone on the beach could see anything, and all they were doing was gathering sticks, but as her mother used to say, "A toad doesn't run in the daytime for nothing." Akilah had always thought her mother was paranoid, but it turned out she wasn't paranoid enough so Akilah had grown up a very wary, very careful young woman.

She felt a weight on her shoulder; Chibi was leaning his head against her. He still had a hard time staying up all night. It was boring, watch, but it was their job. She didn't really need Chibi; she'd been guarding her part of the island alone for at least two years, and honestly it was easier that way. Except for the boredom. And staying awake.

Back in her first months guarding alone, she had regularly hidden herself away in some cozy hollow for a catnap. Strictly forbidden, of course, and not necessary anymore once daytime sleeping became normal for her. Still, she knew every little corner where the leaves piled and made a mattress hidden from view. There were several here in the Gardens where they were sitting. She was tempted to let Chibi lie down for a while; he was really too young for this, and not actually a very good lookout because his attention wandered too much.

But his hearing was good. He had noticed the drone last time long before she heard it, and she was able to give Base a heads up before it even appeared on their scope. They only operated on the darkest nights so they couldn't be seen, of course, but the day will come, Orion likes to say, when camouflage and infrared shielding and signal scrambling won't be enough. "They'll come up with something new, mark my words," he says, "Maybe they already have, some new sensor we don't know about yet. That's why we need you young folks."

She had made sure to give Chibi credit for the save that time, and she for damn sure hadn't told them that the poor little guy had wet himself when he heard it. She knew why without asking. Her folks had been taken too, and she knew: that's the last sound you hear before boots kick down the door.

The first time she'd ever laid eyes on Chibi she had known, had sensed, that they had this in common. He was standing completely still, staring straight ahead, not seeming even to notice the new faces, this strange new underground world. She understood right away that blank look; it wasn't dullness, it was endurance.

Everyone else was staring at Orion. Not every day you get a new security chief, and this one was famous. He didn't look impressive, with his gray fro and bent back, but no one else had survived so many missions; nobody else had managed to stay so long under the radar, operating right under the nose of the V.T.B..

"My grandaddy was a Panther," he was saying. "They marched straight through the streets of Oakland in the middle of the day with their rifles at their shoulders." He paused dramatically and took a deep, slow breath. He looked like a hungry man smelling a roast. "Wouldn't that be nice?

"I'm sick of the shadows; I'll bet you are too. Being on watch is boring, right? You want action, don't you?"

Akilah nodded along with the rest.

"You want to break something? Want to swing that bat, shoot that gun?"

More nods.

"Want to take revenge for the way they treating us?"

"Amen!" It was Akilah. She couldn't help it.

Orion smiled. "I hear you. I feel you." He paused again. His smile faded. He looked straight back at Akilah, right into her eyes. His voice got even quieter. "Revenge. Revenge is sweet, and justice is even sweeter. But I tell you right now, what we're doing here, what Doc is cooking up, is more important than any protest, more powerful than any gun.

"If you want to live in a world where you're not treated like a human donkey, where regular people can breathe and dream, where happiness is not reserved only for the lucky few, then there's nothing more important than standing that watch. Without you, them in there, the doctor and the twins, can't do their work, and if they fail, then God help us all.

"We need you. That's the message The Committee sent me here to tell you. We know you're tired of the dark, but we need you in the shadows a little longer. We don't know how long. But morning will come, I promise you. We'll walk in the light, we'll march right out in the open with our weapons held high. That day will come, I promise you, that day will come."

Akilah couldn't help feeling moved, and she could see the others felt the same. Orion shook each of their hands one by one and introduced himself. When he got to her, he said, "I knew your mother. She was a brave woman." She didn't know what to say to that.

"I'm assigning you a partner. I want you to train him." He put a hand on the boy's back and brought him forward. "This is Chibi. He doesn't talk, but he listens and he understands."

He did talk, though, just not to them. Or to her at first. Akilah wasn't much for chitchat, but it was strange to spend ten hours with someone and never hear their voice. Chibi nodded and shook his head, that was about it. When she asked him direct questions, he just stared straight ahead until she got tired and gave up.

But he did talk. More than once, she had come up behind him when he thought he was alone and heard him muttering quietly to himself in another language. Japanese maybe. His voice was soft and high–pitched. It had sounded like, had the rhythm of, someone telling a story. And she knew he'd lived all his life in Oakland, so she was pretty sure he spoke English as well.

She decided it would be her little project to get him to speak. She started by listening, by shutting up. For three nights, ten hours together at a stretch, she only spoke two words: "check perimeter." The rest of the time they walked and sat in total silence.

On the fourth night, when they were sitting under a tree below the peak, she broke the silence: "I spy, with my little eye, something that starts with G."

Chibi scanned the bushes. His eyes followed the branches of the live oak overhead, then down to the leaves at his feet. He looked at Akilah's black cape and hood, her blue jeans, and then down at his own jacket and pants. Finally, he caught sight of a flashing light far out above the fog. He pointed, but Akilah pretended not to understand what he meant.

"Golden Gate Bridge," he said in a voice surprisingly deep for such a small child.

Akilah bit her lip to stop herself from blurting, "Good job!" She forced herself to stay calm, to not hug him. She had gone to school and knew first hand that easy praise kills the soul.

"You got it," she said in a tone calculated to show no surprise at all. "Your turn."

Chibi hesitated. He gave her the same blank stare she'd gotten used to.

"Come on," she wanted to say. "You can do it!" But she stayed as silent as he was. She looked straight at him, but acted as if she couldn't care less whether he ever spoke again. Above all, she kept all pity out of her eyes.

When he turned away, she thought it was all over, but in a minute she heard, "I spy with my little eye," the same low, croaking voice, "Something that begins with T."

So it began. They still didn't talk, exactly, but they could at least play games, and when he heard the drone that time, he told her, out loud, specifically and clearly enough that she could understand.

She taught him Morse code by tapping and pressing the dots and dashes on his hand, and he could call out the letters one by one. He was a quick learner, and it was not long before she could tap a whole sentence and have him repeat it out loud.

One night, she was bored, and she feared Chibi was dozing off. She grabbed his hand and tapped: "Press press press, press tap, press tap press tap, tap/ tap tap press, tap press press tap, press press press, press tap/ tap press/ press, tap tap, press press, tap"— "Once upon a time." Chibi smiled, and she told him, "Listen to the whole story, then tell me what it is."

Morse is slower than talking, naturally, so it took a while, but Chibi "listened" intently. When she came to "Press, tap tap tap tap, tap/ tap, press tap, press tap tap" she asked out loud, "Okay, what was the story?"

"Little Red Riding Hood, but you got it wrong." he said, "Grandma's not in the closet, she's in the wolf's stomach and the woodcutter cuts her out."

"Okay, your turn" and that became their new "thing", telling stories back and forth. It wasn't long before they ran out of fairy tales and started telling little stories about their own lives—funny incidents about school and such.

Eventually, she told him how she had ended up on this island, about what had happened to her mother. Chibi's hand trembled when he heard it, and when he told his own story, his hand shook so badly that he had to use his left to steady it. If she hadn't already heard the story from Orion, she wouldn't have understood what he was saying.

It was worse for him. She had run, had slipped through the narrow bathroom window and run down the alley, down to the docks. She knew—her mother had drilled it into her—where she could crawl under the fence, which container to knock on, and she'd taught her Morse code and the password she could use if everything went bad.

But Chibi hadn't known anything, or not much. He knew which closet to run to and how to remove the floor panel and squeeze himself in with the cobwebs and the rats. He knew to keep still despite the thuds of boots on flesh. He didn't move, or cry, even when the sledgehammers were busting through the drywall above him. And later, when it was quiet, he still didn't move, first out of fear, then because the fallen wallboard was right on top of the trap door.

He was stuck there for three days.

It was Orion himself who got him out. He was part of the Oakland crew back then, and he knew patrollers were still watching the house, just waiting for The Resistance to come back. Everyone else figured the kid must be dead, and besides extraction in those circumstances was too dangerous. You'd need a crew of at least ten with better weapons than they had, and if even one patroller survived, their whole cell was fucked forever. Gotta take your losses.

But Orion would not listen. He just went and got an old, rusty shopping cart and filled it with blankets and garbage, and then he just walked straight through the door yelling loudly about private property and folks with no respect. They burst in with their stuns of course, and real guns too, but Orion just yelled louder.

"Always remember," he told Akilah later, "No one wants to deal with crazy people. Not even patrollers."

One of the patrollers pulled out his baton, but Orion just smiled, and said, "Excuse me, gentlemen," and then he did something no one expected: he dropped his pants and started taking a crap on the floor!

Patrollers are human too, sort of, and their disgust was greater than their sense of duty. They cleared out immediately, and when they did, he pinched it off, pulled his pants back up, and made straight for the closet, or where the closet was anyway. He shoved the broken drywall aside, and pulled off the trap door. There he found a pale boy with terrified, staring eyes. When he reached in, Chibi bit his hand, but Orion just said, "Chibi, your Mama sent me to help you. You just need to stay quiet a little bit longer," and he pulled him out and shoved him in the shopping cart and covered him with blankets and trash.

By this time the patrollers had gathered their courage, I guess. No crazy old man was going to stop them from doing their job. They came back in with their weapons drawn and saw him still at his business. They ordered him to stand up. He was under arrest, they said.

"No worries, gentlemen," he said, I was just leaving." And he stood, pulling up his pants. One of them reached for him, but before he could grab him, Orion said, "Oh don't worry, I clean up after myself" and scooped up the pile with one hand. He held the hand toward them, as if offering a present, and with a "Good day, gentlemen" he pushed the cart out the door, down the street, and all the way to the safe house. No one followed him.

. . . .

Akilah's shoulder was wet; Chibi drooled in his sleep. What she wanted to do was lay him back in the leaves, cover him with her cloak, let him be the child he was supposed to be. But she knew he had to learn and quick. Ace was being moved; they were upping their surveillance of San Q. Akilah would be covering China Cove, and Chibi would be alone in this sector.

She shoved him maybe a little too hard and grabbed his hand. "One two three four, I declare a thumb war."

Chibi joined in with "Five six seven eight, try to keep your thumb straight." He was fully awake now, up on his knees, swinging his whole arm around, trying to gain an advantage.

Akilah smiled. She swung her long thumb back and forth, pausing as usual in the center to tease. Her eyes scanned the beach below.

Something was wrong; the boat was still there, but where were the people? She looked at the big rock. Maybe they were behind it. She was just about to stop the game, creep forward to the cliff edge for a better look, when a head appeared not twenty yards away. At the same time, she felt a pressure on the back of her thumb.

"I win!" Chibi cried before she clamped a hand over his mouth.

The whole man appeared now, heading straight for them. If he had heard them, he showed no sign. He was tall and very thin. Akilah could make out a big nose and pale skin beneath his stringy bangs. He was dressed in an old hoodie and a pair of jeans, both ragged and filthy. He turned back and said something she couldn't hear, and then the girl, younger than Chibi, stepped out with her hair in pigtails. She was also stick skinny, and also dressed in rags, but she was grinning ear to ear.

He held out his hand to her and when she grabbed it, turned back again and the two of them kept walking straight up the hill, right past their hiding spot.

When they were out of range, Akilah took her hand off his mouth. "Chibi," she said, "I'm going to follow them. I need you to signal HQ then wait for orders, you understand?"

Chibi nodded. She crawled a few feet to a pile of leaves and swept them aside, revealing two small aluminum rods barely protruding from the earth. She reached in her pocket and pulled out her Morse key. Two wires with alligator clips hung from it and she clipped one to each rod and began tapping on the key. Each tap gave off a barely audible buzz. "Buzzbzbuzz, bzbuzz/ buzzbzbuzz, bzbuzz/ buzzbzbuzz bzbuzz"

Each buzz created a phantom pressure on the back of Chibi's hand. He understood her message perfectly: "KA/ KA/ KA," but it made no sense.

Akilah looked up. "KA is code for attention," she said. Send that again every ten seconds until you get an answer, then just tell them a man and child are climbing the hill from Sand Springs. Tell them we may have been spotted. Tell them I'm following at a distance. I gotta go." and she left.

Chibi listened to the crunch of her feet in the leaves fade away, and suddenly he felt the old fear descend upon him. The lights of Sausalito blurred, and he knew he was doing it again—the stare. He could feel a stiffness in his chest and neck, and his mouth began to gape. There was no noise from the Morse key, and he felt he could do nothing but stay stock still, put everything out of his mind and wait, wait for someone else to do something.

But he heard a scolding voice: "*Chibi, kanojo wa anata ni sobani ite hoshii noyo.*" He shook his head violently and squeezed his hands into tight fists, and suddenly the black metal key swam into focus. He placed his left hand over his right to steady it and tapped "Buzzbzbuzz, bzbuzz/ buzzbzbuzz, bzbuzz/ buzzbzbuzz, bzbuzz."

O rion breathed deeply. He smelled crushed leaves and damp earth. Seaweed was rotting somewhere and the smell of decay mingled with the fresh scent of open ocean.

He held the hatch up with one hand and reached back for his rifle with the other. Ace handed it up to him, and Orion could hear him gulping in the fresh air as well. Their intake tube was in a cave at the shore and was completely covered at high tide so for six hours they hadn't had a puff of breeze and you could feel the CO2 building up. Doc said that was nonsense; he had calculated the air volume and said they could last 72 hours completely sealed off, but it didn't feel like it.

Orion's first act as security chief was to drag his mattress out of the dormitory and down the hall, under the main hatch. He told them it was because he snored, but everyone assumed it was to better guard against the raid they all knew would come at some point; they assumed he wanted to be the first to shoot, to take out as many of the bastards as he could when and if security was ever breached.

The truth was that the second he had entered the bunker for the first time, and the hatch had been sealed behind him, he knew he'd be having The Dream again. Although it had been years since had awakened covered with sweat, groaning for release, one breath of the still air of his new underground home made him certain it would happen again. And when it did, the last place he wanted to be was surrounded by a bunch of youngsters who were supposed to look up to him.

Also, he had noticed that first day that the hatch seal was imperfect. In the day, when the lights were out and everyone was sleeping, he could see a tiny crack of light. Wisps of air descended from that crack, And when The Dream did come, same dream for half a century, all those women in hats talking about how she looked "so natural, just like she was sleeping" and holding him up to kiss her goodbye, and then when they screwed the lid down not knowing it was him in the box all of a sudden, screaming, screaming and no one listening as they lowered the box and started shoveling on the dirt—when he woke up sweating, he'd stare at that crack of light and breathe, just breathe.

The rest of the time it wasn't so bad living underground. Doc had rigged up a wave generator so they had lights. There were some old books lying around, and a deck of cards. Once a week or so, the boss would let his guard down a bit and waste some bandwidth on an old movie or holoplay. There were even a few relics from the original warriors here, the guys manning the old Nike Missiles, protecting us from the evil empire. Here and there you could see scratches on walls and ceilings, names and years mostly, a few hearts with "Johnny loves Celeste"—stuff like that. The best was a life–size painting of a beautiful blonde on one wall. The caption said, "The girl can't help it!"

But the strangest, and the one he found himself reading over and over, was scratched in a dark corner. It said:

Lullaby

1963,

Cuban missile crisis

Go to sleep my daughter

go to sleep my son

once this world was water

without anyone

Who wrote it, and why? He showed it to the others, but he could tell their expressions of interest were just politeness. Only Doc had any real reaction. He just smiled sadly and said, "That's true."

The worst part of the job, aside from the claustrophobia, was feeling useless. He had only the vaguest idea of cyber warfare. He knew that when the aperture was open, they were receiving some kind of signal and somehow hacking into various security systems looking for weaknesses. He knew they only hacked any particular system for seconds at a time—too quick to be noticed—and that even with Doc's special algo something, it was nowhere near enough time to explore all the directories, whatever they were, so they had to hit the same systems over and over again at random times, each time sucking up thousands of lines of code, which Marco and Pablo would pore over, looking for what he couldn't say.

Orion tried to learn, tried to understand what the hell they were actually doing, but in the end he had to take it on faith. All he knew for sure was that they played the long game. Over a year ago they had begun hacking into the personal files of one pasty-faced engineer who worked at a small software company in San Jose.

"They write apps for automated locks," Marco told him. "For prisons."

And tonight was the big night, he said. Tonight they were going to aim their magic beam at San Quentin and unlock a door.

"You're going to bust somebody out?" Orion smiled.

"Oh God no, this is a test. It'll only stay unlocked for three seconds. We've got someone on the inside, a jailer, who's going to tell us if it works. He'll send a note with the resupply boat."

Orion bit his tongue. He could hear his grandfather's voice: "How long, O Lord?"

• • • •

The hatch was hidden in a thicket of bushes and couldn't be seen, but Orion replaced it behind him anyway. Regulations. It was his job to secure the inner perimeter. Of course they had sensors on the surface, but you still needed to verify. Only after he had determined it was safe would the other watchers emerge and spread out across the island. He held his rifle in his left hand and wormed his way out of the thicket. The fog was returning like an old friend, and he could smell it before he could see it. They were safer in the fog; soon the lights of the city would fade away and they wouldn't need to worry quite so much. Drones don't do well in fog.

The only way out of the thicket was a little rabbit path that he had to crawl through. He pushed his rifle before him as he wormed his way, hoping to dislodge any spider webs that might have formed since the morning. Orion was a city boy, unused to leaves and branches scratching at him, and he could never quite rid his mind of the thought that these were not bushes he was feeling on his skin, but creatures.

He wanted to get through as quickly as possible out into the open air, but when the tunnel of shrubs opened up, he forced himself to pause and listen. The fog horn was sounding at the gate—Hum, Hum, Hum—and he could hear the wind in the leaves, and fainter still, the distant waves lapping at the rocks. He took from his pocket a thin telescoping pole with a mirror attached and extended it into the clearing. He twisted it back and forth, but saw nothing but leaves and sky. He collapsed the pole, returned it to his pocket, and crawled out.

First, he doubled back to the old fence that surrounded the missile site itself, an open area covered with concrete. There was no place to hide, and if the enemy were there, it would be too late to do anything, but you had to check.

He continued down to the old boathouse. It was just a shack; ages ago it had held supplies and tools for boats that launched from the old pier, now underwater most of the time. The bay lapped and splashed only a few yards away, but at low tide you could see the outlines of a road leading downhill, and when they had a dead low, the pier itself would appear, slimy with kelp, but still solid enough, the old iron cleats still strong enough to tie up to.

Orion took out a small flashlight and carefully shined it on the latch. The rusty old padlock looked like it hadn't been opened in years, which was exactly how it was supposed to look. He grabbed his knife from his belt and slipped it slowly along the crack. Just over his head he felt a faint resistance. He shined the light and could see inside the door that the small piece of transparent tape he had put there last time was still undisturbed.

Tonight was the night, if the fog held. At 4:30 A.M. tide would be -1.1, almost perfect conditions. Full moon, but the fog would take care of that. They wouldn't even get their feet wet. Everyone had been strictly instructed to be back by four. Resupply was an "all hands on deck" operation. All cargo should be on shore within two minutes, and stowed inside the boathouse within five. Not that they'd be likely to forget. The monthly resupply was frankly the most exciting thing in their lives, the one time they knew for sure that there really was a world still out there.

All the guys would compete for who could see it first. The boat was jet black and designed low–slung so the highest point, the captain's head with its black balaclava, was only a couple of feet above water level. Carla's eyesight was the best, but on a foggy night even she couldn't see it usually until was almost at the dock. Then all of a sudden it would materialize, gliding up silently like a shark, and everyone would spring to action forming a bucket brigade to pass the boxes up to higher land, everyone eager for fresh food, for variety, for news from home. Plus every shipment contained at least one item not strictly necessary—a board game, ice cream. No, they wouldn't be likely to forget.

Satisfied, he continued on, heading north towards Quarry before sweeping across. He was conscious of being waited for and tried to hurry, but every now and then he paused and allowed himself the luxury of enjoying these moments with absolutely no one to bother him. The City twinkled across the back water. The fog was already obscuring the smaller buildings, but the outline of the V.T.B. Building towering above them was unmistakable. It was beautiful, he had to admit, although it felt wrong, like admiring the shininess of the bullet that just passed through your best friend's brain.

Climbing higher, he could see the Bay Bridge and the lights of his home town. He didn't miss Oakland, not like he thought he would. He missed his comrades, his fellow warriors, but he didn't miss the war. He knew their mission here was vital; he knew they'd be target number one if their activities were seen, or even suspected, that the chance of having a bomb dropped on his head had never been higher. But here, in the quiet of the island night, where the wind whistling in the trees was the loudest noise, it was easy to forget the struggle altogether.

The calm he felt on the island made him realize he'd spent his whole life in a constant state of tension. Excitement is over-rated, he decided.

But just then he heard something. Something was moving in the bushes across from him—something large. Orion took a half-step back, dropped to one knee, and shouldered his antique rifle. For a second he saw troopers charging him, but before he could take off the safety, the shape had changed. With a clatter of snapped branches, a deer emerged from the bushes and bounded away.

"Jesus Christ!" he muttered aloud, watching the buck disappear over the ridge. He heard a voice in his head saying, "You don't belong here. You're a city boy."

He continued up the hill, pausing at the road to take out his night-vision binoculars for one long look around the entire inner perimeter and all the waters nearby. Satisfied that they were in fact alone, he moved a few yards into the bushes, bending down and reaching without looking until he felt a rock, low and flat with a knobby bump at one end. He put it aside and scratched at the leaf mold beneath it until he uncovered two metal bars barely protruding from the dirt. Reaching into his pocket, he pulled out his "key" and, again without looking, attached the two wires.

"BzbzBuzzbz Buzzbzbzbz" he tapped, and almost immediately came the one letter response, "Bzbuzzbz."

He detached the wires, covered up the metal prongs, returned the stone, and stowed his key before backing out and taking out his binoculars once more and looking down the slope.

Ace was the first to emerge. Dumb, cocky Ace. His courage would save them all one day—or get them all killed. He turned back and offered a hand to Carla before heading off to the remains of old Fort McDowell and then on to China Cove.

Even alone, Carla's face revealed nothing; she did her job well and always answered with respect and intelligence, but Orion couldn't ever shake the feeling that her mind was elsewhere. She went straight up the hill. She'd send a report from the summit of Mt. Livermore, then head down the other side to Ayala.

Finally, Akilah wormed her way out into the open. Even though three team members had already passed through the area, Orion could see her looking cautiously around before signaling to Chibi who appeared carrying the rifle and the machete, both of which looked huge against his tiny frame. But far from being weighed down by all the weaponry, Chibi looked taller than ever, his posture straight and a little smile, almost a grin, on his face.

Orion looked back at Akilah. "That one," he thought, "is a natural leader. She understands reward. She'll run this whole operation one day."

Chibi indeed deserved a reward. He had definitely come through last night. When Orion had first received the message about the people climbing up from Sand Springs, he couldn't understand why Akilah was talking about herself in third person or why she was spelling out every word instead of using the common Morse abbreviations. All he thought about was heading them off, by force if necessary, if they should make a right turn and head towards the base.

He sent a message to shut down operations as a precaution while he set out to see what was happening. Halfway up the mountain, he saw them. They were passing through a treeless section just as the wind whisked the clouds aside and the moon shined through suddenly and showed them clearly. He took out his binoculars and took a good look.

Orion's immediate impression was the same as Akilah's had been: these two scarecrows were not patrollers. They didn't move like either soldiers on the march or spies on reconnaissance. The tall one had a pronounced limp and he held the hand of the small one who let go and scampered ahead when they reached a level section. A parent and child for sure. Which he wouldn't put it past the V.T.B. to use as spies, but still. The rags, those could be a disguise, but there was no faking that thinness. Even at this distance, he could see these two were no threat.

But who were they? Where did they come from?

When he caught up to her, Akilah was waiting in a clump of trees about 50 yards from the peak. It was the last safe place before the top, which was all mesquite bushes too short to hide in. Together they watched the pair reach the summit. The tall one put the small one on his shoulders and did a slow 360° turn. At one point, they were looking directly at them, but there was no hesitation, no double-take, and the same was true when they faced the base.

"If they're spies," he thought, "They're damn good."

Aloud, he whispered, "I wish we could hear what they're saying."

"I know," she answered, "I wanted to get closer, but there's no cover."

"I can do it," said a low voice from behind them. It was Chibi. He had been trying to catch up to Akilah when he saw Orion with the binoculars. He'd followed him up the hill and had been standing there unnoticed for minutes.

Akilah was surprised to see him, but Orion was astonished. The main reason he had lasted so long in this business is that he prided himself on never letting his guard down. People had tried to sneak up behind him before, but no one had ever succeeded.

But it was Chibi's voice that had really flabbergasted him. Since he had pulled him from the floorboards of that ruined house, Orion had been with him every day for the past six months and had never heard him utter a single syllable. He looked over at Akilah as if to get a witness to this miracle, and that's when he saw Chibi crawling into the bushes.

Akilah tried to grab his foot as it disappeared, but felt a hand on her other arm. She tugged away, whispering, "It's too dangerous," but Orion was strong. He pulled her, gently but firmly back.

"Sometimes you have to let people try," he said softly, "To see what they can do." He pulled her to her feet, and together they watched the faint movement of leaves as Chibi made his way to the top.

The visitors didn't seem to notice anything. After a while, he took the child down from his shoulders and they sat for a while on a rock, talking and looking about before heading downhill the way they had come. Akilah and Orion huddled behind the tree as they passed. They could see now clearly that the tall one with a limp was just a teenager with greasy hair and a wispy almost–beard, and the small one was only a little girl.

"Well," said the big one, "What do you think of a view?"

"I love a view! I want to see a view every day of my life!"

They took the right fork back to their little boat. They definitely wouldn't be going any closer to the base tonight.

Chibi crawled out of the bushes and stood up.

"He was just showing her stuff, like 'See that flashing light there? That's Sutro Towers.' Stuff like that. Nothing about us. Nothing about the island."

Akilah started to say, "Chibi I told you" but she felt a hand on her shoulder.

"Good job, Chibi," Orion broke in. "I'm proud of both of you."

They started down the mountain. It would be morning soon.

"I guess there's nothing to worry about," said Orion, "But I do wonder where they came from."

"Don't you think it's strange what he said? 'How do you like a view?'"

Orion said nothing.

"Shouldn't it be 'the view'?"

Carla had a secret.

Actually, she had a lot of secrets. Keeping secrets was the first thing she ever learned from her mother. Looking back, it seemed like the only thing she had ever learned from her. Unless you count lying. Or pretending not to be disgusted when Mom's "friends" came around. Or how to squirt medicine up her nose if she didn't wake up.

"I guess she didn't teach me that too well," she said aloud to the trees on Point Lone where she was keeping her watch. "It didn't work."

Everyone told her—the church ladies at the orphanage—that it wasn't her fault, but she had learned not to believe what nice people told her. That was another lesson her mom had taught her.

They tried to teach her "useful skills" like how to cook, which she loved, and how to clean, which she hated. But they couldn't teach her to sit still—to be "good"—so before long she was out on the street, scrounging for food, sleeping in dumpsters, hiding in the shadows whenever anyone came near.

She'd see the ladies on The Walk come out at night in their shiny dresses. They looked well–fed anyway, and she'd watch them gossiping with each other and laughing. It seemed to her only a matter of time before she'd be joining them. But not yet, she'd tell herself every evening. Not tonight. As long as she could find something to eat, she'd put that off as long as she could. She was cold, and she never got used to the stench of a dumpster, but it still didn't seem as bad as having some stranger press his flesh against you.

One afternoon she was wandering along 5th between the BART tracks and the freeway looking for anything that might have dropped. When she hit Brush Street, she turned east to try her luck on the other side. But as she walked into the shadow of the overpass, she noticed something strange. Where were the people? Yesterday there had been a little city here—boxes and crates with tarps stretched over them. Today it was empty. And no cars were passing either. Even the freeway itself was quiet. The only sound was a far–off buzzing and voices yelling "Stop! Turn around! Don't go in there!"

But she'd learned from her mother not to listen to strangers telling her what to do. She kept walking, but had only gone a few steps when she felt someone grab her arms and wrestle her to the ground. Pinned to the pavement, she was trying to reach for her knife when the sky broke open.

With a blinding flash and a roar she could still hear ringing in her ears, the other end of the overpass collapsed, raining down concrete and rebar. The shockwave slammed into Carla so hard it slid her down the sidewalk, scraping her face against the ground. The person who had tackled her was thrown several yards by the blast. Carla saw her stumble to her feet and was shocked to see a tiny Asian lady maybe 40 years old. She looked at Carla and mouthed the word "Hide!" Blood was running down her cheek, and she took the scarf from around her neck and pulled it over her head and across her face before limping away as fast as she could. A motorcycle whined up and she climbed on the back before it sped away.

Carla stood and looked around. The world was spinning and the dust stung her lungs and eyes. She did the only thing she could think of at the time, she ran back the way she had come. But she had only made it one block when she heard a high buzzing sound and a deep, artificial voice ordering her to freeze. A few seconds later, the armored truck appeared, and two men in black uniforms threw her inside.

And that is how Carla became the first–ever "guest" of the newly–opened CIGTHU, the Center for Information–Gathering and Temporary Housing Unit.

The place was so new that they had to scurry around to clear out the flowers and balloons from the lobby. The governor had just that morning cut the ribbon to inaugurate the facility. She had given a lovely speech about "New, humane methods of dealing with age–old, intractable problems" and vowed that "no small band of malcontents" would be allowed to interfere with the "march of progress." The speech was well–received. It was news–fed out as mandatory viewing for all chip–minuses in the Bay Area, and within minutes had been dutifully "liked" by almost a million people.

The day would have been perfect, except her return was delayed by the collapse of the freeway only a few hundred yards ahead of her entourage.

Of course, Carla didn't know any of this. All she knew was that she was in a padded, rectangular box and that every turn and stop threw her into a different wall. She knew that the trip was not far, that the jostling soon stopped altogether, followed by a grinding, mechanical screech and a low rumbling beneath her feet. Then silence.

The darkness was total; it made no difference whether her eyes were open or closed. She always wondered afterwards how long she had spent in that netherworld. It seemed like days, although she knew it couldn't be because she never gave in to the urge to relieve herself in the corner, although it was obvious from the smell that others hadn't been so delicate. She could remember feeling along every inch of wall, ceiling, and floor, looking for a knob or a latch but finding none. She was less sure if she had slept. She had lain down, that's for sure, and stayed still a long while. It felt like death, and she indulged herself in the fantasy of imagining that she was in fact dead and would feel like this forever.

But she was hungry, and she was pretty sure the dead don't eat.

When the back wall did open, the blinding light nauseated her. She walked into a large, brightly–lit room, very clean, completely white except for the yellow plastic benches lining the walls. The padded door closed again and a white wall slid down from the ceiling to take its place.

Carla took a seat on a bench and waited for something to happen. She was expecting to be questioned, even tortured. What she wasn't expecting was to be left alone.

She sat very still, straight posture, hands on her knees, and stared straight ahead, trying to look innocent, which of course she was. She knew they were watching. After a while she called out, "Excuse me? Hello?"

No response but the ringing in her ears. She stood and walked around the room looking for the cameras that must be there. She tapped her way along the walls, listening for hollow sounds and figured out that there were three doors, counting the one she had entered through, but no knobs, no latches, no cracks big enough to peer through.

She was on her hands and knees looking under the benches when a panel in the wall across from her slid up into the ceiling. She jumped up, banging her head, and spun around. Another armored truck had just disgorged its contents, a chubby teenage boy, older than her, she judged, maybe 16 or 17.

His mouth was bleeding, his left eye swollen shut. Apparently, his capture had been a bit more dramatic than her own. He blinked in the light, swiveling his head back and forth, trying to figure out where the next blow would come from. He couldn't process right away that there were no booted thugs waiting to knock him around, just a dark, skinny girl in worn, dirty clothes. Carla could see immediately that he was scared and trying not to show it, and she wondered if she looked the same.

He sat down across the room as far from her as he could get and tried unsuccessfully to concentrate on everything that wasn't her. But you can only stare at white walls and yellow benches for so long. After a while, he got up and walked over. He gestured at the bench next to her and raised his eyebrows. Carla shrugged, and he sat down.

"Hi," he said. "I'm Ace."

Carla didn't take the hand he held out or offer her name. "How ya doing, Ace?" she said flatly, "What brings you to this fine establishment?" and she laughed.

The laughter startled him. She could see by the look in his eyes that he thought she was crazy. He edged slightly away.

"No, seriously, what are you in for?"

"Nothing! I was just standing on the corner passing out flyers for the EIM—that's legal, you can look it up!"

Carla said nothing. She'd never heard of the EIM, but she was afraid to show any interest. Who could tell who this boy might be working for?

They sat in silence for a while. Finally Ace asked, "What'd they pick you up for"

"Running from an explosion."

"What? I heard that! What was it?"

"Freeway."

Ace's left eye was almost shut now, but she could clearly see his right eye widen. It was only a second before his face flattened back into a stone mask of boredom, but for that one second he looked like a puppy staring at a rolled–up newspaper. "Poor guy," she thought. He knew something, she was sure of it, and that meant that whoever was watching was sure of it as well.

They sat in silence then, staring ahead, but after a few minutes she felt something. Her hand was resting on the bench beside her, and Ace covered it with his own. He started tapping, gently, on the back of her hand.

"NO TOUCHING!" barked a voice that seemed to come from every-where all at once. "MOVE APART!"

And they did. They both jumped up and ran for the opposite sides of the room just as a panel slid down from the ceiling. At the same time, the wall next to Carla opened up, revealing a long, low corridor pure white and brightly lit. She stood still for a while waiting for another command, but none came. Finally, shaping her mouth into a little half–smile that she hoped looked friendly and innocent, and not (as it felt) maniacal and desperate, she called out, "Hello?"

But no voice ever answered her. Her face reverted to its typical expression of vague annoyance, and she began walking down the hallway. She had only walked a few steps when the wall behind her slid down into place again, and she found herself in a world of white. The floor and the ceiling were as spot-lessly white as the walls that stretched before her as far as she could see.

She moved along, tapping the walls as she went and finding them mostly hollow. Both sides appeared to be composed of doors separated by thick walls. Using her foot as a measure, she could see that the pattern was two feet solid, four feet hollow all the way down, although after about 40 feet she gave up and started running when she saw a change in pattern, a different shade of pale, far ahead of her.

She knew that in a place like this nothing good was waiting down the hall, but the monotony was so great that she couldn't wait to get there and see whatever it may be, and when she finally reached the open door and saw the tiny cell where she would end up staying for god knows how long, she felt only relief. Four feet wide, six feet long, it was smaller than the dumpster she'd been sleeping in, but it had what she'd been dreaming about: a toilet.

The door slid shut when she was using it. It was stainless steel, with no seat, and she couldn't figure out how to flush it, but the prospect of having her own private toilet, of not having to dodge the perverts and weirdos of the street, not having to find some bushes whenever she needed a moment of privacy, filled her with a calm that was almost glee. She lay down on the rubberized bench that took up half the cell and stared at the ceiling, thinking for the first time that maybe things would not be so bad after all. And later, when the door slid up two inches and a robot pushed in a bowl full of glop with no taste, Carla slurped it down eagerly and thought, "I can handle this."

During the night, if it was night, she could hear footsteps, and the now–familiar sound of the sliding doors. Once, she heard yelling, scuffling, then thuds and screams followed by the sound of something heavy being dragged.

After that, it was completely quiet, and Carla drifted off to a restless sleep. Her dreams were full of noise: crashes and sirens. She dreamt she was caught in a storm. The wind was sheeting the rain sideways and she was running, looking for shelter. She saw a house, but when she knocked on the door, yelling for help, the whole thing collapsed around her and she knew that if she didn't get out of there, she'd be blamed. So she kept running, endlessly running, and her lungs stabbed her with every breath. She saw a dumpster and climbed inside and finally there was calm and quiet, no more roaring wind, just the gentle tapping of raindrops on the roof.

But when she awoke, just before dawn, she realized that the tapping wasn't coming from inside her head, but from the wall next to her. TAP tap TAP, tap TAP. TAP tap TAP, tap TAP. Over and over.

"Must be the water pipes," she thought, as she drifted back to sleep. When she lived with her mother the pipes had clattered all the time.

The flushing of the toilet woke her. 6:00 A.M. Sanitation experts advising the construction of the new facility had calculated the cost savings of limited flushing versus the relative increase in communicable diseases and had concluded that once a day was optimal. In addition to the water savings, staggering the flush times allowed the builders to use narrower, much cheaper, sewage pipes. The main benefit, however, was psychological. Depriving prisoners of even this much autonomy sent a powerful, unspoken message: you are nothing. Sitting all day long only a few feet from their own filth filled even the brashest with self–loathing. In subsequent years, studies on former inmates revealed that this simple environmental change was more effective than many of the modern techniques ushered in at the new facility. Hardened terrorists who entered full of determination to withstand any torture or deprivation would crumble as their sense of self–worth faded away.

Because they got everyone's secret eventually.

Except Carla's. To be fair, she wasn't pressed as hard as the "high–value" detainees, because it was pretty obvious that no evil genius master plan involved a terrified 15 year old running from the scene of the crime. In the old days, at the Q, they probably would have let her go in a day or two, but they had all this new equipment to calibrate, and it was useful to have a true innocent as a control.

Carla did talk, of course, when the wires were attached and it felt like her intestines were burning. She told them all about her mother and her mother's friends. She spun elaborate stories, and happily confessed to every crime she could think of. They brought dozens of people into the holding cell with her, and afterwards, she claimed to know them all. But she was lying and they knew it. Their facial analysis software was quite clear on this: no recognition, no suppression of emotion, no fear, no love, nothing but a vague curiosity.

Even when they cranked the machine all the way up and she lost all control over her body her story never changed. She was walking, she decided to cross under the freeway, she wondered where everyone was, then the sky broke open and all hell rained down. The girl simply did not know anything.

So in the end, they just gave her the intradermal, notched her ear and shoved her out the door.

She went back to her old life, skulking in corners, living off discards. For a few days, every time she was out in the daytime, she'd see a drone hovering high overhead, but apparently, they tired of her after a while and moved on to other targets.

When someone came to recruit her, she was not at all surprised. She climbed on the back of the motorcycle as if she did it every day of her life, and she showed no fear at the dark shipyard when the door of the shipping container creaked open to reveal the safe house she lived in for a few weeks before they put her on the resupply boat to Angel to begin her new life.

The boatman, an old Chinese man named Norman, greeted her with respect. They all did. She was famous: the girl who didn't talk. They'd had thousands of people brought into interrogation over the years. Some talked and were let go, some talked and were locked up in the Q, some talked and were never heard from again. But they had all, in the end, given up everything they knew. Only Carla had resisted completely. She only had one tiny piece of information, the Asian lady who had tackled her, but no matter how many times she told her story, she never mentioned it.

That kind of loyalty to the cause should be celebrated, they said. It should be rewarded. So she was off the streets; she had free food and a mattress, and she'd never have to go out on The Walk. But she felt like a fraud. That was her biggest secret. She had no loyalty to the cause. She didn't believe in it. She didn't care if the freeway got blown up, but she couldn't imagine it would do any good. When Orion gave his speech about walking in the sun, about a brighter future, she was the only one who wasn't moved. Sure, she had nodded and mm–hmmed along with the rest of them, but inside she was stifling a laugh. She couldn't predict the future, but if she had learned anything from her mother it was that nothing ever changes for the better.

Carla closed her eyes and listened to the distant waves. She knew why she had refused to give up the stranger who had saved her life. It wasn't loyalty. It was just none of their damn business.

A ce was doing pushups when she got there. "You're early," he grunted, and went on counting. "252, 253, 254..." When he hit 300, he stood up, brushed himself off and looked around. Carla smiled at him, he wasn't pudgy anymore.

Pushups, crunches, burpees, jumping-jacks, running in place—any exercise you could do in a confined space without equipment. Ever since his time in CIGTHU, at first a few, then more, as many as it took to fill the hours, to kill the boredom, to numb the pain. After his release, here on the island, he added running and lifting weights—rocks mostly. The pain was pleasant to him; it was the only way he'd found to tamp down the memories, to hold in the shame.

Because he had talked. He'd spilled it all: names, addresses, everything he'd overheard—vague references to explosives, to a plan, to a freeway. And no matter how many times they told him how well he'd done, how he'd held up under pressure far beyond anyone's expectations, that the delays he caused by holding out led to the mission's ultimate success, he could not shake the shame. Even when they admitted to him that he'd been used, that all the "information" he'd given up was false, it made no difference.

He was the designated Patsy. Everyone he had met in his time with the EIM had used a false name around him, even Deshai, the one he thought might love him. The squat—the abandoned office building where she lived, where she had invited him to—was empty when The Patrol raided it, no traces anyone had ever lived there. Because they hadn't. It was a stage set, a fake. And all the "terrorists" he'd met there, whose whispered conversations he'd overheard, not only used false names, they were wearing wigs and the distinctive scars and tattoos he ended up describing at length were nothing but makeup. It was all a ruse, because of course people would be arrested, and of course they'd tell all they knew. The only way to beat them was to feed them a true believer, someone who actually was certain his info was real, to throw them off the scent completely while operations shut down and disappeared.

And they weren't lying to Ace when they told him how well he'd done. He was expected to crack the first day, so when months went by and the squat was never raided, The Committee began to assume that Ace must have been killed, not captured. But sure enough the vid appeared, newsfed to all chip–minuses, the same day as the fruitless raid. And a few months later, after he'd been drained of all his "information," Ace appeared again on the streets with a dazed expression and a bloody bandage on his freshly–notched ear.

Wherever he went, people pointed and laughed at him. They'd all seen the vid, the worst moment of his life uploaded to warn and entertain the masses. Required viewing for Bay Area chip–minuses the first day, it became hugely popular around the world and spawned a whole new genre, all with the same title: "Terrorist Shits Himself."

You can see him in his orange jumpsuit standing with his arms outstretched, wires protruding from each sleeve. The screen tiles: four images shown simultaneously, medium long shots front and back, close up on his face, and a fourth shot of a dial with numbers 1–100. "I don't know anything!" he says as a blue–gloved hand slowly twists the dial past the halfway mark. Sweat breaks out on his forehead and upper lip. When the dial points to 75, his voice quavers, then fades out altogether. His eyes widen, the brows folding as the expression changes from anger to begging.

"No, please!" he shouts. Then, "Okay, I'll talk!" The close–up captures his tears as the hand twists the dial anyway, and the rear view camera captures the results. Ten million viewers liked the video. The number one comment was "Fucking hilarious."

As soon as it was safe, they picked him up and debriefed him. They lauded his bravery, told him he'd done a great service to the cause, and they removed him to the island, started him on a new life, a life he came to love.

But when he was alone, the memories would return, and keeping watch wasn't enough to block them from his mind. Then he'd have to lift a bigger stone, run a little farther than the day before, do one more pushup.

And he liked the result. His posture now, as he stood before Carla, was ramrod straight. He couldn't resist flexing his muscles for her, although he flashed her an apologetic smile when he did it. She wasn't interested, she'd made that clear. But they were friends. She knew he was a show-off and she didn't make him feel stupid about it. She just raised one eyebrow, and said, "Okay, Hercules, let's go."

"You're early," he said again. "Is there news?"

"Didn't you hear? There was a nuclear war." She touched his arm and batted her lashes at him, then purred "We're the only two people left alive."

But she couldn't keep a straight face. "Sucks to be you!" she laughed.

"You too," he answered.

"I suppose." then "Come on, let's go."

"I've gotta do one more perimeter. What's the hurry?"

In response, she pointed right, tilted her head left, then took off in that direction. If they split the perimeter check, they'd save time. She took the path down to the old immigration station, where they'd detained people like her in the good old days.

She never answered his question, even to herself. What was the hurry? It's not like she could make the boat arrive any sooner. And when it did, then what?

Last time, she couldn't even say one word. She'd just stared like an idiot. It was the shock, that's all. The surprise. She was on the dock, ready to unload, to grab the boxes from Old Norman and pass them down the line. But when the boat pulled up, and she looked up after securing the hawser line, the old gonggong had transformed. In his place, she saw long, shiny black hair, glowing dark skin. And the eyes! Too big to be real, too dark, too perfect.

"Are you okay?" because she hadn't taken the box. And all she could do was nod and look down. And pass the boxes.

And after she'd uncleated the rope and the electric whirr of the motor started up, she still couldn't talk, couldn't even raise a hand to answer the goodbye wave.

This time it would be different. She'd be first at the dock again, she could do that, and this time she'd say something. But after a whole month, she still hadn't figured out what. As she walked along, she tried out various ideas. So far, the best she had come up with was, "You're not Norman."

"Idiot!" she said aloud.

• • • •

She met him way past the halfway point and she could see that he was about to object—she couldn't possibly have checked carefully enough—but he clamped his mouth shut and just nodded instead. Without words they turned and headed towards base.

Orion was still on point when they reached him. He looked at them skeptically, but Carla spoke up.

"It was quiet," she said, "So we thought we'd open up the boathouse for you."

Orion was a taskmaster, and he'd introduced stricter regimens than past security chiefs. He wasn't fooled for a minute by this sudden generosity. They were bored, lonely, eager for human contact. He'd been a teenager himself long, long ago, and he knew how any break in routine is treasured by the young.

Carla held out her hand.

"You sure you remember the sequence."

"Yes sir." It was Ace. "I've done it several times, sir,"

Orion reached into his pocket and took out a metal rectangle with three prongs protruding from it. He looked solemnly at Ace, but handed it to Car-la.

"Don't screw up."

As they walked along, Ace went over the procedure in his mind. It wasn't difficult, but the consequences for failure were pretty dire. If you messed up the entry, that was no big deal, but the trapdoor in the floor was booby-trapped.

When they reached the door, Ace held up a hand. He took the knife from his belt and slid the blade slowly along the crack at the top of the door until he felt a soft resistance. The tape was still intact. He put the knife away and nodded to Carla. She took the tool Orion had given her and lined the three prongs up with the screws of the bottom hinge. With a pop and a crash, the magnets inside gave way and fell to the floor. Ace leaned against the door to hold it in place, and she repeated the procedure on the top hinge. Then she and Ace pulled the door open slowly, careful not to scratch the old latch.

Once inside, they turned their flashes on, making sure to shine them only on the floor. The trap door was fitted carefully. It took a keen eye to see the seams even in the brightest daylight, and if someone were to snoop around in the day and find it, they'd have a nasty surprise if they tried to pry up the boards to see what's underneath. The rest of the floor was lined with explosives wired to go off if the entry were ever breached.

"Do you remember the sequence?" he asked.

"Never eat shredded wheat, clock counter clock counter" was her answer.

Ace smiled and nodded and watched as Carla knelt on the floor. She ran her fingernail gently along the north edge. When she reached the spot, she took the metal rectangle and placed it face down. She turned it three quarters clockwise, then moved to the east edge. Same procedure, except only a ninety degree turn counter–clockwise.

On the south edge, she faked a counter–clockwise, just to hear Ace gasp. He really was too easy.

"Take it easy, big man" she smiled. The last two sides went as smoothly as the first two. She moved back to the north edge, this time placing the tool on the trapdoor itself. There was a sound of a bolt sliding and the north edge of the door popped open half an inch. They grabbed it and pulled it open, revealing dark wooden stairs. Quiet, ranchero music could be heard echoing from the lab.

"Okay," she said, "You stand guard here, I'll go watch for the boat." And she skipped out, leaving Ace alone, wondering how he once more had let himself fall into her trap.

Carla followed the old road down to the jetty, staying low and dodging in and out of the shadows, out of habit. The fog was thick now; she couldn't even see the city so it was highly doubtful anyone could see her. And she wouldn't see the boat either, until it was only a few dozen yards away, but that would give her enough time to get in front, to be the one to tie up the boat, the one she'd talk to. It was her chance to say something. But what?

Her mother had been beautiful, before she fell apart. From a very early age, Carla had been aware of the power of attraction—how strangers would smile at her mother, would do things for her. It was something that just happened. She never had to try to get people's attention, and Carla just assumed it was that way for everyone. The only thing her mother had ever taught her was how to discourage people, how to keep a stone face, how to put an icy edge on her voice. For her mother, a look, a smile, was currency, for use only when necessary to purchase something you need.

And since Carla needed only to be left alone, she wore her scowl as armor. Even with Ace, honestly the only friend she'd ever had, her guard was always up. Dark sarcasm was always ready at the tip of her tongue to push him or anyone else away, if they ever began to get too close.

Love was not a word she ever heard her mother mention. Just thinking the word brought a sarcastic chuckle to her throat. She wasn't in love, that's for sure. But what was it? What was this feeling? And why the hell couldn't she think of a single word to say? How could someone you saw for two minutes live in your mind for a month?

Probably just this damn island, she thought, probably I'm just bored.

An inbound freighter was passing the island so she knew the boat, if it was on its way, would be hanging off, hiding in the fog, waiting for it to pass. She looked back to the land. The others were gathered along the fence line. Akilah and Chibi were holding hands, it looked like, leaning together like they were having some big conversation, although she knew that wasn't it—the kid was mute, brain–damaged or something. Orion came down near them, and soon he was joined by the twins—the brain crew, Doc's little proteges.

"I'm just as smart as they are," she thought. She turned her attention back to the water. "Him him him" sounded the fog horn behind her. Carla pulled her cape up over her head and leaned back against the rock. She closed her eyes.

"I don't care," she argued with herself. "Let someone else be up front. I'll stay on shore."

But when she opened her eyes and saw a ghostly movement in the fog, she jumped up despite herself. She hooted once, like an owl, and headed down to the dock. But as the boat floated closer, she could see right away that something was wrong. Where was that shining, black hair? The balaclava was back. Old Norman again.

Carla felt the peculiar pain of losing something she never had. How could she have been so stupid to assume...? But no time to think now, she hurried down the dock, stepping carefully on the sodden boards. She caught the thrown rope and cleated it, then turned dully to accept the first box. She turned to pass it to Akilah, first in line behind her. When she turned back for the second one, she even tried to smile. It wasn't Old Norman's fault after all. But instead of pouched lids and gray brows she looked up into the vision she'd carried for a month. Those eyes! And she was smiling, looking at Carla's fluster with amusement.

"You're not Norman!" It just came out of her. And she was happy she had an excuse to turn away, to pass the box down the line. But when she turned back, the smile was still there.

"Very observant!" and handed her another box.

And so it went, a few words with every box. And she didn't embarrass herself, much, other than forgetting to ask her name or give her own. Still, Carla was a good observer of other people's reactions, and she could see clearly that the other person was enjoying this little chat, but nothing beyond that. She recognized the look she was getting; it was the same one she gave to Ace. When the last box had been taken off, and they'd loaded up the empties from last month, along with a month's worth of garbage, she uncleated the rope again and watched the boat reverse and turn again toward Oakland.

"See you next month!" she called out too loudly and was instantly aware of eyes on her back. She turned toward them with her usual bored expression fixed on her face and went on with the task at hand—getting the cargo into the boathouse and down into HQ as fast as possible. She picked up the heaviest box she could carry and followed the others up the road.

Ace was stacking the goods neatly inside, and Carla handed him her box and turned back to the water, but when she got there she was greeted by a strange sight. Orion, on one knee, had his rifle out. Without thinking, she stopped stock still, pulled out her pistol and turned to see what he was aiming at. There, on the dock stood a very skinny boy with stringy hair. In one hand he held a burlap sack while his other hand held the line of an ancient rowboat. In the boat sat a very pretty, but equally skinny, little girl.

"Live crabs" the boy called out like a seller in a market. He held the sack aloft.

Carla heard steps behind her. She glanced back and could see Ace had his rifle out as well. She could hear the click of his safety being switched off.

"Hold still," he barked as if he was the one in charge.

"Calm down, it's just crabs," said the young man. "Saw you just got supplies and thought you might like to trade." He smiled. "Live crabs."

Carla's eyes were on the little girl. She didn't like children much, but she hated to see people afraid. But this child, no more than seven or eight she judged, showed no fear whatsoever. She just looked amazed, like she was watching a circus.

Without removing the rifle from his shoulders, Ace took two steps towards them. "Just get in that boat and get out of here," he said, putting every bit of menace into his voice that he could.

The smile left the boy's face. He took a half step forward and opened his mouth like he was about to say something, but Ace kept coming. The stranger glanced at the girl in the boat and said, "Okay, calm down." He raised his hands. "We'll leave."

But another voice broke in, loud, but not a bark like Ace. It was calm, almost sad.

"No one's leaving," said Orion. "Carla, grab the boat."

She holstered her pistol and moved forward. As she reached the end of the dock, she looked back. There were three rifles aimed in her direction. Even little Chibi was looking as threatening as he could with his machete. Only the twins were gone, scurried back to the basement.

The tide was rising, and a wave sprayed over the dock. Carla stepped carefully, eying the bag in the boy's hand the whole time. She held both hands up and gestured to the hand with the rope and when he handed it to her, she pulled it taut and knelt down to cleat it.

The little girl's expression was changing by the moment. Her posture did not waver, but up close, Carla could see fear forming behind the eyes.

"Don't worry," she whispered to her. "It will be all right."

"Of course it will," the boy said. He was older than she thought, maybe 19 or 20, with a deep worry ridge between his brows like Doc's. He held his hand out and the girl grabbed it and scrambled out of the boat without tilting it.

"Okay," said Orion, "Put the bag down and walk forward slowly."

"It'll crawl away."

"Drop it!"

So he did, but when the sack hit the shallow water, it came alive, wriggling and squirming toward the sea. The boy stepped on the bag.

"C'mon please. We worked hard for this."

"Step forward."

"Can I at least untie the bag? They'll die."

"It's really crab?"

"Why would I lie?"

"So many, many reasons. Okay, Carla, pick it up. And you all walk forward, slowly."

Carla followed close behind them, the bag squirming in her hand. She could see Orion talking quietly to Akilah. She and Chibi left, back to the boathouse, but as they were going Carla heard her say, "Boss, they're just kids,"

"Okay, close enough." said Orion, "Carla, make sure they have no weapons."

And she did as she was told. Running her hand down the girl's back, she could feel her spine, her ribs. The young man wasn't much different. She felt a sick pain in her stomach. She knew why Orion hadn't let them go. They'd seen too much, obviously. But what he'd do about it, the only solution possible, it made her sick.

"Okay," he said, "The crab is real. But that's not why you're here, is it?"

There was no answer. The stranger was looking around, calculating. He swallowed hard, then said, "The Committee sent me."

"Bullshit!" The gun came up, and Carla saw a side of Orion she'd never seen before. Old and gray as he may be, when his anger flashed, it was terrifying. He left no doubt about what he was capable of.

"Don't ever lie to me! Now, we're going to move out of the open," Orion told them. He pointed up the road with his rifle. "I'll follow you."

The young man took a step forward, but stopped. He looked back at Carla, then down at the girl. She could see his Adam's apple bob when he swallowed. He turned back to Orion.

"No," he said quietly and pulled the girl in close.

"No?"

"We're not going anywhere unless you promise me."

"Young man, you don't seem to realize which end of the gun you're on."

"The sun is rising, the fog is lifting. You don't want to be seen, I get it. I don't either. But you've got to promise, otherwise just do what you're going to do right here out in the open."

"Promise what?"

"You don't hurt the girl." And with this the child began to sob quietly. "No one hurts the girl."

"Okay."

"Swear!"

"Okay, I swear. I give you my word."

"And if anything happens to me, you swear to raise her as your own daughter."

Orion didn't know what to make of this strange young man. "I swear" was all he said.

"And she never goes to the city, she never ends up on the street."

"Okay, I promise."

And with that, The stranger knelt down. "It's okay, Umi. No one's going to hurt you. Your bear's watching over you." And he picked her up, held her to his chest, and walked up the road.

Orion started to follow, but turned back. "You two, take everything useful out of that boat. Then sink it."

It's not as easy to scuttle a boat as you may think. After dragging out various sail cloths and pieces of fishing equipment and placing them up at the edge of the road by the still—squirming crabs, they set about to sink the boat. Ace wanted to shoot holes in the bottom, but Carla just rolled her eyes and said, "Yeah no one would hear that."

But her plan, loading it with rocks, wasn't much better. Load after load of the heaviest rocks they could carry only brought it down an inch. It was Ace who thought of standing on the rim, holding down the edge until it filled with water. And except that they both ended up waist deep in the freezing bay, it worked like a charm. In the end, the boat was hidden from view, lying at the bottom, under 10 feet of water, and they were soaking wet, lugging all the stuff up to the boathouse.

The shed was shut up when they got there, but the hinges were just lined up, not attached. Ace grabbed the door and dragged it open. They brought in the junk from the boat and pulled the door shut. A lantern on the floor cast everything in a strange light. The stranger was sitting on an old crate, and Orion was standing over him. He had slung his rifle back over his shoulder, but he held his stun in his hand and was gesturing with it. The trapdoor was closed and Chibi was gone. Akilah had probably sent him away so he wouldn't see whatever might happen. She was sitting on the floor with the little girl, holding her hand.

"So the V.T.B. killed your grandfather, why?"

He looked up at Carla and Ace. "Seal it," and they went about reinstalling the magnetic bolts and putting up the security tape.

"I don't know. He said they wanted him to play ball. That's what he said. They wanted him to play ball, but he didn't want to. It had something to do with a new chip; they were installing a new chip, but Grandpa said it wasn't ready yet. Unsafe or something."

"And before he died, he told you to come here?"

"Yes. Well, sort of. Maybe. I told you what he said."

"How would he know about this place?"

"I don't know."

"When was this?"

"Long time ago, maybe a year."

"And you have no idea why he said it?"

But the prisoner answered a different question. He had remembered something. "May 15th. It was May 15th. When he . . . when it happened."

"How do you remember the date?"

"It was a week before my birthday."

"And that's when you removed your chip?"

But he never answered. There was a creak, and the trapdoor was opening from below. A gray head emerged. Orion looked back and immediately moved out of the way of Doc's intent gaze. He was looking even paler than usual, and he appeared to tremble as he approached the stranger. When he reached him, he said nothing, just stared with an intensity that made the boy look down.

"Your birthday is May 22nd?"

The prisoner nodded. When he looked up again, he could see tears in his interrogator's eyes. Doc reached out and touched his arm.

"Frankie?" he said.

Franc examined the face in front of him. The gray hair, the wrinkled forehead, was unfamiliar. But the eyes were a piercing blue he'd seen before. And that nose was unmistakable, the prominent bridge almost a hook.

"Dad?"

U mi liked many things about this new underground life. She liked the food, especially the smooth, white dishes they served them on. She liked using a fork and enjoyed stabbing her peas, which she had never had before, one at a time. She liked the soft, white mattress and the warm, fluffy blankets, although it was a long time before she got used to sleeping alone.

She liked being around people and never tired of trying to figure them out. Carla's hair was black and straight like Momma's, but she didn't want to cuddle. Ever. And she'd listen to Umi's dreams in the afternoon, but would never share her own. Akilah was nicer. She was calm and didn't mind Umi in her lap. She'd plait her hair, like Momma used to, and tell her stories about talking animals and Anansi, the clever spider. Ace was tall, bigger than Frankie even, and he'd hold one arm straight out and let Umi hang from it.

But her favorite was Chibi. Chibi taught her games, card games, thumb-wrestling, chess, and would play with her for hours. She could beat him at checkers, but he'd slaughter her every time at chess. She could never concentrate on the game. The little carved horse, the king, the queen, the very word castle—these things would create stories in her head and the stories would push everything aside.

Chibi showed her around the place, not just the rooms they used, but all the dark corridors. He wasn't much bigger than she was and they could climb into spaces no one else could fit in. They would crawl through the air duct all the way to its intake by the water's edge. You could smell the ocean there, hear the "home home" of the fog horn. Umi liked to go there just to sit and listen, and Chibi never hurried her along.

The first night, when the crew left on guard duty, Umi was more than happy to remain behind. She stayed right next to Frankie, listening quietly while he told his story. She didn't interrupt; she asked no questions, even though much of the story she had never heard before, and there were many things she did not understand. She sensed a new seriousness in Frankie, a sadness, and she kept her mouth shut, even when the story turned to Momma and her. She wanted to jump in and describe Frankie gasping for air in the bottom of the boat and the way Momma had tied him up to fix his leg, but Frankie squeezed her hand. He didn't tell much about their life together, only that they lived by fishing and stayed hidden, only coming out at night. He said they had come here after Momma "passed away," an expression she had never heard before and did not like.

Franc had many questions for this man everyone called Doc, but he asked only one.

"How could Grandpa know you were here?"

"He's the one who showed me this place, many years ago. His grandfather, your great-great-grandfather, owned a concrete company, and your grandpa worked for him when he was young. When the government was decommissioning this place—it's an old missile silo, you know—they hired him to fill it with cement. But the old guy ripped them off. He built that ceiling, all held up with those little poles, see?"

He pointed, and Franc noticed for the first time that the ceiling did not match the walls. It looked like plywood, and it was indeed propped up by many, many thick metal pipes.

"That way he only poured concrete a quarter meter deep, saved a bundle. But the real reason was that the old guy was what they called in those days a "prepper." He was convinced that society was going to collapse any day, so he wanted this place for himself. He put in those hidden entryways so he could sneak back in an emergency. He stocked it full of supplies, canned goods, weapons, stuff like that, and when your grandpa showed the place to me, many years ago, before you were born, the stuff was still there. I guess because I was marrying his daughter he wanted to show it to me, just in case.

"So that's why I always thought he must know, or anyway suspect, that I would be here. At first, when I was just hiding out here alone, I expected the patrollers any time. If they compelled him to talk, it wouldn't be long till they burst in. It was even possible he'd volunteer the information. I didn't think so, but I know he was angry with me. When they rejected my chip, my plan, he told me to drop it, said it was time to play ball, told me I didn't know what

I was up against. I guess that was true enough. He said it was time to 'accept the things I cannot change' blah blah blah. But that's just it, it was something we could change! We had in our hands the solution! No more cancer. And they were only going to use it on the chip–plus, going to let 99% of the population suffer and die so a few could live forever.

"I couldn't let that happen, Frankie. People died to make this happen. I let them die." His voice dropped. "I killed them."

There was a long pause. Franc looked over at Umi. She was patiently waiting, examining her fingernails.

"I didn't want to, but it was the only way to rid the world of this suffering forever. I told myself the trade–off was worth it. But then, they weren't going to use it! They were worried about population growth, but there was an obvious solution. I showed them. I made the chip. Chip–minimum. Health functions only for all the currently chipless, and add the health functions to the chip–minus, and of course the chip–plus already had them. It would take some time to ramp up, but in a few years cancer would cease to exist—diabetes too, that one's easy. I showed them how we could do it without increasing the population."

"How?"

"Planned obsolescence. Ninety and out. Instead of a few people hanging around for hundreds of years, everyone gets 90 good years and then the heart just stops. A planned, peaceful end. I laid it all out for Altshuler, but he just laughed. 'Young man,' he said, 'Do you have any idea how old I am?' He didn't even pretend to have an argument other than 'it won't benefit me, so no.' So I lost my temper, I accused him of genocide, said he'd go down in history as a mass murderer and I'd make sure everyone knew it. I didn't say it, obviously, but I had a friend, a schoolmate who was part of The Resistance. I was pretty sure he'd help spread the word, whatever good that'd do.

"He just stayed very calm. He said, 'Tell you what, let's both sleep on this, and we'll talk tomorrow.' but there was a look in his eye, Frankie. It was evil, like I was looking at the devil himself, and I knew right then I was never going back.

"You gotta believe me, there was no other way. If I stayed they might have killed us all. So I took out my chip, like you did, stuck it into a bag of laundry and put it in the car seat and set the destination for work, but I doubled back, hid in the woods all day, and at night, I snuck down to Fort Point. I had a trash bag with clothes and my old laptop and records of my work that I had managed to smuggle out on my last day, and I tied it to my waist. Then, when the tide was right, I just jumped in and started swimming.

"I was a good swimmer when I was young, but the cold and the current was quite a shock. It was windy that night, and the wind was blowing me in the right direction. The bag buoyed me up, and I thought "this won't be so hard after all," but the bag ripped and everything I had, all of my work, began sinking—not to mention my clothes. I ended up cutting it loose, it was dragging me down. So I arrived on this island with absolutely nothing.

"I came here because I didn't know where else to go, but I always knew that if your grandpa said the word, it would be all over for me. When that didn't happen, I had a crazy hope that he'd join me. We disagreed about many things, but I know he loved me. I loved him too, we were very close. So I had this fantasy that he'd show up himself, with you and your mom, and together we'd fight this thing, find a way to end the genocide.

"Well, he didn't join me, obviously. But he didn't turn me in, either. Weeks went by and no troops stormed the building, so I figured he hadn't talked, and wouldn't. There was a big yacht moored at Ayala, and I managed to liberate the dinghy they were towing. I rowed to Tiburon where my contact in The Resistance was and started the arrangements to bring equipment and people here, to build a stronghold against them right under their noses."

He went on to outline their operations. They were part, only part, of a larger resistance movement and were under the orders of The Committee. Therefore, most of what they'd done so far was to provide logistics for various demonstrations planned by different groups connected with The Resistance. Yes, they'd commandeered the buses he'd seen on the bridge, one of their more successful operations. But he didn't sound happy when he talked about it.

"We haven't accomplished much, to be honest. So far, we're just the flea on the dog. The best we can do at this point is to annoy the powers that be, remind them that there is a price to pay for keeping the majority in slavery.

"But what we'd like to be, what I'd like to be," he looked up, a grin on his face, "Is—have you ever heard of Ophiocordyceps?"

"What?"

"It's a fungus, you know, like a mushroom. All fungi send out spores, like seeds, that's how they propagate, but this one fungus, Othiocordyceps lateralis, down in South America, sends out spores that land on ants, okay? And once they're on the ant—this is the good part—once they're on the ant, they burrow into the brain and take over. These spores are microscopic, right? They're millions of times smaller than the ant, but they release a chemical that overrides the ant's brain and causes it to commit suicide. It stops eating and just climbs straight up as high as it can, then bites down hard on the leaf or twig or whatever with a bite that doesn't let go even after death. Then the ant just withers and dies while the fungus reproduces, eventually sending out new spores, starting the cycle over again.

"The point is not the fungus, but the control. We can control little things at a distance, like you saw with the buses, but what does that do really? They just patch the software and we have to start again. But the brain. That's the point. That's what we want to do, take over the nerve system of the V.T.B. itself.

"Because otherwise, we're really just an annoyance to them. A necessary annoyance. They need to know that the people aren't happy, that they won't lie down forever. But until we can actually take over the facilities, manufacture the chips, distribute them to the people, it won't mean much."

He went on to explain the nuts and bolts of the operation itself. Franc nodded from time to time, but said nothing. The twins had plugs in their ears and hardly ever looked up, except to answer an occasional question from the doctor. Once in a while, they'd speak to each other, but it was a strange language Umi had never heard before. They showed no interest in the strangers in their midst, just kept their eyes on the screens in front of them.

Umi was fascinated by the screens as well. They were like a blue fire that gave no warmth. She knew her letters and her numbers, of course, and she could recognize them as they flashed by, but there seemed to be no order or pattern she could detect.

But she didn't interrupt. The only question she asked, when there was a pause and it seemed polite to do so, was, "Where are the ones and zeroes?"

"What?" asked Doc.

"Frankie says it's all ones and zeroes, the computer. Binary."

The doctor looked her over as if he'd just noticed her. "That's an excellent question. An excellent question. Unfortunately, I don't have time right now to answer it, but I will. I promise you."

But he never did, mainly because after a few weeks she was gone at night, on guard duty with the rest of them. Frankie was reluctant to let her leave his side, but he finally gave in to the pleading from her, from Chibi, from Akilah. Even Orion had been observing this unusual child and had concluded that she would not be a liability. She definitely knew how to obey orders, how to keep quiet when necessary.

And she wanted it so badly. She felt she just had to feel fresh air again, but even more, she wanted to help, to be a part of something, to contribute.

But there was something else. She wouldn't say it of course, but she wanted to be away from Frankie. There was a sadness about him now that she couldn't understand, one that her hugs could not erase.

The transition had been harder on him. Of course, he also missed the fresh air. His back was strong now, and he felt cramped sitting all night and most of the day squinting at a screen. His calloused hands felt strange at the keyboard and he fat-fingered all the time now. But she knew there was more to it.

First, there was the news about his mother. His father had put out inquiries. The Committee had some agents on the inside. He told Franc that his mother had indeed been arrested, although he did not know why.

"Questioning, I could understand," he said, "But arrest? Your mother wasn't political, at least not when I knew her. She worked for them, for God's sake! It looks like she's been accused of being a spy, but I think most likely she's got some enemies in her own department, maybe somebody who just wanted her job."

"Where is she now?"

"Unless she just snapped," he went on, "Family gone, heart broken, maybe she just let them have it." He looked off in the distance and a little half-smile played on his lips. "She had a temper, your mother. I remember that. I remember one time. . ." He began to grin, but when he looked back at Franc and saw the pain in his eyes, he returned to business.

"San Quentin," he said. "That's where she is."

Franc said nothing. He walked out of the room, but there were people there. There were people everywhere in this cramped new world. He found a quiet corner and sat alone, trying to not picture his mother locked in some grim cell. He closed his eyes and imagined rowing the boat out under the bridge, though the Golden Gate and past, further and further into the fog until everything disappeared and he could lie down alone on the rolling sea and disappear himself.

But he couldn't do that, and he couldn't storm the prison either and set his mother free. He opened his eyes and looked around. There was a beat–up old sofa against the wall. Akilah was sitting there, under a dim lamp, reading a book. Umi sat on the floor in front of her, playing checkers with Chibi. She was winning, based on the smile on her face. Franc was glad to see her happy, but he couldn't help feeling even more alone.

When they had first arrived, the relief at not being killed was so great it cast everything in a golden light. Steady food, soft beds, clean clothes, work that would tax his brain and not his body: Franc felt happier than he could ever remember. There were people to talk to, and he felt for the first time in his life that he understood his purpose. But claustrophobia was getting to him. It had been almost a month; he hadn't accomplished anything, and he was beginning to feel like he hated every human being on the planet, especially his father.

At first, he had wanted to know so many things about him, about his mother, about their lives together before everything fell apart, but he couldn't ask; he couldn't listen when his father said anything about the subject. He'd harden his eyes and look bored. He'd never been a petulant kid, but still he knew the look: the blank, waiting gaze all teenagers use from time to time, the "This is so stupid!" stare they knew could make their parents explode in anger, and make all other adults dry up, stop talking, feel like an idiot.

Doc was used to being listened to, even by the twins who had to be reminded to look away from their screens when he was giving instructions. He sensed the anger in the young man who'd once been his baby boy, but he couldn't do anything about it. If he tried to address it directly, Franc would just say, "I'm fine, go on with your story" and return to the stare, the polite waiting, until the doctor stumbled to a halt.

Franc didn't like being this way, but he couldn't help himself, the pain was too great. It was like finding a lump, some tumor you've had for years and never noticed, but once you become aware of it the pain throbs and soon you can't concentrate on anything else. How strange it seemed that finding family could make you feel so alone.

Something else was bothering him. He wasn't any good.

The systems they were hacking used internal encryption, something he did not know even existed. Even after the password had been decoded, or the back door had been found, the code was unintelligible, shuffled in a seemingly random order. Only the host server would have the key, the large prime number necessary to sort the commands.

But even after Marco and Pablo had cracked the order problem, had written the override to unshuffle the commands, they still looked like gibberish to Franc. He'd never learned much about these types of machine languages. Each page of code he looked at had terms he had never heard of, and the commands he did know seemed garbled to him, the syntax all wrong. His father was a patient explainer, and Franc was progressing, but something happened that stole his attention completely.

It began with taking out the trash. One morning Ace asked him if he cared if they chucked out his old clothes. He was holding a wad of rags as far from his nose as possible. Water is a limited resource on the island, he was explaining politely, and although they *could* try and wash them, perhaps it wasn't worth it. New clothes would be coming on the next resupply, good news for Ace, who'd get his clothes back, and for Franc who wouldn't have to walk around with a bungee cord for a belt anymore.

"Be my guest," he said, but after Ace walked away, he ran after him.

"Hold on," he said. "Hand me those," reaching for his pants. The once–blue fabric was stiff and dark gray, and the smell of smoke and rotten fish was overwhelming. He looked at the holes in both knees, the fraying at the cuffs, then reached in the left front pocket and pulled out the thing he had been looking for and handed the pants back to Ace.

"Burn 'em," he said and turned back to the lab. He walked past his workstation, past the twins, who of course did not look up, and through the door into the back room where the doctor sat in front of two huge monitors.

"Explain this," he said, throwing the object on the desk.

Doc looked up at him, then down at the piece of plastic in front of him. It looked like just a bit of flotsam, some old piece of trash that he'd found floating in the bay, but when he turned it over he could see, in the mush of gray–brown, a faint design, some sort of picture. He flipped on his desk lamp and held the piece of trash close to his eye. It was a baseball player!

He leaped to his feet and hugged Franc, who had no idea what to do with this explosion of emotion. "You've got it!" he shouted, "I can't believe you've got it!" Franc felt two lips on his cheek, but before he could pull away or demand an explanation, his father had turned his back on him.

He reached into a drawer and removed a round piece of glass as big as his hand, attached to a metal handle. He held the glass between the plastic and his face and looked through it. Looking over his shoulder, Franc could see that the glass made everything look bigger. His father tipped the plastic sleeve on its end and squeezed the edges gently. A thin stream of sand poured out.

"Come on, come on!" he said. He tapped the end on the table, and a dirty strip of latex—some old bandage—came tumbling out. He pushed it aside and shook the card again. This time he found what he was looking for: a tiny wax pebble, resembling a booger.

"You've got it!" he shouted again, leaping up. Franc thought he was going to be kissed again, and he backed away, but his father just looked at him as if he'd just scored the winning goal. "When my stuff sank, I never thought I'd see it again," he said.

"See what?"

But his father had turned away again. He put the glass flat down over the booger. "Don't let that roll away," he said to Franc before dashing to the closet.

Franc peered through the glass, trying to fathom what was so precious. Magnified, it looked more like a booger than ever.

Doc came back from the closet carrying something heavy, some sort of old–fashioned machine. "Now we'll see what we have!"

He put the machine on the table and flipped a switch. A light came on, shining from below. He reached into a little drawer and pulled out a pair of tweezers and a small rectangle of glass. He used the tweezers to carefully transfer the wax pebble to the little pane of glass.

"But what is it?" Franc asked, but there was no answer. Doc was busy putting the little piece of glass onto a table–like structure of the machine. He pulled out two metal arms and used them to hold the glass to the table, then put his eyes on two black cylinders and smiled.

"Take a look," he said.

It wasn't clear to Franc exactly what he was looking at. It was interesting, he thought, to see how what looked solid and brown now glowed a light amber with a couple black spots, but what was so special about it?

He looked back at his father and raised his eyebrows, but Doc was too busy to notice. He was bending a paperclip into a little lasso. He took a lighter from his pocket and heated the loop. When it glowed red, he brought it over to the machine and placed it carefully on the glass plate around the wax pebble. He held it there a few seconds, then looked up at Franc.

"Take a look," he said again.

When Franc put his eyes up to the machine again, the change was already apparent. Amber had faded to pale yellow, and as he watched, it turned to water and dripped away, leaving only the two black spots, which he could see now were clearly not dirt or sand, but two perfect squares.

He felt a hand on his back and looked up. His father was waiting his turn. He pulled a stool out and sat down. He looked through the eyepiece, then adjusted the glass plate before flipping some dials. A sound escaped him, something between a sigh and a groan. He was still so long that Franc turned to go, but when he reached the door, he was called back.

His father was still smiling, but there were tears now streaming down his cheeks.

"Don't go," he said. "I want you to see this. My life's work."

This time, when Franc looked through the eyepiece, what he saw astounded him. It was a bird's eye view of a foreign city, a neat grid of streets and houses, or maybe more like a jungle gym because he could see by tiny shadows that what he was looking at was 3-D, a stack of grids. He knew what he was looking at, and as soon as he saw it, he could hear the music, feel the dark, insistent pounding in his bones. He was filled with a sudden longing for a game after school with Nigel, for some stupid vid to laugh over, for a storehouse of answers at his fingertips, for a life of ease and privilege that had once seemed normal to him.

"A chip?" he asked.

"My prototypes," he said.

'But why would you have put them in a baseball card? How could you think I'd bring them to you someday?"

"No, I didn't think that. I thought someday I'd be back. I hoped, anyway. Maybe one day the administration would change; it would be safe to return. I didn't want it found, and I didn't want your mom to throw it away either. I knew she'd be pissed when I left, would maybe chuck out every sign of me. But she'd never destroy something that belonged to you.

"When that bag sank in the bay, I lost it all—all my notes and plans—my whole design, lost forever. I've tried to recreate it here, on paper, but it's too difficult—too many variables. But now I have these, maybe I can piece it back together, reverse-engineer my own design.

"I know conceptually how it works of course—I was lead on the project—but something like this is so complicated that no one person knows all the elements and how they fit together. I've tried before to piece together what I remember, but it's just been an exercise in frustration.

"But with this, the physical chip, I have a chance. Of course I really need a microscope far more powerful than this one, but it'll have to do."

"But what will you do with it? You can't exactly manufacture new chips here."

"No, but someday. Always plan for success, Frankie; it's the only thing you can plan for. Look, this whole thing may fail; let's face it, The Patrol might find us tomorrow, and if they do, there's no way Orion and his crew—no disrespect—there's no way they're going to stop them. Even The Committee itself, wherever they are—even Orion doesn't know, not really—maybe they'll be meeting and a bomb will drop on their heads. You're intelligent, and you've seen the world. You know how much better the ones on top have it compared to the rest. You know they're not giving up the advantages they have voluntarily. And they control the technology. Every tool can be a weapon, and the chip, the enhancement of the human brain, that's the most powerful tool in history, so of course it's the most powerful weapon.

"Honestly, and I hate to be like this, chances are we won't win. Logically, it's only a matter of time before the doors burst open, or a bomb brings the roof down."

Franc said nothing. The probability of failure was in his thoughts every day, but he'd never heard anyone voice it aloud. "Do you ever regret it?" he asked.

"What?

"Fighting. Not playing ball. Leaving."

"Every day. Every single day for the last 14 years. But there's no going back. We're here, and we can't give up," his father went on. "I never give up." He smiled. "Because maybe, just maybe, we succeed, then what? Right now everything we do is aiding destruction—fine, things need to be destroyed sometimes. But if we can't build, ultimately what's the point? They want revenge, the crew, The Resistance. I guess I do too. But it's not enough. If that day comes, that improbable day when we can finally walk out those doors in the daylight, we need to be ready to provide something, make people's lives better.

"Besides, I'm a chip designer; it's what I trained for. It's who I am."

Franc said nothing. Doc turned back to the microscope and began fiddling with the dials. He was motionless for a long time, the only sound an occasional "Hmm."

What would it have been like if he had never left? Growing up, he'd never fretted overmuch about being fatherless, but there were times, usually involving sports, when he fantasized about having a father who'd take the time to teach him how to throw a ball, how not to strike out. And when Bruno started picking on him in middle school, maybe a father would have straightened that out, taught him to stand up for himself.

But looking at this frail, studious man peering into a microscope, Franc felt sure that none of that would have ever happened. He just knew, without asking, that the doctor had been picked last for the team in his day, that kids had stepped on the backs of his shoes as well. Still, it might have been nice to have some sympathy—Grandpa had never given him any. And maybe he could have helped in other ways, have given him some advice when he was thinking about breaking up with Kelli. Maybe not.

Franc smiled. We're all just ourselves, he thought. We can't be anyone else.

He turned and walked away, but when he got to the door, he turned back. He went back to the table and picked up the round glass. He held it over the old bandage his father had swept aside.

"Hey Dad," he said. "I've got something for you."

S o Franc came to rely on Marco and Pablo to answer his questions, which wasn't easy. When he first started working in the lab, Franc thought it only natural that the three of them would all become friends. He could see right away that they were a bit odd, but who wasn't? Working together day after day, it was only a matter of time before they would get to know each other.

He was the new arrival, so he waited to be asked his story, but that never happened. So he'd ask them questions about their lives, and they'd answer, sometimes with a few words, sometimes at length, but always more like a report than a conversation.

They never asked him about his life. In fact, they never asked him about anything that wasn't work–related, except once. That night, just after dinner, they said they had a question for him.

"We hear you went to SpaceTime," Marco said.

"Um, yeah."

"Is Mr. Pham still there?"

"Who?" He'd never had that teacher, but he had a dim feeling he'd heard the name.

"Hao Pham." He smiled, "The coding teacher."

"Oh. No, he's not. He left after those kids released that malware—you know, the Shudder Bomb?"

There was a groaning sound. It was Pablo.

"That was us!" he said, as if he were in pain. "Was he arrested too?"

"What? No," he lied, "Definitely not. He went to another school. Um, Mitty, I think." He had so many questions, but he could see the looks on their faces. They believed his lie, he could see, but they were still upset. He decided to let it drop.

The rest of the time, their conversations were limited to questions about work. They weren't rude exactly, but like a lot of intelligent people they weren't good at explaining things. They'd leave out most of the steps in any process because they seemed to them to be too obvious to mention.

At first, it seemed to Franc like they were purposely withholding information, sabotaging him out of jealousy, perhaps, of his relationship with the boss, but it soon became obvious that wasn't the case. They were just as indifferent to the doctor as they were to him. It wasn't disrespect, and they were perfectly willing to take orders from him, to drop what they were working on and pursue a new target that The Committee had handed them. But there was no change when they talked to him.

Franc had never been conscious of this, until he saw its absence: the way people changed depending on who they were talking to. But once he noticed it, he knew that it was true. He did it, for sure, and so did everyone else he'd ever known. Your choice of words, your tone, how fast or slow you talked, even where you stood and looked, depended on the audience—who they were and how they were reacting to your words, even how you were feeling inside. We have lots of voices inside us, like an orchestra with many instruments.

But the twins were more like the fog horn, one note without variation. Except when they were speaking to each other in Spanish. Then, their voices were animated, they'd rise and fall, speed up, slow down. They'd laugh, giggle to each other. But never with others.

The only exception was Umi. Like them, she did not understand small talk. One of the first things she ever said to them was "I like your tummies, they're so big and round!"

Rather than being offended, the twins smiled at what seemed to them a very sensible comment. She was fascinated by the fact that they were identical and would stare at them, searching for differences. She reached up and touched a scar Marco had on his forehead where he had run into a door jamb, and then measured Pablo's hair with her fingers. It was longer than his brother's and draped over his eyes.

"Como Angelita," Marco said to his brother.

"What are you saying?"

"He's saying you remind him of our Primita, our little cousin."

"What's a cousin?"

Pablo didn't find this question any stranger than any other. "A cousin is a relative of the fourth degree of consanguinity, in this case, she is my mother's brother's child."

"What's your momma like?"

"That's hard to say."

Back in their school days, when Marco and Pablo told people that their mother had died giving birth to them, many refused to believe it. Even teachers, who of course said all the correct, comforting comments, often looked skeptical. For one thing, it sounded medieval. Death in childbirth conjured up ancient images of desperate peasants squatting in a field or a cave, not the modern world of sterile hospitals. Plus, the twins delivered this improbable news with absolutely no emotion, seeming to have no more personal interest in the matter than if they were talking about last week's weather report.

When a classmate confronted them about this apparent coldness, they were surprised.

"Well, we didn't know her," Pablo had said, and Marco had nodded in agreement. The classmate's face had looked like it was smiling, but he backed away and was soon telling everyone that the new kids were not just weird, but actually psycho.

So they were reluctant to answer the little girl's question, but they did, mainly because they were not skilled in evasion, and lying never crossed their minds.

Umi didn't say anything at all; she jumped up and threw her arms out and tried to hug them both at once, but succeeded only in grabbing both their necks and pressing a wet cheek to Pablo's chest.

The twins were surprised by this outburst of emotion, but they did not pull away. Remembering lessons their grandmother had taught them, they patted her back softly.

"Pobrecita, pobrecita," Pablo cooed. "It's all right. We're all right. We never knew her. How can you miss what you never had?"

"How can you not?" she answered, and the twins nodded.

"Exactamente como Angelita," Marco said to his brother.

The next day at dinner, Marco startled the whole crowd by calling out, "Hey, Primita, come sit with us."

Umi stood without surprise and dragged her chair over to the little table the twins always shared by themselves. As they watched her stab peas one at a time, they asked about fishing. Neither of them had ever been much for outdoor activities, and the only boat ride they had ever taken—the one to the island—had made them both sick. But they both liked the idea of boats, of skimming over the surface of the real world, the world of 71% of the planet.

They had never seen a rowboat and asked her how it worked, and pretty soon Umi was sitting on the floor demonstrating her stroke while the big table looked on with varying levels of interest.

"What kind of fish did you catch most?" they asked her.

"Rockfish, probably," she answered.

"Sebastes auriculatus," Marco said.

"What?"

"Don't pay attention to him," Pablo said. "He's just showing off."

"It's Latin," Marco said. "The scientific name. I'll show you." He went back into the lab and returned with a dusty volume entitled "Peterson Field Guides Pacific Coast Fishes."

Umi stared at the cover. There were fish there that she had never seen, or even dreamed of, orange and blue fish with plumes and stripes. But there, in the corner, was the old rockfish. "That's it," she said, pointing.

She leafed through the book, staring at the pictures, until she reached one that stopped her. "I caught one of these!" she said.

Marco looked over her shoulder and saw the page for Chinook Salmon. "Oncorhynchus tshawytscha," he said.

"I cast the line and everything."

She told them the story of her lucky cast and catching the salmon, jumping up on her chair to demonstrate the cast. Over at the big table, conversations had stopped as they watched her. She even acted out lying down beside her mother, looking at the stars peeking between the clouds, drifting off to sleep, voyaging off into the bright world.

But dreams didn't interest the twins. They wanted to know how someone so small could reel in a fish that big.

"Oh, Momma did that. I just sang my song."

"Your song?"

"She likes me to sing my song to distract her when the work is hard." Then after a pause, "Liked."

Marco had seen that look before. Angelita would look like that just before the water came out of her eyes, before she'd start wailing and wake their father, who worked nights, and he'd come out and yell at the twins for their lack of responsibility even though it wasn't their fault. Pablo saw it too. To distract her, he said the only thing he could think of. "Sing it."

Umi took a deep breath. She looked at the faces at the other table looking at her and felt an unfamiliar twinge, but she began the song anyway. Eyes closed as always, she tapped the rhythm herself with her fork on the table.

No one was talking now, or even chewing. When the last note floated to the ceiling, Umi opened her eyes. Carla was smiling, but her brows were together and she was looking to the side. The rest of them looked kind but puzzled. For the first time in her life, she felt embarrassed.

"I guess people don't sing," she said. "Do they? I guess that was just Momma and me." And as she mentioned her mother, the look returned to her face.

But Marco said, "Don't be silly. We sing." And to the shock of everyone, he and his brother launched into a slightly off-key but full-throated version of "Las Mananitas."

This time the whole table erupted in applause, which the twins barely seemed to notice.

"You're all right, Primita," Marco said softly. "Don't ever be ashamed to be you."

That night, when they were working in the lab, Franc looked at the twins in a whole new light. "That was nice what you did for Umi. At dinner," he said. "Thank you," and Marco said, "For what?"

• • • •

Next morning, without being asked, Umi took Chibi with her and sat at the twins' table. They ate in silence for some minutes, then Umi asked the question she wanted to ask the night before. What was it like to grow up without a mother?

"To us it was normal, of course," Pablo began. "Our father is a good man. He did his best, but he didn't understand us."

Marco giggled, "He named us after Marco Pablo," he said.

Neither Umi nor Chibi had any reaction to this at all so he explained. "Marco Pablo was a football player from Mexico."

"Not football, futbol. Soccer," Pablo corrected him. "He scored the winning goal in the 2036 World Cup."

But this had no more impact on their listeners than the name itself. "He was a guy," Marco said, "From a country we've never been to, who was good at running fast and kicking a ball. It's not a name that exactly fits us."

"It was important to him," said Pablo, and from the tone, Umi could tell that they'd had this argument before.

"But Marco's right. He obviously hoped we'd be athletes, but it didn't work out. Apparently, when we were just toddlers, he'd try rolling a ball to us, but it would always bounce off and roll away, and we wouldn't even notice.

"We crawled and walked late, and we weren't interested in toys much. We didn't like to be held and hugged like other children. And we didn't talk until really late. We weren't normal."

"Normal?" Marco shook his head, but Pablo went on.

"So they were worried. If you can't talk, you can't go to school, and if you can't go to school, no chip. Our family are first generation chippers."

"Chip–minus."

"Okay, chip–minus, but still. My dad picked fruit with his family; that's what we'd be doing but some teacher noticed he was smart and recommended him, so he ended up in Oakland with a real factory job, and he worked his way up. We lived in the top floor of Maia, you know the Seven sisters? And we had a window. Our dad worked really hard."

Marco nodded.

"They took us to some doctor, which must have cost a lot of credits. She said we had brain damage caused by a traumatic birth. She said we'd probably never talk. But Abuelita—our grandmother—said don't listen to them. Obviously, we don't remember any of this. I'm just telling you what they told us. She used to tell us she scared us into speaking by threatening to smack us with her chancla if we didn't talk."

Marco laughed. "She was always scaring us. Remember La Llorona? No wonder we can't swim."

Pablo smiled and went on. "But after she died, our father told us that really she had just noticed something no one else had, that we were already talking. Everyone else thought we were just babbling, but she knew. We had our own language, a language spoken only by two people."

"Really?" Umi said. "Can you still speak it?"

The twins looked at each other, but said nothing. Umi tried to read their expressions, but she wasn't sure, and Pablo just went on with the story.

"What she did, according to our father, was she learned how to speak our language. She'd sit on the floor with us and babble along, and everybody thought she was brain damaged too. But she got our attention, I guess, and she steered us into speaking Spanish.

"Anyway, we did speak finally and we did go to school and we did get our chips. And later, we were the only two students in the entire East Bay chosen for a scholarship to SpaceTime, and that meant a chip–plus, a whole new life.

"They delivered the news on actual paper, an old fashioned certificate, and my family hung it on the wall, but Abuelita—and this was not too long before she died—took it down to that doctor. She didn't speak much English, but she held that paper up to the doctor and said, 'Brain damage, my ass!'"

The Committee was worried. Drone activity was up all over the Bay Area, but especially in a wedge–shaped region beginning with Sutro Tower and spreading out north from the Marin Headlands to the Richmond Bridge. But what really worried them was that this enhanced surveillance coincided exactly with their last operation—crashing an unmanned cement mixer into the lobby of the V.T.B. Building itself.

The operation had been a raging success. Timed perfectly to avoid casualties, it had inflicted dramatic damage, a cascade of broken glass impossible to ignore. Even better, they had smashed into one of the girders, so the entire building was unusable that day as they tested its structural integrity. Shutting down their headquarters, even for just one day, had been The Resistance's greatest achievement so far.

But their swift response showed that the V.T.B. was, if anything, stronger than ever. At any rate, they appeared to have developed more effective sensors. Naturally, Doc and his crew had bounced the signal off Sutro Tower and simultaneously lit up a dozen sensors up and down the East Bay where the V.T.B. expected the attack to originate. This had always worked in the past, and it had always been amusing to watch the drones flock back and forth over the Oakland hills desperately searching for something that just wasn't there.

But this time was different. Detectors showed dozens of drones immediately leaving the roof of the building and heading as expected to Sutro Tower, but instead of hovering there as they had always done in the past, or taking off to the decoy sites in the East Bay, this time the bulk of them turned due north and began zig–zagging off in that direction.

Of course the operation was over by that time, and the first drones to reach the island saw only trees and the same old concrete pad of the defunct missile site. As expected, they buzzed past, seeking more likely targets. But the next night, as soon as the aperture opened, they received a coded message: "Cease ops imm. Orders to follow."

No sooner had they shut the aperture than the radio began to buzz. Carla had spotted drones approaching from the south. Orion couldn't see them yet, but he trusted her sharp eyes and messaged base to shut it down. He wasn't particularly concerned, though; they'd been through this type of thing before. But the tone of the response surprised him.

"Buzz bz buzz bz buzz buzz" it began. An exclamation point. "Stay und cover all ret base imm."

He knew the most vulnerable positions were his own and Carla's at the top of the hill. He made sure Carla had heard the orders before he moved. She'll be all right, he told himself. The only cover near her current position was the stand of oaks where he and Akilah had hidden last spring to spy on the two scarecrows mounting the summit. It wasn't perfect, but it was sufficient if you stayed still in the shadows, and he knew she would. Carla wasn't entirely reliable, but she had an instinct for survival.

Ace's zone had many places to hide—empty buildings he could easily duck into. Unless he was too busy with his jumping jacks or whatever to notice, he should be fine.

It was Akilah he was worried about, or more specifically the two youngsters with her. There were plenty of hiding places in the gardens, but would she be able to corral them into one? He never should have agreed to this, he told himself. The girl was mature, different, but she was still a kid, and she brought out the kid in Chibi as well. It probably wasn't fair to saddle Akilah with both of them.

His own position was the worst by far. Open grassland, a few rocks, a road. He reached in his backpack and removed a large cloth. One side was treated with a sticky substance, and he put this side down on the gras and rubbed it back and forth vigorously until it was coated in bristles and broken stalks. Looking towards the city, he could see them now. They were zig-zagging in a wide arc, but every pass brought them closer to the island.

Orion lay down on the cloth on his back, then grabbed the edge and flipped himself over. He crawled along the grass a few feet from the shoulder of the road until he heard the familiar whine of the approaching drone. He tried to empty his mind of all thoughts of creeping insects and lay as still as possible, but he couldn't help brushing at his face with his hand, and when he took his hand away, it dragged across the entrance to a little tunnel. The thought of snakes drove all fear of insects out of his mind.

But he was disciplined and remained as still as a rock as the noise above grew louder, then began again to fade. When he couldn't hear it anymore, he began crawling, the only sound now the creaks and cracks of his old knees. But he made it less than a 100 yards when the sound returned, further ahead, also coming from the west.

"They're criss–crossing," he thought. He could picture the operation in his mind. This wasn't the random meandering drone they'd usually encounter. There were two of them and they were progressing slowly, sweeping back and forth, mapping out every inch of the island. "That's how I'd do it," he thought.

It was so obvious now that he cursed himself for having moved. If the drone were facing towards him, it might detect that movement. And even if he weren't seen then, he knew that landscape recognition software would be combing over all the footage, looking for any discrepancies from previous passes. Before long the buzzing grew louder, then began to fade away. It didn't hover, which was a blessing.

The gap this time should be longer, he calculated. He was closer to the west than the east end of the island, so it should be some minutes before the first drone doubled back. He decided the risk was worth it and stood up. Wrapping the tarp around him like a cloak, he stepped into the road and broke into a run.

By the time he reached the stand of oaks, he was gasping for breath. Electric jolts were pulsing from his left hip down to his knee. Sciatica. "Old man," he muttered to himself. "When you gonna learn?" He knew sitting wasn't good for it, but he had already decided to hide there until both drones passed and doubled back again, and he was so tired that he leaned his back against the trunk and slid down. He pulled the tarp out on top of him and swept as many leaves as he could reach on top of it, and then he went to sleep.

Orion was, above all, a practical man. Survival always depends on knowing at every moment what you can do and what you can't. On the streets of Oakland, he had a reputation for audacity—for taking chances that seemed crazy to everyone else. But that's not how he saw it. Everything he did was calculated, and he never engaged in any action—no matter how necessary—if he didn't see the probability, even a slight probability, of success. He wanted desperately to get to those children, to make sure they were well-hidden and safe, but with the open terrain between him and the next decent cover, and with the shape of his old man body, he knew that the likelihood of being spotted was too great. The best thing now was to stay still, and because the human body needs rest, the practical action at this moment was to close his eyes and shut off his mind from worrying, so he did.

"Ten minutes" he told himself, and then he was asleep. A light sleep, but definitely sleep and not the anxious stewing that might have troubled another agent in this situation. That was the key to his long life in The Resistance: constant vigilance over his surroundings and constant vigilance over his own mind.

He heard the first pass, from the east, but it was only after the two drones flew past in the other direction that he bothered to open his eyes. He waited a few minutes, then rose and shook off the pile of leaves. His knees, his shoulders, his neck cracked as he stood. His left leg was asleep and sparks of pain radiated up from his foot. But he knew this was only his nerves and forced himself along. Soon he was limp–running and before long had reached Akilah's zone.

He first checked the bushes where he knew the aluminum prongs for signaling were hidden. That was the best hideout, but they weren't there. He then poked his head into every likely spot he could think of, but he couldn't see any sign of them. In the end he decided he'd better radio in and see if there'd been any word from anyone. He crawled back under the bush where he'd started and felt around for two bits of metal, but his hand closed around something roundish and warm. It was a shoe!

He brought his head under the branches and peered into the dark. He could barely make out a grinning Chibi sitting stock still.

"What the hell?" he muttered and a voice broke out behind Chibi.

"Orion loses!" and there was little Umi, sitting on Akilah's lap.

"We're playing the quiet game," she said.

"And you lost!" Umi said again.

Orion shook his head. "I should have known you were the last ones I'd have to worry about."

• • • •

It was almost four when they got back to base. Orion had made them wait until the deep fog shrouded the island before he moved. Carla and Ace were already there, playing cards, when they arrived, and Chibi and Umi went to stand next to them to wait for their turn to join. Akilah sat next to the tiny heater and picked up her book. She was reading *War and Peace* for the fourth time.

Orion went in immediately to meet with the doctor, and when he came back he cleared his throat to get their attention. "Bad news folks. We're on a seven day break. No leaving the bunker for any reason until next week. We're expecting the drones to return, and when they do we want to make absolutely certain that all they see are some pretty trees and a few dilapidated old buildings."

"But what about the resupply?" Carla asked. The next boat was due in two days.

"It'll come next week. We'll use some of the emergency rations."

A collective groan was punctuated by Carla slamming her hand on the table. Ace, Carla, and Akilah had tasted those e–rations before—dry protein crackers with no taste—and the young ones just joined in out of sympathy. Besides, everyone liked the monthly resupply; it was their only break from monotony, and seven days without a breath of fresh air didn't appeal to anyone.

The doctor was giving his crew the same news. Marco and Pablo had no reaction whatsoever. They seldom went outside anyway, and they had mixed feelings about the resupply; they liked seeing the lights of the city, but they weren't terribly fond of manual labor. They turned their attention to their screens without comment.

Franc did the same. He nodded and kept his eyes down, keeping his face a mask. He tried to return to his work, but his heart was pounding. "One more week won't make any difference," he kept telling himself, but it didn't feel that way.

Last month the resupply boat had been delayed. It was supposed to have come at 11:00 PM when the tide was at its lowest, but there was no fog that night, and the moon was too bright to risk it. It was 4:00 AM before the moon set over the Pacific and the morning fog poured through the gate. By that time the tide was in. The dock was completely under and the water had reached the treeline, so the boat had to land on Quarry Beach. This meant a longer walk and more carrying, and Marco and Pablo complained all the way there. Franc did not really mind; he missed the open air, but he grumbled along with them just to be friendly.

When they arrived, Carla and Ace were already dragging the boat ashore. They were wet to the waist, and Franc realized he was glad to be in the back with the "brain trust." He knew how cold that water was. And when the boat was about halfway unloaded, a sudden surge lifted the entire craft and propelled it up the beach, knocking down half the loaders and the boat captain. Franc laughed out loud, then felt bad as he watched the struggle. One of the boxes had broken open and Ace was floundering in the shallow water grabbing bits and pieces before they were ruined or washed away forever.

But when they had unloaded everything, they couldn't dislodge the boat from the sand. Franc looked up and shook his head. It was obvious these folks had never beach–landed before. They were pushing from the prow, and with every heave, they were driving the propeller deeper in the sand. He ran down to help them.

"No, like this." He went down to the stern and grabbed the gunwale. "Come on, help me." Ace came up on the other side and copied his hold. "One two three," and they heaved together. They'd only shifted it an inch or so, but it wasn't stuck any more. "One two three" again and they had dragged it a foot or so. They were up to their knees in the water now, and it was every bit as cold as he expected.

The tide was going out, that's how they got stuck in the first place, but even in an ebb tide there will be surges. Franc held up his hand and waited. Sure enough, the water began to rise. He was up to his thighs now. "Go go go go go go," he whispered and the two of them strode into the water, dragging as hard as they could. The Captain started the motor, but the prow was still stuck on the sand. One more heave and Franc could feel it gain its float.

Ace felt it too and let go sensibly, heading back up the beach, looking forward to changing his clothes. Franc was about to let go as well when he heard, "It's you!"

He looked up and there she was. The balaclava pressed down her hair and distorted her features even more than that damn hairnet, but he knew those eyes.

"You're not dead!" she said "I heard you were dead."

"Not yet," he grinned. He was clinging to the gunwale, his legs floating freely. The motor was still turning, and they were backing their way into San Francisco Bay when the reality of the situation came clear to her. She flipped it from reverse to neutral and turned back.

"You have to go" she said.

"I know, but I don't want to." He was still grinning.

She shook her head. "You're so stupid."

"I know."

"I mean it," She reached over and put her hand on top of his, then pulled it back. "Let go."

And she was right of course, so he did. He treaded water and looked up at her, watched her shift into forward and make a sharp, graceful turn back towards Oakland, calling over her shoulder, "I'll see you next month!"

Franc turned and looked back at the shore. It was farther than he expected. No one was moving; they were all just staring at him. He put his head down and started to swim. Before long he sensed shallowness and gained his footing. When he walked out of the water, people looked at him as if he'd lost his mind. Except Carla, she had a different expression, one he didn't bother to understand.

"Come on," he said to the crowd. "Let's get this stuff inside."

That week the days were long and the nights even longer. Orion tried to keep his crew busy and on their regular schedule, but realistically there was a limit to how much cleaning they could do, and only so many games they could play before they started getting on each other's nerves.

Ace felt the walls closing in, and he upped his exercise routine even more, sometimes recruiting Umi to sit on his back when he did pushups. But all his huffing and puffing filled Orion with dread. He felt like he could almost see the oxygen being sucked out and replaced by carbon dioxide. He spent most of his time sitting as close as possible to the intake duct envying Chibi and Umi who were small enough to crawl down the pipe for real fresh air.

The coding team was used to long hours indoors, but they weren't used to having other people around all night long. It was hard to concentrate on lines of code when you could hear laughter or arguments. With no possibility of downloading any new data to analyze, they turned to other tasks. Once the twins had found out that most of the work Franc had done with his grandfather had to do with storage, they asked him to look at their servers.

"We deleted a ton of stuff," they told him, "But we're still running out of space."

He began by looking through the directories. Nothing was labeled, which made sense considering the type of operation they were running. Of course, he recognized the hack into the truck guidance system, and a few others that he had personally worked on, but most were before his time. Fortunately, Marco and Pablo had incredible memories. They only had to glance at the code to remember when they had written it and what it was for.

They showed him the code they'd written that had stopped all those buses on the bridge that he had seen and the hacks that brought down all the surveillance cameras in the area of a certain span of the freeway that had almost fallen on Carla. There were dozens of other successful operations long before his time, all of which were unusable now naturally since their systems had been patched, but still useful as a reference.

They showed him abandoned operations, as well as hacks that were not yet successful, but that they were still working on, primarily their decade of work attempting to countermand drone guidance or infiltrate the command communications of the V.T.B. itself.

"Those boys really know what they're doing," Marco told him. They had multiple layers of security, and they changed their systems frequently. It seemed they'd never be able to crack it, but they were still trying.

Franc was surprised to find dozens of successful hacks that had never been utilized. They already had the ability to unlock (or lock) any or all of the city gates. They couldn't open the V.T.B. building yet, but they could stop the elevators and shut off the water. They had also successfully stopped a single car from a distance, shutting down its motor and locking its doors with the passengers inside. That one had been tested, although never used in an actual attack, but Pablo had written a very clever program that had never been tried at all. His hack would zombify a car's system, relaying the virus to all the cars nearby. If it worked, it would set off a chain reaction to stop all the city's traffic.

But the one that surprised him the most had to do with San Quentin. They had the power already to unlock any door in that prison at any time, and shut off the power as well. When Franc heard this, he lost control. He went into the next room, but his father wasn't there. He was out in the main hall, teaching Ace and Carla how to solder. He had a box full of old light fixtures, and he was wiring them together to create some sort of spotlight.

"Doctor?" he said as calmly as he could. "May I speak with you?"

But no one was fooled. Franc wasn't good at holding in his emotions, and every conversation came to an abrupt end as they watched the two of them walk into Doc's office and shut the door behind them. Soon raised voices were heard, but the only thing they could definitely understand was, "Your own wife is in there!"

Franc was careful not to slam the door when he left, but still he felt every eye on him as he returned to his computer. Marco and Pablo didn't look up from what they were doing. They seemed unaware that anything notable had just occurred. Franc sat down and stared at his monitor.

His father's words, so calm in the face of his rage, infuriated him. They echoed in his head, a quiet droning that clashed his own incoherent anger, the words he hadn't said.

"You have to remember, we're a part, only a part, of a larger movement. Sometimes that means waiting"

I remember. I remember you said we hadn't done much so far—fifteen years and just a flea on a dog. I remember we're stuck in a hole, and we'll probably never get out. Waiting! How long?

"We can unlock the doors, but then what? The guards have guns. Even with open doors, they'd never make it out, most of them. And if they get out, where will they go?"

"All I know," he had told him, "Is if I were in there, I'd want to try. I'd want a chance."

And it was true, he would. But he knew also that his father was right. He was always right. His mother wasn't the only one in that prison. Of course it would be a huge operation, emptying a huge facility like San Q. Even without guards, even if everything went perfectly, you'd have thousands walking out that gate and where would they go? In his mind's eye, he could see the drones descending, watching all the people, relaying their whereabouts to the men with the trucks.

His father was right, that was the problem. They'd have to wait. And wait. And wait. He tried to control his breathing. He remembered his grand-father's leveling exercises and the sound he used to make, the single syllable stretched out over and over. What was it, he wondered, and did it matter? Then he could feel it in his chest, a low rumbling hum. "Home, home," the sound came out of him, quiet but persistent. "Home, home, home," and he let his mind go back there. His grandfather, sitting in his closet, his back straight as a board. "Home, home, home," and a cat meows to be fed. The wind is blowing, and the trembling leaves cast dancing shadows on the floor, but there is no sound, only the rumbling of his grandfather, the mewing of the cat. Just then he hears a sliding bolt, the sucking sound of seals released, and the door opens, his mother returning from work, and he can see so clear-ly now the worry lines that were always there. "Home, home, home, home," but now he's lying in the bottom of a boat. Everything is pain and darkness and cold and he feels that he will never move again, but a strange woman picks up the oar and smacks him in the side. "Home, home, home, home," and floating still out in the deep, rolling with the swells, erased in fog, it calls him, guides him. "Home, home, home, home, home, home."

He opened his eyes embarrassed as if suddenly startled awake, expecting staring eyes. But the twins paid no attention whatsoever. If they had heard him, they didn't show it. He had a feeling it wouldn't matter if they had heard him. Say what you want about them, they were the least judgmental people he had ever encountered. At any rate, they were both busy with tasks they found fascinating.

Pablo was typing furiously, reams of code flying up the screen. Occasionally, he'd grunt and shake his head, then erase a huge chunk of code, but in a few minutes he'd be typing again. Franc admired his speed, his concentration, his creativity at solving problems.

The simple fact was that both brothers were far better coders than he'd ever be, and once he had accepted that fact, his new life had improved considerably. He'd come in thinking he was some hotshot genius, and it was humbling. Many of the tasks he'd been given were little more than the q.a.ing he'd done for his grandpa when he was ten. But he was learning. If you counted lines of code in their most recent hack, you'd see his contribution was far smaller than his share, but he was quite confident in what he had written. Marco checked it and called it "elegant" in that flat, unemotional voice of his, which somehow made the compliment so much sweeter.

His current job, trying to streamline the servers, was not exactly exciting. He had quickly identified the root problem: the machines were too old. Doc told him that all of their equipment had been supplied by The Committee over a decade before and they weren't new then. Since that time, he had repeatedly requested upgrades, but they were not forthcoming. Getting more would impose an unacceptable risk to human life, and it was hard to argue with that. As a result, they'd gotten good at working with what they had, and that was what he needed to do.

He was doing his best, but he could not see any way to make substantial improvement. Still, he enjoyed the job. He liked seeing the work that had been done before his time, getting a better sense of their progress. The most interesting thing he found looked different from all the other programs. It had to do with video files, he could tell that much. When he had asked the twins about it, their faces had reddened.

"Um, you can probably delete that. It's really old."

"But what is it?

"It's something we did before we came here," said Pablo, sounding pained.

Marco giggled nervously, "It's why we came here."

"The Shudder Bomb?" Franc asked. "Let me see it. How did it work?"

They showed him, their voices a curious mixture of shame and pride. The shudder part was easy, they said. It was based only on the timestamp. Each vid would play normally for 30 seconds, then rewind three seconds, then jump forward to single frames at intervals of .2 sec until it reached the 30 second mark at which point it would play normally for 6 seconds, then repeat the process.

"A child could do it," said Marco.

The part they were proud of, the innovation that got them arrested, was something he called "parasitic tunneling." While the vid played, their code was replicating itself, infecting other video files on that particular server. But the real killer, the thing that hadn't been done before, was the virus would attach itself to the signaling of the server itself. As the first server began to slow, it would send out a signal to instigate load sharing, but the signal was infected and would immediately infiltrate the next server, which would also slow down and send out a signal, etc.

"I heard you guys almost took down the cloud."

"No, that's an exaggeration. They patched it in one day. And then..." He was thinking about the lonely holding cells they'd been put in, the only time in their lives they'd ever been separated.

And even though The Resistance rescued them, hijacked the truck that was supposed to take them to San Quentin, the event had traumatized both of them. Sometimes it still didn't feel real, that one little prank could separate you from your family forever.

"You'd better delete it," he said.

"But why? There may be a way around the patch."

"Yes, there's a way, I think," said Pablo. "But Marco's right. Delete It."

Franc had been forced to go fetch the doctor, to explain it to them, that they wouldn't be in trouble for working on it, that it might be a good thing. In the end, he was forced to point–blank order Pablo to do it, which he was clearly very willing to do, considering how energetically he set to his task.

Doc had a different job for Marco.

Marco had a piece of paper in front of him that the boss had given him, covered in mathematical notations. He was holding an oblong piece of glass and metal, a sort of combined tiny monitor and keyboard. At first, Marco wasn't sure what he was looking at when Doc reached into his pile of antiquities. He plugged in some sort of cord and the black turned to light blue covered with little icons. It was a tiny monitor, apparently. He dragged his finger across the screen and a tiny keyboard appeared.

"We need a stand–alone system. I want you to program this, he gestured with the object toward the paper with the scribbles, to do that."

Marco looked at the paper. He'd always been good at math, and he could follow the lines of logic like a map. The end result, he could see, would be 12 nodes, each pulsating in an offset manner. Obviously a code of some sort.

"Okay," was all he said.

Franc watched him work. He admired the way nothing seemed to frustrate him. He was pecking at the tiny keyboard with one finger, hacking into a system he'd never seen, trying to transform an ancient device into something it was never intended to be. It was a daunting task, but you'd never know it from looking at him patiently exploring one character at a time.

"Hey Marco," he said. "Do you know what he's doing, really?"

"The doctor?"

"Yeah, what's all this for?"

"It's for the light he's building."

"Yeah, but why?"

Marco looked at him and shrugged. To him, work was work, and the problem was the problem. Anything beyond that wasn't his concern.

Franc knew it had something to do with the chips. His father had spent thousands of hours peering through the microscope at his prototype chips, comparing them and writing pages of notes in his scrawling shorthand. But when he turned his attention to Franc's chip, he saw something he did not understand. He had mapped and remapped the nodes of the chip and the various neural pathways they must connect to, but the result made no sense.

Then he remembered Franc's story, about the filtering, about the disappearing chipless folk, about how he didn't know his own grandfather had lost an eye in an industrial accident as a young man. It hadn't made sense to him at the time, and he had made the fatal error so many intelligent people make when they encounter facts that contradict their preconceptions: he had ignored it, pushed it aside, forgotten all about it. Now, staring at this configuration of transistors in front of him, he could see there was only one logical interpretation.

"Hey," he said to Franc. "When you had a chip, could things be recorded without you commanding it?"

"You mean auto–rec?"

"Tell me about it."

The question puzzled Franc. Everyone knew that the Mindsi™ recorded constantly and held that data for 30 seconds before deleting it unless it received the REC command, which would begin recording 30 seconds previously and continue until the STOP command was given.

He looked up and saw a strange look in his father's eyes. "Isn't that how it always worked?" he asked.

"No, and it's a terrible idea. It was proposed when I was working there, but it was rejected out of hand. Too dangerous."

F ranc stared at the ceiling and listened to his own heart beat. For once, Ace wasn't snoring, and he could hear nothing else in the stillness of their concrete tomb that might have awakened him. He recognized the ragged breath of his own anxiety. He had often lain like this, unable to control the swirling of his own thoughts, but this felt different. Usually, he'd see himself before the mirror, razor in hand, then he'd spiral downward in endless loops of regret, his heart filled with useless longing to return to that world of blissful ignorance, but it wasn't the past that woke him this time, but the future. The feeling was unfamiliar to him, so it took him a few minutes to recognize it: hope.

Tonight, he'd see her.

Maybe. Twice now, they'd delayed the resupply.

"No ops. Rem ug 1 wk" was the message they'd received last time as soon as the aperture opened, the same as a week before, but this time Doc had responded, "WE NEED FOOD" and after a pause, as if considering the matter, their handler had returned with, "Tue ni boat 430. No ops. NFC" and then radio silence.

So they'd radioed Orion to bring the crew back, then closed the aperture again and returned to work. Franc noticed that it was some time before the watch made it back. Ace was last, and Orion had a few choice words with him about obeying orders promptly, no questions asked.

No one was happy about being stuck inside again, and there was the bigger problem, that they had already polished off the last of the emergency rations.

Around midnight, Chibi and Umi disappeared for a while before crawling back through the intake tube dragging a huge pile of seaweed. Akilah scolded them for going out without permission, although they swore they had never left the cave.

"What's all this anyway?" she asked.

"Dinner," said Umi calmly, and she and Chibi dragged it into the kitchen area, leaving a wet trail behind them. She pulled a chair over, climbed on the counter, and reached down two large pots, and handed one to Chibi. She climbed down, put her pot on the stove, and gestured with her head to her partner. The two of them headed back to the intake tube. When they got there, Umi turned back with a puzzled expression on her face.

"Okay?" she asked.

Akilah looked over at Orion, but his face betrayed no emotion whatsoever. She hated looking weak as a leader in front of everybody, but she was curious, so she just nodded and watched the two of them disappear, wriggling through the opening.

It wasn't long before they appeared again. Chibi climbed out first, then reached back for the pot, which she slid toward him. He staggered with its weight, and Akilah had to resist the urge to grab it from him. When Umi was out, she took one of the handles and the two of them carried it carefully into the kitchen.

"Watch it!" hissed Carla when they sloshed water on her back as they passed. She shivered involuntarily, but the hand on the soldering gun stayed steady, and she never took her eye off the wires she was joining together. She and Ace were building another light box, although they didn't yet have enough lights or fixtures to fill it. She liked this work; in fact, it was the first work she had ever done in her life that she had truly enjoyed. When Doc explained the dynamics of the electric circuit, and the conductive properties of various materials, it was a revelation to her. She'd never learned any science at all, but once explained, and once her own hands were making the connections, it all made perfect sense to her. On or off, off or on, just a series of switches directing the current where to go. It was beautiful.

"Sorry," said Umi and kept moving. When they got there, they realized they couldn't hoist it onto the counter, so they set it on the floor. Then she got a bowl out, and scooped some out into the pot on the stove. "How do you make the fire?" she asked.

Chibi found the correct knob and soon the orange glow appeared beneath the pot. Umi sat back down on the floor and began separating the fronds and dipping them in the large pot to remove the sand before handing them one at a time to Chibi to drop in the cooking pot. The stems she laid aside after popping the bladders and smiling each time. Once, she found a sea snail clinging to one of the leaves, and she popped it in her mouth and sucked on it meditatively as if it were a hard candy. She hummed as she worked, pausing only once to remove the empty shell and place it carefully on the floor.

From across the room, Orion watched her. He never ceased to be amazed at this self–possessed little girl. He remembered what he had promised Franc that first night, that he would raise her as his own daughter, and his heart stirred with a yearning for the life he had once thought he would lead. His family was working class, and so was everyone else he knew growing up. Life had never been easy, but there had always been children running about, and he had always assumed he'd have some of his own when his time came. But his time had come and gone, and he knew he'd be the end of the family line.

Before long the room was filled with an awful stench. Umi stood on a chair by the stove stirring with a giant wooden spoon while Chibi climbed back down the intake tube with the stalks, except for one that Akilah pulled aside. It was high time, she thought, to teach these kids to jump rope.

"It's ready!" called Umi, and the crowd gathered. There was a great deal of trepidation about this dark green, smelly soup, but in the end everyone tried it, although Franc and Umi were the only ones who finished their bowls. The most common comment was "Interesting," and everyone laughed out loud when Umi said loudly "Mmm, this is delicious!" and went back for seconds.

"Well, at least we won't starve," said Orion, and the rest of them nodded. Spirits were surprisingly upbeat overall. Doc's demonstration, the night before, of his new invention, had changed the mood of the whole staff. Even Carla began to feel something like optimism.

When he first aimed it at the wall and threw the switch, no one knew what was happening. First, there was a series of blinding flashes: all 64 lights firing in unison. Then the lights began blinking separately, asynchronously, creating mesmerizing spirals and undulations. It was beautiful, in a way, but also made you kind of sick to your stomach.

After a few minutes, he shut it off. "Perfect," he said, smiling at Ace and Carla. "Of course we won't know until we test it."

"What is it?" asked Umi.

"It's a weapon," said Ace, proud to see it actually working.

"I don't get it," said Orion. "You going to make them dizzy?"

"Did it make you dizzy?" said Doc, "Hmm, probably oscillopsia. Your eye muscles are unable to keep up with what the brain is perceiving as motion; that can induce vertigo in some people. But this isn't meant to affect regular people at all. It's programming.

"You and I see with our eyes, obviously. But vision is really a process of the brain. Light enters the eye and stimulates the retina, which passes that stimulation through the thalamus to the visual cortex where the image is actually produced. If you look at let's say a tree, you see the geometric lines of the tree and the varying shades of light intensity bouncing off it, but your mind instantaneously combines this a lifetime's worth of visual memory of that tree, or similar trees and forms those geometrical patterns into information that's useful to you. For instance, it compares the tree to other items in your line of sight to give you an estimate of the size. It analyzes the patterns of shadow so you'll know how far away the tree is. And most of the time, your mind will tell you not to pay attention to the tree at all, but to focus on the squirrel running up the trunk. Our visual cortex prioritizes movement. And faces, we love the human face. Anyway, these processes occur mostly unconsciously, though of course if you concentrate, you can choose what to focus on. A similar process occurs with each of the other senses.

"But the chip, the new chip, well new since I left anyway, the new chip bypasses this pattern. Visual stimulation still occurs, of course, but before it reaches the visual cortex, it is processed in the hippocampus, the area normally associated with dreaming. This was proposed when I was still at the lab, but it was rejected—too dangerous and, well, immoral. The psych folks thought it might literally lead to mass insanity.

"It works like this: all of the chips are connected in a neural network, so your perceptions are combined not just with your own visual memory, but with the visual memory of everyone else who ever looked at that object. And this process, as I said, would take place in the hippocampus, where dreams are formed and the mind is highly suggestible. The result, in early testing anyway, was that people quickly ceased to see, really see, common objects, especially of the natural world. An awful lot of people have seen the moon already, and it hasn't "mattered" to hardly any of them, so the network would quickly submerge it to the level of unconsciousness, screen it out. After a while, the moon, the stars, even the structures of the landscape would essentially cease to exist. All people would really notice would be change. That was one of the major selling points: a world with an obsession with change is a fertile ground for selling new products. Why look at the moon when you can look at these new shoes?

"But the worst thing is that all visual information would be digitized before the brain ever got a chance to even see. The people with the chips aren't really seeing reality at all, they're just watching a video of reality, a video that can be manipulated before it ever reaches the conscious mind. So anyone with access to the system, anyone with enough money, can make you see anything at all. And since the hippocampus processes memory, these manipulations not only appear real, but permanent, like they've always been there."

"At least that's how I assume it works. Does that sound right to you, Franc?"

Franc nodded. "Yeah, I guess it does."

"That was the plan I saw presented all those years ago. It seemed like a pipe dream then, but I guess they've made great progress. I hate to say it, but from the perspective of a chip designer, it's a monumental achievement.

"But it has a weakness. Visual imagery is digitized before it ever enters the brain. Millions of pixels create images, trick the brain into thinking they're real, but they're still just pixels, trillions of bits of information, trillions of on/off switches. My device is designed to trick the system. The brightness of the flashes, the speed, and the patterns, which will force the eye to follow, all these will be outside the range that the chip is prepared to handle. It will attempt again and again to process this new phenomenon, each time restarting at a slightly different point. The overlapping patterns will create a moiré effect that will overwhelm the system itself. That's the plan anyway; it hasn't been tested obviously."

"I still don't get it, Doc," Orion said. "How is it a weapon? If I shine it on someone, what'll it do?"

"It will blind them," he answered simply. "It'll shut down their visual processing altogether, at least temporarily, and I think most of their cognitive functions. They'll be left blind and stupid."

This caused a great deal of excitement among the outside crew. All night long, conversations centered around how to use the new technology. Some had fantasies of revenge. Ace wanted to use it to enter CIGTHU and strap his captors to their own instruments of torture. Others dreamed of entering the holy of holies, the V.T.B. building itself. They pictured themselves bathed in a magic light, paralyzing anyone in their way.

Carla was practical; her mind went immediately to logistics. They'd need a lot of these devices. Was there some sort of electronics factory in the Bay Area that The Resistance could commandeer? Her other plan was based on a memory. When she was very young, her mother had once taken her inside a huge home supply store. God knows how she had managed it, probably smiled sweetly and stuck close to some actual chipper family. Carla was in a stroller that she was too old for, and she couldn't understand why she wasn't allowed to walk until her mother started shoving small items under her. She could still remember the discomfort of sitting on a whole set of router bits as they walked out the main door, ignoring the squeaks and beeps of the theft prevention system. But she could also remember the blinding beauty of the lighting section of the store. She had no idea what kind of resources The Resistance had at their disposal, but surely they could rob one store. If they could get the supplies and get her a room and a crew, she'd have them cranking out light boxes so fast it would make your head spin. She closed her eyes and allowed herself to imagine it: she'd make a great boss, she decided.

The most ambitious idea came from Chibi. "What about the streetlights?" he asked. "Couldn't you hack into their system? Command them to flash in the right pattern, hypnotize the whole city at once?"

Doc was pleased with all this imagination, but he just said, "Don't count your chickens; it might not work at all."

Franc knew that was true, but he couldn't help but be caught up with the enthusiasm. He sought out Orion. "How about Quentin?" he asked him.

"We can already unlock the doors and shut off the power. Suppose we had a bunch of these, do you think that would be enough to get the people out?"

"Absolutely" was his answer. "Listen, I already made a proposal—five guys with good old-fashioned guns, but it was rejected. They said we'd need 50, but they're assuming all the prisoners are just sitting passively. Believe me, I know some guys in there and if you unlock those doors, ten minutes later the number of guards is going to be reduced considerably."

Franc didn't like to think about his mother in the middle of that kind of chaos. He couldn't see her strangling some guard, fighting her way to freedom. But maybe the others would fight, and she could just walk out. He pictured her outside the prison, standing on the mud flat by the bay, where he had once trolled for lingcod gazing at the gleaming city across the bay.

And then what?

No matter how hard he worked his imagination he couldn't fashion a happy ending. As long as the V.T.B. were still in power, nothing could really change, and no box of flashing lights was going to change that.

There was only one chance, ultimately. They had to find a way to bring the entire system down. He thought about the twins and their Shudder Bomb. Pablo was pretty confident that his new version would work. He'd found a new way to bypass the patch. But still, the old one was patched in one day, so what was the point really? They were just gnats annoying an elephant. He remembered the high school stories about the kids who "almost broke the cloud." They seemed so silly now. How could something that affected only video files possibly do that? And all those warnings about "the cloud is almost full"—just scare tactics. There were thousands of acres of servers out there, all of them with the latest technology. What chance did they have?

He admired Marco and Pablo. What were they, 16 when they came up with their original program? As far as he knew nothing so destructive had ever been unleashed since. Sure, it was stupid of them to release it, but on a purely technical level, it was really impressive. Their method of spreading server to server was ingenious. It would have worked with enough time, but that's like saying, "I can beat you up, if you just stay still."

Working on the storage code reminded him just how robust servers are, and it reminded him of just how good his grandpa was. He was self-taught, basically, and yet it was he who solved the problem: where the hell would they put all the data they were collecting? Grandpa used to claim he'd invented the cloud, or the modern cloud anyway. He said he figured out how to "put the drops between the drops," and working on these old machines, with their structures of kubernetes packets, he could see it was actually true. Grandpa's matrix system was far superior by an order of two to the fifth.

If he hadn't worked so many years with him, going back to his QA days, Franc would have never been able to come up with his own matrix configuration. It's a hell of a lot easier to copy than to create. His system did not equal his grandfather's, but he was still proud of what he'd accomplished. When he was able to shrink the files to an eighth of their size, that was a moment of great triumph. He had literally let out a whoop, and the twins, who never seemed to notice anything, came over to see what he was doing. He showed them his code and explained what he had done, and they were very complimentary—effusive for them. For the second time, his work was called "elegant."

Grandpa had been a wealthy man, but if you looked at what he contributed, maybe he deserved even more. Their entire society depended on the cloud. In a very real sense, it was where they lived. What would they have done if the storage problem hadn't been solved?

Suddenly Franc was sitting bolt upright. Was it possible? He put on his clothes and went to the lab.

· · · ·

Umi was always the first one up even though she slept longer than anyone else. She'd crawl into bed at six and sleep until four while the rest slept nine to five. And since she was up anyway, they'd given her the job of making the coffee. She enjoyed pouring the water and measuring out the beans. She liked listening to the big machine splutter and fart. And she loved the smell of it, although it tasted terrible.

The first step was throwing away yesterday's grounds and putting in new, but there wasn't any new so she pondered what to do. One time, she had accidentally reused the grounds, and people were not happy. The thought occurred to her to try the leftover kelp, but she remembered how everyone had moaned about that. She thought about her dilemma: old coffee was weak, so she should add more coffee, but there wasn't any. In the end, she dug through the trash for the previous day's grounds, added them to what was there, and turned on the machine.

The coffee maker was old and took a few minutes before it was hot enough to make any noise at all, and in that moment of solitude and quiet she heard something. It was a tapping noise coming from the other room. She followed the noise, and there was Frankie, staring at the big screen and tapping as fast as he could. She could see the line between his eyebrows like when Momma was sick and afterwards. She knew he didn't want to talk, so she said nothing. But she dragged Marco's chair next to him and sat down in it. She leaned against his side and he took his left hand and placed it on her shoulder, still typing with the other.

They sat like that for a long time, watching the lines of code fly up the screen and listening to the coffee spluttering in the next room. Eventually it stopped, and she stood and went back into the kitchen area. She climbed on a chair and got a mug from the cupboard. She filled it at the spout and carried it back to him carefully and set it down on the table next to him.

The smell of the coffee seemed to wake him up and he looked away from the screen. He smiled at Umi like he had just noticed her. "Thank you," he said. Then he did something he had never done before—he kissed her on the cheek and pulled her in for a hug.

"There's a way," he whispered to her.

"A way for what?"

"A way out."

She wasn't alone.

Carla spotted the boat first, as usual, and made her way down to the dock before anyone else. Franc was annoyed, but he just smiled and took his place in the loading line as close as he could. He felt like nothing could dampen his mood after his breakthrough, and what were they going to talk about anyway with all these people around? He really only wanted to say one word to her: *Soon*.

It wouldn't be long now. They'd shut it down—all of it, or at least slow everything down so much that nothing worked the way it was supposed to. They'd overwhelm the servers—break the cloud—and files would drop. Grandpa said they had protocols to distinguish and keep the essential data, but even if that worked as planned, it would still shake people's faith in the system. It would create chaos, and if The Resistance couldn't seize control in circumstances like that, they never would.

Still, Franc didn't like to imagine the anarchy that might follow, the revenge that Orion and the others dreamed of. His old friends, his neighbors, who could say what would happen to them when the world turned upside down? He tried to push all that out of his mind, to harden his heart, but it was no use. "What's wrong with me?" he wondered again, "Why can't I just be happy without thinking about everything?" There are sides, he told himself. In this world you must choose sides, and he was on the side of the ones on the bottom, the hungry masses, the tortured, the prisoners rotting away in iron cells.

He pictured his mother pacing in a concrete box. How could they not unlock those doors? But he remembered what Orion said, about what the prisoners would do to the guards. Visions of blood and gunfire came into his mind unbidden. Would she even survive such a scene? He felt his breath catch with a stabbing pain; it would be his fault again, just like his grandfather.

The boat pulled up, and Franc tried to get a glimpse of her face. If he could see her, he knew his mood would return, but the passenger, a husky figure also clad in black, wearing the same black balaclava, stepped between them. He threw the hawser line to Carla who cleated it and stepped onto the dock. He stomped past them without a word, but when he got to Orion and Doc, he pulled out a piece of paper and gestured toward the boathouse.

They walked off together, while the rest of the crew unloaded the boat. It didn't take long; they hadn't brought much—maybe a week's worth.

"Who's the guy?" Carla asked, but Maya just shook her head.

"Someone important," she whispered and bent to her work, passing the rest of the boxes without speaking at all.

When everything was out and last month's trash had been stowed away, there was nothing to do but grab a box and join the others, but Franc held back. Carla was uncleating the line and holding it while Franc spoke over her head.

"Hey." It was literally the only thing he could think to say.

The smile that began to play on her lips disappeared as she looked past him. The passenger was back, plodding down the dock. He grabbed the line from Carla, stepped aboard, and the boat pulled away. Franc and Carla picked up the last two boxes and headed up the hill.

"What the hell was that?" she asked him.

• • • •

They were the last to reach the boathouse, and Akilah and Ace were waiting to seal the door, but Franc couldn't help taking a last look back at his city before he was locked in again. The fog was low and Sutro Tower stood out clearly with its three flashing red lights. The only other recognizable landmarks were Fisherman's Wharf at the water's edge, and the ominous beauty of the V.T.B. Building towering over everything.

Inside was a hive of activity. Orion had ordered half his crew to cook dinner while the other half put things away. Franc didn't have to do either one. He could have followed Marco and Pablo to the lab. They had work to do. Franc's code worked; he'd found a way to destroy his grandfather's handiwork, to return matrix–structured servers back to the old configuration of packets, instantly making each file 32 times bigger, but it had to be weaponized, joined together with Pablo's "parasitic tunneling." Franc knew he probably should join them, but he was too hungry to concentrate so he headed to the kitchen and helped prepare the meal.

Orion was nowhere to be seen, and that was unusual. They didn't need supervision, but they were accustomed to his teasing fake–bossy way of giving orders while surreptitiously stealing little bites of dinner and shoving them in his mouth. He was still locked up in Doc's office talking to him, something he did occasionally, but not usually for so long. That, combined with the appearance on the boat of the mysterious stranger, gave them plenty to speculate about while they worked.

They didn't appear until dinner was called, and no one was fooled by their "This looks delicious" smalltalk. Something was definitely up, but no one wanted to ask what it was. Thank God Umi was there. She just blurted, "Who was that fat guy, and what were you talking about?"

Doc chuckled nervously. "Well, we thought we'd wait until after dinner to discuss it." He looked out at the expectant faces and went on. "But it appears you're curious, so I guess no time like the present."

He raised his chin toward Orion who said, "That was Bookman, don't know his whole name. He's on The Committee. He came to tell us . . ." His voice petered out. They had promised to keep all emotion out of their voices. This would be an important decision, and they didn't want people choosing one way or other depending on what they thought their leaders preferred.

The doctor filled the silence. "They came to tell us that The Committee has been in talks with the leadership of the V.T.B.. He says they've negotiated a truce."

He pulled out a piece of paper and began to read. "'The terms of the treaty are as follows:'" But he interrupted himself. "This affects all of us, but you young people most of all. I'll read it and then you'll all have an opportunity to comment. Okay? 'The terms of the treaty are as follows:

1. As of Friday, January 12th, all organizations known collectively as "The Resistance" whether directly or indirectly under the control of the entity known as "The Committee" will disarm and cease all activities including, but not limited to: any attacks, whether physical or cyber, against any government or private property or against any person whatsoever.

2. In response, the V.T.B. will immediately disband its antiterrorism unit and suspend all investigations into The Resistance and its members.

3. All current members of The Resistance will be granted complete, unconditional amnesty for any and all previous actions.

4. Resistance members will be reintegrated into society, given food, housing, and receive chips that will allow for gainful employment.

5. This treaty will take effect on January 12th and from that day forward on into perpetuity.'

"Any questions? Comments?"

Carla's comment was one word long. "Bullshit," she said loudly, followed by a murmur of approval from the crowd.

Akilah raised her hand. "Why now?"

Orion answered, "Bookman says we can't fight forever. The Committee feels they're in a position of strength. The last raid, smashing into their headquarters, really rattled them, he says, or they'd never be offering amnesty. They feel they won't get a better offer. He says the next offer will be a bullet in the back of the head, or at best a prison cell."

"What about those who are already in prison?" Franc asked.

"It doesn't say anything about them," his father said. "So I presume they stay where they are."

"What kind of job, and what kind of place to live?" asked Ace.

"Why are we talking as if we believe them?" Carla broke in. "It's bullshit. 'Give us your weapons and we promise we'll treat you nice.' You know that will never happen. We come out in the open and they'll round us up, or just shoot us in the street."

"Did you show them your weapon?" asked Ace. "The light box?"

"I tried to get him to take it with him and test it. I told him we could make more, that it would change the whole calculus, but he wasn't interested."

"How about my weapon?" said Franc.

"What?" said Orion.

"Not mine—ours, Marco, Pablo and me. It attacks the server configurations. All the files will explode in size until the servers overload and shut down. It works. We tested it, and Marco and Pablo are working on attaching it to their weapon, their 'parasitic tunneling' so it will spread from one to another. Isn't that right, Pablo. "

Pablo and Marco were the only people in the room who thought that the treaty might be a good idea. They were hoping to see their father again. Still, Pablo answered truthfully, "Yes it will work."

Orion still seemed unimpressed. "That's not a weapon though, really."

"You don't understand," Franc said. "We'll shut everything down. No communication, no transportation, no security. Everything will start to fail one at a time. People won't even be able to see straight, maybe."

"But you don't know, do you? Same with the light. It's a great invention, but we don't really know if it even works."

Akilah stood up. "This thing begins Friday. What options do we even have?"

The doctor answered, "On Friday a boat will come big enough to take us all away. In the meantime, we're supposed to destroy our computers and our weapons. Option A is we just get on the boat.

"Option B is we pack up and get out of here before Friday. We'd have to steal a boat, but there are usually a few yachts at Ayala. Orion says he knows some folks who won't ever sign the treaty. He says they'll be scattering, looking for new hideouts, a place to re–form. He's pretty confident they'll help us. But we'll be on our own. No Committee to provide logistics, or food for that matter.

"That's it, as far as I can see. We can't stay here. Bookman says they won't reveal our location, but once they've signed all bets are off. So that's it: option A or option B."

"Option C!" said Carla, almost a yell. "We fight. You guys do your work, unleash your viruses or whatever and we fight. If Franc is right, we'll see the chippers crumble before our eyes. No offense, but I doubt it. But it's a chance, and I say give him a chance. And if he's wrong, we kill as many of the bastards as we can before they kill us."

Akilah said, "Carla is right. You all can do what you want, but I'm not getting on that boat. And, no disrespect Orion, but you haven't talked to these people in over a year. Who knows if they'll actually help? Even if they want to, would they be able to? Where could you find a hideout like this one?"

Ace stood up. "I don't trust them. I'm not going back to jail. Ever. I say we fight. Let's put it to a vote."

Orion held up his hand. "Doc and I have already spoken about this. We are not going to vote. We'll abstain. This is about the future, and that means more to the young than to the old."

"Okay," said Ace. "Who says we fight? Raise your hands."

"Hold it!" said Franc. "Before we vote. If we fight, Umi stays out of this. Chibi too. I'll only do it if we find a way to hide them until it's over."

"I can fight!" said Chibi in a voice surprisingly loud and deep.

Orion put his hand on the boy's shoulder. He knelt down and looked him in the eye. "I know you can, Chibi. You've got a warrior spirit. But I need you to stay in the back row, protect the queen. If this all goes wrong, we need you to survive. If we die, you two will be The Resistance. Okay?"

Chibi nodded and they went on. "Okay," said Akilah, "Everybody who wants to stay and fight, raise your hand."

Ace's, Carla's, Chibi's and Akilah's hands were up before she finished asking the question. Umi looked at Franc, and they both raised their hands. Everyone looked at Marco and Pablo. They were looking at each other.

Franc whispered, "We can't do it without you," and both twins, in an identical gesture, bit their lips and raised their hands.

Orion and Doc smiled at each other. "Okay, let's get to work!"

"**O**ne, one zero, one one, one zero zero, one zero one, one one one..." Umi was counting the guns as she and Chibi pulled them out of the storage closet. They hadn't known there were so many weapons. All of the crew, except Chibi and Umi, carried guns, but only Orion had ever fired one. Each of them had been trained on all of the various weapons: cleaning them, assembling and disassembling them, aiming them, using the scope, squeezing the trigger softly but firmly so as to keep the aim true. Everything except actually shooting. That was too dangerous. The sound would be picked up by sensors all around the bay. It wouldn't be difficult for patrollers to triangulate and realize that something fishy was going on. The watch had been told again and again that if intruders appeared, they were to hide and report only. In extreme situations, they had stuns, which could be used only at close range. Guns were to be reserved for preservation of life only.

". . . one one one one zero." They laid the last one in a pile with all the others of the same type in front of Akilah and Orion, who were busy inspecting and cleaning. He sent them back for the boxes of ammunition, but told them not to touch the yellow box with the big round lumpy things. Some of these boxes were heavy and it took both of them to carry them. And they had to really watch their step because the floor was strewn with wires and light sockets. Ace and Carla were trying to make a new light weapon, a brighter one with two bulbs in each of the 64 slots.

Earlier that night they had raided the old buildings at Fort McDowell and pulled out all the light fixtures and wiring that looked salvageable. Umi loved this excursion across the east side of the island. She'd only been there once before, and the whole crew had never gone anywhere together before. As they went, Orion laid out his plan of action for the following night. They'd only be guarding the inner perimeter. Carla and Akilah had the best vision, so they'd be stationed in the highest, farthest positions along the old fire road, one above Four Corners, the other above the Garrison. From there they should be able to pick off any drones hovering over headquarters. Ace and Orion would be down lower at the two sides of Quarry Beach to fend off a marine landing.

When they reached the old fort, Orion drew a deep breath. This was real now, the point of no return. All the time they'd been on the island, they were under strict orders to never enter any of the buildings; if anything were disturbed in any of them, even footprints in the dust, it would be only a matter of time before people would be poking around looking to find out who was on the island. Missing lights and ripped–out wires would definitely be noticed, but hopefully not tomorrow. After that, it wouldn't matter.

The door to the main building was padlocked, of course, and Orion pulled a crowbar out of the bag, but Ace touched his arm and gestured with his head. They followed him around to the back of the building.

"This will be quieter," he said. "Less noticeable." He reached under a nearby bush and pulled out a wooden pallet, which he leaned against the wall. He climbed up and swiftly slid open a large window. "Follow me."

He disappeared through the window, and they followed. Soon the room was filled with activity. They moved through the rooms breaking wallboard, pulling wires, and dismantling everything electrical within reach. The bulbs themselves were the most valuable and they carried them gingerly to the window and passed them through to Akilah who packed them into boxes filled with leaves. These, along with the wires and sockets, which were shoved into sacks, were stashed under bushes as they moved from building to building.

Carla shook her head after they had pillaged the last building in the fort. "It's not enough," she said. "We've got to figure a lot of those bulbs won't work. We need more."

So they continued to the North Garrison at the far end of the island, the old immigration station. As soon as she entered, Umi felt a strange sensation of sadness. She looked around, and she could see that Carla sensed it too.

The rest of them just plowed ahead and went to work, Carla too after a minute, but Umi was distracted. She wandered through the rooms and found one with tiers of bunkbeds, like they slept in. There were strange figures carved into the walls. Akilah saw her staring and came up behind her.

"What is it?" Umi asked.

"It's some kind of writing," she answered. "I wonder what it says."

Carla walked up behind them to see what they were looking at. Her eyes went from top to bottom.

"This one is *Ju*," she said, pointing. "It means daisy."

"How do you know?" Akilah asked.

"It's my mother's name." She turned to make a sarcastic comment, but when Umi said simply, "It's beautiful," the words stuck in her throat. She reached out and touched the carved figure and ran her finger along the grooves.

They stood in silence for a while, then Akilah very gently touched her on the back. "Let's get out of here," she said.

* * * *

By the time they got back to base, carrying all the fixtures and wires in various bags and boxes, they were exhausted, but there was still plenty left to do. They came in through the boathouse, and when they opened the trapdoor, they could hear the sounds of argument, punctuated with a rhythmic pounding and a weird groaning sound. "Absolutely not!" was the first thing they heard. The rest was muffled, although Umi could make out a familiar voice saying, "No you don't. Marco and Pablo can handle it perfectly."

They were stacking their stuff in the main room when Marco came out and handed Carla another one of the black glass controller things for the new light weapon.

"It's all set to go," he told her. The strange thumping and groaning was louder, and she could see through the open door Pablo pounding his head over and over against a pillow on his desk.

"Don't worry about it," Marco said. "He does this when he's stressed."

"So the program doesn't work?"

"No, it works, but he's upset they won't be able to beta test it in a limited target environment first. Doc says there's no time. He'll be fine, don't worry."

He felt bad for Pablo. They were all under tremendous pressure. Even though they tried to push it out of their minds during work hours, the possibility that the virus might not work, and the probability that even if it worked it might make their arrests more imminent, hung over their heads.

Earlier that night, they had opened the aperture and had downloaded thousands of files: video files, audio files, wiki entries, even programs for common household appliances, anything that was not encrypted and fit the metric for popularity. They now had to insert the new code—Franc's code and Pablo's addition to it—into each file. The more files they had infiltrating the system, and the longer each played before anyone noticed, the greater chance of success. And they needed to do it without altering the file size so that later they could replace the originals without being noticed. Video files would also receive the new, improved Shudder Bomb. Altering their file size was easy, usually just by changing the resolution and/or snipping some of the content. But others were more complicated, and with the speed that they were forced to work, it wasn't always easy to see how to change a program for a washing machine, for instance, without breaking it completely.

To make things worse, Marco had been busy programming the new light weapon and had been unable to help. Pablo had had to rely on Franc and the doctor, who were both smart and very competent, but working with them meant constant communication. With the twins, few words were necessary to pose a problem or ask for help, but with others, it was necessary to explain everything, or so it seemed sometimes. Plus, the doctor kept telling him to just skip the difficult ones, that they would come back to them if they had time, but to Pablo, doing things out of order made no sense. And then the other two had disappeared into the next room and started yelling at each other. In the end, the stress had just been too much.

Carla looked through the door again. She didn't like to see anyone so distressed. "Is there anything I can do?" she asked.

"No, he'll be fine. It's time for him to stop. I'm getting him a cup of tea. Want one?"

This was more astonishing to Carla than the head pounding. In the years she'd lived there, they'd hardly ever spoken. "Yes, that would be nice," she said, even though she hated tea.

Franc came in, shaking his head. When he saw the trapdoor open, he ran up the stairs just in time to stop Ace from sealing the door. He talked to him for a minute, then they were rummaging through one of the closets together. They came out with a smelly old burlap sack, two oars and two fishing poles. Ace asked Akilah to seal the door behind him and the two left.

When Ace came back half an hour later, he was shivering and his long hair was dripping wet. Franc didn't come back until almost dawn. He climbed down from the hatch with sore arms but more determined than ever. He knew he wouldn't be going to sleep. Umi and Chibi were sitting on the floor with a pile of ammunition strewn before them. They each had a rag and were polishing the bullets one by one and returning them to the box.

"Come with me," he told them. On their way across the main hall he stopped and borrowed a screwdriver, then the three of them went through the outer lab where Marco and Pablo were in front of the giant screens patiently tapping away and into Doc's office.

He nodded when they came in and shifted his chair to the side. There was a bookcase behind him, though few books were on it, mostly jumbled piles of antiquated electronics. Franc reached behind one of the boxes and pulled a latch. There was a popping sound and he swung the bookcase open like a door. Inside was a small room, a closet really, but it had a light, and when Franc flipped the switch it turned on.

On the wall near the low ceiling was a rectangular grate. Franc removed the four screws holding it to the wall and then dragged a metal chair in from the next room and placed it in front of the duct.

"Climb in there, if you can, and see if it reaches the main intake tube. You too, Chibi."

Even standing on the chair, it was quite a stretch for Umi, but Chibi climbed up with her and gave her a boost. When it was his turn, Umi held his hands from inside the duct and he walked his feet nimbly up the wall.

"Crawl down to the cave, if you can, and come back," he said, then stood waiting for what seemed like too long for them to return. He could picture them stuck in an elbow somewhere; then what would they do? But in a few minutes the noise of banging sheet metal and giggling talk grew louder. He peered into the darkness, but before he could see them, a leaf of seaweed smacked him in the face and the two of them crawled out, laughing.

Franc laughed too, although he didn't want to. He needed to set a serious tone.

"Okay," he said. "I want to show you something." He shut the bookcase door and slid the bolt shut. "Let me see you open it."

Umi dragged the chair over and stood on it. It took both of them to slide the bolt open.

"Good job, but I think I'll put a hammer in here just in case. You too are going in here tonight, before midnight, and you're going to stay a long time. When it's safe, I'll tap a message on the door in Morse code so you'll know it's me, and then you can open the door. But if it's just regular knocking, or any other sound, do not open the door no matter what. Understand?"

They nodded and he went on. "I want you to put two days of food and water in here, and anything you need to be comfortable. Take the couch cushions, maybe some games. If two days go by and no one comes for you, I want you to crawl out the tube. Understand? Umi, do you remember Sand Springs, the beach we landed on when we climbed the mountain?" She nodded. "When you get out of the cave, climb the rocks to the right and you'll come out there. The boat is there, up on the shingle, with our stuff in it. It's covered with kelp, but you'll find it. It's tied high up on the shore, but if you can't drag it, just hide inside and wait for high tide.

"Take Chibi to the castle, okay? The lighter's still there, and wood, and the old pot. You can fish at night, hide in the day; you know how. If it is humanly possible, I will come for you, or send someone who can.

"But if no one comes, I want you to row to Oakland, the other side of the Bay Bridge, and tell whoever finds you that you're orphans, your parents were fishermen and they died at sea. They'll probably put you in school, you'll like that Umi. So go along, learn what you can, and when you're my age, look around. The Resistance will be somewhere.

"What did your momma tell you? What's your verse?"

"The Lord detesteth a quitter," she answered.

He attempted to chime in with Yvette's line "And don't forget it!" but for some reason no sound came out. Umi leaned forward and kissed him on the cheek. She put her arms around his neck.

"It'll be all right," she told him.

• • • •

When Umi got up that afternoon, she found the place as full of activity as when she had crawled into bed. Even Chibi was awake.

"I can't believe you slept through that," he said to her. The blinding flashes of the new weapon had seared right through his eyelids and ripped him from his dreams. It appeared to work perfectly, although as Doc said for the tenth time, "Remember, it hasn't been tested."

"Ready as we'll ever be," she heard Orion mutter. "I'm going to take a nap. Wake me in two hours" and he lay down on his mattress at the end of the hall amid the piles of weaponry. The lights were on, and the room was still buzzing with conversation, but he pulled a blanket over his head and began snoring almost immediately.

Ace, Carla, and Akilah all decided to follow his example and at least close their eyes, even if they couldn't sleep.

"Two hours, then wake us up, okay?" Akilah said over her shoulder as she walked away. "And don't make the coffee yet, okay Umi?"

Then it was quiet. Umi turned off the lights in the big room. She knew other people needed dark to sleep. She and Chibi decided to go to their new secret hideout and play a game of checkers.

The outer lab was empty when they passed through. Marco and Pablo had been asleep for several hours. Franc had convinced them that it was only fair that he stay up later because he was gone for part of the work hours, and he promised to attack the remaining files properly in order, so they had gone to their room.

In the inner office, Franc and his father were going over the order of operations for the hundredth time, deciding which relay towers they'd use for which attack. The first, opening the doors and shutting off the power at San Quentin, they'd use Mount Tam, obviously. That one would begin at midnight to give the crew time to set up their weapons caches and build makeshift emplacements.

Doc said, "I'm just going to say it one more time, it's a terrible idea. We need you here."

Franc didn't argue, just grunted "Uh huh" in a way that seemed to say, "I agree with you," but his father had been a teenager once and he knew the real meaning was "I'm going to do what I want as soon as your back is turned."

But he knew it was pointless to argue, so they went on with their work. Next, they'd shut down the water and the elevators of the V.T.B. building, this time bouncing the signal off the relay at Mount Diablo in the East Bay. This operation was just an annoyance, really, but coming on the eve of the phony peace treaty, it would definitely send them a message. They'd be furious and pull out of the agreement, and if The Committee had any sense, they'd go ahead and claim credit for the attack. Otherwise, it would look like they had no control of their own forces. Their only sensible move would be to strike, take advantage of the chaos that hopefully would come with the next attack.

Uploading the infected files would appear to be coming from dozens of spots all around the Bay Area and beyond. This would take the rest of the night, or as long as Orion and his crew could protect them. And if they hadn't been conquered by morning, they'd unleash the last one, Pablo's chain reaction virus to stop all the cars in the Bay Area. There was no point in doing it until the cars were on the road, but if they pulled it off, they'd definitely capture some attention. Even if they weren't able to "break the cloud," whatever that meant, they'd send a powerful message. The powers that be would have to realize that they could never rest easy, that human ingenuity would always find a way to rebel against oppression.

What would happen after the message was received they chose not to think about.

I t couldn't be morning yet. She felt she had just barely drifted off when she was awakened by a monstrous clank, a groaning scrape

of iron, and all the cell doors opened at once.

"God damn it!" said a voice above her.

"Pig!" said another.

"Doesn't he ever get tired of this?" said the third.

She felt the bile rise in her throat as she recognized the fear in the voices
of her "roommates." There were four of them in what was once solitary con-
finement. She had the bottom bunk out of respect for her age.

"Remember ladies," she said. "Stick together. In the hallway, shoulder to
shoulder."

A pair of feet suddenly dangled next to her head. One by one they
climbed out of their bunks and slipped into their clothes. In a minute, they'd
be called to line up in the hall while the cells were searched. No matter what,
that pig Murphy would find contraband in someone's bed and that poor girl
would be dragged away, coerced into being "nice" to get the charge dropped.

Last week Rosa had the "honor" of being chosen, but the four of them
had linked arms. Susan and Lakeisha refused to let go even when the billy
clubs rained down on them, and miraculously he had given up, moved on to
another cell with easier pickings.

"Pig!" she muttered under her breath, and even though the order had not
yet been given, she leaned her head out and looked down towards where she
knew he and his partner would be standing.

But no one was there, and even stranger, the main gate at the end, the one
leading to the guardroom and the stairs, was also open. That had never happened before! She called the others to her and they all peered out. All along
the cellblock, the word had gotten out and from every cell, curious heads appeared and soon people began venturing tentatively toward the exit.

That's when Officer Murphy appeared from around the corner, wiping greasy fingers on his dirty uniform. "Okay, ladies, fun's over. Back in the cells!"

But nobody moved. Murphy unholstered his pistol. "I'm warning you," he barked. He stepped forward, raising his gun.

Little Lynnie Stevens was edging toward him from the closest cell, the dirty metal bowl from last night's dinner in her hand. Lynnie was in there for killing her husband, but she was so gentle and kind that most of them were certain she was innocent. But she took them all by surprise when she leaped up and smacked Murphy straight in the face.

The gun went off, and at that exact moment, every light in the entire prison snapped off at once. Her first instinct was to jump back, run for her cell, but it was soon obvious that not everyone was so timid. There was a roar, and a rush of feet, then scuffling and kicking. And more kicking. Someone managed to get the guard's flashlight, and in the yellow pool of light, it was obvious that he was dead. No living man would lie so still being kicked like that.

Lynnie grabbed his gun and others his billy club, stun, and handcuffs. "Let's go!" she yelled.

The floor below them was a men's block, and they'd need to pass through it to the stairs at the other end to reach the ground floor. Below them came what sounded like the throaty roar of a football crowd, mingled with cries of pain. As they approached, their lungs were choked by smoke. The prisoners had piled their mattresses on the floor and lit them on fire, and the growing flames bathed the scene with a lurid light.

A guard was handcuffed to one of the cells. Blood was pouring from his nose, and he was clearly terrified. They were trying to get from him the combination to the gun safe. A huge, pock-marked man was waving a homemade knife in his face, but the guard just kept moaning, "I tell you, I don't know!" She was shocked to see how young he was, no older than her own son would be now.

A small, rat-faced man came up. He had the guard's gun and he smashed the big man in the face with it. "Leave him alone! We're wasting time, you think they'd give that pipsqueak the combo?" He grabbed the chair the guards sit in at quiet times and stood on it. "Listen up!" he yelled, and the roar faded to a murmur. "Directly below us, at the end of those stairs, is the guard office. They'll be waiting for us, make no mistake.

"We're going to go in fast, and we're going to go in hard. Every man grab a mattress. We'll throw them down first, then when I give the signal…" He interrupted himself, looking over the heads of his audience to the windows in the distance where he could see a strange, pulsating light. "What the hell is that?"

He gestured to the man closest to the window. "Bobby? Check it out."

"Hey Boss," the man said a minute later. "You should see this."

The crowd surged to the other side and crowded the windows, but they made room when Rat–face came up. There was some sort of strobe flashing in a way that made you kind of dizzy.

"So what?" he said.

"Look at the guard tower. They ain't moving."

Everyone looked up, and sure enough the guards were there, guns in hand but still as statues. Then someone said, "Look down there!"

Below them, at the end of the courtyard, lay the sally port, the dou-ble–gated entry hall that led to freedom. The inside gate was wide open, and five or six heavily–armed guards stood in the breach. They knew that was the only way out, and even Rat–face had an involuntary gasp. They'd never get through there with one measly pistol.

But as they watched, the guards turned away and directed their attention outside as if a greater threat were coming from that direction.

Rat–face grinned. "They've finally done it," he thought. "They're finally busting us out!" He expected to hear a barrage of bullets, to see his comrades dressed in black burst forth in a hail of gunfire, but nothing happened; just the guards milling about and the strange pulsing light seen clearly now through the entrance to the sally port.

The guards didn't seem to know what they were doing. They turned and spoke to each other, then turned back and walked into the tunnel. But noth-ing happened. They heard no shots, but the guards did not return. Two oth-ers, who had been hurrying to help, were stopped dead in their tracks, just outside the entrance, motionless like those in the tower.

The light, which had never stopped pulsing, grew brighter and brighter, until it finally emerged, blindingly bright, from the end of the tunnel, carried by a thin young man. He looked around, as if he didn't know where he was, and swung the light in slow half circles back and forth.

"Guards!" he yelled. "You've been surrounded. Lay down your weapons and we will not hurt you. I repeat, lay down," but he was drowned out by the roar of the prisoners rushing out of every cellblock door.

When he reached the man with the light, Rat-face asked "Where are the others?" and heard in reply, "There are no others."

"Didn't The Committee send you?"

"The Committee doesn't know about this.Yet. Here, take this." He handed him the light. "It only works on chippers, and I don't know how long the battery will last so get these people out quick. I can't stay, I'm just waiting for someone."

He turned and retreated a few steps back into the tunnel where it would be harder for someone to slip by him. The light had left him with blinding red spots in his vision, so he closed them for just a second and rubbed them. He opened them again and was gazing around, blinking, when he heard a familiar voice.

"I knew you weren't dead."

• • • •

They didn't speak again until they were out in deep water, far enough away that they could no longer hear the shouts, the gunfire, the approaching sirens. Franc knew he still had so far to go and so much to do before morning, but he allowed himself one moment of joy. He pulled the oars out of the water and let the boat drift. He always loved that feeling, and he breathed deeply and slowly and looked at her face. She was all gray now, and the creases on her face that he had seen for the first time not that long ago were deeper. Tears stood in her large, dark eyes. She was beautiful.

And she looked at him. His long, stringy hair, the sparse beard on his chin. Those beautiful blue blue eyes. "I knew you were alive," she said again. "They told me you were dead, but I knew it was a lie."

Franc shrugged and grinned. There was so much to say, but not now. He dipped the oars again and put his back into his stroke.

"Where are we going?" she asked.

"Out of the frying pan," he answered. "Into the fire."

• • • •

She helped him pull the boat up the strand and tie it to two large rocks and cover it with kelp. She knew where they were; she had been to Angel Island as a girl, back when people used to still go out in nature, but she couldn't figure out what they were doing there. Still, she said nothing, just followed him up the narrow trail from the beach.

It was steep and the earth was crumbly and from time to time he reached back and offered his hand. They moved quickly despite his limp and it embarrassed her that she had so much trouble keeping up. She'd had no exercise for a long time.

When they crested the hill, they could hear gunfire in the distance, and some strange buzzing sound she could not identify, but Franc did not pause. They came out of the trees into an open area. Down the road, behind a pile of wood, a young woman in a hooded cloak crouched with a gun. As they approached, she turned towards them and pointed her weapon. Amanda threw up her hands just before she saw a flash from the muzzle, heard a tremendous bang and then felt the rain of plastic and metal falling all around them. She tried to run, but Franc held her hand firmly.

"Trust me," he said.

"Like I have a choice?"

Meanwhile, the girl with the gun had turned away. To their right, down the hill there was another buzzing sound, louder than before, and this time she saw it, a massive drone with what looked like rockets hanging underneath. The girl stood and fired, but the drone kept coming. Then from farther down the slope another shot rang out and a giant fireball lit up the sky.

For just a moment, the entire landscape was visible, and they could see a gunboat approaching the shore with its cannons out. Then the shockwave knocked them both down.

There was a series of blasts coming from far below them. The cannons were firing. Then suddenly the scene was lit up with a pulsing light like the one she'd seen in the prison but even brighter. The massive guns of the boat were still firing, tearing huge holes in the hillside below them. Between them and the boat, with missiles flying by him, one young man stood stock still holding up the light.

They had to crawl the next few yards to where Akilah crouched, reloading her rifle. "Got an extra gun?" Franc asked, and his mother said, "Got two?"

*T*he water was rising faster, *the island must be shrinking.*

He'd been climbing for hours it seemed, but the sand kept crumbling and he kept sliding back down to the approaching waves. Each time the water lapped at his heels, he'd start up again in a panic.

"Help!" he cried, but no one answered. "Help! Help! Help!"

Without turning his head, he could see the sharks behind him circling round, getting closer, waiting for him to slip again.

"Help!"

• • • •

"**N**igel!" It was his mother standing in his doorway. "For God's sake, get yourself up, you're going to be late!" and she stomped away, her high heels clicking on the tile floor.

Nigel blinked his eyes and gulped for breath. His heart was pounding, and he couldn't remember why. What was going on? His curtains were still closed. Was there a time change?

His morning routine was carefully programmed: the curtains would slowly open, the wave sounds he slept to would fade away, and his music would fade up. The screen on his Mindsi™ would brighten and his notifications would appear, all the texts and vids he'd received while he was asleep. Nigel liked to catch up on what he was missing before he ever opened his eyes, but there was no time for it this morning.

While he brushed his teeth, he scrolled through his notifications. Jasleen had sent a vid, of course. Puppies, of course. He'd only seen five seconds before he had responded with the honey emoji. If it was from anyone else, that's all he would have watched, but since it was from her, he thought he'd better hold on until the end. But about half a minute in, it slowed down. Frames started repeating. The little Shar Pei who had jumped off the sofa was suddenly on it again.

Nigel chuckled. "The Shudder Bomb, back again!" This would give them all something to talk about at school. He'd heard that last time, it slowed down vids for a whole day!

He was planning to run into the kitchen and grab some coffee and rolls for the road, but when he came out and saw his mother still in her party clothes standing in front of a chair with a man's coat draped over it, he changed his mind. "She wants the place to herself," he thought, disgusted. He couldn't get out of there fast enough.

The drive to school was quicker than usual, less traffic for some reason. He really wasn't feeling well, though, and he only got through half his messages when he started wondering if there was something wrong with his eyes. The light was different, brighter somehow, and even after he dimmed the visors, he still saw flashes like fireworks floating in front of him. A migraine.

He lay down on the seat and wondered if he should turn around and go home, but the thought of the scene he might encounter when he got there made him even more queasy, and he decided to just keep going.

When the car door opened, and he stepped onto the moving sidewalk, he was dazzled by the sunlight. The school banner—"Spacetime™ Academy for the Gifted (A Subsidiary of V.T.B. International): The Future Is Now!"—seemed to flicker as he looked at it. He decided his problem must be low blood sugar, so the first thing he said to Jasleen was, "Let's go get a cookie." She shook her head at him indulgently as if he were a naughty child, but didn't mention his lateness or or the fact that he hadn't messaged her yet that day, or even about the dangers of poor nutrition, her latest crusade.

They walked into the building hand in hand. Everyone they passed seemed to be involved in an animated discussion about all the things that were going wrong. It seemed everyone had some story about their garage door or toaster oven.

"I heard," said a freshman as they passed, "That it has to do with solar flares."

The door of the snack shack wouldn't open when he pulled on it, so he tried pushing.

"God damn it," he muttered as the signal for first period sounded. His blood sugar level would just have to wait. He gave Jasleen a kiss and hurried off to class.

Fortunately, his first class was Health and Hygiene, the one that took the least concentration. He started to breathe easier as soon as he entered. Nothing could be more soothing than the eternal sameness of Ms. McGreechy's class. Same "Five minutes! Back in the gym in five." Same "Hurry, everyone! Take your spots," when they strolled in ten minutes later. Same vacant look as she watched her kitty–cam. Apparently the solar flares weren't affecting that important technology. And then the same groan from the students when the Classi™ took control.

Before long, his headache began to fade as he ran through the exercises with the rest of the class. But when they were out at the track, something strange happened. They were only on their second lap when the wolves that were chasing them began to splinter and disappear, leaving only a bunch of teenagers in ugly shorts. They all giggled, embarrassed, and looked over at their teacher, but she was paying no attention whatsoever, so they just stood still and chatted about the strangeness of the day.

By the time they got back to the gym, everything was back to normal, the soothing voice of the T-voi™ warning them about the importance of deleting unnecessary files while in the split screen a young lady led them through their planks and stretches. Then the actual teacher's voice yelling, "Up on your feet. Face your partner! Come on, 'Socialization *is* Education.'"

Nigel faced his partner, a dimwitted young man named Randy. But something was wrong, the Classi™ began shorting out, dividing into disappearing diagonals, while the Mindsi™ glowed brighter behind it. Notifications were popping up all over his display: texts, emails, videos, even calls. His mother had called him! She never did that.

He looked at the boy across from him. Something was definitely wrong, he looked pale suddenly, and his eyes were jerking back and forth out of control. Nigel opened his mouth to say, "Are you okay?" but found he was unable to do so. He couldn't move his tongue.

K nock knock KNOCK, KNOCK KNOCK, knock knock.

Umi laughed and jumped up. Chibi had to help her slide the heavy bolt and push open the iron door. Frankie was standing there grinning. He held out his hand.

"I want to show you something."

She took his hand and started out. Franc turned to Chibi.

"You too."

The three of them went down the dark corridor, and Umi could see that no one was in the room with the screens—no twins tap–tapping. The dormitory was empty also, though she was sure that daybreak must have been hours before.

"Where is everybody?" she asked.

Franc just squeezed her hand. "Come on," he said.

The door to the store room was open. Bright light shone on the narrow stairs. When Chibi saw the light, he started to draw back, but Umi took his hand. She was scared too, trembling despite herself, but she was smiling.

"Come on, Chibi," she said, "It'll be all right." And so, holding hands, they followed Frankie up the stairs, out the door and into the perilous light.

The warmth of the sun shocked her. She saw a flood of blue, the color of her dreams, before she shut her eyes and lowered her head. Franc could feel her hand trembling. When he looked down there were tears in her eyes. He moved his body between her and the blinding sun and pulled her into a hug.

Chibi, no longer afraid, moved out into the light, but Franc and Umi stayed where they were. There was no hurry; he leaned down and smelled the top of her head.

When she finally raised her head, the grin was back. She had been peering beneath his arm. Chibi was standing next to Akilah on a pile of metal and plastic wreckage, holding up what looked like to Umi a twisted oar. Marco and Pablo were there too, combing through for recognizable bits of electronics. She walked out of Frankie's shadow and went to join them, but she was stopped, startled by the beauty of the bay. A giant fogbank was sweeping in over the Marin headlands, but everything else was bathed in sunshine. The sky seemed immense, an impossible blue that transformed the black waters into a darker version of the sky itself.

She looked for home, for her castle, but it didn't seem to be there at all. She was about to cry out, to call Frankie over, when she saw it: a tiny pile of rubble, a chip broken off the end of the prison. It didn't look like a place where anyone could live.

The wind was up and whitecaps were forming at the gate. She looked for the Farallons in the distance. It was like she could hear the sea lions setting up a racket at seeing strangers in their midst, a small boat with a child and a very determined woman who had rowed so far against the current that she was soaked in sweat despite the cold, all for one tiny rockfish, just enough to keep off the hunger pains for one more day when they would try again.

The orange bridge stood out against the blue. She'd seen it before in the daylight, peering through a crack, but not like this: the whole graceful span at once. But something else was different. Nothing was moving. Her sharp eyes could see a line of cars all the way across to the tunnel, all standing stock still. She followed the roadway with her eyes past Fort Point, across the Lombard Highway. Nothing was moving there either. She turned and looked at the Bay Bridge, and it was the same: a line of buses on the way to Oakland just stopped dead in their tracks.

She turned to Frankie, to ask him a question, but something else caught her eye. A boat had crashed, it looked like, onto the beach below. It was large and black and had huge guns protruding from it. The crew on board, dressed all in black, stood perfectly still, staring straight ahead, while Ace and Carla and Orion tied them up with ropes.

And there was Doc, sitting on the sand by the water's edge, talking to some lady.

Her eyes went back to the beautiful, forbidden city. The tower on the big hill was different; there was no red light flashing. A huge plume of black smoke rose straight up, then turned and stretched out towards Oakland. It was coming from an oddly-shaped, pointy building that towered above all the others.

Frankie had come down next to her and, like her, was staring at the gorgeous wreckage.

"What's going on?" she asked him. "What's happening?"

He put a hand on her shoulder and said, "It's raining."